Stick in th

Also by Leo McNeir

Getaway with Murder (ISBN 978 0 9524052 6 9)
Death in Little Venice (ISBN 978 0 9524052 7 6)
Kiss and Tell (ISBN 0 9531742 1 2)
Devil in the Detail (ISBN 0 9524052 2 0)
No Secrets (ISBN 978 0 9531742 4 9)
Sally Ann's Summer (ISBN 978 0 9531742 5 6)
Smoke and Mirrors (ISBN 978 0 9531742 7 0)
Gifthorse (ISBN 978 0 9531742 6 3)

and published by enigma publishing.
See the author's website: www.leomcneir.com

enigma publishing

PO Box 1901, Milton Keynes, MK19 6DN

First published 2012

Text © Leo McNeir 2012

Cover art © Garth Allan 2012

The moral rights of the author have been asserted.
The events and characters described in Stick in the Mud are entirely fictitious, and any apparent resemblance to real people, companies or occurrences is entirely coincidental.
All our Rights Reserved. No part of this publication may be reproduced, stored in a retrieval system, or transmitted, in any form or by any means, electronic, mechanical, photocopying, recording or otherwise, without the prior permission of the publisher.

A CIP record for this book is available from the British Library.

ISBN 978 0 9531742 9 4

Prepared by *specialist* publishing services, Montgomery

Printed in Great Britain by Bell and Bain, Glasgow

Stick in the Mud

Leo McNeir

enigma
publishing

The author

Leo McNeir is a linguist and lexicographer and has edited eleven dictionaries in fifteen languages in the past decade, the standard works in their field.

Stick in the Mud is his ninth novel, following the successful publication of *Getaway with Murder* (2000), *Death in Little Venice* (2001), *Kiss and Tell* (2003), *Devil in the Detail* (2004), *No Secrets* (2006), *Sally Ann's Summer* (2007), *Smoke and Mirrors* (2009) and *Gifthorse* (2011).

With his wife, cookery writer Cassandra McNeir, and their cat, Mog, he lives in a 300-year-old cottage in a Northamptonshire village.

They have a narrowboat on the Grand Union Canal.

Dedication

For Roger and Anne Everest-Phillips

and for Mike and Chris John

Prologue

The young woman with short pale-blond hair was sitting comfortably as she opened the book at random at a chapter entitled *The Killing Ground* and began reading.

Condemned on Wednesday, 9 April 1752, Jacob Pepper was led out of the notorious Clink Street prison two days later. With hands tied behind his back, he was dragged on board a river launch and rowed to Horselydown on the south bank of the Thames, opposite the Tower of London. With him were two custody officers from the Clink, the prison chaplain and two guards armed with muskets.

Word had spread rapidly that the infamous river pirate known as Daring Jake was to be executed, and a fair-sized crowd had gathered by the riverside. When they caught sight of the prisoner and his guards a cheer went up from the throng, and the escorting officers were at first anxious that the onlookers might be supporters of the pirate. However, the shouts soon turned to jeers, and some members of the crowd began throwing rotten fruit at the man who had become a legend of wickedness over several years.

The execution party alighted onto the bank. Some members of the crowd were surprised when the prisoner, the chaplain and the two prison officers mounted a small horse-drawn cart. The scaffold was, after all, barely thirty yards along the wharf. The wagon trundled over the cobbles, and the horse was guided through a wooden arch, halting once the cart was immediately below the structure. Now the purpose of the cart became clear.

One of the prison officers picked up a coil of rope from the floor of the cart and hoisted it over the cross-bar. At this, the crowd cheered again, and the prisoner grew deathly pale as he saw the noose dangling before his eyes. The chaplain spoke up in a voice loud enough to be heard by all, asking the prisoner if he truly repented his sins. Daring Jake made one last gesture of defiance to authority. He spat on the floor and cried out that they could all rot in Hell. At this, the chaplain began incanting prayers for the pirate's soul.

One of the officers slipped the noose over Jake's head and tightened the loop. Both men held Jake firmly by the arms, and one nodded at a guard who was holding the horse's collar. The horse walked on, the guards released the arms of their prisoner and Jake was left dangling on the end of the rope. No record was kept of the time it took him to die, but it was believed to be some minutes that he danced on the air while his eyes bulged in their sockets, his tongue protruded from his lips and his face turned a livid purple.

When his writhing ceased, the cart rolled back, and one officer bound the body in chains while the other coated him in pitch from head to foot. Independent sources from those times testified that the body of Daring Jake Pepper was still hanging there a year later, rotting and swaying in the breeze as an example to all who might contemplate a life of river piracy.

1
The Dead

Marnie Walker was obviously in high spirits as she walked across the car park. This did not go unnoticed by her friend and associate, Anne Price, who was sitting in Marnie's Land Rover Discovery waiting for her. They had agreed to rendez-vous at Willards Brewery in Leicester, where Marnie had a meeting with board members of the company, her largest client. Initially Anne had wondered if it was a good sign that Marnie was emerging later than the expected time of three o'clock. But Marnie clearly had a spring in her step as she spotted the Disco, gave a cheery wave and veered over in Anne's direction.

From a first floor window, one of the directors observed Marnie crossing the tarmac. He estimated correctly that she was in her early to mid-thirties. She was above average height for a woman, with wavy shoulder-length brown hair and a figure that looked good in a trouser suit. She was popular with all the directors for her clear presentations in meetings and the interiors she designed for their hotels, restaurants and pubs. They were stylish and original, but possessed a quality that would not quickly go out of fashion.

The director looked on as Marnie reached her car. He saw another woman get out from the driver's side. This one was younger, probably still in her teens. She was wearing a T-shirt and jeans, ideal for the early summer warmth of mid-June, and had a figure that most people would describe as *boyish*. The uncharitable would say she was skinny. But in her favour, she had a pleasant face with sharp features and pale-blond hair almost sculpted to her head.

The two of them exchanged words briefly, and the thin girl resumed her place behind the wheel as Marnie climbed in beside her.

'I think you've got an admirer,' Anne said, fastening her seat belt.

'Really?'

'Blind twitching on the first floor. How did the meeting go?'

'Fine.'

'Only fine?'

Marnie looked thoughtful. 'Fine's good, it's … fine.'

'That's fine, then.' Anne looked at the controls in front of her and took a deep breath before turning the ignition key. The Disco was like a truck compared with her Mini. She looked sideways at Marnie. 'Home, James, and don't spare the horses?'

Marnie hesitated. 'Did you find a good bookshop?'

'Yes. This is a university city.'

'Can you find your way back there?'

'I think so.'

'Then let's do that. I need some reading matter.'

While Anne manoeuvred her way through the traffic, Marnie phoned home on the mobile. The call was answered by her lover, her *fiancé*, Ralph Lombard – to be precise, Professor Ralph Lombard of All Saints College, Oxford – who was working on a research paper on his latest hot topic, the economic situation in the Far East. Marnie told him they should be home within an hour or two, and Ralph promised to have a meal ready for them. He was one of the brightest academics of his generation and knew how to take a hint.

In little more than ten minutes Anne had retraced her journey back to the bookshop and then took another ten minutes finding somewhere to park.

Anne caught up with Marnie at the till and cast an eye over the voluminous carrier bag filled with books that Marnie heaved onto the back seat when they regained the car.

'Next stop IKEA?' said Anne with a deadpan expression.

'What for?'

'A new bookcase?'

Marnie nodded. 'Perhaps I did get a little carried away. Shall I drive us home?'

Anne was grateful to hand over the keys and ride shotgun. The thought of steering through city traffic when the schools were turning out did not appeal. She asked if she could look at the books Marnie had bought and dragged the bag onto her lap as they drove off.

The variety of Marnie's purchases surprised her. There were a few novels of the kind people bought at airports to take on holiday, predictably some art and design books, two books on the history of London and the Thames, plus a further two books about … pirates.

'*Pirates?*' Anne said. 'Since when have you been interested in them?'

'I have hidden depths.' Marnie pulled up at a red light.

'But seriously,' Anne persisted.

'Tell you later.'

'Okay.' Anne noticed that one of the books dealt with river pirates, the other about the myth and reality of pirates in the Caribbean. She flicked open the former. 'May I have a look?'

'Go ahead.'

For the next few miles the car plodded from one hold-up to the next. Anne normally got car-sick if she tried to read while on the move, but she was able to peruse the book without discomfort. It told the story of piracy in the port of London around the eighteenth century. Trade was then so brisk and the port so busy that vessels could be tied up often for weeks on end, waiting to unload, an easy target for thieves.

Anne found herself immersed in the tale of one man, Jacob Pepper – known as *Daring Jake* – a notorious gang-leader in the mid-1700s. They broke into one ship after another and amassed a fortune in stolen goods: carpets, tapestries, brandy, rum, port, silks and silver, spices and gold. They struck at dead of night, off-loading booty onto their own boat. Anyone who got in their way was likely to be murdered and thrown into the river.

'What a scurvy mob,' Anne murmured, 'especially their leader.'

'Who was that?' Marnie asked between gear changes.

'This pirate ... *Daring Jake Pepper*. I wonder what became of him.'

'Probably came to a sticky end.'

Marnie was right.

So successful was Daring Jake, and so elusive, that the port authorities offered a substantial reward for his capture. Jake was eventually betrayed by one of his own crew. Brought to trial and confronted with his crimes, Jake had no credible defence to offer, and was condemned by the testimony of his betrayer. There was only one sentence possible. Anne read on. The account of Daring Jake's hanging left her enthralled and appalled in equal measure.

'... cut across country, I think, and go down the A5.'

Anne looked up in surprise. 'What? Sorry?'

Marnie glanced at her. 'You okay? I was just saying, I don't think it's a good idea to head for the M1 with all this traffic.'

'No,' said Anne, her voice flat.

'What's the matter?'

'I was just reading about that river pirate.'

'Daring Jake? What about him?'

Anne grimaced. 'He was hanged and his body ... *ugh!*'

'Where was that?'

'In London, some place called ...' Anne consulted the text. '... Horselydown. I've never heard of it before.'

'Well, you may be hearing about it again,' said Marnie, 'and sooner rather than later.'

Anne closed the book on her lap. 'It's a horrible story.'

'A sticky end?' said Marnie.

Anne thought of Daring Jake's slowly rotting tarred body, hanging for weeks, months, perhaps longer.

'Very sticky,' she said.

It was almost six o'clock when Marnie turned off the dual carriageway and took the narrow country road to their home village of Knightly St John. Both she and Anne relaxed as they cruised along the high street past stone cottages, some of them thatched, past the shop-cum-post-office, the pub – *The Two Roses* – and the primary school. The street then made a long right-hand turn leading out of the village. Rounding this bend, Marnie steered the car through a field gateway on the left and followed a track down the sloping meadow.

Marnie smiled across at Anne as chimney-tops came into view above a cluster of trees. Now Anne was looking happier. Marnie wondered when would be a suitable time to break the news to Anne that would make her less cheerful.

Arriving at a group of stone outbuildings, Marnie swung left and turned into an open-sided barn comprising four bays. She parked the dark blue Disco between a lighter blue elderly Volvo and a shining red Mini, Anne's pride and joy. The end bay housed a small vehicle under a tarpaulin, Marnie's classic MG sports car dating from the 1930s.

As soon as they climbed out of the Disco, Marnie and Anne paused to take deep breaths of clean country air.

'It's great to be home,' said Anne.

Marnie laughed. 'Anyone would think you'd just got back from the South Pole instead of an outing to Leicester.'

Anne was unrepentant. 'I don't care. I always feel like this when we come home to Glebe Farm. *And* we've got a welcome committee.' She knelt down as a large black cat trotted up and rubbed its flank against her legs. Anne stroked the animal's head. 'Hallo, Dolly. Caught any big fat mice?'

The cat made an enigmatic warbling sound and turned its attentions on Marnie.

'Pity we can't train her to carry parcels.' Marnie reached down to stroke the velvety head. 'These books are heavy. Come on, I want to check the answering machine before we eat.'

The three of them walked round to another stone barn. It faced onto a gravel courtyard, on the opposite side of which stood a row of three cottages, each having a front door of dark blue, with white-painted window-frames. Set back at the end of this terrace, to the right of the office barn, stood a double-fronted farmhouse. All the buildings at Glebe Farm were of pale local limestone under roofs of Welsh blue slate.

The cottages had been renovated and modernised and were let to tenants.

The expense of refurbishing so many buildings had led to only slow progress with works on the main dwelling, but now after three years, they were approaching their final phase. Marnie planned to move into the house with Ralph that autumn.

The facade of the office barn was enclosed by large wooden doors. When shut, they gave the appearance of a double cart building. When opened and folded back, as now, they revealed a tinted plate glass window like a shop front. Marnie unlocked the single front door and went in.

The office contained two desks equipped with computers. Filing cabinets and other storage units lined the wall to the right. At the rear was a kitchen and beyond that, an internal wall concealed a utility area comprising a laundry room, shower room and toilet. The colour scheme of tinted white walls and blond-wood furniture was light and airy. On the left was a wall-ladder leading up through an open trap-door to a large attic room. This loft was Anne's domain, another pride and joy.

Marnie pressed the button on the answerphone and listened while Anne made notes of the messages. One of them, significantly, was from Marnie's former employer, Philip Everett, a senior partner in the London firm of architects, Everett Parker Associates. After clearing the messages, Marnie checked her e-mails while Anne went outside and closed the barn doors.

It was time to join Ralph for the evening meal.

Behind the office barn a spinney extended for about fifty yards, with a footpath running through it to the canal. To their left as Marnie and Anne exited the spinney, a docking area joined the canal at ninety degrees. It was occupied by Marnie's narrowboat, *Sally Ann*, in its livery of navy blue, red and yellow. Ahead of them, moored on the canal's main line was Ralph's boat, *Thyrsis*. Marnie had once compared its livery of deep sage green and gold with a Harrods carrier bag.

Waiting for the farmhouse to be ready, Marnie and Ralph slept on *Thyrsis*, which also contained Ralph's study. They normally used the galley and saloon on *Sally Ann* for eating, but that evening was to be an exception. Even before they emerged from the spinney their noses announced the meal that Ralph was preparing. The unmistakable tang of a barbecue was in the air.

Ralph himself appeared from behind a swirl of smoke, fanning the fumes away with one hand, using tongs to rotate sausages with the other. At six feet tall, with regular features and dark hair, he had kept in good shape for a man in his early forties. Under a red-and-white striped apron he was wearing a light blue silk shirt and navy slacks.

Beside the barbecue, under a large cream parasol stood a round table. Marnie noticed with some surprise that Ralph had put out five safari chairs and five place settings.

'I perceive, Watson, that we appear to be expecting guests,' Marnie said quietly.

'Not in the diary, Holmes,' Anne replied.

'I hope I don't have to be Moriarty.' Ralph kissed Marnie on the lips. 'All that twirling of moustaches and falling over waterfalls can be *very* wearing.'

'Okay,' said Marnie, 'I'll let you off, but you have to reveal who's coming.'

'Fair enough. I'll give you three guesses and a clue.'

'You're on,' said Marnie.

'The clue,' Ralph paused for effect, 'is that I invited them on condition they don't insist on saying grace.'

'Got it,' said Marnie. 'The Archbishop of –'

'Randall and Angela,' Anne interjected.

'Give the girl a coconut!' Ralph exclaimed with a flourish. 'Actually, they virtually invited themselves. They have something important to tell us.'

'Perhaps Randall's going to make an honest woman of Angela,' Marnie mused. 'It's about time.'

'I've never thought of rural deans making honest women of lady vicars,' said Ralph. 'I can't imagine Angela as a vamp in fishnet tights.'

'Pleased to hear it,' said Marnie. 'And while we're thinking of such practical matters, is that all the salad you've made for supper?'

On the table stood a bowl of sliced tomatoes in vinaigrette with chopped basil leaves scattered over them.

'I did wonder about that myself,' Ralph admitted.

Without a further word, Marnie and Anne repaired to the galley on *Sally Ann*. Marnie dug out lettuce, cucumber, spring onions and baby beetroots from the fridge. A mixed salad was in the offing, but she wondered if that would mean too much French dressing in the side dishes. Anne had two suggestions.

'We could use soured cream in the oil and vinegar to make a German-style dressing. We've got some in the fridge in the office barn.'

'Good idea,' said Marnie. 'And what about garlic bread for starters? I know we've got some baguettes in the freezer over there.'

'And if we need another side dish, what about Russian eggs? We've got plenty, and there's mayonnaise in the cupboard.'

Marnie had the oven heating up and six eggs in the pan before Anne reached the spinney. When she returned, she found Marnie threading chunks of onion with green and red peppers on wooden skewers as kebabs ready to join the meat on the barbecue. By the time the Reverend Dr Randall Hughes and the Reverend Angela Hemingway walked arm-in-arm through the spinney, the smells wafting round the table were mouth-watering.

For the evening they were both out of uniform. In place of Angela's habitual grey costume and clerical collar, she was wearing a summer dress of pale primrose with a white cardigan over her shoulders. Instead of his full-length black cassock with buttons down the front, Randall was in jeans and a suede jacket. They looked relaxed and happy together, and Marnie was in no doubt about their *important news*.

Randall proffered a bottle of claret, which Ralph gratefully placed in the centre of the table alongside an Aussie *shiraz*.

Kissing Ralph on both cheeks and eyeing his apron, Angela said, 'Ralph, you're amazing. Just look at all this *wonderful* spread. I don't know how you do it.'

Ralph gave the most Gallic of shrugs, using both hands. 'Sometimes I even amaze myself,' he declared with a brave but unconvincing attempt at looking modest.

Marnie and Anne flashed each other the heavy eyelids but refrained from comment.

In anticipation of Randall and Angela's announcement, Marnie had a bottle of champagne chilling in the freezer. Neither of the guests referred to their *something important* during the meal, and Marnie wondered if Ralph could have misunderstood. By the time they had advanced to chilled stewed rhubarb with Greek yogurt, she decided they needed a little prompting.

'So,' she began, 'what news, then? Is everything well in church circles?'

Randall and Angela looked blank.

'I think so,' said Angela.

'The usual mixture of piety and back-stabbing.' Randall grinned. 'All good clean fun.'

Marnie looked across at Ralph. It was his turn to take a hint.

'Do I remember rightly that there was something important you had to tell us?'

More blank looks until suddenly Angela lit up.

'Oh *that*! Yes, of course.' She turned to Randall. 'Shall I tell them or will you?'

Marnie moved her chair back from the table in preparation for going to fetch the champagne. She was putting her napkin down beside her plate, when Randall spoke quietly.

'We've got the final go-ahead to move Sarah into the churchyard.'

The statement was met with an initial silence. Ralph was the first to speak.

'That was the news you meant when you phoned this afternoon?'

'Yes,' said Randall.

'At last,' said Angela. 'It's great news, isn't it?'

Marnie stood up. 'Wonderful. Would everyone like coffee?'

It was warm enough to sit outside until Randall and Angela rose to leave. Marnie walked with them through the spinney to their car while Ralph and Anne cleared the table.

In the sleeping cabin on *Thyrsis* later that night, Marnie sat on the bed, brushing her hair. She asked Ralph if, on reflection, Randall had given any clue about the *something important* when they spoke on the phone.

'No. Those were his exact words.'

'I suppose it is important in a way,' Marnie said. 'After all, Sarah has been outside the churchyard for three hundred and fifty years. Even so, it's not quite what we expected.'

Ralph did not contribute further to that topic of conversation. As Marnie began peeling off her dressing gown, he had other things on his mind than the reburial of a woman who died in the seventeenth century.

Sarah Anne Day had taken her own life at the age of twenty-three, had in fact hanged herself from a beam in what was now Marnie's office. They believed she was suffering from remorse following the murder of the vicar and the part played in his killing by her own father. Angela, as the new incumbent, had been determined to have Sarah re-interred in consecrated ground. In this she was supported by Randall, who was not only rural dean but had also served as rector in the parish. Permission had now finally been received from the bishop, despite strenuous opposition from the local archdeacon.

All this was fascinating to anyone with an interest in local history, including Ralph at other times, but not as he watched Marnie's long back come into view as the dressing gown rolled away from her elegant shoulders. She slipped it off, laid it across the foot of the bed and turned to put out the light on the shelf above them.

Ralph was just reaching out to draw her towards him, when he heard a sharp intake of breath in the darkness. Marnie had suddenly remembered the champagne in the freezer. By morning, the bottle would undoubtedly have shattered. She leapt out of bed, leaving a bemused Ralph clutching the sheets.

'Don't start without me,' Marnie called over her shoulder as she skipped naked along the passage to the galley.

2
Setting Off

The following morning after breakfast, Anne realised she had overlooked something. It was Saturday. Ralph had set off early to chair a weekend seminar at his college in Oxford, and Marnie was catching up on work in the office. Anne was in her attic room doing some serious reading for her college course when Marnie's words hit her.

... you may be hearing about it again ... and sooner rather than later ...

What had she meant? Anne scrambled up from her giant beanbag, thinking back to their conversation. They had been preoccupied with finding a way across Leicester to avoid the heavy traffic, and the subject had gone out of her mind. The need to prepare for dinner and the arrival of Angela and Randall had completed the shut-out.

Almost sliding down the wall-ladder, Anne found Marnie absorbed in a design, writing notes on a pad. Not a good time to interrupt. Marnie's concentration in that kind of work was always intense. Turning back to the wall-ladder, Anne heard Marnie's voice behind her.

'Yes, you're right. We need to talk.'

They sat by the canal on safari chairs with a picnic table between them. It was a fine, warm morning, and Marnie had suggested they take their work outside. They had changed into shorts and T-shirts and had settled down comfortably with mugs of lemon tea, and the furled parasol standing by in case of need.

'I love mornings like this,' Anne said. 'It's so quiet here, and there's that lovely watery smell from the canal.'

'It's perfect,' Marnie agreed, 'though there were times last winter when I thought we'd never sit outside again.'

They both shivered at the memory.

'It was great eating here last night,' said Anne. 'One of my favourite things. Though I thought it was a pity we had to have Sarah's reburial brought up again.'

'So did I.' Marnie stretched and yawned. 'I've had quite enough of witchcraft and lugubrious goings-on to last me a lifetime.'

Anne became serious. 'That's why I was rather surprised that you bought those books about pirates and hangings and bodies being covered in pitch.'

Marnie smiled. 'Bet you're glad we didn't produce sticky toffee pudding for dessert last night.'

Anne groaned. In her mind's eye she saw a body hanging in chains beside the Thames. She heard the gallows creak as the corpse swung in the breeze, while its eyes were pecked out by crows. She shook herself.

'Go on then, Marnie, tell me about it. Let's get it over with.'

'There's not a lot to tell, really. And ideally I wanted to give you and Ralph the news at the same time.'

'I thought you would've done that already,' said Anne, 'last night after we'd gone to bed.'

'No,' said Marnie. 'We were ... bushed. It was too late to go into all that by then.'

Anne looked at Marnie over the top of her sunglasses. 'Really?'

Marnie ignored her. 'Okay, here's how it is. We have a new contract from Willards. They're part of a consortium developing a site in London. There'll be a *boutique* hotel with a wine bar and a bistro. We'll be handling the interior design for Everett Parker.'

'Wow!' Anne exclaimed. 'That's terrific. When do we start?'

'The site works are already underway. It seems they've been preparing the ground for some weeks.'

'And they've only just now appointed you to do the interior design?' said Anne. 'Why the delay?'

'It's London. They have to allow time for the archaeologists to do their thing.'

'So it's central London?' Anne asked.

'Yes.'

There was something in Marnie's tone that sounded an alarm bell for Anne.

'This is where the books about pirates come in, isn't it?'

'Well ... yes.'

'Where is this site, Marnie?'

'It's that place ... Horselydown.'

Anne repeated the name.

'*Horselydown ... on the south bank of the Thames, opposite the Tower of London.*'

'You know it?' Marnie was surprised. 'I'd never heard the name before it came up at the meeting yesterday.'

'I was quoting,' said Anne, 'from your river pirates book. It's one of the places where they hanged them.'

'I thought that was further along, the other side of Butler's Wharf ... St Saviour's Dock.'

Anne shrugged. 'That's what it said in your book.'

'Well, that's all going to change. Willards are building a beautiful hotel. There'll be a small gallery, too, a sort of *living museum* at basement level. We'll get stuck in to the design and you can forget all about pirates and hangings and such.'

'So what happens next?'

'We study the brief and start putting some ideas together.'

'When do we get to see the site?' Anne asked.

'Philip wants us to meet there as soon as possible.'

Anne ran through the diary in her mind. The early part of the following week was clear. The same thought was occurring to Marnie.

'Are you thinking what I'm thinking?' she said.

Anne was in her element, working through her to-do list. She and Marnie quickly packed their bags for London. Marnie wrote a list of instructions for the builders working on the farmhouse and arranged for tenants to feed Dolly over the weekend. Anne tidied the office and recorded a new message on the answerphone. After hitting the supermarket for provisions, they returned home via the garage where Marnie filled the Disco with diesel and put it through the car-wash.

Marnie phoned Ralph at college during the seminar lunch break to tell him of their spur-of-the-moment plan. Promising to leave him food for the time of their absence, she asked him to check the post each day in case anything urgent arrived.

In the early afternoon they made their final preparations. With last-minute instructions to Dolly – *You're in charge* – Marnie checked the boats and the office barn while Anne loaded the car. They climbed aboard the Disco. Marnie put the key in the ignition and looked sideways at Anne.

'All set?'

'Let's do it.'

Marnie gunned the engine and pointed the car up the field track. As on so many occasions when they travelled together, Anne felt the world was full of promise and new beginnings. She smiled to herself. It was not the same as setting off on *Sally Ann*, but it was good to feel the call of the open road.

3
Sticks in the Mud

Marnie woke to what she considered a typical London Sunday morning. For all its vastness and its population of nearly eight million, the city was bathed in an almost eerie silence. She climbed out of bed and stood at the bedroom window, looking down at the river. The tide seemed to be ebbing, with a swift flow towards the Thames Barrier and beyond it the estuary and the sea. Away to her left she could see occasional traffic on Tower Bridge, but no sound penetrated the double glazing. She sensed that London was not yet ready to throw off its duvet of pale grey cloud and get up to face the new day.

In the bathroom Marnie looked at the marble tiles and heavy chrome fittings as she stepped into the shower and thought how good it was to have modern facilities. The past three years living on *Thyrsis* and *Sally Ann* had been fun, but that phase of her life was now coming to an end. She was looking forward to moving into the house at Glebe Farm.

Towelling herself dry, she became aware of a faint hissing in the background. Anne was up and about, taking a shower. It was time for them both to face the new day.

The plan for Sunday morning was simple: a walk and generally mooching about. A few phone calls to friends and family, a look at the Sunday papers, a chance to catch up on reading, then lunch at a riverside restaurant. A relaxing break before embarking on the new project.

It was not to be.

The first part of the programme followed the plan. Marnie caught Ralph for a quick chat after breakfast at his Oxford seminar, while Anne used her mobile to ring her parents. Marnie's next call was to her sister.

'Hi Beth. Hope I'm not disturbing a lie-in.'

'Cheek! We've been up for ages. How are things in the wilds of the country?'

'Fine. I'm standing in the bedroom looking out over the water.'

'No bodies floating in the canal?' Beth's flippant tone concealed a hint of anxiety.

'Not that I can see, especially as the water in question is the Thames. I'm looking at Tower Bridge, with a glimpse of the Tower of London behind it.'

'You're in Simon's flat? Sorry, I mean ... your Docklands flat.'

Marnie felt her stomach turn momentarily and paused to catch her breath before replying.

'Anne and I are here. We've got meetings tomorrow, a new project just down the road. Look, I know it's all rather last-minute, but would you and Paul be free to join us for lunch?'

'Sure, why not? We haven't anything else planned. It'll be a good excuse to drag Paul away from his computer … and me away from the kitchen.'

'Good. I'll book us a table somewhere.'

'Marnie, there's one condition …'

'No, Beth, this is my treat.'

'What? Oh, we can argue about that later. No, I was going to say let's keep it simple. No talk of murders, mayhem, dead bodies or –'

'See you at noon, Beth.'

One call later, Marnie had a table reserved for twelve-thirty in one of the restaurants at street level of the Butler's Wharf building. The ease and convenience of city living struck her as in marked contrast to the environment she had chosen in what Beth had called the *wilds of the country*.

It was time to wander out and pick up the Sunday papers. Marnie and Anne both chose shirts, slacks and sandals for this first outing as they took the lift down to the lobby and exited the building.

'Shall we have a look at the site?' said Anne. 'I'm bursting with curiosity to see the place.'

They made their way between the twin blocks of the restored Victorian wharf buildings, on cobbled paving beneath the overhead network of wrought-iron bridges linking the upper floors. A pedestrian subway led them under the traffic on the approach road to Tower Bridge and brought them out onto the bankside facing across the river to the Tower of London.

Barriers had been erected to guide passers-by round the development site that had been fenced off with tall green chain-link panels clipped together. Through the mesh Marnie and Anne could see large areas of excavation. Mounds of spoil were dotted about like rubbish tips. In the foreground a row of grey huts lined the access road, forming a short street of offices and changing rooms. Beyond them a collection of diggers painted bright yellow were lined up like dinosaurs at rest. A faint odour of damp soil hung in the air.

'All this?' said Anne. 'It's a big site.'

'It's a big project,' said Marnie.

The fence panels beside them were festooned with signs. The names of the various contractors filled one of them, listing the builders, structural consultants and architects. Anne was intrigued by one of the names: Capital Archaeology. She was thrilled to see Walker and Co, Interior Design Consultants, just below Everett Parker Associates, Architects.

The next panel carried a series of instructions and announcements: hard hats were mandatory; steel-capped boots were required; hi-visibility jackets were to be worn at all times; all visitors were to report to reception; no unauthorised access was permitted. And so on, and so on.

Concluding that they had seen all there was to see, Marnie and Anne were turning away when they heard raised voices from somewhere inside the compound. Men were shouting, apparently calling out instructions. It was strange as no-one was in sight. They scanned the whole area and were about to give up when a man appeared about thirty yards away, reaching the top of a ladder from a hole in the ground roughly the size of a tennis court.

As soon as the man cleared the ladder another head appeared. Then another and another. The men, all hard-hatted and clad in the same bright yellow jackets, streamed towards the huts. One man seemed to be arguing with the others. Marnie and Anne strained to hear them, but the men were speaking in a heated undertone that was drowned out by the noise of the traffic approaching Tower Bridge.

The first man had now reached one of the huts and was taking hold of the door handle when his arm was restrained by the man behind him. The other men caught up with these two and the discussion continued on the threshold. The second man, who had restrained the first, seemed to be pleading with the others, pointing back towards the deep excavation. The first man was shaking his head in a manner that was unmistakably adamant. The others looked on.

'What's that all about?' Marnie muttered.

Before Anne could comment, the pleading man took off his hard hat in a gesture of exasperation and ran a hand over his head. While he did this, the first man opened the door and went into the hut. Moments later the two silent men followed him, leaving the bare-headed man outside, fuming.

'Oh.'

Anne's utterance made Marnie turn to look at her.

'What is it?'

Anne pointed. 'That man.'

'What about him?'

'Don't you see? Don't you recognise him?'

Marnie turned back and stared into the compound. The bare-headed man seemed to be uncertain of his next move.

'Now that you mention it, there is something familiar about him ...'

'It's that archaeologist. He was at Glebe Farm last summer. You know, Marnie ... the one with the name like a highwayman or a ... pirate.' Anne was wringing her hands in frustration. 'A dashing sort of name.'

'Dashwood?' Marnie murmured. 'Or was it ...'

'Blackwood!' Anne exclaimed. 'Dick Blackwood!' She felt like adding, *special agent*.

'I do believe you're right,' said Marnie.'

Without warning, Anne called out, 'Dick!' and waved her arms.

The man's head snapped round. Anne shouted again. He looked in their direction and after a few seconds began walking towards them. Quickening his pace, he reached the fence and peered through.

He was a little taller than Marnie, slim, in his twenties, with a brown crew cut and intense grey eyes. He looked from one to the other.

'Marnie …' He grinned at them in recognition. 'Anne … with an 'e', if I'm not mistaken.' He gave a roguish laugh.

Marnie, beamed. 'Well, this is a surprise.'

'For me too.' Dick looked delighted to see them. 'What brings you here?'

'We're involved in this project.' Marnie indicated the building site.

'Interior design consultants, no less,' Anne added.

Dick's eyes narrowed. 'You're with Philip Everett's team?'

'That's us,' said Marnie.

'Well I wish he was here now. I'd get more sense out of Philip than I do from those clowns.' He gave a nod over his shoulder towards the huts. His tone was bitter.

'What's going on?' Marnie asked.

Dick hesitated. He seemed to be wrestling internally with some sort of dilemma.

'Look, Dick, if it's something you can't –'

'No, it's just … well, it's supposed to be confidential, but … oh, what the hell.' He gestured towards the site entrance. 'Since you're part of the project anyway, come on in. I'll show you.'

Once he had padlocked the entrance behind them, Dick led the way to a hut bearing the sign STAFF ONLY. Inside, he ferreted in a cupboard and produced two packs wrapped in cellophane. Marnie and Anne pulled them open and slipped on the yellow jackets. He showed them how to adjust the light blue hard hats to fit and handed each of them a lantern.

As he turned to leave the hut, Anne said, 'What about our feet?'

Dick looked down, grinning. 'They're very nice feet.'

'But aren't we supposed to wear steel-capped boots?'

'They have to be ordered in your sizes. Don't worry for now. You'll be better in sandals today. The boots take some getting used to, and we'll be climbing ladders.'

They were standing in the shade on sopping wet ground several metres below street level, where the sounds of the outside world barely reached. They had descended two tall ladders, with Dick leading the way. He had insisted that only one of them should be on each ladder at a time. The rungs were muddy, and the ladders swayed gently with every step. With lanterns switched on, they scanned the excavation around them in the gloom.

'What's that smell?' Anne asked. 'Is it some kind of gas?'

Marnie sniffed the air. It was suffused with a damp odour combining rotting vegetation with wet soil. Dick looked initially as if he had not understood the question.

'You'll get used to it,' he said eventually. 'Soon you won't even notice it.'

'But what is it?' Anne persisted.

'That ...' Dick said, pausing for effect, or as if seeking the right words, 'is the smell of history.'

'What do you mean?' said Marnie.

'Where we're standing would've been the bank of the river fifteen hundred years ago.'

Marnie stared towards the top of the upper ladder, high above them.

'Surely we're below river level down here.'

'It's low tide, otherwise this section would be flooded out,' Dick said. 'All the ground from here up to the present-day surface has been deposited over the centuries. Fallen leaves, dead vegetation like trees and bushes, silt from the movement of the river, all of these have made ground level rise to where it is now. That's what you can smell, now it's been exposed for the first time in a millennium and a half.'

'It's quite ... what's the word? ... quite *fetid*,' said Marnie.

'I love it,' Dick said simply.

'You seemed to be arguing with those men,' Anne said. 'What was that about?'

'That was the point.' Dick stared at her, his gaze intense. 'That's why I'm here on my day off instead of tucked up in bed with ... never mind.'

'But what *is* the point?' Marnie prodded. 'I don't get it.'

'Let me show you.' Dick walked a few yards away and held up his lantern. 'What do you see?'

Marnie and Anne raised their lamps and looked around them.

'Mud,' said Marnie. She noticed Dick frowning. 'Sorry. I don't mean to be obtuse. I realise this ... whatever it is ... means a lot to you, but you're going to have to give us a clue. We don't know what we're looking for.'

Anne squatted down swinging her lantern from side to side in an arc. She duck-walked closer to where Dick was standing and pointed at the slimy surface.

'Is it this?' she asked, looking up at him.

'What can you see?' said Marnie.

'Anne's got it!' Dick's tone was triumphant. 'That's it.'

Marnie advanced a few steps to stand beside Anne, who got to her feet. She bent forward and guided Anne's arm to concentrate the light of both lamps together.

'All I can see is what looks like ... some sticks, lodged in the mud.'

'Precisely,' Dick said, as if they had corroborated his findings.

'The argument was about these sticks?' Anne said. 'I'm none the wiser.'

'Look closer.' Dick squatted down. 'I don't want to touch them, but can you see how they're located?' He pointed. 'Here ... here ... and here.'

The sticks were evenly spaced out, protruding from the soil with a distance between them of less then an inch. They emerged from the ground at an oblique angle, rising just a fraction above the surface, each one about the thickness of a thumb.

'Could they be ... ribs?' Marnie asked uncertainly.

'Oh yes,' Anne murmured.

They looked at Dick, who nodded, a smile spreading across his features in the dim half-light.

Back in the staff hut it was time for explanations. Dick took their hard hats and put them in a steel locker, but told Marnie and Anne to keep the yellow jackets for future use. They sat round a table at one end of the hut.

The interior walls were hung with site plans, architects' drawings and a detailed timetable of works. From the felt-tip notes added to some of the plans, it looked as if the first phase of ground works sought to identify and divert underground services, electricity cables, water and sewage pipes.

Marnie recalled one project handled by Everett Parker Associates where a pile driver had struck the national grid in the east end of London. It had knocked out a connection to Deptford power station and put part of the London Underground system out of action for half a day. It transpired that someone years before had removed and failed to return a service plan from County Hall. The contractor had no idea he was piling down through an old street under which the cables were running.

There was no danger of that happening here. Every inch of space was plotted on the site map. Marnie asked Dick to show her where they had been looking at the ribs, and he took up position in front of the plans like a teacher in a classroom. Running a finger down one edge of the works, he indicated the course of the river. On Friday while making a routine check of the exposed surface below ground, he and a colleague had spotted what appeared to be a change of colour in the sub-soil. At that depth and in poor light they were unable to be sure exactly what they had seen. In dry conditions and at surface level Dick would probably have recognised a grave site immediately. Something about this discovery was different.

Dick had spent all of Saturday poring over maps of early London. A medieval specialist himself, he had spent hours phoning friends and colleagues who were experts in the history of London. No-one had been able to clarify what he had uncovered. From earliest pre-history, through Iron Age to post-Roman periods, no explanation made sense. The most likely scenario was that he had stumbled upon a one-off burial or the site of an accidental death.

Unable to rest and burning with curiosity, Dick had checked the tide charts and realised the river would reach its lowest level early on Sunday morning. As one of the archaeological site directors, he had keys to the compound and had let himself in before London was stirring. He had returned to the bones in the depths of the excavation. They seemed to be taunting him.

'Why?' Marnie asked. 'This is London. People have lived here for thousands of years.'

Dick shook his head. 'It's a question of levels. Where we are now is post-Roman. There's never been a graveyard on this site.'

'Didn't they hang river pirates here?' Anne asked, grimacing, thinking of Daring Jake Pepper. 'Couldn't they just be bones that had been left hanging in chains?'

'Too deep for that,' Dick said.

'How deep is it, then?' said Marnie. 'I mean in terms of timescale.'

'Post-Roman, pre-Norman. I'd put it roughly between the sixth and tenth centuries.'

'Anglo-Saxon times?' Marnie suggested.

'Exactly,' Dick said firmly. 'London had been a city for centuries by then, so you wouldn't expect to find isolated graves, not here in such a central position. These people were Christians. We know where they buried their dead.'

For several minutes they discussed the possibilities, and Dick set out the reasons for dismissing each one. The Saxons did not locate burial sites in residential areas; no recorded battles had been fought on that spot; isolated burials were not unknown but not in populated areas; if the dead person had been of major importance, thereby meriting an individual burial site, the experts would probably have known about it. The discovery made no sense.

There it was again. Watching Dick as he spoke, Marnie and Anne saw that glint in his eyes, the spark of enthusiasm bordering on the fanatical. They had seen it before when Dick had been leading the excavations at Glebe Farm. Faced with an impenetrable mystery like this, Dick Blackwood was in his element.

Sensing that they had exhausted all the potential for discussion of the bones, Marnie steered Dick back to his argument with the other men that morning. She guessed they were annoyed at the find because it would hold up progress with the construction works. To her surprise, she was wrong. It was just the opposite. The site agent was not only pleased with the uncovering of the remains, he wanted to announce it publicly.

'This has got to be a first,' Marnie said in bewilderment. 'In my experience, builders usually go ballistic when they hit an archaeological find. They start screaming about delays, loss of earnings, disruption of the sequence of operations, cash-flow problems, you name it. Why should this job be different?'

'You left out the archaeologists' worries,' said Dick. 'We're more concerned about intruders, treasure-hunters, metal detectorists and the like. The last thing we want is a load of amateurs trampling all over our finds, disturbing the ground, destroying evidence.'

Marnie looked thoughtful. 'That's right. And surely the contractor wouldn't want that either. Imagine what would happen if someone unauthorised was injured ... or worse.'

'That's the line I'm taking,' said Dick, 'apart from the fact that we don't yet know what we've found.'

'Could they be animal bones?' Anne asked, 'a wild boar or a wolf or something?'

Dick shook his head. 'These are human. No doubt about it. But there may be a possibility that we haven't considered. We just don't know what this is, and until we do ...'

Marnie broke the ensuing silence. 'I still don't see why the contractor would welcome the find and want to go public. It defies logic.'

'I know what he's thinking,' said Dick. 'A find like that on a site in this location would justify delays, which would mean compensation. Not only that, it would give him something to blame for running late.'

'Is the job running late?' said Marnie.

'They always run late, don't they? You know the score, Marnie. Builders are terrified of liquidated and ascertained damages. They want to cover their backs.'

'That still doesn't explain why they want to make a public announcement.'

'It's the same thing,' said Dick. 'If the discovery becomes public knowledge, it underlines the problem and helps his case. Everyone knows about it, so it can't be denied later. QED.'

'So you're trapped,' said Marnie.

'I wish I'd never brought it up.' Dick sighed. 'I didn't think they'd react like this. I should've thought about it before telling the site agent. I just didn't want builders' boots treading all over my find when they started work on Monday morning.'

At Dick's suggestion they went to find the site agent, but were dismayed to find his office locked. The agent and the other suits had left the compound. Dick was sure their first job on Monday would be to issue a press release. By the time the early editions of the London papers went on sale at lunchtime, the find would be public knowledge. Then the problems would begin.

Marnie scanned the site. On all sides it was securely fenced in, but with chain link that was meant to be more public-friendly, giving visibility all round. At little more than two metres high, the fencing presented scant protection against determined intruders. The find would be blown up in the public imagination. *Could it be the grave of a Saxon king or queen with a buried hoard of silver or gold?*

Dick must have been sharing the same thought. 'If the word gets out, we'll be sitting ducks here. And there's nothing we can do about it.'

Marnie imagined every nut-case with a metal detector for miles around being drawn to Horselydown. She reached into her shoulder bag and pulled out her mobile. Dick shot her a questioning glance.

'I'm not sure you're right about that,' she said, pressing buttons.

Beside her, Anne had already taken out a notebook, and her pencil was poised.

Having booked the table only that morning, there was no chance of getting a view out over the river, but none of them cared. Marnie and Anne spent their lives beside water, and Beth and Paul were glad just to be invited to lunch.

Marnie looked over the top of her menu and asked if everyone had chosen. For Beth and Paul, it had to be the Sunday roast. Anne, the herbivore of the party, opted for asparagus tart. Marnie chose baked salmon and asked the wine waiter for a spritzer. Anne followed her lead, while Paul suggested a robust red Navarra for the beef-eaters.

While waiting for the food to arrive, Marnie noticed Beth looking at her in a speculative way.

'It's good to see you relaxing like this,' Beth said.

'Why wouldn't I be relaxing? It is Sunday, after all.'

'I know, but I'm always worrying that you never let up, never take time off.'

'Well, I'm here, aren't I?' said Marnie. 'We're having a nice restful Sunday.'

Paul laughed. 'Beth was saying on the way here she was convinced you'd have a last-minute excuse for crying off. She was sure some urgent business matter would crop up.'

Marnie stared at her sister in mock indignation. 'Shame on you! I don't know how you could think –'

'Marnie,' Anne interrupted. 'Sorry to break in, but I think the waiter wants you.'

Marnie turned to find a waiter hovering at her shoulder. 'Is there a problem?'

The waiter bent forward and spoke quietly. 'Mrs Walker? Marnie Walker?'

'Yes.'

'There's a telephone call for you, madam.'

'For me? How would anyone know ...? Ah, yes.'

'Would you like to come this way, madam.'

Marnie arrived back at the table while the starters were being served. As they focused on plates of avocado with mushrooms, Beth noticed Anne glancing enquiringly at Marnie. Marnie studiously avoided eye contact.

'Mm, this is good,' Marnie said.

'Is everything all right?' Beth asked.

'Yes. The avocado's just right. Sometimes they can be rather too firm and –'

'Marnie, you know what I meant.' Beth spoke softly, but her voice had an edge to it.

'Everything's fine,' Marnie insisted calmly.

'Then why did Anne look at you like that?'

Marnie sipped the spritzer. 'Am I a mind-reader?'

Paul chuckled. 'Come on, Marnie, out with it. Amaze us. Tell us they've found a dead body in your building site.'

'So Anne told you about that?' Marnie said.

At adjacent tables several heads turned momentarily as Beth dropped her fork onto the plate with a clatter.

After lunch they adjourned to the flat and settled on Simon's comfortable cream sofas, while cups of coffee steamed on low mahogany tables, watched over by abstract paintings of the Thames and Docklands.

'You probably won't want to talk shop,' Beth began, 'but you hinted that this project was out of the ordinary. What's so special about it?'

'It's complicated,' said Marnie.

'Cretins guide version will do.'

Marnie paused. 'Okay. Here goes. We always knew we were likely to find archaeology here because of the location. Someone at Willards suggested we should if possible include any archaeological finds in the design. The site had once been an island in the river in the Bronze and Iron ages, so Philip suggested that water could feature prominently below ground level. Willards agreed and said that if anything significant was found, Philip should explore *imaginative new ways* of incorporating it.'

'Had anything been found at that time?' Paul asked.

'No. It was just an idea. But soon some small finds were made. Encouraged by this, Philip came up with an original concept. The flow of tidal water would be incorporated into the scheme, with glazed panels allowing visitors to see the exhibits while at the same time protecting the remains.'

'That hadn't been done before?' said Beth.

'Not the way Philip planned it. The panels and related lighting would make it look as if the remains were being submerged by the tides. He consulted experts at London Barbican University who were highly enthusiastic. Willards were ecstatic.'

'How would they keep the glazed panels from silting up?'

Marnie smiled. 'That's the beauty of it, Paul. The glass would have a special diamond-hard coating and high-speed jets would flush off any impurities.'

'Brilliant.'

'Absolutely. Willards were getting a world class design that would confirm them as a company with world class credentials. Any large finds will remain *in situ*, and smaller objects will be displayed in the gallery.'

Beth looked doubtful. 'Forgive me if I'm being thick, but did they commit to the scheme before finding anything?'

'It's a win-win,' said Marnie. 'We've got to excavate deep foundations because of the sub-soil. If we find nothing, we've lost nothing. The hotel will still have one of the best locations in the country.'

'Are there extra costs involved?'

'Only if we find something worth displaying. And if that's the case, the costs will be covered by grants from the Heritage Lottery Fund, a private foundation and English Heritage.'

'You seem very confident you will find something,' said Paul.

'Not me ... the experts at LBU. Their professor said if they didn't find something important he'd emigrate to Timbuktu.'

Paul grimaced. 'I hope for his sake he's right.'

'Don't worry. He won't be needing an airline ticket.'

'They've found something?' Paul was agog. 'Something major?'

'It's strictly confidential at this stage, but the first remains were located early this morning.'

Marnie described the events that had led Dick to excavating ancient bones lying in mud deep below street level.

'That was your phone call in the restaurant?' Beth asked.

'That was Philip,' said Marnie. 'When I phoned him earlier I'd mentioned the name of the restaurant where we'd booked a table. That's how he knew where to find me.'

'What was so important he had to interrupt your Sunday lunch? The remains were hardly an urgent case for Scotland Yard.'

'I needed him to issue an instruction to the contractor not to go public.'

'Why would they take orders from him?' Paul asked.

'I figured that Philip could offer to make a note in the file of the exact date of the find. That would protect the builders if it caused delays. He would tell them he'd also be contacting Willards first thing tomorrow.'

Beth looked sceptical. 'My guess is they'll still leak this to the media, if they think that's in their interests.'

'My guess is, they won't,' said Marnie.

'What makes you so sure?' Paul said.

'Philip made it clear this was a formal instruction and he was putting it in writing. I expect a fax is already sitting on the machine in the contractor's site office.'

'You think that's enough to hold them back?' Beth asked.

Marnie nodded. 'Sure. He pointed out that any leak could only emanate from one source. If word got out and intruders broke into the compound, the contractor would be liable in the event of any injury. You know how hot everyone is these days about health and safety on building sites.'

'So the contractor was cornered.' Paul smiled. 'That's neat.'

'That was the idea,' Marnie said.

'So what happens now?' Beth asked.

'We have our progress meeting on Monday and then go home.'

Beth shook her head. 'No. I meant about … the bones.'

'That's a question for Dick Blackwood,' said Marnie. 'After all, they're his baby. We'll have to wait and see.'

4
Zoë

Marnie was surprised how many people came for the management group meeting on Monday morning. Arriving at the compound, she and Anne were directed to a minibus that would take them to a hotel across the river. The journey was only a few hundred yards, but even such a short trip qualified for an executive Mercedes with leather upholstery and air conditioning. Marnie half expected a stewardess to serve cocktails on the way. She noticed that Anne was striving not to look overawed, and almost succeeding.

On arrival, they were conducted to the Convention Centre one floor down by a wide staircase and guided into a spacious room by a young woman in uniform. Its walls were lined with ivory drapes, and deep-pile red carpet covered the floor. Around the tables laid out in a square formation, comfortable chairs in royal blue upholstery were set out. At each place notepads were provided, plus pens, pencils and glasses, all bearing the name of the hotel. A conference microphone was positioned before each delegate, rising up from its console to face them on a slender black stalk. Bottles of mineral water and fruit juices were clustered within reach of every participant.

Marnie walked slowly round the table until she found their places. Anne struggled to suppress a smile at the sight of her own nameplate.

> **Miss Anne Price**
> **Walker and Company**
> **Interior Design Consultants**

'Who are all these people?' Anne whispered, taking her own notepad and pen from her bag.

'We'll soon find out,' Marnie said quietly. 'The chairman will invite us to introduce ourselves. Just say your name, followed by *Walker and Co* and then *interior design*. Okay?'

'Just like on the card,' said Anne.

'Exactly. And before you speak, press that button there on the console. You'll see a red light come on like a collar round the microphone. As soon as it lights up, the mic is live. When you've finished, press the button again and the light will go out.'

'Got it. Who's chairing the meeting?'

'Over there on our right in the middle at that end of the table. He's Malcolm

Cawdrey, deputy chairman of Willards Brewery.'

Anne saw a tall burly man in his fifties with greying hair wearing a dark grey suit, shaking hands with one of the other men.

'So he's our client?' she said.

'Strictly speaking, Philip Everett's our client and we're his consultants, but yes, Malcolm's the big cheese here today.'

At that moment Philip Everett arrived, placing a hand on each of their shoulders. He kissed Marnie on the cheek, winked at Anne and took his seat beside Marnie.

Anne watched the other participants arriving. It occurred to her that nearly everyone present was middle-aged, wearing a dark suit. The world was run by such men. For that day Marnie had chosen a jacket in deep emerald green and navy stripes over a white shirt and a skirt of dark blue. Anne was wearing a cream silk shirt and black trousers.

There were only two other women in the assembly. Anne guessed that one was about forty and obviously a personal assistant to one of the senior executives. The other was much younger, probably in her twenties. She looked vaguely familiar. Anne wanted to check this with Marnie, but she was now locked in conversation with Philip, studying a book of floor plans.

The young woman was standing on the opposite side of the room and had become the centre of attention. Surrounded by a group of suits, she was listening to one man who appeared to be telling a story. The other men were watching her, as if gauging her reactions. She was wearing a fawn linen safari shirt and cream slacks. Her hair was golden-blond, falling to her shoulders, and she was lightly tanned.

The image she conveyed was fit and wholesome, an outdoor type who had not lost her femininity. In fact, Anne could see that in subtle ways she sought to emphasise it; a gesture with her hands, the toss of her head when she laughed, the hint of a coquettish smile as she listened to the narrator.

Anne was still puzzling over where she might have seen her before when she noticed Dick Blackwood standing behind her, a little to one side. He was the only man present not wearing a suit. In an open-necked check shirt, he looked out of place in this company, and although he joined in the laughter of the others, he seemed uncomfortable as if unsure of himself.

The tapping of a fingernail on a microphone – and a *shall we make a start, ladies and gentlemen?* – brought the meeting to order, and a hush descended on the gathering as everyone took their seats.

Attending such a meeting for the first time, Anne was fascinated to see how the world of big business functioned on a major project. Until then, she had not fully appreciated that Willards Brewery was such a big league player. She was overwhelmed by the weight of finance and power gathered round the table, feeling as if she had wandered in like a child from the playground who had no right to be in such exalted company. Suddenly the room had become unbearably warm, and she found breathing difficult. *Calm down*, she told herself, *take deep breaths, relax. It's just a meeting like any other.*

While Anne strove to maintain her composure, the chairman ran through the preliminaries, drawing attention to the agenda. He asked everyone to press the button on their consoles to check that the microphones were all operational. Then, as Marnie had predicted, he asked the participants to introduce themselves briefly and mention at the same time any matters not contained in the agenda that they would like to be discussed at the end under *Any Other Urgent Business.*

The chairman introduced himself simply as Malcolm Cawdrey of Willards before indicating the woman sitting to his left.

'Jane Bennington, personal assistant to Mr Cawdrey.'

And so the baton was passed to the man on her left, and the introductions proceeded. Anne saw that Marnie was noting the names round a square that she had drawn on her pad. Quickly, she reached forward and took a bottle of sparkling water. Having second thoughts, she replaced it with still water. A hiccup while introducing herself would be a disaster from which she might never recover. Carefully pouring water into her glass, Anne took two sips. The moment when she would have to speak was approaching like a tidal wave.

She heard Philip introduce himself as she put down the glass with as much serenity as she could muster. Then Marnie spoke clearly and calmly into her microphone. When she finished, Marnie inclined her head slightly in Anne's direction. Anne extended a hand towards the console and pressed the button. The light glowed red.

'Anne Price ... Walker and Co ... interior design.'

Thank god for that! Anne pressed the button again and the microphone light went out. She realised that she had stopped breathing and hoped it would be only a temporary phenomenon.

And then it happened. The man sitting to Anne's left was reaching for the console when Malcolm Cawdrey intervened.

'One moment, if you would, please. Just a word for Anne.'

Anne's heart stopped beating. Her major organs seized up and ceased to function. The breath was sucked from her lungs and all brain activity stopped. She was dead before she slumped to the ground.

At least, that was how it felt as Anne sat rigid in her place. By a miracle her sense of hearing continued to work. She heard the voice of the chairman as if from a great distance.

'This is the first time Anne has joined us at a formal meeting. We've had contact with her on numerous occasions when dealing with Walker and company, and she has always proved to be a most helpful colleague.'

Anne could feel the red tide rising up her cheeks as every person in the room stared at her, but was fortunately paralysed and therefore unable to writhe about in desperation. Marnie turned slightly towards her and murmured three words under her breath. Anne swallowed hard. The chairman continued.

'So I'd just like to welcome you formally to the management group, Anne. It's a pleasure to meet you in person at last.'

Making every effort to conceal the shaking of her hand, Anne deftly hit the button on the console and in a robotic trance repeated the words Marnie had whispered to her.

'Thank you, chairman.'

She made a brave effort to smile but her face muscles had solidified and her jaw was locked. She sat back in the chair, trying not to slump, and began breathing again, peripherally aware that Marnie leaned over and pressed the button to extinguish the microphone light for her.

'Well done,' Marnie whispered with an encouraging smile.

The chairman said, 'Sorry to interrupt you, Mr Jackson. Please continue.'

The man sitting beside Anne switched on his microphone and said, 'Terry Jackson, clerk of works.'

When he sat back he extended a hand to Anne who shook it, hoping her own hand was not cold and clammy.

'Good to meet you, Anne,' he said softly.

Anne nodded in reply, not trusting her vocal chords to perform correctly. By the time she resumed normal breathing, the roll call had turned the corner and was making its way along the next run of participants. Soon the people on the opposite side were making their introductions. Anne listened carefully when Dick's turn came, as he was sitting beside the young woman.

'Dick Blackwood, Capital Archaeology, joint site director.'

The young woman switched on her microphone, paused and spoke in an authoritative tone.

'Dr Zoë Tipton, Cambridge University Institute of Archaeology, site director.'

Dick's head twitched perceptibly and he looked down at the table, frowning. The man on the other side of Zoë Tipton introduced himself.

'Dr Miles Fennimore, London Barbican University Department of Archaeology, Senior Research Fellow and Horselydown project director.'

After the introductions, the chairman embarked on the agenda. He guided the assembly briskly through the early points, matters arising from the previous meeting, ground survey results, a report from the structural consultants, the resolution of some outstanding planning issues.

Eventually they reached the item entitled *Archaeology*, and Dr Fennimore was invited to report on progress. Anne spotted the reaction of one of the contractors, who glared in the direction of Dick Blackwood, who seemed not to notice.

Fennimore had a nasal voice and an accent that Anne thought was northern. When he called on Dick to present the report, Zoë Tipton uttered a faint sound that might have been surprise or disapproval.

Dick began by stressing that everything he revealed was to be treated as strictly confidential. He looked across at Philip Everett who confirmed that he had sent written instructions on confidentiality to all contractors and consultants. Philip had evidently briefed Malcolm Cawdrey about this, as he too weighed in, pressing home the point about potential claims for damages if intruders incurred injuries on site.

The senior executive from the construction company asked that the date of the discovery of the human remains should be recorded in the minutes. This was agreed.

Dick returned to his report, explaining that he had made a discovery on Friday that could be archaeologically significant. As he outlined his findings, Zoë Tipton turned and began speaking quietly to Dr Fennimore. Anne was impressed at how succinctly and clearly Dick presented the facts. He concluded with an assurance that he would work on the remains as quickly as he could to minimise any possible delay to the contract.

Malcolm Cawdrey asked if anyone had any questions in a tone that suggested he hoped they did not. There was an immediate reaction. Zoë Tipton raised one hand while pressing the microphone button with the other. The chairman acknowledged her.

'Just a point for clarification, please, chairman. These remains ... are they the ones I pointed out on Friday?'

Cawdrey gestured to Dick, who looked momentarily wrong-footed.

'Er, yes.' He sounded uncertain. 'Zoë did ... that is, Dr Tipton did see them, but thought at the time they might not be important.'

Tipton's microphone was still live. 'I thought there was no evidence to suggest –'

'Sorry, Dr Tipton,' Cawdrey interrupted. 'Would you please address your remarks to the chair.'

'Of course. Sorry, chairman. I was just rather surprised that there now seems to be such certainty about the bones. We have yet to ascertain precisely what they are. When I left to return to Cambridge on Friday afternoon that had not been established, and here we are on Monday morning making unequivocal assertions about them.'

'Mr Blackwood?' said the chairman. 'Have there been further developments?'

'Yes, chairman,' Dick said. 'I spent most of Sunday morning on site – before the tide rose – and carried out further excavation of the bones. There's no doubt they are human. Other dating evidence suggests they're probably Anglo-Saxon.'

Dick fielded questions from around the table, while Zoë Tipton said nothing. In fact she did not even look up, but spent the time writing rapid notes. Eventually the chairman glanced at his watch and brought the discussion to a close, asking Dick and his colleagues to keep everyone informed if any other significant finds were made.

Over the next hour technical reports were presented. Philip was called on several times to contribute to the discussions, sometimes on design matters, sometimes on phasing and timing of building works.

Marnie did not have to speak except to confirm that she had received a full set of floor plans from the architects. She would begin work on the interior design immediately and would be putting forward her proposals at the next monthly meeting. Anne admired Marnie's calm tone and confident delivery and noticed she was listened to in respectful silence.

The chairman paused the meeting mid-morning for what he called a *comfort break*, and participants took the opportunity to stretch their legs in the lobby, where coffee and pastries had been set out. Marnie said she wanted to phone Ralph, so Anne nipped along to the *Ladies Powder Room*, where the sign on the door depicted a lady wearing full-length Victorian dress. After powdering her nose and adjusting her crinoline, Anne bumped into Jane Bennington on the way out.

'Hallo, Anne. Lovely to see you. I hope you're not finding it too boring.'

'Not at all,' Anne said, shaking hands. 'It's interesting to see how everything fits together.'

'You made a good impression this morning. Well done.' The PA pushed the restroom door open. 'Must dash. We're due back in five minutes.'

In the lobby Anne could see Marnie still talking on the phone. In need of fresh air, she hurried up the stairs, crossed the hotel reception area and went outside. Tower Bridge loomed up before her and, right on cue, a Thames barge slipped out of Saint Katherine Docks, its brown sails furled, and headed downstream.

Anne realised that the hotel rooms in their project across the river would have a spectacular outlook and skyline. The feeling that she was privileged to be part of it all flooded over her. Standing there beside the Thames, she recognised how great a part luck had played in her life. Everything she did, everything she had, she owed to a chance meeting with Marnie three years earlier one summer's morning by a bridge on the Grand Union Canal in Bedfordshire.

Anne wanted there and then to rush back inside to hug Marnie tightly and thank her for her life. Suddenly she recalled some advice Marnie had once given her. *Never be late for a meeting, especially if you're a woman.* Anne knew the session would resume in one minute and was determined not to fall short of her or Marnie's standards. Turning on her heel, Anne strode towards the hotel entrance and as she did so, saw Zoë Tipton speaking urgently into her mobile near the door. The young archaeologist failed to notice Anne as she sped past, so absorbed was she in her conversation.

People were talking together in small groups round the table when Anne entered the meeting room. The chairman had left his place and was standing beside Marnie and Philip, with the other architect in attendance. Marnie spotted Anne and signalled with a nod of the head for her to join them. Philip's colleague was a slightly-built man in his thirties with thinning mousy hair. He was tall with a hint of a stoop and wearing John Lennon glasses, which combined to give him a scholarly air. He passed Anne a spiral-bound A4 book containing a site plan, floor plans and elevation drawings, a useful volume covering the whole project. She saw that among the names listed on the front cover was *Project architect – Nigel Beardsley.*

'Hallo, Anne,' he said in a low voice. 'I'm Nigel. This is your copy.'

Anne silently mouthed her thanks as she heard the chairman speaking to Marnie.

'… your initial thoughts, though I realise that's an unfair question at such an early stage.'

Without hesitation Marnie replied.

'I've been thinking about the job ever since we talked about it in your office on Friday. Most guests in the hotel will have a busy schedule, either seeing the sights of London or attending business meetings. They'll appreciate a welcoming entrance probably in muted colours with imaginative lighting. I'd like them to feel they've come back to an oasis of calm in a hectic world.'

'I'm with you there, Marnie,' said Cawdrey.

'But,' Marnie went on, 'and I think this is important, they should also feel inspired by their environment, so I'd like to feature a mural facing them as they enter, a riverscape scene of London as it was in times past, filled with sailing ships at anchor in a bustling port, with wharves and cranes as a backdrop.'

'Do you yet have a colour scheme in mind?' Cawdrey asked.

'The style would be like a pen and ink drawing over a single colour wash … possibly in a faded blue or perhaps cream, depending on the scheme for the rest of the entrance.'

Cawdrey was nodding. 'I like it. What do you think, Philip?'

'Murals have become a popular feature of Marnie's designs in your waterways pubs. This would be a continuation of that theme, a sort of extension of the house style.'

'Good, good.' Cawdrey beamed at Marnie. 'I can't think of anywhere else using that kind of design. Any other thoughts?'

'I'm thinking of having a key colour for each floor, restful colours to soothe the guests at the end of their day. And perhaps we could continue the mural theme in the dining room, bistro and wine bar.'

The chairman looked at his watch. 'We'd better get started. Thank you, Marnie. That all sounds very promising. I'm looking forward to seeing your proposals in detail later on.'

Malcolm Cawdrey looked up from his agenda as the meeting drew to a close. The participants now appeared rather less alert than when proceedings started. He thanked everyone for their contributions and declared that his PA would be distributing the draft minutes later in the week. The management group would reconvene in one month's time. His last task was to invite everyone to stay on for a buffet lunch which was waiting for them in an adjacent room.

There were no windows in the convention centre, and Anne found the air-conditioned atmosphere weighed down on her. When the chairman rose from his seat, she muttered to Marnie that she would see her at the buffet and made for the exit.

She was not alone. On reaching the external courtyard, she found herself followed by half the participants, all of them performing the same act. As if choreographed, they each took out their mobile phones and began pressing buttons, pacing up and down like dancers in a surreal modern ballet. Anne turned to look out at the river. A few minutes of watching the tourist boats passing by restored her spirits, and feeling revived she returned to the basement.

Marnie, Philip and Nigel were chatting in one corner of the room, and it was clear that the gathering had split into groups of shared interests. Anne headed for the buffet and studied the name-plates, looking for the non-meat offerings.

At the end of the table she joined the drinks queue and found herself close to Dick Blackwood and Zoë Tipton. They were engaged in conversation with their backs turned to the rest of the room and seemed oblivious to everyone else. Although speaking in lowered voices, Anne heard every word.

'... and thanks for upstaging me in front of everybody,' Tipton was saying.

'That was *not* my intention,' Dick protested.

'Well you could've at least told me what you'd been up to while my back was turned.'

'I wasn't *up to* anything. I was *concerned* about the find.'

'The find that I'd seen first.' Tipton's voice had an edge to it. 'I seem to remember that *I* pointed it out to *you*.'

'And immediately dismissed it as *probably nothing significant*,' Dick reminded her. 'Probably a still-born calf, you thought, buried where it was dropped.'

'Not unreasonable,' Tipton protested, 'seeing as there wasn't likely to be a cemetery in a Saxon residential area.'

'No. That bothered me, too,' Dick admitted. 'Which is why I went in yesterday to check it out.'

'You could've informed me,' said Tipton.

'I had no chance. You were surrounded by your circle of admirers as soon as I got here.'

Tipton gave an exasperated sigh. 'Well keep me in the loop from now on.'

At that moment Dick seemed to become aware of Anne's presence. She stepped smartly forward to the drinks table and asked for a fruit juice.

Much as Marnie enjoyed visiting London, she was always glad to shake the dust of the capital's streets from her shoes – or in this case her tyres – and head for the country. As soon as lunch was over, she led Anne back to the flat where they packed their overnight bags. Marnie was giving the place a final check-over when her mobile rang.

'Where are you now, Marnie?' It was Philip.

'Just getting ready to go home. Why?'

'Is there any chance you could be around tomorrow? I've got Dr Fennimore, the archaeology project director, coming. He wants to talk about the gallery-museum area. We need to make sure the decor blends in with the rest of the development. What d'you think?'

'Well, I … yeah, I suppose we could stay another day.'

'Thanks, Marnie. I appreciate it. About eleven on site?'

Marnie ended the call and explained the change of plan to Anne while pressing Ralph's number on the speed-dial. She told him not to kill the fatted calf – Anne the vegetarian grimaced – or the fatted aubergine, until the next day.

'Girls night in?' Marnie suggested.

Anne nodded. 'There are some food shops somewhere round here. I remember them from last time we came.'

They bought lettuce, spring onions, tomatoes, cucumber, new potatoes and

French beans from a greengrocer. At a mini-market they bought a few basic stand-bys plus yogurt, eggs, tuna, olive oil and wine vinegar. A wine shop supplied a bottle of Italian Orvieto. Back at the flat they spent a happy half hour in the kitchen putting together a *salade niçoise*, and for this meal they had a river view from their table.

Afterwards, they took coffee over to the sofas, where they settled down to look at the books of plans given to them by Philip and Nigel. Anne had already set up a file for the project back at the office. Looking at the layouts, a thought occurred to her.

'Marnie, this is different from most other jobs, isn't it?'

'It's all new build,' Marnie said.

'So what do we do about claiming fees and expenses? We haven't talked about that side of things. Have we been given a budget?'

'It's all done on a percentage basis. We'll agree phasing of payments with Philip.'

'Okay. Shall we talk about it with him tomorrow?'

'Sure. It's all quite straightforward. Everett Parker get six per cent of the total build cost as their fees. We'll get ten per cent out of their commission.'

Anne sat working out the sums. The total cost was tens of millions of pounds. She could not remember how many. Six per cent of that went to Philip's company. Ten per cent of that amount to Walker and Co. Every way Anne looked at it, the fee element came to a vast sum. Yet there was Marnie, calmly leafing through the plans, sipping her coffee as if this was just another job for Walker and Co.

Marnie looked up, smiling. 'Anne, I can hear your brain humming from here.'

'Marnie, do you realise –'

'Yes, I know.'

'Have you worked out how big our fee will be?'

'No. I try not to think about it. It could become a distraction. Better just to concentrate on the work in hand and let the money take care of itself.'

'But we've got to know how to organise the payment schedule.'

'Easy. The first instalment will come when our scheme design is accepted. Then it's just a matter of phased payments as work progresses.'

'But the sums involved ...' Anne's voice petered out.

'I know,' said Marnie. 'With that kind of money I can afford bonus payments. You know what that means, Anne.'

'A tin of that luxury cat food for Dolly?'

'Exactly.'

5
Donovan

Marnie and Anne rose early as usual on Tuesday. After a shower and breakfast they decided to take a stroll along the Thames bank. It was a perfect summer's day. Gulls were dipping low over the river that reflected the clear sky. The sun, climbing steeply above the hills on the eastern horizon, was already easing the coolness from the morning air. Traffic was flowing steadily across Tower Bridge.

They stopped to lean against the parapet and look towards Saint Katherine Docks on the opposite bank, where masts extended upwards from yachts in the basin.

'It's amazing to think we're part of all this,' Anne said quietly.

'Part of all what?' said Marnie.

'You know ... the world of big business, developers and all that. We work in a little office barn in a small country village, yet we can play a part in what goes on here.'

'Only because the business people like what we do for them.'

'They like what *you* do,' Anne said. 'Otherwise we wouldn't be here at all. Actually, why are we here? I mean, why doesn't Philip just use his in-house design group, the one you headed up?'

'It's like you said, Anne. Willards asked for me to continue handling their projects when I set up on my own, and Philip puts their work my way.'

'So Philip gets a major job like this because Willards like your style.'

'And he's a very good architect, Anne. Don't forget that. There's no room for sentiment in this world. You saw how radical the project is in the book of plans. He's designed something that hasn't been done before, as far as I know.'

Anne nodded. 'It's quite an achievement.'

Marnie chuckled. 'It will be if it works.'

Anne's eyes widened. 'You think it might not?'

'Don't look so worried, Anne. He's brought in some of the best structural engineering consultants in the country to make sure it does.'

They walked back to the flat in silence. As Marnie was using the key card to open the access door, Anne's mobile chirped. She pulled it from her pocket and pressed the phone to her ear.

'Donovan,' she mouthed.

Unable to use the mobile in the lift, she took the call on the pavement while Marnie wandered along the cobbled walkway to look in the window of an estate agents. It was a decision she soon came to regret. She was reading the details of a flat in the same part of Butler's Wharf as her own, and trying not to boggle at the asking price, when the door to the agents flew open and she was joined by a smooth-looking man in a three-piece suit.

'Mrs Walker! How nice to see you. I was thinking of you – or rather your flat – just the other day.'

'Good morning, Mr Blunt.'

'Indeed it is. Do I take it that your presence here means you were coming to see me with a view to letting the flat, or perhaps putting it on the market?'

'I'm afraid not. I have a project here in London and I'm using the flat myself.'

'And when the project is completed?' He flashed a wheedling smile.

'Too early to say. It's a big project and will be running for a year or so.'

'Ah …' Blunt looked deflated. 'Such a pity. The market's picking up again. With the new government installed, there's a feeling in the air that things might start going forward.'

'Sorry to disappoint you.' Marnie glanced over her shoulder and saw that Anne had finished the call. 'Time to go. Good-bye, Mr Blunt.'

Marnie walked briskly back to the entrance, where Anne was slipping the mobile into her pocket.

'How's Donovan?' she asked.

'Fine.' Anne looked serious. 'Marnie?'

'Yes?'

'Do you think it would be possible for Donovan to come and see us? And I do mean us, not just me.'

'Why not?' said Marnie. 'Do I get the feeling this wouldn't be just a social visit?'

'That's right. He's doing a project for his university course. It involves making a short film on how progress impacts on heritage and the environment … something like that.'

'And you told him about the Horselydown job?'

'Hope you don't mind. If you'd rather he didn't –'

'No, no. That's okay. When's he coming?'

'I said I'd phone him back to let him know what you thought.'

'Tell him he's welcome. Does he want to come today?'

Anne grinned. 'You know Donovan.'

They all knew Donovan. To call him Anne's *boyfriend* would be the nearest to a description of their relationship, but it was more complicated than that. Everything about Donovan was usually more complicated.

Ralph had known Donovan since he was six years old, when his father, Dr William Donovan Smith, had been doing research at Oxford about fifteen years earlier. Unable to secure a tenured post there, Bill Donovan Smith had obtained a part-time lectureship at Reading University and another at one of the London University colleges. For that reason Bill and his German wife Greta had bought a house in west London, convenient for commuting in either direction.

Donovan was ten when the family was on holiday in South Africa and they were involved in a coach accident. Both his parents had been killed but by a miracle Donovan survived and went to live with an aunt and uncle in Germany. The family kept the house as a *pied-à-terre*, and now it was Donovan's home. Having dropped out of one university course when he found it unsuitable, Donovan had taken a year off and was now studying Media and Communications at Brunel.

He had come into their lives two years earlier at a time when the far right had been fighting a European parliamentary election in Northamptonshire. Fiercely opposed to the extreme right-wing – his German family had suffered greatly under the Nazi regime – Donovan had taken part in activities aimed at thwarting the fascist campaign. When the far-right leader had been shot dead, Donovan left town in a hurry and had been careful not to be seen too often in the area.

Donovan had a habitual preference for dark clothing, a taste which extended to his narrowboat, which was painted all over in battleship grey. This led Anne to compare it to a U-boat or even a *stealth narrowboat*. The interior was similarly monochrome, decorated in shades of grey. The boat bore the name *XO2*, which was Donovan's cypher for *exodos*, Greek for *exit*. It was typically cryptic of Donovan to choose such a name when he dropped out, and he had lived on board, travelling around during his gap year.

When they had first got to know him, Marnie and her friends had suspected he might be a Nazi sympathiser, given his enigmatic style and uncommunicative manner. Subsequent events had proved them wrong, and he was now an important part of their lives, albeit on a peripatetic basis.

Marnie and Anne presented themselves at the entrance to the compound shortly before eleven. A burly man whose jacket sported the logo of a security firm asked them for their passes. Marnie explained this was their first visit to the site during normal working hours and they had yet to receive them. She handed him a business card and suggested he check his list of *authorised persons*. Satisfied as to their *bona fides*, the man stood aside to let them in, reminding Marnie they should collect their passes before leaving.

As Marnie walked past the guard, she said, 'Oh by the way, we have another colleague joining us this morning. You may not have his name on your list. Donovan Smith.'

'He'll be easy to recognise,' said Anne.

The security man looked at her. 'Would he be a little taller than yourselves, slim, with short fair hair?'

'That's extraordinary,' said Anne. 'How did you know that?'

'He's already arrived?' said Marnie.

The guard's expression was deadpan. 'He's standing behind you.'

Marnie and Anne whirled round to see Donovan straddling a black mountain bike, smiling, removing wrap-round sunglasses. He wore a black T-shirt, dark grey cargo pants and black trainers. Over his shoulder was slung a small black rucksack.

'Sorry to cut it fine,' he said. 'Heavy traffic.'

Marnie knocked on the door marked STAFF ONLY and they went in. The hut was empty. She checked her watch: five to eleven. Leaving Anne and Donovan in the hut, she jogged back to the entrance to ask the security guard if he knew anything about the site meeting. He recalled that several people had arrived, including the architects, about half an hour earlier. They had met some of the other 'suits' and were somewhere within the compound, he knew not where.

Back in the hut, Marnie related the conversation.

'Where was your other meeting held?' Donovan asked.

'Over the river in the big hotel. I'm sure this is the right place.' Marnie looked concerned. 'Something's happened.'

Anne looked anxious. 'What d'you mean?'

'Just that maybe something unexpected has come up.'

Donovan stood and opened the door to look out. Contractors were moving purposefully about the site, operating diggers and dumpers, carrying equipment. There were no 'suits' anywhere to be seen. Murmuring that he would be back soon, Donovan slipped outside, leaving the door to close behind him. He was back within less than a minute.

'Something's going on,' he announced.

'What is it?' said Marnie.

'Not sure. I only got as far as the big holes in the ground when a guy came up and said I should be wearing protective clothing.'

Anne got up and opened a grey metal cupboard. She handed Donovan a pack containing a hi-vis jacket, and took a hard hat from the top shelf. Suitably equipped, Donovan went back out and this time was gone for several minutes.

'D'you think we should go with him?' Anne said.

'Not if the others are coming here. He'll keep us posted if anything's going on.'

When Donovan returned he looked puzzled.

'You know those big holes ... the deep ones? There are lots of voices coming up from below, but I can't see anyone down there. Are there any women on site?'

'There's a female archaeologist,' said Marnie. 'Why d'you ask?'

'Whoever she is, she's got a lot to say for herself, and something's rattled her cage. She's spouting off at quite a rate. I wouldn't like to be on the receiving end.'

'Doesn't sound very professional.' Marnie looked at her watch again. 'Nor is it very professional for no-one to have shown up for the meeting. It's nearly ten past.'

'You were right, Marnie,' said Anne. 'Something has happened. I bet it's to do with those bones in the mud.'

'Bones?' said Donovan.

Marnie was about to explain when they heard voices outside the hut. Seconds later the door was pulled open and Philip Everett entered, followed by Nigel Beardsley.

'So sorry to keep you waiting, Marnie.' Philip smiled at Anne and offered a hand to Donovan.

'Something's come up?' said Marnie.

Philip nodded. Before he could speak, the door opened behind him and Zoë Tipton burst in. She was breathless as if she had been running. Right behind her was Dr Fennimore and two men, the site agent and the clerk of works. Bringing up the rear was Dick Blackwood, his expression hovering between bewilderment and annoyance.

Philip suggested they start the meeting. There were two round tables in the hut, which they pulled together. Each person grabbed the nearest chair, and there was a general rustling of notebooks. Philip welcomed everyone, pointing out that they all knew each other with one exception and invited Donovan to introduce himself.

'Good morning. My name is Donovan Smith and I'm here with Walker and Co. It has yet to be established if I have any role to play, so I suppose this morning is a watching brief.'

'Would you like to add anything, Marnie?' Philip said.

'I had hoped to have a word with you before the meeting got underway, Philip. The fact is that Donovan is working on a university project, which he'll be able to explain much better than I can. If there are no objections, we'd like him to keep a record on video of how the building works progress.'

'Any comments?' said Philip. One finger was raised. 'Yes, Dr Fennimore?'

'Would that include the archaeological aspects of the work?'

Philip glanced at Marnie who in turn nodded at Donovan to reply.

'Certainly, unless you objected. I would say, though, that I couldn't guarantee to film every aspect of the excavation. I wouldn't be here full-time.'

'Any objection, Dr Fennimore?' said Philip.

'It would have to be cleared with my head of department, but I think it could be useful to have a visual record of progress. I would say this, however, any filming must be kept strictly confidential. There must be no leaking of material to the outside media. Is that clear? Are these proceedings being minuted?'

Philip indicated Nigel Beardsley who was taking notes beside him. 'Your points have been noted, Dr Fennimore. Donovan, would you like to add anything before we move on to the agenda?'

'Just one or two points. Any material gathered by me would be primarily for the purposes of my project. Nothing would be passed to any third party. I can guarantee that. I'm sure the archaeologists would be welcome to have a copy of my video material for their records. I'll just have to get that cleared with my tutor. I don't see a problem.'

Dr Fennimore nodded his approval and looked at his two colleagues. Dick Blackwood smiled and gave a brief nod at Donovan. Zoë Tipton stared at Donovan and declared she would be happy to co-operate. Philip announced that it was time to tackle the agenda.

'Sorry, Philip,' Marnie interjected. 'We don't actually have copies of the agenda.'

'That's because there isn't one, strictly speaking, at least not on paper. The meeting has been called to discuss matters raised by Dr Fennimore.'

The academic cleared his throat. 'I originally asked for a meeting to discuss the design of the gallery-museum area, but I've now heard about your proposals for the interior, Mrs Walker, and I'm entirely happy with them.'

'Does that mean you don't need me here?' Marnie asked.

'I think it's important for you to know about the latest developments.'

'Of course.'

'Please continue, Dr Fennimore,' said Philip.

'We believe we've made a find of some significance. Late on Friday afternoon, Mr Blackwood discovered some remains which he believed to be human.'

Zoë Tipton interrupted. 'I'm sorry, Miles, but as the meeting is being minuted I want it made clear that I was the one who found the remains.'

'And identified them as probably animal bones,' Dick interjected rapidly before Fennimore could reply.

Fennimore raised both hands as if in surrender. 'Please ... please.' He looked at Philip and began speaking very slowly. 'Perhaps it could be noted that *both* joint site directors came upon remains which at the time were not identifiable with any certainty.' He paused. No-one spoke. Nigel Beardsley scribbled rapidly. Fennimore turned to Dick Blackwood and nodded.

Dick continued. 'It was very murky down there and we didn't have much to go on, but I suspected the bones might be human rather than animal and I returned to the site to examine them further at low tide on Sunday morning. There was no other time when I could view them properly that day.'

Marnie raised a finger, and Philip gave her the go-ahead.

'As I understand it, the lower level is to be enclosed to protect the site from tidal erosion and preserve it as a kind of *living museum*. Will that be taking place soon? I'm thinking that these bones could be seriously damaged now they're exposed to tidal water.'

Philip replied. 'Screens are going to be installed to seal off the area completely, but only temporarily. We're gradually going to incorporate the lower levels into the overall scheme in a way that I believe has never been done before.'

'Such procedures have in fact been carried out previously,' said Zoë Tipton. 'Some are to be found here in the City of London.'

Philip agreed. 'Yes, but in this case there's one significant difference. Here, the river tides will ebb and flow around the lower level and the water will be seen through glazed screens. The idea is that whatever we find should remain visible as a kind of living exhibit.'

'The bones need immediate protection,' Dick said. 'In their present situation they're highly vulnerable.'

'But *they* are *not* the object of the exercise.' Zoë Tipton spoke rapidly, her eyes blazing. 'They're almost an irrelevance. We have to –'

Philip stopped her in her tracks. 'Dr Tipton … Zoë … please.'

Fennimore smiled indulgently. 'Both my young site director colleagues feel passionately about their subjects. Please forgive their exuberance. It's not a weakness. It's their great strength. I ought to remind everyone that planning permission on this site stipulates that the archaeology must be respected, and every step must be taken to preserve and protect it … all of it.'

'That goes without saying,' said Philip, 'Dr Fennimore, could you just spell out the background, please.'

Fennimore looked at each person present. 'London as a settlement began not far from here, probably on the other side of the river. Where this site now stands used to be a series of islands. By the time the Romans established themselves here, there was probably a ferry crossing nearby. As time passed, land on this side of the river became assimilated into *Londinium*. It's not clear exactly what was located here back then, but we do know that the town continued to grow after the Romans left during the fifth century.'

'An Anglo-Saxon settlement,' said Dick. 'And we've come upon it.'

'And it's absolutely definite that these remains couldn't be Roman?' Philip asked.

'Not at this depth,' said Fennimore.

'We *have* to go deeper,' Tipton said. 'One set of bones shouldn't interfere with our excavations. It's imperative –'

Philip held up a hand as if to stop traffic. 'I think we know your views on that subject, Zoë. The point is, we're bound to deal with *these* remains before we can do anything else. We have no alternative. It's both a legal and a planning requirement.'

Zoë Tipton made a sound somewhere between a snort and sigh. In the few seconds of embarrassed silence that followed, Donovan intervened.

'Can I ask a practical question?'

'Certainly,' said Philip.

'These remains ... the bones ... are they exposed at present?'

Fennimore looked at his watch. 'Slack water is coming to an end any time now. The tide will begin turning, and they'll be covered soon.'

'Would it be possible for me to get a sight of them and maybe some initial footage?' Donovan asked.

Dick got to his feet, staring at Philip like a gun dog waiting for instructions.

'I suppose so,' said Philip.

Dick had the door open in a flash, as Donovan grabbed his rucksack from the floor and followed him out.

The sun was warm on their backs as Dick and Donovan descended the first ladder. At the bottom they climbed down the second ladder and reached its base where the air was noticeably cooler and the light more subdued. Dick produced a torch from his belt and led the way.

'Perhaps I shouldn't be dragging you away from the meeting,' said Donovan.

'Nah.' Dick was dismissive. 'I'm fed up with endless bloody meetings. They'll only be going over the same old ground.'

'Then why meet?' said Donovan. 'What's the point?'

Dick pointed the beam of the torch at the muddy ground before them.

'There's your answer. Those bones have stirred everything up. We're trying to dig down to Roman times, but with archaeology you never know what might turn up.'

Donovan reached into the rucksack and withdrew a compact video camera.

'I'm still not sure you've answered my question,' he said.

'Miles Fennimore wants to place on record that archaeology at every stage has to be protected. That includes non-Roman finds.'

'Why is your Zoë chum so upset about that?' Donovan asked. 'It's all archaeology, after all.'

'She's Roman ... I mean that's her subject. She doesn't want anything to distract us from that.'

'But it can only be a temporary blip if you're excavating further, surely.'

Dick shrugged and watched Donovan circling the bones, checking the angles with the camera. After further excavation the whole skeleton was now visible.

'Like I said, with archaeology anything can happen. We could, for example, come upon a major Anglo-Saxon settlement. That might prove that London expanded and grew here, where significant traces have never been found before. That would change our whole perspective.'

'Isn't that rather unlikely?' Donovan asked.

'Very. So if we did find something like that, it would seriously rock Zoë's world.'

Donovan chuckled and aimed the camera at the ground. A faint humming sound was heard as he began filming in short bursts of about ten seconds each. Dick held the torch steady on the remains while Donovan shifted position, squatting to shoot wide-angles and close-ups from every side.

Between shots, Dick said, 'Is the torch helping? Just tell me if you want me to alter its position.' He lowered his voice. 'Sorry, perhaps I shouldn't be talking.'

'No, you're fine,' said Donovan. 'The light's okay for now.' He stood up. 'If it's all right with you, I'd like to film you up at street level, talking to camera, explaining what's going on here, how the bones were found, what you think they might be and ...' Donovan looked him straight in the eye. '... anything else you think we ought to know about.'

Dick gave Donovan a sharp look. 'What d'you mean?'

Donovan returned his gaze. 'I think you know what I mean, Dick.'

A roguish smile crept across Dick Blackwood's face.

When they returned to the surface, Dick insisted he was perfectly ready to be filmed there and then, explaining what had been discovered so far. Most people have no idea how difficult it is to appear relaxed when confronted by the unforgiving stare of the camera lens, but Dick proved to be a natural.

He paced himself well, describing the project, how it would be, literally and metaphorically, ground-breaking, how he had almost literally stumbled upon an articulated human skeleton in the mud several metres below the ground. To his credit, he related that it was his colleague, Dr Zoë Tipton on secondment from the Institute of Archaeology at Cambridge University, who had first noticed the remains. He explained how they had first "been thought" – no mention of by whom – possibly to be animal bones, but how they had preyed on his mind so much that he had returned over the weekend and identified their true nature.

Donovan was delighted to have found Dick, regarding him as a great asset. His delivery was cool and underpinned by detailed knowledge, yet his enthusiasm shone through. Donovan placed him at the top of the upper ladder, speaking from the heart of the excavation. He stood him beside the dig, pointing down into the ground and had him pacing the periphery of the site with the Thames, Tower Bridge and the Tower of London as impressive historic backdrops.

The footage shot below ground would be edited in later to illustrate what had been discovered. Donovan was convinced he could produce an interesting documentary, but also tell a story filled with drama. The human remains had not seen the light of day for well over a thousand years.

Donovan declared that he had enough footage for the first shoot. As they wandered back towards the meeting room, the site agent and clerk of works came out of the hut followed by Zoë Tipton. She paused on the threshold and veered towards Donovan.

'Donovan, hallo.' She extended a hand. 'Zoë Tipton, site director. Call me Zoë.' She glanced fleetingly at Dick. '*Joint* site director. Will you be doing much filming here?'

'I hope so.'

Zoë still had hold of Donovan's hand. 'Let me know when you need me.' She released her grip and quickly produced a business card. 'Contact me ... any time.'

Turning away, she joined Miles Fennimore and they headed for the site exit. Behind them, Marnie, Philip and Anne came out together. They too walked towards Dick and Donovan.

'Did I miss much?' said Dick.

Philip shook his head. 'Nothing you didn't know already. The main thing is we've kept the main contractor on board. They know where they stand and also that they can't make any public utterances about what's found ... now or in the future.'

Philip excused himself and dashed off to his next meeting. For a few seconds the group stood quietly together in the sunshine, looking at the bustle of building work, with the sound of traffic in the background. Dick broke the silence.

'Anyone fancy a coffee? I mean a *proper* coffee, not the stuff from that machine in the hut.'

The four of them occupied a table in *Fellini's*, in a quiet side street. The staff who ran the establishment sounded like Londoners, except when they spoke to each other. Then, they used rapid-fire Italian, their conversation punctuated by the hissing and slurping of the coffee machine. The walls were hung with tasteful black-and-white photographs: the Coliseum, the Mount Palatine, the

Forum and the Trevi fountain.

Settled with their cups of cappuccino, mocha and americano, Dick's guests thanked him for his hospitality. In reply, he nodded and chuckled to himself.

'What's the joke?' said Marnie.

'I was just thinking ...' Dick looked up at the photos. 'It should really be Zoë here now. This is just her scene.'

'She's a coffee fan?' Marnie said.

Donovan replied. 'She's a Roman fan, right, Dick?'

'Absolutely. Did you notice the brooch she was wearing?'

The others gave this some thought.

'Quite a small one ... like a bunch of grapes?' Anne ventured.

'You got it. Romano-British, found in a field in Cheshire last year.'

'How did she get it?' Anne asked. 'And should she be wearing it for everyday use, just like that?'

'It was found by a metal detectorist who didn't know who owned the land, so he gave the brooch to Zoë.'

'Why?'

'Because ...' Dick shrugged, 'she has ways ...'

'You mean she's used to getting her own way,' said Marnie. 'That doesn't seem to be the case here, at least not for the moment, does it?'

Dick smiled enigmatically. Marnie continued.

'I suppose you're happy because you've got in first and found something that captures everyone's attention. I didn't realise there was such rivalry.'

To Marnie's surprise it was Donovan who replied.

'That isn't what it's all about.'

Marnie and Anne studied his face. It had been a typical Donovan utterance, and they could see the hint of a smile about his eyes.

'Go on,' said Anne. 'Don't keep us in suspense. What do you know that we don't?'

'It's not my story to tell,' said Donovan, turning to Dick who was still smiling.

'Looking at you, Dick, thoughts of the cat who got the cream spring to mind,' said Marnie. 'Come on, spill the beans.' They all laughed at the hopelessly mixed metaphor. 'Time to tell us what you've already told Donovan.'

Dick put on an innocent look. 'I haven't told him anything and I'm not sure what he's found out. Why don't *you* tell *us*, Donovan?'

All eyes turned towards him. Donovan lowered his voice.

'The person Dick found in the excavation was murdered.'

6
Loose Ends

It was a different kind of silence. That was Marnie's first thought on waking that Wednesday morning. She lay in bed for a short while in the sleeping cabin on *Thyrsis*, wondering if that thought made any kind of sense.

Back in the flat in Docklands, the silence had been an enclosed variety. She had been insulated by walls lined with rockwool panels behind plasterboard, by thick double-glazing and by a structure fortified with steel and concrete. Here on a canal boat in Knightly St John, she was enclosed in a shell comprising a steel outer layer with expanded polystyrene sheets behind tongued-and-grooved pine cladding.

The silence she could hear now was not absolute. She could feel the air moving around the boat, catch the occasional hint of birdsong. She could almost sense the fish swimming a few feet from where she lay.

Ralph was oblivious to these flights of fancy, lying beside her, still sound asleep, and she would never reveal such thoughts to him. Not that he would mock them or chide her for them, but because they were part of her private relationship with the world of the waterways and she wanted them for herself alone. No doubt Ralph had his moments too.

She swivelled her legs out from under the duvet and lowered her feet to the floor. Her toes immediately made contact with clothing, jumbled in a heap where she had dropped everything the previous night. They had hastily pulled each other's clothes off before falling into bed to make love after their protracted absence over the weekend.

Stooping to gather up the abandoned items, Marnie smiled inwardly. Yes, Ralph definitely did have his moments.

Donovan rang during the morning to say he had completed editing his video material and wondered if Anne and Marnie would like to see it. A plan was formed: Donovan would come up by train that afternoon, and Anne would collect him from Milton Keynes Central.

By the usual standards of Walker and Co, the office closed early that day. Instead of their last session from six to seven o'clock, they switched on the answerphone and decamped to Ralph's study to view Donovan's footage on the television. With coffee mugs in hand, they sat around while Donovan plugged various leads from the video camera into the monitor. He switched on the equipment and operated the remote control.

With Marnie and Anne on armchairs and Ralph seated at his desk, Donovan knelt on the floor beside the machine.

For a first cut, the material was impressive. Donovan had edited the interview with Dick Blackwood into a clear exposition of what was happening at Horselydown. Beginning with a series of location shots showing the river, the historic buildings around and the construction site itself, Donovan homed in on Dick, who gave a good account of himself as a presenter. Donovan varied the image with cutaways to the lower-level finds to illustrate the points Dick was making.

When they came to the end of Dick's talk, the sequence ended with views of the scene below ground.

'Can you run that last sequence again,' Marnie asked.

Donovan gave a hint of a smile and rewound the tape to a point where Dick was speaking to camera.

... much work still to be done, but we've made a good start and the best may yet be to come. In the days and weeks ahead we should be able to shed light on what really happened here at Horselydown in what are sometimes called the Dark Ages.

The image resolved itself into a series of shots moving in on details of the skeleton from different angles before fading to black. Donovan switched off and sat back on his heels without comment.

'*What really happened here,*' Ralph repeated. 'That's a rather enigmatic statement.'

Still, Donovan said nothing. Marnie spoke next.

'You said the person Dick found – the skeleton – had been murdered, Donovan. What did you mean and how did you reach that conclusion?'

Donovan pressed buttons on the remote, and the image reappeared on the screen, running backwards. When he reached Dick uttering his last words, he pressed the forward button.

'Watch carefully,' he said, 'and tell me when to stop.'

The images ran on in the dim light, bones in the mud, torchlight reflecting off the wet ground.

'There!' Anne called out, pointing. 'What's that?'

Donovan smiled at her. '*That ...* is what it's all about.'

'Can you run it again,' said Ralph. 'I'm missing something here.'

Donovan muttered *Play it again, Sam* and rewound the tape.

'Look!' Anne pointed again.

Donovan paused the tape and began running it in slow motion.

'*There,*' said Marnie. 'Is that what we're supposed to be seeing?'

'What is it?' Ralph asked, squinting at the screen.

By way of reply, Donovan lay on the floor on his back and extended his arms and legs outwards like Leonardo Da Vinci's Vitruvian man diagram of human proportions.

'What you have there is the skeleton's left arm,' Donovan said. 'The Horselydown man – or perhaps woman – is lying more or less like this.' He resumed his kneeling position and pointed at the screen. 'The significant detail is this.' He ran his fingertip across the image, close to the screen. 'It's the same for the other arm and at least one of the legs.'

'That isn't bone, presumably,' said Ralph.

Donovan turned to look at Ralph over his shoulder. 'No. It seems to be leather.'

'Which could be why it's been preserved in the mud,' Marnie added.

'Exactly. That's what Dick thought.'

'And it's why you think the person was murdered,' said Anne.

'Yes,' Donovan agreed. 'Or it might have been a ritual killing or something like that.'

'Did the Anglo-Saxons practise sacrifice?' Ralph sounded sceptical.

'Apparently not,' said Donovan. 'But they did have a legal system.'

Ralph narrowed his eyes. 'Meaning?'

'One possibility is this might've been an execution.'

They considered this for a long moment. In their imagination they saw the figure staked out on the ground at low tide, with leather thongs attached to wooden pegs hammered into the ground. They could imagine the horror experienced by the victim as he or she felt the rising water touch their skin, first tentatively and then in a steady surge, inexorably sweeping over them, knowing that the flood tide could not be halted and that death by drowning was inevitable, just a few minutes away. They gave a collective shudder.

'It's *horrible*,' Anne murmured. 'Like what pirates did in the Caribbean.'

'Perhaps that was the reason for what happened here,' said Ralph.

'You think this might've been a pirate?' Marnie said. 'I somehow never associated Anglo-Saxons with piracy, least of all down there in London.'

'Do they know what that area was like in post-Roman Britain?' Ralph asked.

'It might've been a ferry crossing point,' said Donovan.

Ralph thought back through his studies of economic history and tried to recall how London developed as a port after the departure of the Romans.

'Perhaps trading vessels tied up there waiting to be unloaded,' Ralph suggested. 'There was brisk business between Continental Europe and Britain even in those precarious times when the stabilising influence of the Romans had waned.'

Marnie chuckled. 'You sound like an economic history textbook, Ralph.'

'That's what I am,' Ralph laughed, 'a textbook on legs.'

'And you think our skeleton might once have been a robber, who stole from trading ships?'

'It's only a guess,' Ralph said. 'We'll have to wait and see what Dick turns up, if anything. But whatever it is, it certainly isn't a casual attack or a mugging gone wrong. There's a certain amount of ceremony involved here, a ritual of some kind. This man – and I suspect it was a man – was probably put to death in accordance with some kind of legal procedure.'

Another silence followed while Donovan began disconnecting the equipment. He gathered together the leads, bound them with plastic fasteners and stowed them in the rucksack with the camera.

'A killing ground,' he said quietly.

'You think so?' said Ralph.

Donovan nodded. 'The robber, the pirate ... whatever, was executed there as an example of what happened to thieves, and he was left to rot for all to see forever and ever.'

'And he only disappeared from view when the channel shifted and he was covered over with silt and then soil,' Ralph added.

'It's all very grisly,' Marnie said.

'And now we can understand Willards' attitude,' Donovan said calmly.

'Willards?' Marnie said, puzzled. 'Where do they come in?'

Donovan shrugged. 'They don't want the outside world knowing about this discovery, do they?'

'They don't want nighthawks getting in, injuring themselves and making a claim on safety grounds,' said Marnie.

Anne raised an eyebrow. 'Nighthawks?'

'Unauthorised metal detectorists,' Marnie explained. 'This would be like a magnet to them. Think how many thousands there are in and around London.'

'I think Willards' concern probably goes deeper than that,' said Donovan.

'What do you mean?'

'People have been executed on that spot for centuries, haven't they? Dick's skeleton might go back almost fifteen hundred years.'

'And they hanged river pirates there in the seventeenth and eighteenth centuries for sure,' Anne added.

'Think about it,' said Donovan. 'If you were looking for a hotel in London, would your average visitor want to stay in a place with the tradition that criminals were put to death there since time immemorial?'

Donovan stayed for the evening meal. No-one could have been blamed if talk of killings, corpses and skeletons had blunted their appetite, but the aroma of cucumber and spring onions, tomatoes and peppers being sliced and chopped in the galley on *Sally Ann* soon revived their spirits. Outside on the bank, Ralph had rigged up the barbecue ready for grilling tiger prawn kebabs, and he busied himself with opening a bottle of Chilean chardonnay while the briquettes heated up.

By common agreement they avoided further discussion of the Horselydown project or of putting criminals to death for the rest of that day. Instead, they turned their thoughts to plans for the summer. Sitting round the large circular table under the cream parasol, hearing birdsong in the warm evening air, it seemed a fitting way to spend their time.

Ralph had taken a major decision: no lecture tour abroad that summer. For years such tours had been an important, and lucrative, part of his annual timetable. For the past few years, since living with Marnie, they had taken him away at times when she had found herself embroiled in all manner of dangerous situations.

That year would be different. The BBC had invited him to write and present a series of television documentaries on the changing world of economics. Most of the filming would be done in Britain. But that was for later in the year. In the immediate future Ralph had a new contract from his publisher and was about to start work on another book.

'That's you nicely sorted out, Ralph,' Marnie said. 'It'll be lovely to have you around for the whole summer.'

'What about you, Marnie?' Anne said. 'Beth's always nagging you to take a break. You haven't had a holiday since you moved up here.'

'Every day is like a holiday to me,' Marnie replied. 'I just love what I do.'

'But Anne does have a point,' Ralph said. 'And so does Beth. All work and no play can lead to serious burn-out. Being self-employed, you can't afford to run yourself into the ground. You need to recharge sometimes.'

Marnie agreed to give it some thought. 'But I can't just up and away like that, not when my biggest ever project is coming on-stream.'

Ralph conceded the point. 'I suppose not. But take a lesson from me. I got so bound up in what I was doing a few years ago, I ran myself into the ground. Now, I'm more careful.'

'Ralph, when did you last take a holiday?' Marnie protested. 'I haven't noticed you packing a bucket and spade when you set off to tour America or the Far East.'

There was laughter round the table at the thought of Ralph making sand castles on the beach at Martha's Vineyard or Penang. Again, Ralph acknowledged the argument.

'Okay, fair enough, but I do take days off for rest and relaxation in between lectures. And I always use hotels instead of accepting invitations to stay with my hosts. That way I can switch off in the evenings instead of being on duty all the time.'

'Sensible,' said Marnie, 'but it's not an option for me, is it?'

Before Ralph could respond, Donovan interjected.

'The option for you is even simpler, Marnie.'

Heads turned. Donovan was making one of his pronouncements again.

'I'd love to know how,' said Marnie.

Donovan grinned. 'Surely, it's staring you in the face.'

Marnie knew she should have thought of it first. Donovan had been right; the answer was staring her in the face. She turned off the shower on *Thyrsis* that night and began towelling herself dry. *Sally Ann*. The boat had come to her rescue before when she was desperate for a break from the stress of work. That sabbatical summer three years earlier had changed her life. What she needed now was nothing so drastic, just a short spell of freedom, a breath of fresh air. Nothing she knew could provide that better than a holiday on the waterways.

Ralph had already showered and was sitting up in bed correcting the first draft of an article he had written for a specialist journal. As soon as Marnie entered the sleeping cabin, she sensed he was not happy.

'Something wrong?' she asked.

'Mm ...'

'Really? You don't say. I'd never have thought it.'

Ralph looked up and caught her grinning at him. He smiled wanly.

'I think, Marnie, you're not the only one who could benefit from a change of routine. Reading this article, I get the impression I've already written it before.'

'Put it away and sleep on it,' Marnie said. 'It'll seem different in the morning. Better still, lock it away for a week and come back to it afresh. I do that sometimes with designs. When I see them again, I know straight away whether they work or not.'

Ralph stared at her, standing by the bed in her white towelling dressing gown, running a brush through her hair.

'You have hidden depths, Marnie. And you're absolutely right.'

'Are we going on this canal trip together?' Marnie asked. 'We didn't actually talk about details.'

'I half assumed I'd be staying here working on the TV series.'

'Don't you think we deserve some time together, Ralph, you and I?'

'Absolutely!'

Marnie put the hairbrush on the shelf and sat at the foot of the bed. She kicked off her slippers and peeled off the dressing gown. Laying it down beside her, she slid under the duvet from the foot of the bed and began wriggling up towards Ralph.

'Ah!' he cried. 'That tickles. What are you doing down there?'

He lifted the duvet and saw Marnie peering up at him with a devilish smile.

'Just like you said,' she whispered playfully.

'Like I said?'

'Absolutely. Hidden depths …'

Anne turned out the light in her attic room, yawned and rolled onto her side. She had concluded that evening that her life was made up of a number of loose ends. It did not bother her, but she knew she wanted to resolve them sooner rather than later.

She had had two phone calls that evening since driving Donovan to the station. The first was from her parents, who were planning to go camping, this time in north Wales. Her mother had asked if she would like to go with them, and Anne had explained diplomatically that the work situation made it difficult to commit herself.

The second was from Donovan, ostensibly phoning to thank her for the lift to the station and to let her know he had got home in good time. His real purpose was to make the point that she too needed a holiday, something that no-one had mentioned over supper. That was one of the loose ends. What would she do that summer? Would she be spending some of it with Donovan? Another loose end.

Did she really want a holiday? The most exciting part of her life at that time was in Docklands. More than anything, she wanted to immerse herself in the project and play her part in making it a huge success.

Immerse herself, she thought. Yes. Her breathing settled into a slow, steady rhythm. All around her was darkness and silence, acres of quiet countryside where the barn had nestled for hundreds of years. Anne was drifting off now, but her thoughts floated on. One image slipped into her mind. She saw the wet ground in the lower levels of the building site at Horselydown. She saw the terrified face of a man, hearing the water of the river as the tide seeped closer to his tethered arms and legs. She felt the river flow over her while she fell back through the ages into a restless, troubled sleep.

7
Plans

On Thursday morning at breakfast Marnie noticed that Anne seemed a shade less alert than usual. As Anne raised a hand to her mouth, Marnie looked up at the galley clock.

'At the third yawn it will be seven fourteen and thirty seconds,' she intoned in the clipped voice of the speaking clock.

Anne's yawn turned into a splutter, which morphed into a hiccup.

'Marnie!' she exclaimed. 'You nearly made me choke.' She laughed and added. 'Sorry about the yawning.'

'Bad night?' said Marnie.

'Sort of. I kept having weird dreams and waking up.'

'Did those dreams involve people being tethered to the ground so the tide washed over them by any chance?'

Anne looked as if she did not want to continue the conversation. 'Possibly.'

Ralph poured her some coffee. 'It does all seem rather gruesome. Why don't we concentrate on something more pleasant?'

'Such as?' Marnie asked.

'Planning the summer?' Ralph suggested. 'None of us can afford the time to be out of the country for weeks on end, but Donovan was right about our having the means to take a break.' He raised his hands to indicate the boat.

'I think that's a great idea,' said Anne. 'You and Marnie could at least fit in a week on the canals and maybe another week later on in the summer.'

'But what about you, Anne?' said Marnie. 'You're in as much need of a holiday as any of us after all your hard work in the office, plus your college course.'

'Well …'

'You have an idea?'

Anne sighed. 'On the phone last night my mum said she and dad were going camping in north Wales. Richard's going too, and she wondered if I'd like to go with them … a real family holiday, she said.'

'But? I sense a *but* creeping in here.'

Anne smiled ruefully. 'Can't say I really fancy it. Last time we went camping we were flooded out.'

'That was in Scotland,' said Marnie. 'Wales is usually milder.'

'Positively sub-tropical,' Anne agreed.

'It's got wonderful sandy beaches,' Marnie pointed out.

Anne nodded. 'We could trek across the central desert region, find a nice oasis and camp out under the palm trees at the coast.'

'I take it you're not overly keen, then,' said Ralph.

Marnie suddenly exclaimed. 'Bulb!'

Ralph and Anne boggled at her.

'I've had one of those light bulb moments,' she said.

'Fetch the brandy,' Ralph said to Anne across the table, 'the cooking sort, not the Courvoisier.' He turned to face Marnie. 'Explain?'

'Where would any sophisticated, fashionable, culturally discerning young woman wish to spend her time?' Marnie asked.

'Can't we get back to me?' Anne said, deadpan.

Marnie gave her the heavy eyelids. 'Think about it.'

Anne looked at Ralph. They reflected, then spoke together in unison. 'Docklands?'

The plan was formed there and then. Marnie and Anne would aim to complete the scheme design stage of the project by the end of the following week. Marnie would then set off with Ralph on one of the boats, probably *Thyrsis*, with her more modern facilities, and travel down to London. She would phone the BW office in Little Venice and try to get a mooring there for a few weeks.

Anne would travel to London by car and stay in Butler's Wharf. With Marnie's flat as a base, she could visit the capital's museums and galleries, go to the theatre, see the sights and soak up the atmosphere. They all spotted that the plan had two drawbacks.

The first was that Anne would be taking her holiday alone, which was not much fun. Marnie suggested an obvious solution: Anne could invite a friend to stay with her. The second was that a holiday of that kind could be expensive. Another obvious solution: Marnie would deal with Anne's credit card bill for the trip. It would be a holiday with pay or, given that Anne would be on hand for the construction site, if needed, partly an extended business trip. Their accountant could decide what was appropriate.

Both holiday plans seemed sound and proved to be so, at least until the first disaster struck.

8
Gold

Donovan had once told Anne he thought Marnie's way of working could be compared – kindly – to *Blitzkrieg*. In the week or so that followed the decision about holiday plans, Anne had occasion many times to remember that comparison. While she handled most routine matters, Marnie applied herself with fierce concentration to finalising the design of the Horselydown complex, often charging on at lightning speed.

It seemed to Anne that Marnie worked like an artist. First she applied a colour wash, choosing a base colour for each part of her canvas, each area in the building. Then she mixed the palette, creating nuances and shades to blend together to give tone and depth. Finally, she picked out the details with contrasting tints and textures, coverings, surfaces and fabrics.

By applying herself virtually non-stop for just over a week, Marnie laid out the whole scheme. Floor by floor, section by section, she passed the designs to Anne to examine and give her comments. In between these exercises, Anne was given the task of identifying images from books and the Internet that might serve as the basis for the murals that would eventually enhance and embellish the main entrance, the bars, lobbies and hallways. There was no shortage of material, and Anne fell upon her assignment with much the same application as Marnie. The atmosphere in the office in those days was focused and intense, but by no means frenetic.

On the following Friday, when Marnie pushed her chair back and stretched her arms towards the ceiling, the first phase of the *Blitzkrieg* was concluded.

In the meantime, Anne had kept the office running and had helped Ralph prepare *Thyrsis* for the trip to London. The two of them had worked happily together, washing down the topsides, checking all ropes and equipment in readiness for the journey. The engine had been serviced in the spring, and the diesel tank had been kept full throughout the winter. It only remained to clear the weed trap, check fluid levels and sluice out the fuel filter.

On Friday afternoon, while Marnie was gathering her designs into folders and labelling them, Ralph and Anne took *Thyrsis* on a trial run for a pump-out and to fill the water tank.

They were ready for off.

After supper that evening, Anne was in the utility area of the office barn ironing clothes for her London trip when Donovan rang.

'You might want to switch on the TV in about ten minutes,' he said. '*Timeline* is on tonight. It could be of interest.'

'Any drowned corpses or public hangings?' Anne's tone was suspicious.

'No, a Roman villa.'

Anne could not think why Donovan believed this would interest her. 'Just up my street,' she said.

'Actually,' said Donovan, 'it's up Ermine Street, somewhere near Peterborough. The point is, there's a group of archaeologists from Cambridge taking part.'

'Cambridge?' Anne made the Roman connection. 'Would that include Zoë Tipton?'

'I'd put money on it. Anyway, you said you were keen to *bone up* on archaeology. Here's your chance. I'm going to record the programme.'

'You're very keen, Donovan. You're sure it's the archaeology that interests you?'

'Professional interest,' he said. 'I'm keeping a record of how the experts film excavations. It'll help my project.'

Timeline was a very popular series on archaeology that the BBC had been running for several years. Every year they took a single theme and followed excavations on that subject around the country. The current topic was the changes to the way of life in Britain brought about by the Roman occupation.

The previous year they had focused on witchcraft. That had brought one of the *Timeline* excavation teams to Knightly St John, including work on Marnie's land at Glebe Farm.

The main presenter of the series was Professor 'Barny' Guthrie. Now in his early sixties, he had a talent for making complex subjects understandable by the average viewer. It was no wonder he had become one of the first *celebrity archaeologists*. He deliberately cultivated a highly individual style. Tall and rangy, with craggy features and a mane of abundant white hair, he had brought mass appeal to a subject that might otherwise have been regarded as dry and dusty. Barny Guthrie brought archaeology to life.

He also possessed formidable qualifications. After setting up one of the best university departments in the country, he had resigned at the age of fifty to concentrate on research, writing and television. He was the only archaeologist in Britain who had received awards both for academic achievements and television shows.

The professor had a talent for hand-picking colleagues who brought glamour to the subject. This not only gave the programmes a distinctive style, but added to Guthrie's personal *mystique*. Naturally this brought him a considerable degree of envy in the academic world, but most detractors were wary of openly criticising a man who had brought the subject a national following.

Anne sat on her giant bean-bag at the foot of the bed and watched as

Guthrie introduced the subject for that evening. On the screen a map showed the location of digs all over Britain before homing in on a remote field in the flat Cambridgeshire countryside. Talking to camera, Guthrie explained that they had identified a substantial settlement, a village that had grown up on Roman foundations but had been wiped out by the Black Death in the thirteen hundreds. He introduced a *local archaeologist* involved in the excavation, who would tell the story in more detail.

And there she was.

The scene cut to an overhead panoramic view of the entire site. Anne remembered the enormous crane used for such shots that had towered over Glebe Farm like a monstrous dinosaur. Gradually the image had zoomed in towards a lone figure standing among mounds of excavated soil.

Zoë Tipton looked the epitome of *archaeology chic*. In the opening shot she was wearing a leather bush hat. A pale blue skinny top revealed bare arms and shoulders, as she pointed out different features of the site. The camera steadily homed in on her. Zoë must have been a cameraman's dream subject, Anne thought, as she took in the long legs, made even more shapely by the briefest of shorts and the chunky boots with rolled down socks that completed the *ensemble*. At the bottom of the screen Anne noticed a scurrying group of figures and was not surprised when the image cut to a view from field level.

Another crew had taken over filming and, as if cued by a director, Zoë turned to face the camera while at the same time removing her hat to expose golden-blond hair, tied back in a ponytail. A few errant wisps played about her face, and she brushed them aside with an insouciant, languid gesture that Anne guessed she had rehearsed beforehand. With her lightly-tanned face, limbs and shoulders, everything about Zoë was golden.

The camera reluctantly abandoned her and returned to Barny Guthrie who took over the narrative to interview other members of the team. The content of the programme was lost on Anne who found herself looking out for Zoë. She was not hard to find.

Each time the director resorted to close-ups to give variety to the scenes, there were the smooth features of Zoë Tipton, sometimes in profile, sometimes in flattering shots with face looking down and eyes averted. On occasion, Anne could tell the cameraman was having to restrain himself from dwelling on glimpses of cleavage.

The whole team came together at the end of the programme to sum up the action, and Zoë gave a good account of herself when invited to contribute to the discussion of experts. As the credits began rolling, the final image before fading out was of Zoë in smiling conversation with Barny Guthrie. The late afternoon sun was shining in her golden hair. With consummate ease, Zoë Tipton had stolen the show.

9
Timbers

On Sunday morning the residents of Glebe Farm awoke to a cloudy sky, with a cool breeze blowing from the west. By the end of breakfast, the clouds were giving way to a hazy sun, and the temperature was climbing.

While Marnie and Ralph swabbed down the gunwales on *Thyrsis*, Anne descended on the red Mini, armed with sponge and chamois leather. Soon, both boat and car were gleaming, ready for departure. For one, the trip to London would be a voyage, a serene progress over hills and dales. For the other, it would be half a morning's drive down the motorway.

At journey's end, new opportunities awaited them, but not in the way they expected.

By mid-day, *Thyrsis* was halfway round Milton Keynes. Marnie chose a secluded spot to tie up for lunch under shady trees that could have been miles from anywhere. In fact, they were little more than a short walk from the centre.

Meanwhile, Anne had stowed the Mini in the underground car park in Docklands and made her way up to Marnie's flat. Donovan arrived minutes later, having cycled across London. He had somehow managed to bring a small overnight bag strapped to the bike and a rucksack. From the latter he unpacked numerous items of food and drink from Germany, ranging from *Pumpernickel* and *Bockwurst* to *Melitta Kaffee* and *Warsteiner Bier*.

That night, Marnie and Ralph revelled in the tranquillity of the Bedfordshire countryside and a sense of freedom from everyday cares.

Anne and Donovan wallowed in the spaciousness of the Docklands flat, each of them luxuriating in their own individual bathroom before collapsing into each other's arms under a lightweight duvet of Hungarian goosedown.

Thyrsis proceeded calmly across country in the days that followed. For Marnie and Ralph it was the perfect way to relax together. In settled summer weather, they covered the miles to the capital at a soothing pace, all their thoughts and energies devoted to running the boat and living the simplest of lives.

On Monday morning the plan was for Anne to visit the British Museum and go on to the Courtauld Gallery. She would return late afternoon to take a short rest – or, as she put it, *collapse in a heap* – before preparing supper with

Donovan. For Donovan, it would be a day of filming, mainly with Dick Blackwood, laying down as much material as he could for his project.

At supper time they looked back on the day and realised that their plans had gone awry within minutes of leaving the flat.

They stepped out into the shady canyon formed by the Butler's Wharf buildings. Walking along the cobbled way in the cool morning air, both felt elated at the prospect of the day before them. The underground passage led them to the building site beneath the traffic approaching Tower Bridge. They emerged into bright sunlight and turned to face each other. Anne was kissing Donovan temporarily goodbye when over his shoulder she noticed some kind of commotion beyond the perimeter fencing.

'What's going on over there?' she said.

Donovan turned to follow her gaze. All attention inside the compound seemed to be centred on a cluster of people standing between the builders' huts and the deep excavation. Some others were rushing over to join them, while a few were detaching themselves from the group and heading for the ladders leading down into the ground.

'Another discovery?' Anne said. 'Perhaps they've found a second skeleton down there.'

'I don't think so,' said Donovan.

Anne was surprised by his reaction. 'Why not?'

'Look. You can see for yourself.'

Donovan pointed at the group by the huts, where an intense discussion was in full swing. At the centre of the scrum, a head of golden hair was clearly visible. One of the participants had removed her hard hat.

'Zoë?' said Anne.

Donovan nodded. 'I don't think the *Golden Girl* gets excited by Anglo-Saxons. Only the Romans are good enough for her.'

By now, Anne was already reaching into her shoulder-bag for the security pass, as they started walking towards the site entrance.

'I think we'd better take a look,' she murmured, and they quickened their pace.

They flashed their passes at the security guard, and were admitted into the site. The hubbub from the group was now separating into a number of distinct voices. Neither of them was surprised to hear the only female voice loud and clear as they drew nearer.

'... so you'll just have to shift operations for the time being to another part of the site. You've surely got plenty to do.'

Male voices clamoured together in protest, each one drowning out the other. In the midst of the whirlwind, Zoë Tipton raised a hand.

'You're not *listening* to me. This is *important*. It's in the contract that this part of the work has *automatic priority*. You know that *perfectly* well. I'll get an architect's instruction or a variation order, or whatever you call it, straight away.'

More protests rained down on her, but Zoë was resolute. She would not be moved. One of the builders spoke up in a firm voice.

'Without a formal instruction, we're carrying on as set out in the programme. Have you *any* idea of the penalty clauses on this contract if we fail to meet the target deadlines?'

Everyone turned to look at Zoë, who momentarily fell silent.

'But you'll act accordingly if you have an instruction from the architects?'

'That's right,' said the builder, 'but only then.'

'Verbal or written?' Zoë was staring him in the face. 'From any member of the architect's team?'

'It's all the same to us ... makes no difference.'

Suddenly, Zoë turned and stared directly at Anne. 'You're with Everett Parker, aren't you?'

Anne could feel her face redden. 'We're the interior –'

'I know that,' Zoë interrupted. 'But you are part of the team, right?'

'Er ... well, I suppose ...'

'Careful,' Donovan said quietly. 'This could be trouble.'

Zoë persisted. 'If you're not part of the team, why are you here?'

'I am –'

'Right, then.' Zoë's voice was hard as rock. 'I want you to issue an instruction to –'

'Just hold it there,' said Donovan. 'The interior design team can't issue that kind of instruction to the main contractor. Think about it.'

Zoë's eyes blazed. 'So you're saying there's nothing you can do to stop this blatant *vandalism* taking place.'

'No, I'm not.' Donovan stood firm. 'I'm saying you're probably both in the right, but neither of you is talking sense.'

Zoë glared, while the contractors regarded Donovan with suspicion. He continued.

'We can resolve this here and now ... with a little goodwill on either side.' He turned to Anne. 'Got your mobile?' She nodded and produced it from her pocket. 'Can you ring Philip Everett at the architect's?'

Anne pressed buttons and, when it was ringing, Donovan held out his hand to take the phone. He pressed it to his ear.

'Hallo. Is Philip Everett available? ... I have to speak to him, please. It's

Donovan Smith, calling from the Horselydown site. There's a problem. It's urgent.'

After a pause, Donovan handed the mobile to Zoë. 'You can explain,' he said.

The conversation that followed was brief and to the point. It appeared that something significant had been identified at the lowest level of the dig. The builders needed an instruction to stop them excavating further. Zoë handed the phone to the contractor who confirmed what had been said and agreed to act on a verbal instruction pending the issue of an order in writing.

With honour satisfied on both sides, the builders withdrew. Zoë handed the phone back to Anne without a word before turning to Donovan. For some seconds she looked at him appraisingly.

'I suppose I should thank you for that,' she said in a flat tone.

'No need,' said Donovan. 'It was obvious what had to be done.'

Zoë turned to Anne. 'I, er … look, I'm sorry. I shouldn't have put you in an awkward position like that.'

'That's okay.'

'No, it's not okay,' said Zoë. 'But I was feeling desperate. You've no idea what's at stake here.'

'Suppose you show us,' said Donovan. 'Can you do that?'

Zoë's expression changed instantly. Her eyes lit up.

Equipped with hard hats and yellow jackets, they descended the ladders and continued on past the skeleton, which now lay covered in a thick white plastic sheet. Zoë did not even glance in its direction as she led Anne and Donovan to a new ladder plunging further below ground. This deeper hole was protected on all sides by new shuttering supported by a framework of scaffolding.

The lower level was in shadow, and all three were using torches. Zoë indicated that they should stop, and she stepped cautiously forward, placing each footstep with care. When she was several feet away, she knelt down and swept the torch beam over the wet surface. Without looking back, she raised a hand and signalled to Anne and Donovan to advance. They squatted down beside her as she pointed at the ground before them.

'Do you see that?' Her beam swung in a slow arc across the slime. 'There … and there?'

'Is it wood?' said Anne. She spoke quietly, suspecting they were in the presence of coffins, relics in an ancient burial ground.

'Yes,' said Zoë, '… timbers. Do you know what they are?'

'Roman.' Donovan spoke less quietly, his tone firm and definite.

'Yes.' There was surprise in Zoë's voice. 'How could you tell?'

'It was easy … by the tone of your voice. Nothing else would turn you on like that.'

Anne chuckled. Zoë made no reaction. A few feet away, the timbers lay in strips protruding from the muddy ground, standing on edge like the border of a flower bed.

'Coming back to your question,' said Donovan, 'what are they?'

'I thought you'd be able to tell me.' There was a challenging tone in Zoë's voice. 'Well?'

Donovan hesitated. 'You said *timbers*, so I'm guessing they must be parts of a building or a vessel.'

'Take a leap into the unknown.' This time Zoë added a hint of mockery. 'It's really rather obvious.'

Anne realised that Zoë was playing Donovan at his own game and she wondered how he would take it. Without answering, Donovan crawled forward, reached into his rucksack, pulled out a video camera and aimed it at the timbers. A soft humming could be heard as the tape began running. After a few shots, Donovan gave his verdict.

'A vessel. That would be my guess.'

'How did you know?' Zoë sounded incredulous.

'Surely it's obvious,' he said.

Returning to the surface, Anne and Donovan stood together, while Zoë spoke on her mobile a few steps away. They heard her ask for Dr Fennimore and guessed she was reporting that morning's find. Anne wondered if she should call Marnie and bring her up to speed, but Donovan thought otherwise.

'Does she really need an intrusion into her holiday when it's only just begun?' he asked.

Anne agreed it would be unfair, though she asked herself if Marnie might take the opposite view. Donovan suggested they wait and see how the situation developed. In the background Zoë was raising her voice again. It seemed to be her default setting.

'No, I can't call back later.' Zoë was gesturing with her free hand to emphasise the point. 'I need to speak to him … *now*. Please interrupt his meeting. Tell him it's *very* urgent.'

Anne pulled a face at Donovan. 'What do you think it is down there?' she whispered.

Donovan shrugged. 'Whatever it is, it's certainly got her excited.'

'It wasn't very big,' said Anne. 'I wonder …'

It looked as if Zoë had got her way, as she turned and began pacing up and down, waiting for the project director to come on the line.

'I think perhaps I'd better stay here a while to see what happens,' Anne said, 'at least until Philip arrives.'

'Yes. You are after all representing the architect's department.' Donovan gave Anne a wry smile. 'I suppose that means technically you're in charge.'

Anne stared back at Donovan. 'Blimey,' she muttered.

'Ah, there you are, Miles.' Zoë was back in contact. 'Listen up. I've made a find ... yes, this morning ... absolutely ... well perhaps the departmental estimates can wait for a bit ... whatever, this is big, potentially *massive* ...'

She began pacing again, her head turned away. Anne and Donovan could no longer make out what she was saying. Whatever it was, she was leaving Dr Fennimore in no doubt about her views.

'Is this Fennimore guy her boss?' Donovan asked quietly.

'He's director of the archaeology project,' Anne said.

'She makes it sound like it's the other way round,' said Donovan.

Zoë was on the move again, this time walking back towards Anne and Donovan. She stopped within a few feet of them, smiling and confident. Removing the hard hat, she shook her hair free. The smile broadened as she rounded off the call. Everything was as she wanted it. Zoë Tipton had got her way again.

'Good,' she declared. 'Fennimore's on his way. In the meantime, Donovan, you can film me by the find, as if I'm making the discovery. Okay?'

'Sure. I'll need a power supply for lighting. Can we arrange that?'

'Yes,' said Zoë. 'What about sound? I want to give an *in situ* commentary as I work.'

Donovan frowned. 'With the equipment I have, that could be tricky –'

'Could I help?' Anne said.

'What about your plans for the day?' said Donovan.

'No probs. I can go later ... or tomorrow, even.'

Donovan positioned the lights around the timbers while Anne unpacked the sound equipment. They had agreed to meet Zoë up at surface level when everything was in place for a briefing on how she wanted the shoot to be organised. In the meantime, Zoë had absented herself for a few minutes on the grounds that she had *things to attend to*. Anne suspected that meant going to the loo, but Donovan thought she had other things on her mind. He was proved right.

They arrived at the top of the ladder just as Zoë was coming out of the staff hut. She immediately began explaining the order of the shoot while Donovan scribbled notes on a pad.

'I want you to note what is unacceptable. Absolutely no shots of me from behind bending over. I don't want viewers peering at my backside, okay?'

Donovan grinned and nodded. Zoë continued.

'Also, no shots of me talking from below the face, with the camera pointing up towards my chin. Got that?'

'Of course.'

Anne looked puzzled. 'Why's that?'

Donovan said, 'Zoë has a slightly crooked tooth. An upshot would emphasise and exaggerate it.'

Zoë flushed momentarily and blinked several times. Donovan handed her his notebook.

'Would this be a running order?' he asked.

Zoë studied the list of shots, concentrating hard. There were about ten points on the list, and she worked each one through in her mind. While Zoë was reading, Anne noticed the change in her. Donovan had been right; she had had other things on her mind when she had left them to set up the shoot below ground. Anne observed that Zoë was wearing subtle make-up, a delicate shading of lavender around her hazel eyes, a faint touch of mascara to emphasise the lashes, a hint of pink on the lips. Each of these combined to complement the lightly-tanned skin and complete the *ensemble*. Zoë Tipton was ready to face the camera ... on her terms.

They were halfway through filming beside the timbers when a sound from higher up announced the arrival of Dr Miles Fennimore. They broke off while Zoë revealed the find that was so important she had insisted the project director abandon his finance meeting to join her at once.

The two archaeologists went into a huddle, crouching over the timbers while a few steps behind them Anne and Donovan reviewed the filmed material on a small portable monitor.

'She'll love this,' Anne murmured quietly. They were watching a series of close-ups: Zoë in profile; Zoë's eyes concentrating hard; Zoë turning to face the camera. 'You'll presumably be cutting these in between shots of the boat, or whatever it is?'

'That's the idea,' said Donovan. 'Cutaways to add variety, pace and visual interest.'

'She's very attractive,' Anne said.

Donovan agreed. 'Telegenic. Not necessarily the same thing, but in her case ...'

'You've obviously studied her very closely.'

'The crooked tooth thing, you mean?' said Donovan.

'Exactly,' Anne said. 'I hadn't noticed it at all.'

'When you're filming something or someone you've got to be aware of all the little details that can spoil the results.'

Anne gestured over Donovan's shoulder; the archaeologists were coming over.

'Okay,' said Zoë briskly. 'Let's get back to the filming. We'll do that last scene again, the one that Dr Fennimore interrupted.' Beside her, Fennimore pulled a guilty face. Zoë smiled forgiveness at him. 'Then we'll bring Miles in and I'll explain the find to him.'

'Just Dr Fennimore?' said Donovan. 'You're not involving the other site director?'

Zoë stiffened. 'Why do you ask?'

'Just a thought. It would be a shame to have to do that part of the shoot again if you decided you wanted anyone else included.'

'Fair point,' Zoë agreed. 'But no, we're not including anyone else at this stage.'

'He's away today working on his own research,' Fennimore said.

'Medieval stuff,' Zoë added in a tone that Anne thought rather dismissive.

By lunchtime they had completed the shooting schedule for the day. Zoë had called up a group of archaeologists and wanted to spend the afternoon excavating the ship's timbers. Dr Fennimore was allowed to go back to finalising his estimates at the university. Before he left, Zoë swore him to silence.

'Even to Dick Blackwood?' Fennimore had protested.

'*Especially* to Dick Blackwood.' Zoë laughed. 'Otherwise he'll be claiming this was *his* find.'

'It's a matter of professional courtesy, Zoë. Dick *is* the joint site director, after all.'

Zoë stood her ground. 'Look, Miles, he'll be here tomorrow. I can bring him up to speed then. In any case, we'll have a better idea of what we're dealing with by that time.'

Fennimore was mollified. 'I suppose that's fair enough.'

'Frankly, Miles, if Dick can't spare the time to be on site …' She left him to draw his own conclusions.

'That's a bit unfair, Zoë. He does have his own research to do. No-one can accuse Dick of being unconscientious.'

'Whatever.' Zoë smiled and walked away.

Dr Miles Fennimore, senior research fellow and project director, realised he had been dismissed.

Anne and Donovan found a pub in a side street for a sandwich lunch. It had a small sunny terrace at the rear, and they sat out under a parasol advertising Carlsberg beer. Anne said she had found it interesting to watch Donovan filming while she handled the rifle microphone and kept an eye on sound levels. She had also been impressed with Zoë's approach to the shoot.

Instead of complaining or *throwing a wobbly*, as she put it, when Donovan asked her to repeat a scene that needed improvement, Zoë had born every demand with patience. She complied with every request without demur and followed all Donovan's advice closely, obeying every instruction.

'Why does that surprise you?' Donovan asked.

'It isn't Zoë's usual style to follow someone else's orders. She likes to be in charge. You know that.'

'She *was* in charge,' said Donovan. 'Everything we did this morning was about *her*. I was working for Zoë, not the other way round. She did what I said because it was in her best interests.'

'Even though it was only a bit of filming by a student working on a college assignment that –' Anne put her hand to her mouth. 'Oh, sorry. Donovan, I didn't mean it to come out like that.'

Donovan grinned. 'That's fine. I know what you meant. It is just a college project that hardly anyone will ever see.'

'Even so, I shouldn't have said –'

'You're right in one sense, Anne, but not in every sense.'

'Go on.'

Donovan took a mouthful of lager. 'Zoë will use this shoot in a number of ways for her own purposes.' He put down the glass. 'At the very least, she'll treat it as an opportunity to gain a little more experience in front of camera. Even with an unknown film-maker like me, it's useful extra practice.'

'But you're a very good photographer, Donovan. That comes through in everything you do.'

Donovan nodded. 'And she can tell that. Otherwise she wouldn't stick with it, believe me.' Another sip of beer. 'Next thing is, she'll want a copy of the finished film, at least the part that features her work on the excavation.'

'Will you let her have it?'

'Sure. Why not? Unless the university forbids it, which they won't. And I'll make sure I have a credit on the tape I hand over.'

'What will Zoë do with it?'

'Use it as an example of her work, I expect … and prove this find was hers, of course.'

'So it'll be like part of her CV,' said Anne.

'In a way, yes; a stepping stone on the way to becoming *the* new star in the world of archaeology.'

'You think she sees everything in those terms?'

'Don't you think she does?' said Donovan.

'So she has a master plan?' Anne said.

'I think so. You can never be certain about other people, but I have a pretty good idea of what she has in mind, and it doesn't involve spending the rest of her life scrabbling around in the dirt, scraping up sherds of pottery.'

'What do you think she has in mind?'

'I think it's fairly simple. She wants to be the next Barny Guthrie ... an archaeologist, sure, but in the public eye on television with her own series.'

'She's certainly well qualified for it,' Anne agreed, 'with her doctorate and reputation. And she's got the looks for television, all right.'

'And the determination,' Donovan added. 'In that way, she's rather like you, Anne.'

Anne started and almost spilled her spritzer. '*Me*?'

'Yes. Why are you surprised? You're ambitious. You want to be like Marnie. I'd say you were quite determined in your own way.'

'But I ... I just –'

'I know. You just want to do the job. Nothing wrong in that. The difference between you and Zoë Tipton is, you're not ruthlessly pushing yourself forward all the time.'

Anne looked reflective. 'What about you, Donovan? Would you say you're ambitious?'

Donovan gave a brief wistful smile. 'I'm not as fortunate as you, Anne. I don't have a clear goal. I just like to do interesting things. I'll have to wait and see where they lead.'

'So what's next for you?'

'One step at a time. Today, it's filming here ... my project.'

'And tomorrow?'

'More of the same. My guess is, Zoë will want to be filmed at surface level, talking to camera, wearing full equipment.'

'Hard hat and hi-vis jacket?' said Anne.

Donovan shook his head. 'Eye shadow and lipstick.'

Anne laughed. They both drank and imagined Zoë preening herself in front of the camera, standing beside the top ladder by the excavations. But in that regard they would be proved wrong.

10
Mega

Marnie could hardly believe it was only Tuesday as she prepared breakfast in the galley on *Thyrsis* while Ralph used the bathroom. Through the window she could see the Chiltern countryside through a faint mist under an opaque sky. She felt as if they were suspended in a parallel world, far removed from everyday reality, and had lost track of time and place. Ralph came into the galley looking refreshed and tanned and kissed Marnie on the lips.

'Ralph, where are we?'

'Oh god, she's gone doolally. That didn't take long. Two days away from the drawing board and her brain's ceased to function.'

Marnie gave him the Death Stare. 'Seriously. Where is this?'

Ralph shrugged. 'Somewhere in Bedfordshire or Hertfordshire, I presume. Hadn't thought about it.'

'I suppose that's a good sign,' Marnie said. 'Proves we're benefiting from the holiday. All the same, I'd like to have a rough idea of where we are.'

Ralph poured hot water into the cafetière. 'We can check the cruising guide with the map after breakfast.'

They took their seats and helped themselves to orange juice, toast and marmalade. Outside, they could see the light was already improving. It would be another sunny day.

'I wonder what Anne and Donovan are doing,' Marnie said, spreading butter on a slice of toast.

'Having a nice time, I hope,' said Ralph. 'Anne's probably soaking up the culture in the museums and galleries. Donovan's no doubt filming Dick and his bones.'

'Interesting that Anne hasn't phoned.'

'Were you expecting her to, Marnie?'

'Not sure what I expected, really.'

Ralph poured Marnie more coffee. 'My guess is, she's giving us time to ourselves and enjoying a relaxing break in the Metropolis.'

Anne was in no rush to set out on her quest for culture that morning. She knew that some cities in the world were early starters, but London was not one of them. People were still heading for work after nine, and she wanted to let the tubes and buses settle down to off-peak running before crossing the capital.

She and Donovan had a leisurely breakfast by the window, watching the sky gradually clearing in the distance downstream over the sky-scrapers of Canary Wharf. Anne had assembled her guidebooks and street maps the evening before, and she observed Donovan as he put together his equipment and removed the batteries from the charger. Living with him for just that short time, she was learning about him.

For all his self-assurance and confidence in his own judgment, he was an easy-going companion. She had feared he might be so used to living alone and taking account of his own wishes that he would find her presence intrusive. She remarked on this as he fastened the straps on the rucksack.

Standing up, he looked at her for a long moment. 'It's not me, it's us.'

Anne pondered what he meant. 'You mean we get on together?'

'Partly. You're a tidy person, though not obsessively so. If you'd been messy, you'd probably have driven me mad.'

Anne grinned. I feel the same way. But you said *partly?*'

Donovan reflected again. 'You're fun to be around.' Donovan grabbed the rucksack. 'Are we ready for off?'

'Let's go for it.'

It was cooler as they stepped out that morning. Anne, who was wearing blue cotton slacks and a fawn linen shirt, hesitated on the threshold, wondering if she should take a jacket.

Donovan looked up at the sky. 'By the time you reach the British Museum it'll have warmed up. You might not want to lug a jacket around all day.'

Anne could already see sunlight falling obliquely in the street beyond the wharf buildings. She agreed with Donovan's assessment and said she would go with him as far as the other side of the underpass.

When they climbed the steps and looked across to the construction site, they experienced a sensation of *déjà vu*. Inside the compound men were rushing in all directions. Their voices could be heard even from fifty yards away. Like a scene from an animated cartoon film, figures were bustling and scurrying about, some carrying ladders, others arc lights, some were pushing wheelbarrows, others carrying sheaves of picks and shovels.

And there at the centre of operations, surrounded by a small coterie of men in suits, was inevitably Zoë Tipton.

'I think I'd better come with you,' said Anne, 'at least as far as the gate. I ought to know what's going on.'

Zoë spotted Anne and Donovan as soon as they entered the compound and waved them over. Even before she spoke to them, they sensed a marked change in her manner. Whereas the previous day she had been excited, on that morning she was on a higher plane of exultation.

'Donovan, do you have your equipment with you?' There were no preliminaries. She spoke breathlessly.

'Yes.'

'Good. Get geared up ...' She glanced at Anne for the first time. '... both of you.'

'Anne isn't due to be here today,' Donovan said.

Anne touched his arm. 'It's okay. I'll stay if it's important.'

Zoë appeared not to have heard either statement. She stepped forward and placed both hands on Donovan's shoulders.

'Why is it only you, Donovan?' she said.

'Why is what only me?' He seemed baffled. 'What d'you mean?'

'Why are you the only one who seems to understand the importance of what I'm doing here?' Her eyes were sparkling.

Because I'm the only one pointing a camera at you and making you look good, he thought. He said, 'Do I take it you've made another discovery?'

'What have you found?' Anne asked quietly.

Zoë released one hand and placed it on Anne's shoulder, as if they were conspirators.

'You won't believe it, Anne,' Zoë said. She pronounced the next three words slowly and distinctly. 'It is *mega*.'

Marnie glanced down at the exhaust as *Thyrsis* pulled slowly away from their overnight mooring. Only light grey fumes emanated from the tailpipe as the engine burbled and the water boiled around the rudder. They had checked the oil levels in the engine and gearbox and adjusted the stern gland the night before on arrival. Now, everything seemed to be running smoothly, as Ralph made his way along the bank to climb aboard beside Marnie after pushing the bows free.

They had tied up for the night in an isolated stretch of water in a long pound between locks at the southern end of the Tring summit. As usual, they had woken to find other boats moored in line with them on both sides. Marnie smiled to herself, wondering if boats were naturally gregarious or just afraid of the dark. She steered *Thyrsis* slowly into mid-channel, waited until they had cleared the line of moored craft and accelerated up to cruising speed.

The morning air was cool, and for that first stint Marnie had draped a long navy blue cardigan over her shoulders. By the time they were approaching the first lock of the day, the sun was shimmering though high clouds and the air was warming. Marnie removed the cardigan and dumped it on the gas bottle container while Ralph strode along the bank towards the lock, windlass in hand.

Waiting for Ralph's signal to advance, Marnie again wondered how Anne was enjoying her holiday in London. She looked forward to hearing what discoveries Anne had made in the abundant galleries and museums of the city. She knew there would be a collection of postcards to admire, together with guidebooks and probably a few textbooks on artists and architects that would be useful to Anne's studies.

Marnie also wondered how Anne and Donovan were getting on together. They were not accustomed to being with each other on a day-to-day basis, and living in close proximity would be an interesting experience for them both.

Up ahead, Ralph waved. Marnie pushed the accelerator and guided *Thyrsis* forward, through the still water, into the waiting lock chamber with practised ease.

Donovan was faced with a problem. By now, the excavated area was much too big for his lights to cover overall. The only solution was to divide the space into individual sections and film them separately. He would later edit them together with shots of Zoë and detailed cutaways.

In her hyped-up state, Zoë was keen to make a start in front of the camera, but Donovan persuaded her he had to have the total site *in the can* before anything else. He asked Anne to start recording sound while he filmed, and when she asked what sound he wanted, he surprised her.

'Just wild sound.'

Anne looked blank. Donovan explained.

'I want a constant, consistent background sound level that I can build on. Give me about ten minutes' worth, okay?'

Anne grinned at him in the subdued light. Her reply was delivered in a deep, gruff voice in an accent straight from Hollywood central casting.

'You got it … ten minutes … on the wild side. Yo!'

Connecting two cables together, Donovan shook his head, chuckling. Beside him, Zoë was champing at the bit.

'Ten minutes?' she said in disbelief.

Donovan turned to face her. 'Don't you have something you can do in that time … make-up, perhaps?'

Zoë's expression hardened momentarily, but almost immediately relaxed. She left without a word.

By the time she returned, Donovan was setting up lights around the original timbers, having worked back in his filming to the starting point for that day's exposition by Zoë. She walked straight up to him.

'I hope you're —'

'We can begin now,' Donovan said quietly. 'First, I want you to tell me what all this is.'

Zoë's eyes flashed as she glanced at the unprepossessing wet soil. 'I've made more discoveries since yesterday.'

Donovan positioned her under the lights and saw that she had applied the same subtle make-up as the day before. She looked like the proverbial *million dollars*, though he would never tell her that. He noticed she was wearing perfume, and she saw that he had noticed.

'Morale booster,' she murmured.

'Okay. You were telling me what you'd found.'

Zoë pointed. 'You can see more timbers there ... there ... and there.'

'More vessels?' said Donovan.

'We now have three in all, *three* Roman trading ships.'

'Definitely Roman?'

'Beyond any doubt.'

'They couldn't be ferry boats?' said Anne.

'Is my judgment being called into question here?' Zoë's tone was icy.

'Not at all,' said Donovan. 'We just need to establish the facts.'

'Those *are* the facts. Three ships ... Roman ... trading vessels. All extremely rare and well preserved in the mud. This could be the site of the original port of Roman Londinium. Do you understand how important this is?'

'That's why I'm asking the questions,' said Donovan. 'I need to know what to stress, particularly when I'm editing the film together.'

Zoë became calmer. 'Of course. Are you ready to begin filming me?'

Donovan nodded. 'We're ready.'

'The light's better at surface level,' Zoë said. 'Shall we do some shooting down here and some up top?'

'We need to shoot everything down here,' said Donovan. He knew why Zoë wanted it different. 'Sound levels,' he explained. 'We need to keep clear of traffic noise up there.'

'Okay.'

Donovan sensed her disappointment. 'Perhaps by way of introduction we could shoot some footage of you at ground level before descending to the remains.'

Zoë considered this. Donovan continued.

'If we filmed outside the compound, looking in to establish the scene, you could appear in camera without the hard hat and hi-vis jacket. Then I could film you getting togged up to go below ground. How would that be?'

Donovan knew she would like that. He would be able to film her at her best.

'I like it,' she said. 'Let's get started.'

'One last thing,' said Donovan. 'Where's Dick Blackwood this morning?'

'Why d'you want to know about *him?*' The edge was returning to Zoë's voice.

'I don't want him blundering into the scene while we're filming.' Donovan's tone was even. 'That's why I need to know if he's likely to arrive out of the blue.'

'No idea.' Zoë frowned. 'That's odd, actually. He should be here today. Never mind. This isn't his kind of thing. Now, where shall I stand?'

For the next hour Zoë produced a presentation worthy of mainstream TV. Donovan backed her up with precise, unfussy filming. Avoiding the excessive zooming in and out and panning of amateur film-makers, he compiled a clean, clear series of images that kept the viewer's attention focused on the subject matter.

And what a find Zoë Tipton had made!

She guided Donovan around the timbers, pointing out details of the ships' construction, indicating the fine points that gave clues as to where the ships had been built, what cargoes they had carried and in what period they had operated. Anne and Donovan were impressed. Donovan was announcing that they had probably achieved all they could that morning, when Zoë produced her trump card.

'One last thing,' she said, pointing at one of the vessels. 'Over here.'

Donovan moved the camera on its tripod and realigned two of the lights, indicating to Anne where she should position the microphone.

'Tell me when you're ready,' Zoë said.

'What are you going to do?' Donovan asked. Zoë shook her head. 'Zoë, I need to know what I'm shooting … head and shoulders … big close-up …' He grinned. '… full frontal?'

'I'm going to kneel here and point at that part of the ship. Then I'm going to reach forward and pick something up.'

'Okay. I'll follow you in with a zoom, then a close-up on your hand. Keep it steady.'

He lined up the shot, told Anne to run sound and gave Zoë a countdown to action. After a brief pause, she began speaking.

'Perhaps the most interesting find is right in front of us, what every archaeologist needs above all else … dating evidence *in situ.* How old are these vessels exactly? What can we deduce without waiting for results from the laboratories? The answer is here.'

She leaned forward, while Donovan zoomed in smoothly. Her long slim fingers reached into a gap in the timbers. Withdrawing her hand, she held up a tiny object, turning it slowly in the light as she spoke.

'The Romans had the custom of placing a coin in the caulking in the bows at the time of construction. This is a golden *solidus*, beautifully preserved, clearly depicting the head of Theodosius the Great, who was emperor from 379 to 395. This ship therefore dates beyond doubt from the last years of the western Roman empire. That probably explains why they're here now. When we examine them in the laboratory, I'm sure they'll give up more of their secrets.'

Zoë held the coin still. Donovan counted to ten in his head.

'And cut,' he said.

'Wow,' said Anne, switching off the microphone.

'Wow indeed,' Zoë said in triumph.

Marnie handed over the tiller to Ralph and went below to change into a T-shirt. The afternoon had warmed up considerably, even though huge fluffy clouds were sauntering across the sky. She came up on deck clutching her mobile and hitched herself up onto the roof beside the stern door, pressing a button on the speed-dial.

'Hi Beth, it's me.'

'Marnie? I don't believe it. You've actually found time to phone your big sister? How can this be?'

'Easy. I'm on holiday.'

'I must be hallucinating,' said Beth. 'I think I have to lie down.'

'Ha … ha …' Marnie said slowly. 'But I'm serious. Ralph and I are taking some time off.'

'That's great. So where are you? Thailand? Acapulco? The Riviera?'

'Actually, I think we're somewhere in Hertfordshire.'

'What is it, some kind of mystery coach tour? Doesn't seem like your style, or Ralph's.'

'I think you know what we're doing, Beth. We're on *Thyrsis*, having a week on the canal.'

'Well, that's better than nothing.'

'What d'you mean? It's perfect, and so is the weather. We're having a *wonderful* time.'

'Sure. I'm only kidding. So Anne's in charge of the office?'

'No. Dolly's in charge this week. Anne's having a cultural break in London, staying in the flat. Donovan's keeping her company.'

'Very nice. So you're all just mooching around.'

'Yep.'

'Well, I'm pleased for you. You all deserve some R and R. It's nice not to have a care in the world.'

'You can say that again.'

'It's nice not to –'

'Beth!'

While Marnie and Ralph were wrestling with the thorny problem of where to stop for dinner that evening, Donovan was making a Spanish omelette, and Anne was preparing a mixed salad. Working together in the kitchen, they sipped spritzers.

After their meal, Anne and Donovan took coffee to the sitting area to watch the day's footage. Anne tried to imagine the final edited version showing cutaways interspersed with Zoë talking to camera. When they reached the end, Donovan pronounced it as okay.

'You didn't doubt it would be, did you?' Anne asked. 'You take a lot of care to get things right.'

Donovan shrugged. 'I'm never sure until I've had a chance to view the footage afterwards.'

'I don't think you make mistakes, Donovan.'

'Huh! I once set up an interview at college as an exercise. It looked fine until we watched it on the monitor in class.'

'Something went wrong?'

Donovan nodded. 'You could say that. I'd got the lighting lined up poorly around the subject's head. He came out looking like a chimpanzee with luminous ears.'

Anne shrieked with laughter. When she subsided, she added, 'But this shoot went well, didn't it?'

'Yeah, I think so.'

Anne watched Donovan as he disconnected the cables and packed the equipment away. By now, having known him for almost two years, she felt she could sense how he was feeling.

'Donovan, is something bothering you? If it's the footage, you've got no reason. It looked great to me.'

He stowed the equipment in the bedroom and returned to sit beside Anne on the sofa.

'It's Dick Blackwood,' he said.

'What about him?'

'Didn't it strike you as odd that he failed to show up today? He was due on site.'

'Is it such a big deal?' said Anne. 'Didn't Dr Fennimore say he was working on his thesis?'

'That's what he *suggested*.'

'What else would he be doing?' Anne said.

'That's the point.' Donovan looked thoughtful. 'I wouldn't be surprised if there was more to it than that.'

Anne wondered if this was another of Donovan's mysteries. Maybe. But he rarely made mistakes.

11
Pied-à-terre

On Wednesday Donovan had an unexpected day off from filming. When they left the flat, he told Anne he would only be doing establishing shots and general views of the archaeologists at work. At the end of their session the previous day, Zoë had told them Dr Fennimore was returning that morning with a team of students. They would spend as much of the day as possible scraping mud from around the Roman timbers under Zoë's direction.

'It'll give you a great chance to watch me – I mean *us* – in action,' she had said.

'So you'll be getting your hands dirty?' Donovan had asked.

Zoë had fixed him with an unblinking stare that lasted several seconds before giving him the benefit of the doubt. 'Sure ... at some point.'

That morning Anne and Donovan walked up from the pedestrian tunnel to be greeted by a familiar sight. In the building compound a small crowd was involved in what looked like some kind of disturbance.

'It's becoming a daily ritual,' Donovan said quietly. 'Messiah Zoë casting the money-lenders out of the temple.'

'I can't see Zoë in that crowd,' Anne said.

'Nor can I, in fact, but you can bet she's in the thick of it. Come on.' Donovan turned to Anne. 'Unless you want to beat it while the going's good?'

'I think I'd better come.'

Once inside the compound, Anne and Donovan went straight over to the crowd. Donovan was spotted at once by the site agent, who was looking flustered.

'Donovan, I'm sorry but I must insist you hold back from further filming, at least for today. We have to make the site secure.'

'Fine by me,' Donovan said in an even tone.

The contractor added, 'And it's in everyone's best interests. The boats have to be protected from tidal erosion.'

'*Ships.*' The voice came from behind the agent. Zoë emerged from the pack. 'They're *ships* not boats.'

'I don't care if they're the Battlestar *Gallactica*, young lady. They have to be protected, and we have to install more shuttering around the deep excavations. It's not stable down there.'

'It seems fine to me,' said Zoë. She looked as if she was on the brink of exploding. 'The archaeology gets priority. It's in the contract and –'

Donovan raised a hand. Everyone looked at him.

'Zoë, we already have a mass of unedited material.' His tone was reasonable. 'I'm sure the builders wouldn't hold us up for nothing.'

'It's health and safety,' the site agent muttered.

It was the familiar catch-all mantra. He was going to say more, but Donovan gave him a *don't-chance-your-luck* look and he wisely desisted.

'I can see I'm outnumbered here.' Zoë sounded deflated. 'So where does that leave us? What happens now?'

Donovan replied. 'The builders make the site secure and protect the ships. I get on with editing the footage. You presumably need to write up the results so far and bring the students up to speed.'

'That sounds like a plan,' Zoë conceded, but with little grace. 'When can I see the material?'

'I should get it edited today,' said Donovan. 'If you like, we can take over the staff hut so that everyone can watch at the end of the afternoon.'

Zoë turned to the site agent. 'I don't want to hold you up. You can be getting on with your health and safety works.'

The builders turned as one and marched off. Zoë took Donovan by the arm and walked him away from the rest of the group. Anne fell into step beside them.

'No-one sees the edited footage until I've had a chance to view it,' Zoë said under her breath.

Donovan acquiesced. 'Okay. Where d'you want the viewing to take place?'

Zoë frowned. 'That's the problem. We need somewhere private.'

'The university?' Donovan suggested.

Zoë shook her head. 'Can't go all the way back to Cambridge.'

'I meant Barbican,' said Donovan.

Another frown from Zoë. 'No guarantee of keeping it private at LBU.'

'You could come back to our place.' Anne spoke for the first time. 'It's just a few minutes' walk from here.'

Zoë considered this. 'Student digs,' she muttered. 'Okay.' A weary sigh. 'That'll have to do.'

Anne and Donovan traded glances but made no comment.

As they turned to leave in different directions, Donovan said, 'No Dick Blackwood again?'

Zoë's only reply was a *who-cares* shrug as she walked away.

Marnie watched Ralph power-walking along the towpath towards the next lock, over a mile away. For a man whose only exercise was walking, he was in good shape. A few times each day he chose to follow the towpath between locks rather than travel on *Thyrsis*. It gave Marnie time for her thoughts. Relaxing at the tiller, she let her memory float back to her first long solo journey on *Sally Ann* a few years earlier.

It was on this stretch that she had spent part of a day with Anne, who was then running away from home to ease the pressure on the family finances. Her father had been made redundant for the second time in as many years, and Marnie encountered the fifteen-year-old schoolgirl on the journey, desperate and depressed. Noticing the name of the boat, she had told Marnie she was also an Anne … Anne with an 'e'. The nickname had stuck and was still used on occasions.

That day had been a turning point for both of them. Anne found a role-model for life; Marnie found a friend who was to become her greatest support and ally.

Marnie smiled inwardly at the memories from that journey – a time she always thought of as *Sally Ann's summer* – and she felt the waterways working their old magic on her. Every mile she travelled lifted her spirits. She could think of no better way to relax and unwind.

Up ahead, she saw Ralph turning the windlass at the next lock. Marnie's last thought before concentrating on her approach to the chamber was the hope that Anne too was having a relaxing time in London.

Anne was lying flat out on the biggest cream sofa, a mug of tea steaming on the low table beside her, when the bell rang. She sat up, clambered over the pile of catalogues and brochures and padded to the hall. On the video screen she saw Donovan in the entrance at ground level. She said a cheerful *Hiya!* into the microphone and pressed the entry button. Opening the front door to the flat, she left it ajar and went to the kitchen. As soon as Donovan shut the door behind him, she called out.

'Tea?'

'Great.'

They met in the sitting area and kissed. Anne looped her arms round Donovan's neck and went limp.

'So you've done the tourist thing, I gather,' Donovan said.

'I'm putting my feet in for a retread,' Anne whispered into Donovan's shoulder, without loosening her grip or looking up. 'How did your day go?'

'I got the editing done.'

Anne moved her head to look into Donovan's face. 'How did it turn out?'

'Okay … usual form.'

Anne broke off her embrace and went into the kitchen area where the kettle had switched itself off. 'You don't sound too ecstatic.'

'The camerawork was all right. The zooms were smooth enough. The lighting wasn't brilliant. The sound quality was a bit below par.'

'Oh dear ... was that my fault?'

Anne returned with a mug, which she deposited on the table beside her own.

'Thanks, Anne. No. It was nobody's fault ... a limitation of the equipment. I expected as much.'

They flopped down onto the sofa. Donovan eyed the museum catalogues and the small pile of postcards.

'You've had a busy day, too.'

Anne rolled her eyes. 'Tell me about it. What time did we agree to meet Zoë?'

Donovan checked his watch. 'In about half an hour. I'll go and collect her from the site.'

Anne grinned. 'And bring her to the, er ... *student digs.*'

Donovan met Zoë in the staff hut where she was hanging up her jacket in the locker. Across the back was printed the title, *Capital Archaeology*, and below it were the initials ZT. She asked for a minute to change out of her boots and thick socks and sat on a chair flexing her toes. Donovan noticed her feet were neat and slim as she put on her sandals.

'Hard day?' Donovan asked.

'Mm ... I could really use a shower,' Zoë said.

'We have one in the flat. I'm sure you'd be welcome to use it.'

'I don't have any towels with me.' Zoë sounded as if that was final.

'Believe it or not we have towels.' Donovan smiled at her. 'There's even shower gel and shampoo. You'd be amazed how civilised we are.'

Zoë gave him a look that spoke of reserving judgment.

On the way to Butler's Wharf, Zoë asked how the film editing had gone, and she paid little attention to their surroundings as Donovan gave an account of progress. It was only as they ascended in the lift that she became aware they were in a modern building.

'Where is this?' she asked.

'It's a conversion,' said Donovan. 'Used to be a warehouse or something.'

'It doesn't look bad.'

'Uh-huh.' Donovan led the way across the lift lobby on the fifth floor, opened the front door and stood aside to let Zoë enter the flat. 'After you.'

Zoë was stunned. She stopped in the middle of the open-plan living space and looked across to the dining area beside the large windows with their view of the river, the City and Canary Wharf beyond. From the adjoining kitchen area Anne called out a greeting and emerged to meet her.

Zoë regarded Anne appraisingly, as if seeing her for the first time.

'You live here?' she asked, her voice dripping with incredulity.

'It belongs to Marnie, actually.'

'But …' Zoë seemed unable to find the right words. 'But I thought … you hung out in some barn in the sticks. That was the impression I got from Dick.'

'This is our London *pied-à-terre*,' Anne explained.

Zoë closed her eyes and let out a long slow breath. She could feel grit between her toes in the sandals and dust on her skin. She knew there was grime under her fingernails and dried mud in her hair.

'Donovan, is that offer of a shower still on?'

'Sure. I'll get you some towels.'

'You can stay for supper if you'd like to,' Anne added. 'It's only something simple. I'm making a Greek feta salad to go with baked trout. Oh, and there are strawberries from the market.'

'And a white wine from Bordeaux,' Donovan chimed in. 'Nothing grand.'

With eyes still closed, Zoë thought of the little room in the student hostel where she was staying, the tin of soup in the cupboard and the ready-meal with her name on in the fridge in the communal kitchen. She smiled wearily and let out a sigh.

'I will lay my bones here forever.' She turned to Donovan. 'Lead me to the shower.'

The evening went well, much better than Anne or Donovan could have imagined. Zoë was surprisingly good company, relaxed and friendly, showing genuine appreciation of the meal. She regaled them with a stock of humorous anecdotes about her experiences on digs all over Europe.

After the meal they all three cleared away then retired to the sitting area where Donovan had connected the camera to the television for viewing. Zoë watched his film of the dig with intense concentration, saying nothing, merely nodding her head from time to time. She reserved all comment until the last image faded to black.

'*Remarkable*,' she said. 'You were right about your equipment not being up to professional standard, but your average viewer would scarcely have known.'

'The sound quality's pretty ropy,' said Donovan. 'Not much I can do about that.'

'It's the images that count,' said Zoë. 'Less than perfect sound is okay in such a restricted space … adds to the atmosphere.'

'I've got hold of a better microphone and recorder for the next time. I'm assuming there will be more filming. Is that right?'

Zoë smiled. 'Oh yes. That's right, all right. You wait till you see what I've got in store for tomorrow.'

12
Disaster

Anne had a long-awaited phone call after breakfast on Thursday. She had expected Marnie to make contact at some point during the week, but had been surprised that she had held off for so long. It was a sure sign that Marnie was enjoying her break and putting all thoughts of work behind her.

'How's the culture vulture?' Marnie said. 'Worn your trotters off yet?'

Anne, who was not sure that vultures actually had trotters, could hear an engine rumbling in the background.

'Not quite. I've spent some of the time helping Donovan with his filming. I'm now a sound engineer. How about you and Ralph? Trip going well?'

'Great. We're on the outskirts of London … should reach Little Venice tomorrow. Is Donovan still filming? I thought he'd have finished by now.'

'No. He's assembling a lot of material. You remember Zoë?'

'How could I forget?'

'Quite. Well, she's discovered the remains of these Roman ships at the bottom level, three of them no less. Donovan's been making a record of the dig. It's apparently very important.'

'But you're supposed to be on holiday, Anne.'

'That's okay. It's quite fun, actually.'

'What do you have to do?'

'I mostly spend my time squatting in the mud pointing a microphone at Zoë.'

'Sounds a gas.'

When they ended the conversation they agreed to be in touch over the weekend.

The plan for the day was that Anne would spend the morning visiting the National Gallery and would return to assist Donovan around lunchtime. Anne would have stayed on site all day, but Donovan insisted she should have at least a partial holiday. He had once told her the saying in military circles that all plans fell apart once contact was made with the enemy. That morning they learned that something similar also held true for archaeology.

Anne and Donovan were wondering what would be the subject of the daily dispute at the building site. Whatever it was, the hot money was on Zoë once again being in the middle of it. They were right, but the atmosphere was much more low-key that morning. As they waved their security passes at the guard on the gate, they could see Zoë remonstrating with one of the students, a thin girl with a thick brown pigtail down her back. The girl looked less than pleased as she walked over to the staff hut. Zoë was shaking her head with a wry smile as she saw Anne and Donovan approaching.

'She knows the rules,' Zoë said in exasperation. 'No jewellery on the dig.'

'The diamond tiara interferes with the hard hat?' Anne suggested.

It was a measure of their improved relationship that she felt able to make such a remark.

Zoë grinned. 'Something like that.'

'Is that the usual rule at an excavation?' Donovan asked.

He had a clear recollection of seeing archaeologists wearing small items of jewellery on the Glebe Farm dig the previous summer.

'It's one of *my* rules,' said Zoë. 'And there's a good reason for it. A year or two back, one of the students on our summer dig in Staffordshire thought she'd found a Roman pendant. Turns out it had been dropped by one of the girls on the team who'd snagged the chain on some stonework.'

'And you seriously mistook it for *Roman*?' Anne said.

Zoë sighed. 'In fact, it was a replica from that company, *Past Times*, and it almost fooled me. Caked with dirt and mud, it was a pretty good imitation at first sight. So now I make a rule … no exceptions.'

Zoë's grin changed abruptly to a scowl. Turning to follow her look, Anne saw Dick Blackwood walking towards the compound.

'Quick,' Zoë said. 'Get your protective clothing and follow me down to the dig.'

Donovan began to speak. 'Actually, Zoë, Anne is going –'

But it was too late. Zoë was already hurrying towards the first ladder. Donovan turned to Anne.

'Look, there's no need for you to –'

Anne interrupted. 'This sound equipment you've brought … it needs someone to operate, doesn't it? I mean, you can't film and record sound single-handed, right?'

'It's not ideal, but this morning I was just going to film the students on site, plus cutaways with wild sound in the background.'

'Looks like Zoë has other ideas,' Anne said. 'Let's just get on with it.'

Entering the staff hut, Donovan was surprised that Dick had not yet appeared. He looked out towards the entrance gate and saw him in conversation with Dr Fennimore. Dick was gesticulating in excited fashion. Donovan went inside and quickly dressed for the site.

'This doesn't look good,' he said wearily to Anne, who by now was ready to go.

'What's the matter?' she asked.

'I think we're about to have *two* hyper archaeologists to deal with. Dick's out there bending the ear of the project director. Something's got him going.'

Anne groaned. Grabbing their gear, they exited the hut and hurried towards the excavation. Dick was still explaining something to Dr Fennimore, but now his style was more restrained, as if pressing home the detailed points of an argument. Fennimore was listening intently, his expression hovering between impressed and startled.

'I wonder what that's all about,' Anne said.

She engaged the top rungs of the ladder and began her descent with the equipment bag over her shoulder. When her feet touched bottom, she followed Donovan across the sodden ground on which some kind of tracking had been laid to create a footpath. Even in the half light of the dig area, she could see that Zoë was more animated than usual. *Hyper*. Donovan was right. She wondered what Zoë would do if she, Anne, simply announced that she had other plans for the morning and could not stay.

Too late. She hesitated, and the moment passed. Donovan was already being briefed, and Anne quickly joined them. Zoë was in mid-flight.

'... even more significant than I at first thought possible.' Her eyes were sparkling again. Anne knew that look. 'The others are over there.'

They all peered into the dimness.

'What are we looking for?' Anne asked.

Zoë turned and placed her hands on Anne's shoulders. She spoke slowly.

'We have now uncovered *five* Roman vessels ... not *three*, Anne ... *five*.'

'Why are they here?' Anne said. 'Presumably, they wouldn't just abandon them, would they?'

'That's what makes them so *special*, Anne. They've probably been here since the Romans began moving back to defend Rome against the Visigoths in around 410.'

'You mean they just left them behind?'

'Exactly. After the Roman empire collapsed in the west, a lot of trading ceased. The Romans dumped a lot of things when they left.'

'But wouldn't they have needed all their boats ... er, ships?'

'That has never been clear, Anne, at least not until now. This discovery may well prove that they took what they could in their biggest vessels and left the smaller ones behind. With no crews to operate them, they were just abandoned.'

Anne thought of old photographs she had seen of decaying narrowboats and barges left rotting in backwaters of the canal system after the bulk of commercial carrying had ceased.

'So this is an important discovery,' Anne said.

'That, Anne, is the understatement of the year. This is *huge*.'

And it will make your name, Anne thought.

Zoë's eyes refocused to a point over Anne's shoulder.

'Ah, good,' said Zoë. 'Just the man I wanted …' Her voice tailed off.

Anne and Donovan turned to see Dr Fennimore reaching the bottom of the ladder. He stopped and looked up, as if expecting someone to be following him. After a few moments he checked his watch and scanned the lower level. Spotting Zoë, he waved to her to come over. Anne and Donovan went with her, but Fennimore shook his head.

'Sorry,' he said, 'I need to have a word with Dr Tipton in private.'

He led Zoë a short distance away while Anne and Donovan withdrew to give them space.

'Something's going on,' Donovan murmured.

'I wonder what,' said Anne.

'My guess is, Dick's got something up his sleeve.'

'It will have to be pretty big to trump Zoë's finds down here.' Anne looked over at the group of students busily engaged on the ship remains. 'What d'you think it could be?'

Donovan shrugged. 'I don't know enough about archaeology to know what's hot.'

'He's probably found … King Arthur's round table,' Anne said, with an impish smile.

Donovan grinned. 'Even if Camelot ever existed, I don't think it was supposed to be in these parts.'

They had a clear view of Zoë's reaction to whatever Dr Fennimore was saying. She looked completely subdued, as if he was telling her the Roman ships were replicas from *Past Times*. Fennimore repeatedly looked up the ladder, but no-one came down. When he ended the conversation, he began climbing to the surface leaving Zoë standing in silent contemplation.

Donovan spoke under his breath. 'I think you're going to get your visit to the gallery, Anne.'

'You think so?'

'We'll see now.'

Zoë walked slowly over to where they were standing. 'Er … I don't think we'll be filming this morning after all. Something's … come up.'

'Will you be needing us later on?' Donovan asked.

Zoë avoided eye contact. 'Probably not, I think.' She glanced up quickly. 'If you'll excuse me …'

Zoë hurried back to the excavations.

'I wonder what's the archaeological term that's bigger than *mega*,' Donovan said quietly.

'You think Dick has discovered something of that order?'

Donovan shrugged. 'What else could it be?'

Marnie was sitting on the roof, dangling her legs over the side of the boat while Ralph steered. Rubbing sunblock on her arms, she was thinking about fetching cold drinks from the galley, when her mobile rang.

'That's only your second call all week, Marnie. It must be a record.'

Marnie smiled and pressed the green button.

'Hallo? Marnie Walker.'

Anne told her of the strange happenings at the site that morning. Marnie was equally baffled and rapidly outlined the situation to Ralph.

'Sounds like Dick has come up with something significant,' he called over the sound of the engine. 'I suspect it must be something like that.'

'Any idea what?' Marnie asked.

Ralph shook his head.

'You haven't been able to ask Dick direct?' Marnie said.

'Not so far,' said Anne. 'He's been in a huddle with Dr Fennimore. They've shut themselves away in another hut on site. Strictly no admittance.'

When Marnie disconnected, she went down into the galley and brought up glasses of sparkling water with chunks of ice and a wedge of lemon. While they sipped, they tried to guess what might have happened.

'I suppose Dick might have come across a hoard of some kind,' Ralph suggested. 'Do you know what's the subject of his thesis?'

'I only know he's a medievalist,' said Marnie. 'And would a hoard be more important than those Roman vessels?'

'Depends what was in it.'

'Any other ideas?'

Ralph pondered. 'A burial, perhaps? The lost tomb of some king or other?'

'Surely they know where all the medieval kings are buried,' Marnie said. 'What about Boudica's tomb? That's never been found, has it?'

'Not Dick's field of study,' said Ralph.

'Maybe not, but that wouldn't prevent him finding it if he was digging somewhere.'

'True. Whatever it is, it must be … what's the best way of describing it?'

'Mega?' Marnie suggested.

Anne and Donovan went back to the staff hut to change out of their protective clothing. While Donovan was putting the hard hats up on the shelf, Dr Fennimore looked in.

'I think we need to have a word,' he said. 'Can you hang on for a minute or two?'

'Sure,' said Anne.

Fennimore went out, and the door closed silently behind him.

'My guess is we're about to sign the Official Secrets Act,' Donovan said, hanging up his yellow jacket.

He held out his hand to take Anne's jacket and joined her at the table.

'I wonder what's going on,' Anne muttered. 'It's all very mysterious.'

'It has to be about Dick,' Donovan said firmly. 'He's been away from the site for most of the week. Then he turns up in an excited state and gets Fennimore jumping. He tells Zoë what's happened, and that bursts her bubble.'

'So where do we fit in?' Anne asked.

'I don't think we do.'

Before Donovan could continue, the door swung open and Fennimore entered, followed by Dick, whose eyes were alight. Anne thought this was how scientists must have reacted when they first split the atom or discovered the double helix of DNA.

Dick winked at Anne as he took his place at the table. She gave him a questioning look, but his only reply was to beam at her with raised eyebrows. Dr Fennimore cleared his throat and adopted a serious expression.

'How should I begin?' he said.

He was evidently not expecting an answer, so everyone waited for him to continue. He steepled his fingers and bowed his head as if about to say prayers.

'In the coming days you're likely to hear things through your contact with the archaeologists here.' He spoke slowly and quietly. 'Certain matters will inevitably be mentioned in your presence. I want you to understand that nothing you hear is to go beyond this compound. Do I make myself clear?'

'Are you going to tell us what kind of thing is in question?' Donovan asked.

Fennimore reflected. 'No. I can't do that.'

'Dr Fennimore, we aren't experts in this field. We may not realise what of all the things we hear might need to be kept secret.'

'Oh, you would,' said Fennimore. 'Believe me.'

Beside Fennimore, Dick Blackwood was staring down at the table, trying hard to contain himself.

'What have you found ... the Crown Jewels?' Donovan said in a flippant tone.

Anne and Donovan were astonished at the reaction of the two archaeologists. Their heads snapped up and they glared at Donovan. He looked sideways at Anne, who was as baffled as he was.

'I meant that in a light-hearted way,' said Donovan. 'Obviously.'

Dick opened his mouth to speak, but Fennimore cut him off.

'I think enough has been said on this subject.'

'So you're not going to give us any idea what's happened?' Donovan said.

Fennimore shook his head. 'We're not ready to make any announcement at the present time. We're not even giving exact details to our own colleagues.'

Donovan persisted. 'Even though we've promised to respect confidentiality?'

'This is about academic protocol,' Fennimore said. 'We'll make known what has happened when we've ascertained all the facts.'

'Do we get back to filming Zoë and her ships?' Donovan asked. 'I want to get footage of the students on the dig. I hoped that might include shots of you talking to them as they work, Dr Fennimore.'

'I'm going to be otherwise engaged this morning,' said Fennimore. 'Mr Blackwood and I have things to discuss.'

Donovan took that as a sign that their meeting was concluded. He stood up and shouldered his pack. Anne did the same and they left the hut.

'Amazing,' said Donovan as they walked across to the ladder.

'The secrecy bit, or their reaction to your Crown Jewels remark?'

'Neither. The fact that Dick didn't utter a single syllable all through.'

Anne stopped and turned to Donovan. 'What did you make of their reaction to what you said?'

Anne knew that face. Donovan was working through the possibilities in his mind.

'It must be about some kind of treasure, I suppose,' he said, 'something really major.'

They looked across to the Tower of London, where the Crown Jewels of England were on display in secure cabinets in a heavily-protected gallery. 'I don't think even Dick would tunnel his way in there and claim them.'

'What then?' Anne said.

'Two things. I think the first question we have to ask is where Dick has been this week. Also, we know his field is the Middle Ages, but we don't know the subject of the thesis he's working on.'

'Can we find out?' Anne said. 'Who would know?'

'I expect if we asked –'

At that moment students began emerging from the dig hole. One after another they scrambled off the ladder and assembled in the yard. A dozen of them formed a group, chatting among themselves. Then their number grew to about twenty, then thirty. Eventually, Zoë emerged from below, followed by two more students. She looked annoyed, weary and despondent in equal measure.

Anne and Donovan went over to where she was standing.

'What's up?' said Donovan.

Zoë was like a different person. The lively, dynamic young woman of the previous evening had gone. Now she looked as if she had not slept for a week. The light in her eyes was extinguished.

'First there's this new business with Dick Blackwood,' she said. 'That's going to get in the way of everything I'm trying to do here. Now this ...' She waved an arm towards the excavation.

In the background builders were descending the ladder, and a crane had swung round to lower equipment and materials down into the hole.

'What's going on?' said Donovan.

Zoë sighed. 'The wretched site agent has intervened, playing the health and safety card. We're out of there for the rest of the morning. He wants yet more shuttering to protect the site.'

'Isn't that a good thing?' said Anne. 'I mean, won't that help preserve your ships?'

'It's just one more annoyance, Anne. There's nothing wrong with the site as it is. These people are *obsessed* with health and bloody safety. They're *always* going on about it.'

Donovan joined in. 'You mentioned this new business with Dick ...?'

Zoë shook her head. 'To be brutally frank, I have doubts ... *serious* doubts. We shall see ...'

With that, she walked away, head bowed, avoiding eye contact with everyone.

'If they're out, we're out,' Donovan said, watching Zoë pull open the door of the staff hut. 'I suppose that means you're free, Anne. The cultural fleshpots of London await you.'

'What about you? What will you do, Donovan?'

'Good question. I suppose I ought to write up my work on the project so far. I've got the laptop with me. Perhaps I could go back and work in the flat?'

'Of course you can.' Anne looked at her watch. 'How about coffee first?'

Marnie yawned and stretched. She had not felt so relaxed in weeks, months ... probably years. She made a mental resolve to take at least one holiday every year from then on. From her perch on the boat's roof, she smiled at Ralph who was leaning comfortably against the tiller. They had passed through the last lock of their journey south at Cowley and knew they now had a clear run all the way to Little Venice.

'You look happy,' said Ralph.

'Do I normally look miserable?'

Ralph grinned. 'Like an ogre.'

'Thank you for that generous assessment, kind sir. But seriously, Ralph, I feel *great*.'

'You look great, darling, especially in those shorts. Has anyone ever told you, you have exceptionally fine –'

Ralph's compliment was interrupted by the trill of Marnie's mobile. She picked it up and pressed the green button.

'Hallo? Marnie Walker.'

'Marnie, it's Anne.'

Even on the mobile Marnie could detect the tension in Anne's voice. 'Something wrong?'

'Oh, Marnie. Something *terrible* has happened.'

Leaving *Thyrsis* near Uxbridge, Marnie and Ralph crossed London by tube and reached Horselydown in just over an hour. They went straight to the flat, noticing in passing that all activity in the building site had ceased, and found Anne still in a state of shock. Donovan was beside her on the sofa.

'It was all so unreal,' Anne murmured. 'We'd been talking to him about the work. It was an ordinary morning ... apart from Dick's new discovery ... whatever that was. I went for a coffee with Donovan. When we came back, Dr Fennimore was ...'

Anne sat staring ahead.

'Can you bear to talk about what happened?' Marnie asked gently.

Donovan took up the story. He explained about Dick's discovery, and how Dr Fennimore had insisted on confidentiality.

'We were just making plans for the day when the students started coming up out of the dig. Zoë was annoyed that the builders insisted on carrying out more reinforcements to the shuttering. They said they had to protect the walls down to the lowest level.'

'Where was Fennimore at that time?' Ralph asked.

'Donovan said, 'He'd gone off with Dick for further talks in one of the huts.'

'Didn't they know about the extra shuttering works?' Ralph said.

'There was a *Health and Safety – Keep Out* warning sign by the ladder, but they must've assumed it was just a routine inspection.'

'What happened then?' said Marnie.

Anne continued the narrative. 'We'd gone for coffee at a little place round the corner. As we were coming out we heard a loud siren coming from the site, so we rushed back. Builders were running to the dig ladder. A cloud of dust was coming up from below. We could see part of the shuttering and scaffolding had collapsed on the far side.'

'That was the deepest part of the dig,' Donovan said, 'the bottom level by the Roman ships.'

'That's where Dr Fennimore and Dick had gone,' Anne added. 'It seems they'd finished their meeting and decided to go down to inspect the ship excavation. They seem to have ignored the warning sign and just climbed down. Then the scaffolding gave way. Part of the shuttering collapsed and ...'

Anne put her head in her hands. Donovan put an arm round her shoulders.

'It's all right,' Marnie said quietly.

'Dr Fennimore was ... killed outright?' Ralph said.

Donovan nodded.

'What about Dick?'

'He was on the opposite side from Dr Fennimore. When the walls came down, apparently he dived out of the way.'

'Was he injured?'

'Not a scratch,' Donovan said.

'What happens now?' Marnie asked.

'The site's closed down for the day,' Donovan said. 'Inspectors are going in tomorrow. They'll produce a report and there'll be an enquiry.'

'How long will that take?' Marnie said.

Anne looked up. 'I spoke to the clerk of works. He said they'd have a crew in over the weekend making the dig site secure. Building work would probably resume on Monday.'

'That's quick,' said Marnie. 'I would've expected them to take much longer.'

Anne shook her head. 'The builders said they had to make the site safe without delay. They can't risk any more collapse. It could compromise that whole central area.'

'And the excavations?' Ralph said.

'Probably the same. Remember, they only have a limited time to complete the dig.'

'So at least Zoë will be happy,' said Marnie.

Anne shook her head. 'She certainly didn't look happy.'

Marnie was anxious to see the site for herself and talk to Philip Everett. Ralph went with her, leaving Anne with Donovan in the flat. It was only as they drew up to the site entrance gate that Marnie realised there was a problem with Ralph. She took the security pass from her bag and held it up. The guard waved her in, but looked pointedly at Ralph.

'This is my colleague, Professor Lombard,' Marnie said in a confident tone, stressing the *Professor*.

The guard consulted his list. 'Professor ...?'

'Lombard,' Ralph said, equally confidently. 'Ralph Lombard.'

The guard frowned. 'There's no-one of that name on the list, miss. I've got a Professor de Groot.'

'De Groot is here?' said Ralph. 'He's head of archaeology at London Barbican University. I'm from All Saints' College, Oxford.'

The guard looked dubious and checked his list again.

'Look, I'll vouch for Professor Lombard,' said Marnie. 'He's ... oh, just a minute.' Looking beyond the guard, she waved an arm, once, twice, then made a beckoning gesture.

Philip Everett arrived a moment later. His expression was grim as he kissed Marnie on the cheek and shook Ralph's hand.

Marnie explained the security problem, and Philip assured the guard that Ralph was not a security risk or sightseer. He would authorise his admittance. The guard asked Philip to print Ralph's name on the sheet and sign his own name alongside.

Philip left Marnie and Ralph to equip themselves with protective clothing and dashed off to see the site agent and other contractors for a hastily-convened meeting. Marnie pushed open the door to the staff hut and stopped in her tracks.

Seated at the table was a stocky man in his forties wearing a dark suit. Beside him sat a younger man, Afro-Caribbean, in a black leather jacket. On the other side, two students were sitting, young women. One of them looked as if she had been crying. The stocky man eyed Marnie with a look bordering on suspicion. The Afro-Caribbean got to his feet and began gesturing to Marnie that she should withdraw.

'It's all right, Ray,' the stocky man said, not taking his eyes off Marnie. 'It's interesting that *you* should be here, Mrs Walker.'

'Good morning, chief inspector,' Marnie said. Turning a little towards Ralph she added, 'Ralph, this is DCI Bruere of the Metropolitan Police.' She turned back to Bruere. 'This is Professor Ralph Lombard, my fiancé.'

'And your business here?' Bruere asked.

'I'm part of the architect's team for the building project.'

Bruere looked at Ralph. 'And yours, sir?'

'Moral support for Marnie.'

'You're not one of the archaeologists?'

'No.'

Marnie said quickly. 'Sorry to interrupt your discussion, Mr Bruere. We need our protective clothing from the lockers. If we can just take what we need, we'll get out of your way.'

'Okay, go ahead. But don't leave the site until I've spoken to you. Got that?'

Marnie and Ralph were out of the hut in less than a minute. As they hurried across to the dig site, Marnie was muttering under her breath.

'What was that, darling?' said Ralph.

'I said that was all I need ... bloody *Bruere*.'

'Not your favourite policeman?'

'He's interviewed me in the past. Don't you remember, Ralph?'

'Come to think of it, the name is familiar.'

Marnie stopped abruptly. 'Wait a minute ... what's he doing here? This is an industrial accident. I'd expect health and safety inspectors to be crawling all over the place, but he's CID.'

'You think the police are treating this as a suspicious death, Marnie?'

'They must be. I mean, why else would he be here?'

'Presumably, there has to be –'

Marnie cut Ralph off with a gesture. 'Come on.'

She set off, leaving Ralph trailing along in her wake. Ralph understood her intention when he saw Dick Blackwood standing by the perimeter fence talking with some of the students. Dick caught sight of them and broke off from the group to meet them halfway.

'Dick, I'm really sorry about Dr Fennimore. This is *awful*. Is it true, you weren't hurt in the accident?'

'Yeah. Thanks, Marnie. I was dead lucky.' He paused after the unfortunate choice of words. 'We were taking a look at the ships when the scaffolding just started falling down around us. There was no warning. I'd moved a short distance away and managed to throw myself clear, but Miles had no chance.'

'Anne said you'd made some sort of major discovery,' Marnie said.

Dick nodded, his face sombre. 'Miles was almost as excited as I was.'

'Was he a medievalist too?' Ralph asked.

'Not exactly. He was a landscape archaeologist, a brilliant one.'

'Am I right in thinking your discovery was elsewhere?'

'Yes.'

Marnie wanted to bring the conversation back to the immediate questions.

'Dick,' she said, 'why are there detectives here?'

Dick shrugged and shook his head. It occurred to Marnie that like Anne he too was in a state of shock. And there but for the grace …

'Is Zoë not around?' said Marnie.

'Zoë?' Dick repeated, as if he had forgotten who she was.

'I thought everyone was supposed to wait to be seen by DCI Bruere.'

'I think …' Dick began. 'I think Zoë went off to get some lunch.'

'But surely the police required everyone to stay on site.'

Another shrug from Dick. 'You know Zoë …'

Marnie looked at her watch, then scanned the site. Students were scattered about in clusters, talking together in subdued voices.

'Has anyone done anything about food for the diggers?' she asked.

Dick looked blank. 'Not that I know.'

Marnie dug out her mobile. 'I'm going to ring Anne … get her to meet us at the mini-market … we'll bring some sandwiches and stuff. The students must be starving.'

'Good idea,' said Dick, to whom the thought had obviously not occurred.

'And I think you could use a brandy, Dick,' said Ralph.

'No alcohol allowed within the compound.' Dick sounded as if he was quoting from a rulebook. 'But you're absolutely right.'

'Perhaps that's what Zoë went to get,' said Marnie, pressing buttons on the mobile

'I couldn't blame her if she did,' Dick said. 'And in any case, I wouldn't. Zoë saved my life.'

❖ ❖ ❖ ❖ ❖ ❖ ❖

They descended on the sandwich cabinet in the local mini-market and cleared it out like the plague of locusts attacking the Pharaoh's crops. While Marnie and Ralph filled one trolley with sandwiches, Anne and Donovan piled packets of crisps, boxes of fruit pies and soft drinks into another. Ralph added a half bottle of brandy for medicinal purposes. When Marnie explained the circumstances to the somewhat bewildered Indian lady in charge of the shop, she readily agreed to let them take both trolleys away, with the promise that they would return them very soon.

They trundled along to the building site in convoy, like working narrowboats, a motor trailing its butty. With some difficulty they humped the trolleys down the steps to the subway and up again on the other side of the road. Once admitted into the compound, Marnie signalled to the students to help themselves from the trolleys. They needed no further prompting and gratefully crowded round the food supply, declaring that they were indeed famished.

Ralph had slipped the brandy into his back pocket and, when he was sure no-one was watching, offered it to Dick, who gratefully swigged a mouthful and handed it back to Ralph.

'You hold on to it,' Ralph said. 'You may need it again.' He took a tube of Polo mints from his pocket and handed them to Dick. 'You should take these, too. Not a good idea to smell of brandy when the police interview you.'

To Ralph's surprise, Dick reached forward and hugged Ralph tightly to him, holding on for several seconds. Ralph could feel him trembling, as if on the brink of tears. When he eventually released Ralph, Dick stood back with eyes closed and took a series of deep breaths.

'Are you okay?' Ralph asked gently.

'Yes,' Dick breathed the word. 'Better now, thanks, Ralph.'

Marnie had come over to them, seeing Dick holding on to Ralph and she laid a hand on his arm.

'You ought to eat, Dick,' she said. 'You need something inside you.'

Dick took the sandwich she held out to him. It was ham with salad. He took a bite without looking at it. Marnie suspected he did not taste it, either. She felt moved that he was simply doing what he was told, like a child obeying his mother. The thought came to her that with his enthusiasm and curiosity he was in some ways like a boy with a hobby, a passion that dominated his life. He was probably only a few years older than Anne, and at that moment while he stood eating his sandwich, he seemed young and vulnerable. Marnie could well understand why he had needed to hug Ralph.

'Is that better?' she asked quietly.

'Much better,' Dick said with a grim smile. He took another mouthful.

'Dick,' Marnie began, 'I don't want to pester you with questions …'

He swallowed. 'I'm not supposed to talk about my project, Marnie. All I can say at the moment is that it's about … treasure.'

Marnie frowned. 'Treasure? You mean like *buried* treasure?'

'In a way, yes. That kind of thing … sort of. But I promised Dr Fennimore –'

'No, that's fine,' Marnie interrupted. 'I wasn't going to ask about that. It was something else you said … about Zoë saving your life?'

Dick nodded. 'Yeah.'

'How did she do that?'

'I told you.'

'No, you didn't.'

Dick looked confused. 'It was when I went down with Miles to examine the ships. We were going round to the far side of them when my mobile rang. The signal was poor … too close to the scaffolding. I had to move to avoid the interference. I was walking away from Miles when the scaffolding crashed down. If it hadn't been for that call …'

'I see.'

'It's weird,' Dick said. 'I never did find out what she wanted.'

'What's going on?' A loud voice from behind them made Marnie and Dick start. 'Well?'

They turned to find DCI Bruere and the younger black man staring at them.

'Lunch,' Dick said simply.

Bruere glared at the trolleys. 'Where's this come from?'

'The corner shop down the road,' Marnie said. She could feel her anger rising. 'They're all bought and paid for, and the shop owner lent us the trolleys.'

'Did you go out for them?' Bruere said to Marnie.

'Yes, I did.'

'I distinctly told you not to leave the site without my permission.' If possible, Bruere's voice was even louder. 'Which part of that didn't you understand, Mrs Walker?'

'No, you said not to leave without talking to you. There's a difference. I'm here and I am talking to you.'

'But you left the site.'

'And you overlooked the fact that the students hadn't had anything since breakfast. That was negligence.'

Bruere looked as if he was going to explode. By now all the students had formed a group behind Marnie and Dick, while Anne and Ralph came to stand beside them.

'Chief inspector …' Ralph's tone was calm and relaxed. 'Surely you'd acknowledge that you owe these young people a duty of care. They are after all not suspects or even witnesses.'

Bruere focused his attention on Ralph, who stood quietly beside Marnie, commanding the moral high ground. With a movement so brusque it made Marnie flinch, Bruere turned and strode off. After three paces and without breaking stride he called out over his shoulder.

'Mrs Walker! In the office … now!'

In the silence that followed, Ralph's voice could be heard clearly by everyone present.

'We're taking the trolleys back to the shop, as we promised.'

Bruere growled some sort of reply, but it could not be understood. Judging by the expression on the face of the other detective, that was possibly just as well.

Ralph kissed Marnie on the cheek and added, again in a clear voice, 'Don't be too hard on him, darling.'

This drew laughter from the students, which did not go unnoticed by the police officers, who had now reached the staff hut. Anne invited the students to remove the last remaining packs from the trolleys, which they did with alacrity. She gave Marnie an encouraging smile as she set off towards the staff hut for her interview with Bruere.

It was only when Anne turned to push her trolley that she realised Donovan was nowhere to be seen.

Marnie could not really understand why Chief Inspector Bruere was in such a bad mood where she was concerned. She had, after all, committed no crime, withheld no evidence, not been obstructive. When he invited her to sit down he merely grunted and pointed at a chair. Marnie remained standing. Bruere took his seat and looked up, surprised to see Marnie still on her feet.

'Sit down, Mrs Walker.'

Marnie did not move. 'Aren't you forgetting something?'

'What?'

Without a word, Marnie walked round the table and extended a hand to the other detective.

'Hallo, we haven't been introduced, but I'm Marnie Walker. Nice to meet you.'

A large black hand enveloped Marnie's slim pale fingers. 'And you, Mrs Walker. DS Robertson.'

Releasing Marnie's hand, the detective moved past her and withdrew a chair from the table. 'Won't you take a seat?'

'Thank you.'

As Marnie sat, the officer guided the chair under her. Marnie noticed that Bruere was looking down at his papers.

'Why are you here, Mr Bruere?' Marnie asked.

Bruere's head snapped up, but Robertson replied first.

'We always attend a fatal, Mrs Walker. This could be a crime scene, in which case it has to be handled strictly in accordance with procedure.'

'But a chief inspector?'

Bruere quickly raised a hand to stop Robertson. 'I happened to be on duty and available when the call came in. Now, if you don't mind, I'll ask the questions.'

'Of course. I was only curious.'

'You said you were part of the architect's team.'

'I'm responsible for the interior design.'

'And where were you when the incident took place?'

'I don't know exactly, probably somewhere north of Uxbridge.'

'*Uxbridge?*' Bruere looked confused.

'Ralph and I were travelling down by boat. I got a call from a colleague on site and we came in straight away.' Marnie attempted a smile. 'If you have a list of suspects, inspector, I think you can safely remove my name.'

Bruere remained silent for a long moment.

'By leaving the site without my permission, you set a bad example, Mrs Walker, and you undermined my authority.'

'I'm sorry. That wasn't my intention. But you should've thought to get food for the students.'

Another long moment passed.

'Yes.' Bruere's tone had softened. 'I didn't realise …'

'Shall I go now,' Marnie asked, 'or do you have more questions?'

'No more questions.'

'It was an accident, wasn't it?' Marnie said.

'What makes you so sure, Mrs Walker?'

'I, er … I had a talk with one of the archaeologists.'

'Which one?'

Marnie hesitated. 'Dick Blackwood.'

'Why did you question him about it?'

Bruere's phrasing put Marnie on her guard. 'I didn't *question* him. We were just talking together … as friends. He was upset.'

'What did he tell you?'

Marnie stood up. 'I think he should tell you himself, in his own words.'

DS Robertson rose from his seat and opened the door for Marnie. She thanked him and went out.

Anne and Ralph pulled the mini-market trolleys over the uneven ground to the site exit; it was easier than pushing them. Two of the students, one of each sex, helped lift them over the roughest section. When Anne turned to thank the students, she was surprised to find that Donovan had materialised beside her. He indicated they should waste no time in leaving the compound and took over

Ralph's trolley. Ralph returned to wait for Marnie with Dick Blackwood and the students.

They were well clear of the site before Anne spoke.

'Where did you get to? One minute you were there, the next, you'd vanished. Was it your natural aversion to the police?'

Donovan glanced over his shoulder as they neared the kerb. There was a gap in the traffic and, rather than take the subway tunnel, they raced across the approach road to Tower Bridge. Once on the opposite side, Donovan did not slow down, keeping up speed until he turned the corner of the side street. Anne struggled to control her trolley as she jogged along and found Donovan waiting for her round the corner. She stopped beside him, panting and grinning.

'What's funny?' Donovan said.

Anne laughed. 'A supermarket trolley as a get-away car ... it's gotta be a first! And of course I get the one with a wonky wheel.'

Donovan smiled at her. 'And I'm guessing you probably didn't get a sandwich, either.'

'You're right, I didn't. Did you?'

Donovan shook his head. 'Come on. Let's take these back to the shop and see what that café has to offer.'

They were in luck. After reuniting the trolleys with the Indian lady in the shop, they walked to the Italian café, and Donovan guided Anne to a table in the corner away from the window.

'So what did happen to you?' Anne said when they were settled.

'I made a couple of phone calls. I rang the library at London Barbican University, said I was filming the dig here and writing it up for my project. I said I needed the title of Dick's research thesis for the appendix to my report.'

'Brilliant! So you found out what he was researching, so you could work out what he'd discovered.'

'It was a good idea,' Donovan said, '... in theory.'

'But?'

'The LBU librarian said the title was something like, *Repression and resistance: uprisings in the wetlands of north Norfolk and south Lincolnshire in the early Norman period.* Something like that.'

'Oh ...'

'Exactly.'

Silence descended on them as they started on their sandwiches. Donovan spoke first.

'Of course, I hadn't expected it to be like, *Buried treasure in the outskirts of London*, but even so ...'

'Disappointing,' Anne muttered between bites. She swallowed and took a sip of coffee. 'You said you made a couple of calls?'

'Yeah. I rang Dick's department to find out where he'd been those days he was away.'

'And they told you?' Anne sounded surprised.

'I said I was filming his research as part of my own media project and I was planning to go with him on his next field trip. I needed to book accommodation, but with all the hassle surrounding Dr Fennimore's accident, I didn't want to bother Dick when he was being interviewed by the police. I was speaking to the departmental secretary, and she said she'd give me the information if I faxed her my request in writing on my own department's headed notepaper.'

'She treated you as suspicious?'

Donovan nodded. 'I expect she thought I was a journalist.'

'So can you do what she wants?'

'Sure. I'll go in this afternoon.' He grinned. 'No probs.'

Marnie was surprised that Dick was kept waiting by the police before being interviewed at length. Instead of seeing Dick at once, the detectives sent for the students, leaving Dick cooling his heels in the compound. Marnie noticed he had taken a bottle of mineral water from Donovan's trolley but had not even opened it. She walked over and suggested it would do him good if he had something to drink.

'You don't want to get dehydrated,' she said. 'You'll need a clear head once Bruere gets started on you.'

Dick looked alarmed. 'What d'you mean, Marnie?'

Marnie took the bottle from his hand, unscrewed the top and gave it back, indicating that he should drink. He took a mouthful and a deep breath.

'The chief inspector will ask you all sorts of questions about what happened.'

'There's not much to tell,' Dick said. 'We were looking at the ship remains when the scaffolding came down. That's it.'

'Not entirely. He may want to explore other areas, for example, your relationship with Dr Fennimore.'

Dick looked baffled. '*Relationship?* Why?'

'The police have their methods,' Marnie said. 'They're very thorough.'

'I can only tell them what I saw.'

'Dick, they'll want to look at all the angles.'

'What *angles*? They ought to be looking at why the scaffolding collapsed.'

'They will. They'll probably also want to know why you and Fennimore were down there together at that time and why he was standing under the scaffolding and you weren't.'

'I told you … we didn't realise it was risky.' Dick looked flustered. 'Why are you telling me all this, Marnie?'

'Because I've been questioned by the police about other cases and I know how easy it is to get drawn into saying the wrong thing. You can learn from my mistakes.'

'What do I have to do?'

'First, stay calm and try to relax.'

Dick pulled an *easier-said-than-done* face. Marnie continued.

'Answer each question accurately and simply. Just stick to the facts. Don't embellish. Don't fall into conversation. Don't offer opinions. Don't speculate.'

'I wasn't expecting anything like this,' Dick said.

'It may not be as bad as I'm making out, but it's as well to be on your guard. Remember, anything you say could be misconstrued and even turned against you.'

Dick looked worried. 'You make it sound as if they'll be trying to catch me out.'

'Not really, but it may feel like that. They're just doing their job.'

'You think they regard this as a suspicious death, Marnie?'

'They'll probably treat it as such until they're convinced otherwise.'

Dick took a gulp of water. 'I thought I was just a witness, but you're telling me they may well regard me as a suspect.'

Marnie looked him steadily in the eyes. 'Until they're convinced otherwise.'

On her way back to the compound, Anne encountered Ralph going in the opposite direction. He said he had asked for permission to leave as he had work to do. Bruere had responded reasonably on the grounds that Ralph had not been present when the accident took place and could be contacted later if the need ever arose.

'What about Marnie?' Anne said. 'The same applies to her.'

'She wanted to stay with Dick. He's in a very nervous state, and she thinks he needs supporting. Where's Donovan? I thought he was with you.'

Anne explained about Donovan's attempts to learn more about Dick's mysterious find. With Ralph working on his papers in the flat and Marnie in the compound, Anne decided that her time was best spent shopping for their evening meal. Ralph watched her go, the thin waif of a girl who took control of practical matters and held everything together.

The Indian lady in the mini-market greeted Anne like a friend and joked that she hoped Anne did not want a sandwich – the shop had run out! Anne rummaged around until she found pizzas in the freezer. She chose four on the off-chance that Donovan might return, and supplemented them with lettuce, garlic, peppers, spring onions, cucumber and tomatoes. She found some passable Spanish red in the wine section and took two bottles. Dessert was a pineapple.

Weighed down like a bag lady, Anne sighed as her mobile began ringing while she was saying goodbye to her new shopkeeper friend. She carefully set the bags down near the doorway, pulled out the phone and pressed the green button.

'Have they applied the thumbscrews yet?' It was Donovan.

'Can't talk,' said Anne. 'I'm a bit stretched at the moment. I'm on the rack.'

Donovan chuckled. 'Any news?'

'I'm at the mini-market getting food for tonight. Can you join us?'

'Thanks, but I've got a lot of editing and writing-up to do. I'll be along first thing in the morning.'

'Okay. We'll throw yours in the bin. How d'you get on?'

'I sent the fax to LBU. They said to phone back for a reply in half an hour.'

'D'you think it'll be okay?'

'I've got my fingers crossed.'

'I'd do the same if I could,' Anne said, eyeing the shopping bags at her feet.

Dick was calmer now. After walking around the site with Marnie, going over all the questions the detectives might ask him, he felt less stressed. When DS Robertson came out of the staff hut – now known as the *interview room* – and waved him over, he thanked Marnie for her help.

'Just take it gently and you'll be fine,' she said.

'Sure.' Dick grinned broadly, popping a Polo mint into his mouth. 'I'll probably go in, pass out and then confess to everything.'

Marnie smiled back. 'Good idea. I'll organise the firing squad.' Her expression changed. 'Seriously, Dick … take care.'

He was making his way across the site when his mobile rang.

'Dick, this is Sarah Lockyer, Professor de Groot's secretary.'

'Hi Sarah. This had better be quick. I'm just going in to be questioned about the accident.'

'Then I'll be brief. Do you know a Donovan Smith?'

'Sure.'

'Is he at Brunel?'

'That's right.'

'And he's filming your work?'

'Yes, for a special project.'

'Will he be going on your next field trip?'

Dick realised they had not talked about that, but he liked the idea, and they got on well together. It could be a real bonus.

'I'd like that, Sarah, but we haven't actually discussed any details.'

'I think he wants to make travel arrangements.'

'Great. Look, Sarah, I've gotta go now, okay?'

'Of course. Leave it to me.'

Dick arrived at the door of the interview room, which DS Robertson was holding open.

'You're going to have to switch off the mobile, please,' the detective said.

Dick complied with the request and stepped inside.

When Donovan rang the departmental secretary, he tried to sound relaxed. As soon as he announced himself he could tell by the tone of her voice that his ruse had worked. Sarah Lockyer told him she had spoken with Mr Blackwood who had confirmed they were indeed collaborating on his project. Donovan took down the name and address of a B and B run by a Mrs Yarrow. The surprise came when Ms Lockyer gave the address as a village in the vicinity of King's Lynn.

'That's Norfolk, presumably,' Donovan said.

'Of course,' said Lockyer, her voice edged with suspicion. 'I thought you'd know that.'

'I always check with addresses,' Donovan said calmly, his mind racing. 'I don't trust these postcodes. You have a phone number for Mrs Yarrow?'

The secretary's voice relaxed again. 'Yes and actually I seem to recall it comes under the Wisbech exchange in Cambridgeshire.'

'I rest my case,' Donovan said, smiling.

'Will you be checking with Gerald Parfitt?' Lockyer asked.

Who the hell is – Donovan was back in overdrive. 'We haven't really discussed more detailed arrangements, and with Dick so taken up with the police enquiry ...' He hoped Lockyer would pick up the thread.

'Of course,' she said. 'If I give you his university contact details, you can do whatever seems appropriate.'

Yes, that would be best,' said Donovan. 'Thanks.'

'The University of East Anglia?' Anne said. 'I don't get it. Dick's a postgrad here at Barbican. And who's this Gerry Parfitt?'

'*Gerald*,' Donovan said. 'He apparently insists on Gerald.'

'Okay, so who is he?'

'Research Fellow in the Centre for Local History. Look, Anne, my battery's running low. Find Dick and ask him when he's next going on a field trip. Get the dates. My guess is, it'll be soon.'

'All right, but we're still no nearer to finding out what's going on.'

'Really?' said Donovan. 'But it's staring you in the face.'

'What d'you mean?'

'I would've thought it was fairly obvious.'

'Donovan, you're always doing that, coming out with these gnomic utterances. Why can't you just … Donovan? Are you there?'

Anne found herself listening to silence. The connection was dead.

Ralph had installed himself in the master bedroom, reading in a Victorian button-back nursing chair, with his papers spread out on the bed, and Anne did not think he would wish to be disturbed. With no-one to share her thoughts, she sat at the dining table, gazing down at the broad river meandering into the distance. She had barely begun trying to work out the conundrum set by Donovan, when she heard the front door open and Marnie call out.

They exchanged news. After her interview with DCI Bruere, Marnie had received a message from DS Robertson. It was good news for Ralph: the police would not be wanting to question him at all.

Anne relayed her conversation with Donovan and was relieved when neither Ralph nor Marnie could see what was supposedly staring them all in the face.

13
The Last Great Mystery

The next morning was Friday, and all was eerily quiet when Anne went out before breakfast to visit the building site. She stopped several yards short of the perimeter fence and looked in. There was no hum of generators, no diggers tearing at the ground, and the cranes were standing at rest, silent sentinels.

Anne was turning to leave when she spotted Nigel Beardsley coming out of the staff hut. She advanced to the site entrance, called out and waved him over. A new security guard was on duty, one Anne had not seen before, and he advanced in her direction.

'Can I help you, miss?'

Anne pulled the security pass out of her shirt pocket and waved it at the guard. He insisted on taking it from her, studying it carefully, then checking her name against his list of *authorised persons*. By the time he handed it back with a grunt, the architect had reached the fence, and Anne told the guard there was no need to let her in.

'Hi, Nigel. You're an early bird.' Anne spoke through the chain-link fence. 'What's happening?'

'Philip's down there now with the health and safety inspectors.'

'But not you?'

Nigel shook his head. 'It's still so unstable below ground they want as few people as possible in the area.'

'What's the feeling?' Anne asked.

'Well … hard to say, but it seems the contractor ordered everyone out. Then Blackwood and Fennimore climbed down afterwards by themselves.'

'And no-one warned them?' Anne said.

'Well, a warning sign was in place, but they thought it was just for a routine inspection and ignored it.'

'An avoidable but unfortunate accident,' Anne said. 'Is that what they're saying?'

'That just about sums it up.' The architect looked despondent. He added quietly, 'Wrong place … wrong time.'

When Anne returned to the flat with her news plus a carton of milk, she found Donovan chatting with Marnie and Ralph at the dining table. The skyscape visible behind them through the window was dramatic, a thin veil of high clouds through which the sun was poking long fingers down into the river.

Donovan accepted Marnie's invitation to join them for breakfast, and they positioned themselves round the table so that each of them could enjoy the view. When Anne was pouring orange juice, she could contain herself no longer.

'Well?' She looked pointedly at Donovan. 'Is our *man of mystery* now ready to reveal all?'

'Yes,' Donovan said simply. 'I think so.'

'Mystery?' said Ralph. 'Have I missed something?'

'We all have,' said Anne, 'apart from Donovan, that is.'

Ralph turned to Donovan. 'Reveal away,' he said. 'But first, can someone tell me what actually *is* the mystery?'

Marnie said, 'It's this business about Dick apparently discovering something important. Neither he nor Dr Fennimore was willing or able to talk about it.'

'Yes, yes, I was aware of that,' Ralph said. 'But that's no great surprise. It's normal for the academic world. Information has to be kept confidential until such time as the facts have been verified by independent peer group assessment or a report has been published ... all quite routine stuff.'

'Just a question of being patient for a while,' said Marnie.

'Exactly,' said Ralph. 'I thought that was the case here.'

'Donovan thought otherwise,' said Anne.

'Any particular reason why?' Ralph asked.

'This is the world of archaeology,' Donovan said quietly. 'It's all about digging up the past, uncovering ancient relics. It's also about fierce academic rivalry.'

'You think that's what we have here?' said Marnie.

'I'm sure it's what we have here. Think about it. Zoë believes these Roman vessels could point to the original port of London. That's quite a significant discovery ... major league. But Dick obviously thinks he's found something that trumps her ace.'

'And you believe you know what that might be?' said Ralph.

Donovan nodded. 'I tried to work it out. Several possibilities immediately came to mind, all rather obvious.'

'Staring us in the face,' Anne said with a hint of a smile.

'Yes,' said Donovan. 'I thought so.'

'Go on, then.'

'Well ...' Donovan took a sip of coffee. 'I dismissed things like the discovery of King Arthur's tomb or his round table or Avalon or the tomb of Joseph of Arimathea. They're all just myths. I ruled out a Viking ship burial or a Saxon king's tomb like the Sutton Hoo treasure. They'd be important but not so as to rival Zoë's ships.'

'And they'd be outside Dick's field of interest, presumably,' Ralph added.

'Quite,' Donovan agreed. 'This initially left two important unsolved mysteries as far as I could tell. It was a while before I realised there was a third.'

Ralph chuckled. 'Would Boudica's tomb be one of them?'

'Yes.'

'And the remains of the lost Roman Ninth Legion?'

For once, Donovan looked wrong-footed. 'Yes. I did say they were staring us in the face.'

'But surely they'd both fall into Zoë's field of study,' Anne said. 'Or were you thinking that would rub salt into the wound … Dick stealing a find she might regard as rightly hers?'

'I did wonder about that at first,' Donovan said. 'But I reckoned that that wouldn't account for Dick's level of excitement. Then I asked myself what would be the greatest unsolved mystery of the Middle Ages, Dick's area of interest.'

The phone began ringing. Marnie reluctantly got up to answer it.

'Hang on a minute,' she said. 'I don't want to miss anything.'

Donovan took advantage of the hiatus to eat his toast, while Anne and Ralph sat lost in thought. Marnie took the call in the kitchen area and a minute later called out across the peninsular unit.

'Donovan, it's for you.' As Donovan rose from the table, Marnie put her hand over the receiver and said quietly, 'It's Dick Blackwood.'

Donovan crossed to the sitting area and picked up the cordless phone by the sofa, returning slowly to the others as he spoke.

'Hang on a sec, Dick.' He held the phone down at his side. 'Dick wants to meet. I think he's intrigued by my enquiring into his travels yesterday.'

'Would he like to come here and join us?' Marnie said, making no attempt to disguise her curiosity.

Donovan put the invitation to Dick, who said he would come at once.

'Are you going to tell us what this unsolved mystery is, then?' Anne said.

'I'm almost a hundred per cent convinced I know what it is,' Donovan said, 'but perhaps we might just wait a few more minutes so that Dick can confirm or deny it?'

Anne and Marnie sighed in unison.

Ralph said, 'You can at least tell us where your enquiry about Dick's travel arrangements fits into the scheme of things.'

'And have Anne accuse me of trying to be a *man of mystery* again?' he smiled.

'A small price to pay,' said Ralph.

Donovan nodded. 'For the moment, let me just say I think the whole thing became clear when I was given a telephone number from the Wisbech exchange in Cambridgeshire.'

Three blank faces looked at him.

'Now I'd better go downstairs,' Donovan said. 'I told Dick I'd wait outside to show him where to come.'

Anne and Ralph cleared the breakfast table while Marnie brewed a fresh pot of coffee.

Anne looked up from loading the dishwasher. 'He's a strange one, isn't he?'

'A rum cove,' Ralph said with a grin.

Anne shut the dishwasher door. 'Sometimes I think he just enjoys playing a part.'

'Oh, I think there's more to it than that,' said Ralph.

'Now *you're* starting to sound like Donovan,' Marnie said.

Anne looked in the store cupboard. 'Anyone seen the evaporated milk?'

'Tried the fridge?'

'Thanks, Marnie.' Anne took out the tin and opened it, pouring some of the contents into a small jug. 'I got it for Donovan. He likes it in coffee.' By way of explanation she added, 'It's a German thing.'

Marnie lit a nightlight in the base of the coffee stand and placed the cafetière on it. 'What were you saying, Ralph, about there being more to it?'

'Well … to be fair to Donovan, I don't think he's deliberately keeping us dangling for the fun of it, not *just* for the fun of it.'

'But that's always his way,' said Anne.

'Yes, but in this instance, I think he's using guesswork to a greater extent than usual. Remember, he's investigating something apparently major in a field that isn't his own.'

'You think he wants to hear more from Dick before committing himself?' said Marnie.

'I do. And I get the impression that that throw-away remark about the telephone number in Cambridgeshire was perhaps his way of telling us how precarious his thinking is.'

'Have you worked out what's the third great unsolved mystery, Ralph?' Marnie asked. 'You were on target with Boudicca and the Ninth Legion. I was impressed.'

Ralph reflected. 'That telephone reference has got me foxed. It might help if we had another clue.'

'How about the Crown Jewels?' Anne said.

'Where do they fit in?' Marnie asked.

'No idea, but you should've seen Dick and Dr Fennimore's reaction when Donovan mentioned them.'

'The Crown Jewels ...' Ralph repeated thoughtfully. 'Could he have meant that metaphorically, perhaps?

Marnie considered this. 'In what way *metaphorically*? And the *Cambridge* connection ... what's *that* all about?'

Donovan saw Dick coming along the cobbled walkway between the wharf buildings and waved to him. Dick quickened his pace and the two young men shook hands.

'Is this it, where you're staying?' Dick looked surprised and impressed.

'Marnie has a flat here,' Donovan explained. He turned towards the entrance lobby. 'Before we go up, is there any news from the site?'

'Industrial accident,' said Dick. 'That seems to be the verdict.'

'Is that what you think it was?'

Dick looked wary. 'What d'you mean? What else could it have been?'

'You can never tell with the police,' Donovan said casually, '... what slant they put on things.'

'No,' Dick relaxed. 'I see what you mean.'

Donovan keyed in numbers on the pad and held the security card against the touch screen. A buzzer sounded and Donovan pushed the lobby door open.

The lift was waiting for them, and as its doors closed, Dick said, 'I need to talk to you some time about my project ... the other one, the one you seem to have been enquiring about.'

'Sure.'

'You know I can't really go into any detail about it.'

'That's okay.' Donovan looked down at the control panel. It showed they were passing the third floor. 'We know what it involves,' he said simply.

Floor Four ... Floor Five. The lift came to a gentle stop, and the doors slid silently open. Donovan gestured to Dick.

'After you. It's the door opposite.'

Dick remained where he was, his expression suspicious, puzzled, concerned.

'What d'you mean, you know what my project involves?'

Donovan stepped out into the hall and indicated that Dick should do the same. He followed, not taking his eyes from Donovan's face.

Donovan inserted the key card into the lock. 'Let's talk about it inside, shall we?'

Dick grabbed him by the elbow. 'No, wait a minute. Who is *we*? Who knows about it? How did you find out?'

'I think you mean, who *are* we?' said Donovan.

Dick looked puzzled. 'Whatever. Tell me what you know ... and *how* you know.'

'Of course.' Donovan's tone was reassuring. 'But perhaps not out here in a place where we might be interrupted at any moment?'

Behind them, as if underlining the point, the lift doors closed and it descended with a faint hum. Donovan pushed the front door and held it open for Dick to enter. The smell of coffee created a welcoming atmosphere in the flat, and three smiling faces completed the picture. But their expressions faltered when they saw Dick's worried countenance.

'Come in, Dick,' said Marnie, stepping forward to take his hand. 'Is everything all right?'

'I'm not sure,' he said hesitantly.

Marnie led him towards the spacious sitting area. 'Come and have some coffee. Make yourself at home.'

He sank into a deep-cushioned sofa while Anne poured coffee and set it down beside him.

'Is there a problem?' Ralph said, taking a seat opposite. 'Has there been a development concerning the accident?'

Dick shook his head. 'No. That is the official decision, I believe ... an accident. The announcement will be made some time soon, but I've heard unofficially.'

'That's good. At least we now know for sure.'

'Have you eaten?' Marnie asked. 'Perhaps I can get you something?'

'No ... I mean yes, thanks. I have eaten.' He took a sip. 'This is great coffee. Look, I need to know ...' He looked at Donovan. 'What were you saying in the lift?'

'You mean about knowing what your other project involves?' said Donovan.

Dick frowned. 'Only Miles Fennimore knows ... *knew* about it. So how do you all know?'

'We don't, actually,' said Ralph. 'But Donovan thinks he has a good idea.'

'Go on, then,' Dick said to Donovan. 'Tell me what your *good idea* is.'

'You gave me a number of clues,' Donovan said. 'First, your absence from here for some days in a row. That struck me as odd, given how excited you were over your find in the excavation. No-one knew that better than me, filming you.'

'It's true, and I still am excited about it. But I could have been away for any number of reasons.'

'Dick, you came back even more excited than when you left, and Dr Fennimore told us something important had happened … something secret.'

'We could see you were bubbling over,' Anne added.

Donovan continued. 'So I asked myself where exactly you'd been.'

'No-one knew that,' Dick said firmly, 'no-one at all.'

'Aren't you forgetting the departmental office?'

'What about them? They have no idea what I've been working on.'

'Maybe not, but they handle your travel and expense claims. They know where you've been and where you stayed.'

'So? That wouldn't give them any clues.'

'But *you* did, Dick. Or rather you let your guard down. You and Dr Fennimore jumped like startled rabbits when I made my quip about the Crown Jewels.'

Dick's eyes narrowed. 'Why don't you just come out with it?'

'Okay.' Donovan collected his thoughts. 'You seem to have made a major discovery, something obviously monumental, somewhere in East Anglia up near King's Lynn. At first I thought it might have had something to do with Queen Boudicca. Her tribe, the Iceni, lived in that part of the country.'

'That was my first guess, too,' said Ralph.

'But,' Donovan went on, 'I suspected it would have to be a medieval find to get you so wound up. I've noticed that you archaeologists seem to think yours is the only period that matters.'

'It's the only one that matters to me,' said Dick.

'Quite. Then came the Crown Jewels thing. I think I struck lucky there. I only made the joke because we were just opposite the Tower of London, where the modern Crown Jewels are on display. It just slipped out.'

'You didn't do it deliberately?' Marnie said.

'Not at all. But Dick's and Dr Fennimore's reaction got me thinking, and then suddenly it all became clear.' Donovan counted on his fingers. 'East Anglia, major mystery, the Middle Ages, the Crown Jewels …'

'King John's lost treasure,' Ralph said quietly.

Donovan smiled. 'Exactly. The last great unsolved mystery of the medieval period, and you've solved it, Dick. Am I right?'

Dick was unsettled. Looking down, he seemed to be wrestling internally with a dilemma. He reached for his cup, and they noticed his hand was trembling.

The restaurant was busy with the usual Friday lunchtime crowd. Philip

Everett had booked a table that morning and had invited Marnie and Ralph, Anne and Donovan. On learning that Dick Blackwood was with them he was happy to extend the invitation to include him, too, but Dick declined. He had a meeting arranged with Professor de Groot.

Philip had spent the entire morning in back-to-back meetings with the contractors and consultants, the health and safety inspectors and the police. He looked exhausted when they met in the entrance to the restaurant. Marnie could well understand why he was so drained. As principal architect in charge of the project, he might easily find himself being held responsible, at least in part, for the fatal accident.

They took their places at a table with a view of Tower Bridge and Saint Katharine Docks across the river. On any other occasion it would be a cause for delight, but none of them felt in a festive mood that day.

'How did it go?' Marnie asked as soon as they were seated.

'It went,' Philip sighed. He attempted a smile. 'An industrial accident. No blame. The contractor had informed me he was clearing that part of the site for remedial works. I'd agreed on safety grounds. It was put down to bad luck that Dr Fennimore went below with Dick during a brief lull in the works. No-one disputes they ignored a warning sign.'

'That's a relief,' said Marnie.

Philip accepted a menu from the waiter. 'Yeah, but poor Miles Fennimore is still dead.'

'But you could hardly be held responsible, surely,' said Ralph.

'Don't you believe it.' Philip looked grim. 'We take dozens of decisions every week, and any one of them could have dire consequences if things went wrong. It's something they don't teach you when you sign on at college to study architecture at eighteen.'

'It's true,' said Marnie. 'Architects carry a huge responsibility. Ever since the Summerland disaster of 1973 –'

Philip waved a hand. 'D'you mind if we change the subject?'

Marnie nodded. 'Yes, of course, Philip. Sorry.'

They studied the menus, made their choices, and Philip ordered the wine. A waiter fussed discreetly over cutlery and glasses, brought a basket of mixed breads and two bottles of mineral water which he began pouring. Gradually the atmosphere at the table became more relaxed. The waiter went away and returned with a bottle of white wine. He invited Philip to taste it and, when approved, placed it in an ice bucket on a stand beside the table.

Eventually Philip said, 'Do you know what all this carry-on's about … this business with Dick Blackwood?'

The question was addressed to Marnie, but it was Donovan who replied.

'We worked out what it was,' he said.

'*Donovan* worked out what it was,' Marnie said.

'Worked out?' said Philip. 'Didn't he tell you?'

'No,' said Marnie. 'He was sworn to secrecy. No-one was supposed to know what it entailed.'

Philip looked at Donovan. 'How did you work it out?'

Donovan outlined his method, during which time the first course arrived. Conversation ceased as they began eating, and the waiter served wine. When he withdrew, Philip looked over at Donovan.

'That's very interesting,' he said. 'Sherlock Holmes would be proud of you. But you've missed out the main point. What had Dick actually discovered?'

Donovan glanced at Ralph.

'This is the difficult part,' Ralph said. 'It's a question of academic confidentiality, you see.'

'Hang on,' said Marnie. 'I don't think Philip should be kept in the dark, not when the rest of us know what's happened.'

Ralph hesitated. 'You're right, of course.' He nodded at Donovan.

'Dick thinks ... in fact he's certain, he's discovered the lost treasure – for want of a better word – of King John.'

Philip screwed up his face. 'It got lost in the Wash or something ... is that it?'

'Yes,' Donovan said. 'We've just got the whole story from Dick. Apparently, the king was travelling in the east of England between Lincolnshire and Norfolk when he was taken ill.'

'When was this?' Philip asked.

'It was ... 1216, I think,' Donovan said. 'Yes, the year after Magna Carta. It was autumn ... October. He decided to return to Lincolnshire.'

'Why not go home to London?'

'That was tricky. King Louis of France had invaded the south of England with the help of the English barons who opposed King John. Going back north was a safer option, and the most direct route involved crossing the Wash.'

'By boat, presumably,' Philip said.

'No. In those times the Wash was quite different, penetrating much further inland. It was a shallow marshy region with mudflats and quicksands. If you knew the route, it was possible to ford it in various places. The King and his entourage crossed by Wisbech, seemingly fording the mouth of the river Wellstream.'

'Wellstream?' Philip repeated. 'Never heard of it.'

Donovan explained, 'It's all changed now. It roughly coincides with the place where the river Nene enters the Wash. Anyway, the King and his cohorts got across safely, but the baggage train ran into difficulties. It was travelling more slowly and, by the time it began crossing the ford, the tide was turning. By some accounts they were caught by a kind of bore, a powerful wave that swept in and overturned everything.'

'And this baggage train was carrying what exactly?'

'Opinions differ on this, but it now seems fairly clear that the goods included the royal regalia ... what we'd call the Crown Jewels ... plus similar items that he'd inherited from his grandmother, the Empress of Germany.'

'Might've known there'd be a German connection,' Anne said, grinning.

Donovan smiled back at her.

'Okay, so what happened next?' Philip asked.

'The king travelled on to a monastery, Swineshead Abbey in Lincolnshire, where –'

'Hold on,' said Philip. 'You're saying he just abandoned his treasure, made no attempt to recover it ... just like that?'

'I think there were probably several reasons for that,' said Donovan. 'First, the tide was racing in and the whole expanse of land would soon have been flooded. There was nowhere to hang around in that wilderness. The water would've covered a *huge* area. Also, don't forget, the king himself was unwell and needed to be taken care of.'

'There was another factor,' Ralph joined in. 'That part of the country had long been hostile to the Norman kings. John was immensely unpopular with his subjects, but nowhere more so than in those parts. This was dangerous territory, and they had to move quickly to get him to a place of safety.'

'And he never went back to try to reclaim his lost treasure?' said Philip.

'No,' Donovan said. 'In fact, he was dead within a week. There were few reliable maps of the area in those days, and it mainly comprised water courses that were constantly shifting.'

For a while they ate in silence until Philip spoke again.

'And Dick thinks he's located this treasure? This episode sounds like it's being scripted by Robert Louis Stephenson.'

They collectively resisted the temptation to mutter, 'Arr, Jim lad,' though they all thought it.

'It isn't quite as fanciful as it might appear,' said Donovan. 'Dick didn't just go out with a metal detector and strike lucky.'

'Metal detectors don't work in water, do they?' said Philip.

Donovan shook his head. 'I'm not yet sure if water actually comes into it. The topography in all that part of the country has changed beyond recognition. For example, Wisbech used to be on the coast; now, it's miles inland.'

'And therefore easier to survey,' Philip added.

Another shake of the head from Donovan. 'Not quite. What in those days was ground – or sea – level, could now be as much as ten metres below the surface.'

'Like the lower levels in our building site.' Philip inclined his head towards Horselydown. 'So how did Dick find this treasure? Strikes me as being a bit of a long shot that he just happens to come along and dig it up when people have been searching for it for nearly eight hundred years.'

A waiter cleared away the dishes from the first course and adjusted the cutlery while another poured the remains of the wine. After a subtle exchange of glances with Philip, he went to fetch a second bottle. Moments later, the main courses arrived, and they settled down again. In between mouthfuls, Donovan continued the story.

'Dick wasn't in fact working on King John's lost regalia. It was one of those instances where you study one subject and turn up something completely different.'

'Like Alexander Fleming's discovery of penicillin,' said Ralph.

'Quite. Dick was investigating the impact of Hereward the Wake's revolt on the governance of eastern England when he came upon documents referring to King John. He became interested in these and read further. Then, by chance, at a conference he met a landscape archaeologist from the University of East Anglia, who was researching something like wetland development in the Middle Ages.'

'That was Gerald Parfitt,' Marnie said.

'That's right. Dick described what he was working on, and Dr Parfitt offered to show him aerial photographs from the drought summer of 1976.'

'What was the point of that?' Philip asked.

'To show how volatile the region was. It made it clear how Hereward was able to operate without being detected for so long. The photographs showed all sorts of patterns of watercourses, causeways and tracks that had been covered up for decades, even centuries.'

'And presumably Dick spotted something in the photographs?'

'No. It didn't work like that. He kept in touch with Parfitt and spent a weekend at his place outside Norwich. Among other things Parfitt showed him more aerial shots, this time from the long hot summer of 1975. He was able to compare them with '76 and see how patterns changed even from one year to the next. Dick decided to trace a route across the Wash using the aerial photos plus ancient maps and field plans.'

'But he couldn't be sure he was on the right track, surely?' Philip sounded sceptical. 'Not if there were no real fields.'

'The king's itinerary was documented to a certain extent and by comparing different accounts, Dick was able to make an educated guess at his route back to Lincolnshire. What had started out as a casual enquiry was turning into a serious study. Dick outlined his ideas to Dr Parfitt, and eventually the two of them set out to retrace the king's steps.'

'And they actually found the lost baggage train?'

Donovan nodded. 'Apparently a few weeks ago. They'd spent the winter building up a theoretical model of the topography of 1216 in relation to the tidal patterns of early October that year. Quite a lot of work had been done by others, taking into account such things as leap years, the lunar cycle, exceptional tides and so on. Now, Parfitt has a yacht that he keeps at King's Lynn.'

'I thought you said –'

'I know, but their calculations put the position of the baggage train somewhere around the present-day mouth of the river Nene.'

'But doesn't that fly in the face of the evidence you described earlier?' said Philip.

'Potentially, yes. But Dick factored in two elements that no-one seemed to have taken on board. More than one account of what happened that day stated that the king himself witnessed the destruction of the baggage train and was dismayed at what he saw.'

'So he wasn't miles ahead of it.'

'No, and remember, the landscape is very low-lying up there. There's no chance he was looking down from a hill and seeing the train in the distance.'

'Okay. And what's the other element?'

'They knew roughly what time of day it was, what time the tide would flood in and what time the king's party arrived at Swineshead Abbey.'

'So they could pretty well pinpoint the position of the king from those cross-references,' Philip said.

'It wasn't all plain sailing,' said Donovan. 'They had to plot three different routes because of minor variations in the recorded accounts of eye witnesses.'

'Presumably, this is where the sailing – plain or otherwise – comes in,' said Ralph.

Donovan nodded. 'And diving.'

'Surely that would be no task for amateurs,' Philip said. 'I thought those waters were treacherous.'

'They are,' Donovan agreed. 'But I've done some investigating of my own and come up with something potentially interesting.'

'About the location of the treasure?' said Marnie.

Donovan shook his head. 'No. That's out of my league. But I checked the

UEA website and found the archaeology department has some of the most experienced marine archaeologists in Britain.'

'You think they were involved, too?' said Philip.

'I'm guessing, but it must be a possibility.'

'I knew about them,' Anne chimed in. 'They were on the *Timeline* programme a couple of years ago, when they were looking for wrecks of the Spanish Armada.'

'Did Dick say those divers were involved?' Marnie asked.

'No,' Donovan said, 'not exactly. He was fairly coy about the details, but he did say he'd made some significant finds. The first of these were animal bones.'

'So not boxes filled with jewels,' said Philip.

'Sadly not, but when analysed in the lab, they turned out to be remains of heavy horses dating back around ... eight centuries.'

'So they'd found the baggage train?'

'They couldn't be certain, at least not until earlier this week when Dick produced more finds.'

'Some actual artefacts?' said Philip.

Donovan nodded. 'Three actual artefacts. They'd found a plate, a cross and a chain.'

'All of them preserved and recognisable?' Philip sounded sceptical again. 'After all those centuries under water in mud?'

'They were all made of gold,' Donovan said simply.

'My god ...'

'And they've been authenticated by experts from the British Museum.'

With the implications of the latest developments hanging in the air around them, they ate on in silence. Philip was first to finish that course and put his knife and fork together on the plate. Picking up his glass, he spoke quietly.

'I seem to be playing the part of devil's advocate, but it's just ... I suppose I'm lagging behind the rest of you in this matter.'

'No harm in that,' said Ralph. 'As an academic, I spend much of my life questioning people's opinions and judgments. Do you have reservations about Dick's story?'

'Not exactly. In any case, I'm not qualified to raise doubts about any of his findings. It's only that ... I'm not sure ... there's something in all this that I don't quite follow.'

'Is it the different accounts of eye witnesses that lead to three different locations?' said Marnie. 'I must admit, that bothers me.'

'The names vary,' said Donovan. 'I know that a Norman knight in the entourage referred to a place by the name of a nearby village, while a chaplain used the name of the marsh they were crossing. There was more than one route, apparently, so that gave rise to different possibilities.'

'That didn't bother me so much,' said Philip. 'No. I found myself thinking, so what? Why all the secrecy?' Why did Dr Fennimore insist on that?'

Donovan was the first to reply. 'Again, I'd have thought that was pretty obvious. There were probably two main reasons. One is, they didn't want to be overrun by treasure hunters.'

Philip looked doubtful. 'Out there in the middle of the Wash?'

'Why not? There's potentially a king's fortune – literally – waiting to be raised. Archaeologists are always careful about naming sites on land for fear of intrusion by metal detectorists. And there are their counterparts who dive on wrecks around the coast, all hoping to find an Armada galleon. The personal effects of an aristocratic Spanish captain would be small change compared with the discovery of the Crown Jewels of a Norman king.'

'And a German empress,' Anne added.

'Quite.'

'Did you say two main reasons, Donovan?' Philip said.

'At least. Another reason is, they don't want to release information until they're absolutely certain of what they've found.'

'But I thought they were convinced –'

'Not the same thing,' said Ralph. 'They'll want more artefacts. They'll want them all to be authenticated by independent experts and, ideally, they'll want an identifiable piece, something they can put on show that proves beyond any doubt that what they've found was part of the king's regalia.'

'That makes sense,' said Philip. 'They wouldn't want their discovery to be held up for criticism before they've had the chance to evaluate everything.'

Donovan spoke again. 'But having said all that, they do know what they've found. My guess is, Dick wants to prepare the ground carefully before revealing that he genuinely has solved the last great mystery of the Middle Ages.'

Philip stared into the distance. 'Bloody hell!'

That Friday afternoon was a time for regrouping, ready for work starting again the following week. Philip spent the rest of the day on health and safety matters. Hugely relieved that he had not been singled out for blame, he threw himself energetically into getting the project back on track.

Marnie found herself rather at a loose end with her design work largely completed. Reminding Ralph that they were supposed to be on holiday, she asked if he had any ideas about how to spend the rest of the day. He pointed out that they had each had a couple of glasses of wine and neither had brought work with them.

'Compelling arguments for easing off,' Marnie conceded.

'And there's the small matter of *Thyrsis*,' said Ralph. 'We still have to bring her into Little Venice.'

'That's true.' Marnie turned to Anne. 'What about you, Anne? Have you actually had any time off this week?'

'Well ...'

'She's spent most of the time working with me on the filming,' Donovan said.

'Which was very interesting,' Anne added.

'But not the cultural programme you'd planned,' said Marnie.

'We could rectify that.' Anne pointed beyond Butler's Wharf in the opposite direction to the building site. 'The Design Museum is just down there. I was hoping to visit it some time. Anyone fancy going?'

'Why not?' said Marnie. 'We could treat it as a works outing. Any takers?'

The plan was accepted, and the four of them strolled along in the sunshine, two couples on holiday without a care in the world. Or at least that was how it appeared on the surface.

As they approached the museum, they were surprised to find a large crowd of Japanese tourists gathered in front of the entrance. Rather than push their way through the group, Marnie suggested they walk on a little further to the point where a small tributary joined the Thames. She had spotted a display board and wanted to see if it gave any information about the history of the district that might be useful for her murals in the hotel complex.

While Marnie, Ralph and Anne read the panel, Donovan walked the few yards to the end of the bank and looked up the inlet where the tributary joined the main watercourse.

'Any idea what this is called?' he asked, looking back over his shoulder.

'It's the river Neckinger,' Anne replied.

'Neckinger?' Donovan repeated. 'How odd. It sounds German.'

'Well, it isn't. It's a short form of the *Devil's neckinger*, meaning neckerchief. Apparently, that was the nickname for the noose on the gallows. They used to execute river pirates here.'

The last words stuck in Anne's throat as she realised she was standing in the place where Daring Jake Pepper had been hanged with his own Devil's neckinger. On that very spot all those years ago he, and others like him, had danced in the air and swung in the breeze as an example to passers-by. Here he had come to a sticky end.

14
Images

On Monday morning construction work at Horselydown was back in full swing.

The Glebe Farm team had split forces for the day. Marnie and Ralph had spent the weekend together on *Thyrsis* in Little Venice, catching up with friends from the time when Marnie had kept *Sally Ann* there. On Sunday evening she had returned home by train to take charge of the office.

Anne had offered to go with her, but Marnie had insisted she should at least have the weekend off. They would review the work situation on Monday. In the meantime Donovan was welcome to stay with Anne in the flat at Butler's Wharf.

This left Ralph on *Thyrsis* in Little Venice, where he happily resumed his research. He suspected, rightly, that he was probably the only academic economist in the world whose duties for the day included filling a boat's water tank, having its fuel tank filled with diesel and its holding tank emptied at the nearest pump-out.

That Monday morning was cooler than before with high clouds obscuring the sun and a fresh breeze wafting between the old wharf buildings. Anne and Donovan left the block for the short walk to Horselydown, prepared for any eventuality. Donovan carried the filming equipment in his rucksack. Under her arm Anne held the project file.

They entered the compound soon after nine and found the student archaeologists already gathered beside the excavation hole. In full safety gear they stood talking quietly as if waiting for someone. The atmosphere was subdued. It was the first time they had returned to the site since Dr Fennimore's death.

Anne and Donovan were heading for the staff hut to collect their own safety equipment when Zoë came out accompanied by a man. Both looked solemn.

'I think that must be Professor de Groot,' Anne said under her breath, 'head of archaeology.'

Donovan acknowledged with a murmur, and they quickened their pace to the hut. Moments later they emerged to find the professor in mid-flow addressing the students. They attached themselves to the group to listen.

'... so I cannot stress strongly enough that safety is paramount. The lower levels are now completely sealed off from tidal intrusion, so you can work all day without interruption. If a safety warning is given, you should clear the site at once. You may take only your trowel. Leave any finds behind. Waste no time. Climb the ladders in an orderly fashion. What happened here was a dreadful accident. There should be no risk of a recurrence, but we'll take no chances. If anyone is anxious or unhappy, they are free to leave now. I assure you it won't count against you.'

The professor paused. No-one moved. He continued.

'Today, you will be under the supervision of Dr Zoë Tipton. If you have any problems, go to her. You are to follow all her instructions without question or delay. Dick Blackwood will be joining us later today or tomorrow to resume examination of the human remains at the middle level.'

Zoë leaned forward and whispered something to de Groot. He listened and nodded.

'I am informed that some filming may take place during the day. Dr Tipton will give any instructions concerning this when the time comes.' Another pause. 'Any questions?.'

There was a general shuffling of feet by the students, but no-one spoke.

'Finally,' de Groot said, 'I would ask for one minute's silence before the excavation begins, in memory of Dr Fennimore.'

The students regarded each other self-consciously. The only movement came from Donovan at the edge of the group. The students looked on as he slowly removed his hard hat, held it to his chest and bowed his head. They immediately began to follow his example. Professor de Groot and Zoë Tipton did the same.

No-one was sure who was counting the passing of time, but eventually Donovan raised his head and replaced his hat. The group again took its lead from him, and the solemn moment was concluded. Glancing at the assembly, Anne saw that some of the students of both sexes were brushing tears from their eyes, all of them deeply moved.

Professor de Groot cleared his throat. 'Thank you everyone. And now let's go to work.'

Zoë at once stepped forward and began organising the students into groups, allocating their tasks, organising their day. She divided them into units of six, with one person designated to be responsible for safety matters. The professor's instructions were being followed to the letter.

Anne and Donovan stood to one side, waiting for their own orders. With Zoë now in charge, Professor de Groot was free, and he walked over to Donovan, extending a hand.

'Bernard de Groot.'

'Donovan Smith.'

'Thank you for your, er … gesture. It was very appropriate.'

'Not at all, professor.'

De Groot looked at them both. 'You're not part of the student group, are you?'

'We've been filming as part of a project of mine,' said Donovan. 'I'm at Brunel.'

De Groot frowned. 'Ah yes. You understand that everything here has to be treated in strictest confidence.'

Donovan smiled faintly. 'We've signed the Official Secrets Act ...or your equivalent.'

De Groot nodded and turned his gaze on Anne.

'This is my colleague, Anne Price,' Donovan said. 'We've been doing the filming together.'

Anne spoke as they shook hands. 'Technically, I'm part of the architect's team. I'm with Walker and Co, interior design consultants.'

'You're with Marnie Walker? Very good, very good.' He looked at his watch. 'Well, I'd better be getting back.'

With a muttered goodbye, the professor took his leave, touching Zoë's elbow in passing. She barely spared him a glance as she continued addressing the students. Anne and Donovan walked slowly over to stand nearer to the group. Zoë was bringing her instructions to a close.

'... and I want you all to be clear about that. The slightest doubt or uncertainty, you come to me without hesitation. This is going to be one of the most important – possibly *the* most important – archaeological finds of the year. I want no mistakes ...'

As Zoë continued, Donovan leaned towards Anne and murmured softly in her ear.

'You'd almost think ...'

Anne was looking puzzled. 'Surely it can't be.'

Under his breath Donovan said, 'She's either blotted Dick's discovery out of her mind or dismissed it entirely.'

Fifty miles north of London, at her desk in divisional police headquarters, something was troubling WDC Cathy Lamb. She had been involved in the investigation the previous summer of two bodies found in shallow graves on Glebe Farm land close to the docking area of *Sally Ann*. The bodies had eventually been identified as those of navvies, ostensibly killed in a brawl at the time the Grand Junction Canal was being dug in 1794.

Mention of the archaeologists in the media following the death of Dr Fennimore had led Lamb to study the reports more closely than she might otherwise have done. She had recognised the name Dick Blackwood, whom she remembered as the highly personable young site director of the Glebe

Farm dig. Watching the early evening news on television the previous day, Lamb had been astonished to recognise Marnie Walker in the background at Horselydown. When she also spotted Ralph Lombard and Anne Price at the scene, she had pressed the *Record* button on her VCR. She recorded subsequent reports and examined them with forensic care.

But it was not just Marnie or her immediate associates who had pricked Lamb's interest. She quickly transferred her focus to a young man who appeared in almost every shot with them. Something about him made alarm bells ring. Had she seen him before?

Watching the recorded bulletins, she spotted someone on a mountain bike outside the perimeter fence. Its rider was wearing a baseball cap and rode with an ease and fluency as if he and the bike were one unit. Lamb studied the recordings over and over again. *Mountain bike ... young man ... baseball cap ...*

Then it struck her. *Yes!*

It was not about the excavations at Glebe Farm, the archaeologists, the shallow graves or anything to do with Marnie Walker. It had been the previous year during the European Parliament by-election. The charismatic candidate, Garth Brandon, leader of the far-right Britain First Party, and a former minister under Mrs Thatcher, had been shot dead in a quiet Northampton street. Lamb remembered how the incident had stunned the political world. The police suspected he might have been killed by someone who had infiltrated his inner circle.

The investigation had found no trace of the killer, and revealed few clues as to his identity, but one of these had been a number of reports of a young man cycling away from the crime scene. A street camera had for a few fleeting seconds caught on film someone who answered his description. The young man seemed to be wearing a black uniform. One witness had remarked tellingly that he looked like an officer from Hitler's SS. Studying the TV news reports, Lamb could not help hearing that description in her mind.

Searching the archives, she had located a video-cassette taken from traffic cameras at the time of what the media had dubbed the *assassination* of Garth Brandon. Watching it now, Lamb tried to bring together the images of that young man. The more she thought about it, the more she began to see a connection.

But what could she do about it? She was well aware that if she put the suggestion to one of her senior colleagues, she might look foolish. She could imagine their reaction to her suspicion that someone glimpsed in the background of a news report might be directly linked to an unsolved murder from two years ago.

So what's your point, constable? *He reminds me of someone I saw on a traffic camera, someone dressed like a Nazi.*

Is this person dressed in Nazi uniform? *He's dressed all in black, sir.*

So, on your days off, are you Lamb. It's called fashion. What other *evidence* do you have? *He sort of looked like the man caught on camera after the shooting, sir.*

Sort of? What is this, feminine intuition?

It's a kind of hunch, sir.

Lamb sat staring dismally ahead of her. No, no, no. She risked making herself look like a stupid amateur. In her few years in the Criminal Investigation Division she had not been treated like some of her female counterparts in other forces. DS Marriner had always listened to her opinions, and even DCI Bartlett had treated her with respect, though it sometimes bordered on patronising. Now, for the sake of a gut feeling, she risked undoing all her good work. If she was to make any headway with this idea, she would need to present her superiors with tangible evidence or at least verifiable facts to link the cyclist in black with the killing of Garth Brandon.

Her breakthrough came in the unlikely setting of the staff canteen when she found herself queuing for the coffee machine behind PC Derek Flannigan, a veteran of the force now serving out his time as custody officer. Lamb enquired about his family.

'And how's your daughter getting on? Sharon, isn't it?'

'Karen,' he corrected her. 'She's doing well, second year at university now.'

'Was it archaeology, her subject?'

'You've got a good memory for detail.' Flannigan had a twinkle in his eye. 'You ought to become a detective.'

Lamb let it go. 'I'll bear that in mind. Actually, Derek, I was wondering ...'

By the end of her coffee break, Lamb had persuaded Flannigan to ask his daughter if she still had her photos from the Glebe Farm dig. She had visited the site several times and always took her camera. As luck would have it, Karen was at home earning money stacking shelves in a supermarket before going to Greece for an archaeological summer school.

As Flannigan got up to leave the table he said he thought Karen might have had some video footage from Glebe Farm. Would that be of any interest?

Zoë Tipton asked Donovan and Anne to wait up at ground level while she made a tour of inspection down below. By the time she returned, Donovan had decided where to set up the camera and how he was going to shoot the exterior scenes.

'What if Zoë wants to film around the boats – er, ships – instead?' Anne asked.

'She'll agree to film up here when I explain the advantages,' Donovan said.

'Advantages? What do you –'

Donovan gestured over Anne's shoulder. Zoë was stepping off the top of the ladder. She spotted them and walked over with a purposeful stride.

'Right, now let's get you sorted out.' Her tone was decisive, authoritative. 'We'll begin with the nearest ship – the first one I discovered – and move on to the others in chronological order of finding.'

Anne glanced quickly at Donovan, who made no reaction. Zoë continued.

'I want you to set up –'

'Not really,' Donovan said in a quiet tone.

Zoë hesitated as if she had not caught the words. 'Sorry?'

'I said, not really.'

'What d'you mean?' Zoë's tone was impatient. 'Not really what?'

'In my view we need to shoot the exterior scenes first while the light is good. The sunlight will bring out the colours in your hair and show you to advantage.'

'Colours?' Zoë seemed doubtful.

'Everyone has a variety of shades to their hair colour. Copper-gold hair like yours is particularly rich in tones. It's going to cloud over later this morning. We can film the ships then, when the light isn't important.'

Anne sensed that Zoë was struggling internally between personal vanity and this challenge to her authority as site director. Eventually, she nodded.

'Okay. That makes sense.' She turned and pointed at the excavation. 'We'll start with me standing by the ladder going down into the ground. You can film me from over there.'

Donovan looked where she was pointing.

Zoë began turning. 'Okay?'

Donovan did not move. 'Not really.'

Anne suppressed a smile. Zoë's expression was hardening by the minute.

'What is it now? You have a good reason for not filming the way I said?'

Donovan nodded. 'Two, actually.'

Zoë placed her hands on her hips in a classic confrontational posture. Anne began to worry they were about to be on the receiving end of one of Zoë's tirades. Donovan seemed unconcerned and continued speaking calmly.

'The first is that if we film inside the compound, you'll have to keep your hard hat on. We'd lose your hair, and your face would be in shadow.'

Zoë opened her mouth to speak, but no words came out. Donovan went on.

'The second is that if we filmed you as you suggested, you'd have cranes sticking out of your head, and the background would be a row of huts.'

Zoë turned to examine the scene. Grudgingly, she had to admit Donovan was right. When she turned back, she found Donovan and Anne heading towards the site entrance. She hurried after them.

Cathy Lamb was at her desk writing a report on a series of burglaries in villages west of Northampton, when she received a surprise phone call. The duty sergeant informed her she had a visitor in reception. Her curiosity piqued, Lamb made her way to the main entrance. At first, she failed to recognise the young woman sitting in a visitor's chair by the door. Seeing Lamb arrive, the girl stood up and held out her hand.

'Hallo. I'm Karen Flannigan. Remember me from the Glebe Farm dig?'

Lamb would never have recognised her.

'Of course,' she said warmly.

'My father rang home to tell me you wanted to borrow my photos and stuff.' She looked down at a cardboard box on the floor beside the chair. 'I wasn't sure what you wanted, exactly, so I brought the lot.'

'That's very kind of you, but it wasn't desperately urgent.'

'That's all right. Dad knew I was coming in anyway to do an afternoon shift, so it was no bother.'

Karen picked up the box and handed it to Cathy Lamb.

'I don't know what you need this stuff for, but you can borrow it for as long as you like. I'm going away next week and I'll be away till the end of the summer.'

'There are just some things I need to check.' Lamb hoped she did not sound too evasive.

Karen smiled. 'That's okay. 'Growing up with dad in the police, I've learnt not to ask questions.'

Lamb escorted her visitor off the premises and carried the box back to her desk. She was relieved that none of the other detectives saw her.

Donovan told Zoë to collect her thoughts. She appeared to have given up all notions that she was in charge of the filming and seemed happy enough to submit to his direction. He told her to divide her commentary into a series of brief statements: how she had discovered the first ship, how she had identified it, how she had come across the other examples, their significance for the history of London, and so on. They would deal with smaller finds, details of construction, conservation matters and the progress of the excavation when they filmed at the lower level.

'Try to keep your sentences short,' Donovan advised, as he fitted a lapel microphone to her tank top.

Zoë made no objection when he put his hands inside the flimsy garment to run the lead round to exit at the back of her waist.

'When you come to the end of what you want to say on a given subject, just stop and look steadily at the camera. I'll count mentally to five and say *cut*, so you'll know I'm switching off and you can relax.'

'I have been filmed before, you know.' Zoë spoke without animosity.

'Sure, but you need to know how I work, and that I know what I'm doing.'

Zoë looked Donovan in the eye. 'I don't have any doubts on that score.'

'Do you need me to do anything?' Anne asked.

Her rifle microphone was lying in its container. Donovan handed her a headset.

'We'll do a sound test for levels, and I'll need you to keep an eye on them throughout the session. If Zoë's voice tails off, and the meter shows a drop in volume, say *cut*, and I'll stop running.'

'Anne can stop the filming?' Zoë said in a dubious tone.

'Sure. The sound engineer can do that.' Donovan turned to Anne. 'Keep an eye on traffic noise, too, and aircraft. If anything noisy approaches, you'll hear it first. Just raise a hand.' Back to Zoë. 'If that happens, you can either bring your speech to a fairly rapid cut-off point or just scrap it and we'll go again.'

Zoë digested the new instructions while Donovan looked up at the changing sky, and Anne adjusted her earphones.

'Ready to go for a sound test?' Donovan asked.

Anne checked her dials. 'Sound ready.'

Zoë cleared her throat. 'Ready when you are.'

Lamb was impressed with Karen Flannigan. The progress of the Glebe Farm excavations was written up in the form of a diary. There were pages and pages of notes in neat handwriting, organised in ring binders, each bearing a number in Roman numerals and a date on the cover. Lamb skimmed through them.

Two further binders contained Karen's photographic records. Flicking through the pages, Lamb watched the dig develop through its various phases, with general shots of the whole field, plus numerous close-ups of archaeologists, pits and trenches. She was initially surprised that Karen had been allowed to take shots of the shallow graves and their human remains, but that was before they had been declared a crime scene.

One binder contained nothing but individual photos of the archaeologists, each with a name under the image and sometimes a phone number and/or an e-mail address. The person Lamb was hoping to find, the young man dressed in black, did not feature in any of those pictures.

Finally, there were two video-cassettes. One of them was a recording of the *Timeline* television series of digs all over the country on the subject of witchcraft, that year's theme. The other was labelled *Odds and Ends*.

Lamb placed Karen's items back in the box, shoved it under her desk and took the two video-cassettes down the corridor to a meeting room. Finding it unoccupied, she hastily switched on the television monitor in the corner and loaded the first cassette into the video machine. With a finger on the remote's fast-forward button, Lamb raced through the material, pausing from time to time when she thought she saw her target.

And there he was, average height, lightly built, with fair hair, dressed in black. She had taken him originally for an archaeologist, on seeing him with the site director when a find had been made. One of the students had held up a tiny fleur-de-lys, gleaming like gold in the sunshine. The site director and the *man-in-black* had for some unknown reason shaken hands. Lamb froze the image and stared at it. Could he be the phantom cyclist, fleeing the scene of Garth Brandon's murder?

Lamb ejected the cassette and fed the *Odds and Ends* tape into the VCR. It was well named, containing a hotchpotch of sequences, mainly snippets from news bulletins, national and regional. The BBC's *Look East* programme had used the image of the handshake as a backdrop to one of its reports on the Glebe Farm dig and the discovery of the shallow graves.

Lamb finished the tape and sat back in her chair. One young man in black; a cyclist who may have been the same person; his sighting – if it was him – near the scene of the Brandon murder; the connection with Glebe Farm, Marnie Walker and the archaeologists; the reappearance of the man in London. There had to be something to it all.

Suddenly, the door flew open and Lamb nearly jumped out of her seat, woken from her concentration with a start.

'There you are, Cathy.' It was DS Marriner. 'Got that burglaries report done?'

'Yes, sarge.' It was close to the truth. 'I want to check it over, but you'll have it this afternoon.'

'Good.' He looked at the TV monitor. 'What're you doing in here?'

Lamb thought quickly of the material she had assembled, the images from London, Glebe Farm and the road traffic camera. Taken together, it was all evidence, all verifiable fact, even if it was open to interpretation. No-one could call it intuition. She took a breath and summoned up her courage.

'Sarge, there's something I want to show you.'

At the end of the lunch break, Zoë gathered the student archaeologists together at surface level by the top of the ladder. Donovan had been right about the weather. The sky had turned a dull grey.

While Zoë gave a summary of that morning's progress, Anne rang the office. Marnie took the call after two rings. For a few minutes they discussed their local interior design projects before Anne gave an outline of her morning as sound engineer.

'We're filming by the ships this afternoon,' Anne said.

'Well be very careful,' Marnie warned. 'After what happened to poor Dr Fennimore ...'

'Don't worry, Marnie. I'm sure everything's fine. Zoë's just giving the safety lecture to the students as we speak.'

At the end of the *safety lecture*, Zoë despatched the students to their various stations, standing beside the ladder, giving words of encouragement to them all as they returned to work. Finally, she signalled to Donovan and Anne, who followed her down the ladder.

Arriving at the lowest level, Zoë went straight round to the students to check everything was running correctly. Anne was the last to arrive and found Donovan standing quietly to one side with his head bowed, as if lost in deep reflection. Then she saw it.

In a part of the site that had been cleared and installed with reinforced shuttering, a tiny light glowed. Anne walked over to Donovan and took hold of his arm. On the muddy ground a candle was burning in a jam jar. Around it, a few bunches of flowers had been laid, a final tribute to Dr Fennimore from his students. Anne felt deeply moved at this simple offering. She swallowed hard and felt her eyes welling.

As they stood together in the grey light, Zoë came to join them.

'Not an imposing monument,' she said softly.

Donovan replied without looking up. 'Its strength is its sincerity.'

'Yes,' Zoë agreed. 'D'you know what happened here this morning when they did this? One of the builders told them they weren't allowed to litter the site with flowers like this ... *litter the site* ... unbelievable.'

'What did they do?' said Anne.

'They stood staring at the man in total silence. One of the girls knelt down and lit the candle. The builder went away.'

'A health and safety hazard,' Donovan murmured. 'Articles likely to cause an obstruction or hindrance to passage.'

Anne thought it sounded as if he was quoting from a safety manual.

Donovan reached into his rucksack, removed a small object and placed it beside the jam jar. Anne saw it was a glass ball with a flat base and a gap in the top. Into this, Donovan slotted a nightlight and lit it with his Zippo. Anne felt her cheeks tingling as he stood up.

'Thank you, Donovan,' Zoë said.

Without another word, they moved away to set up their next sequence.

DCI Bartlett sat in the meeting room in divisional HQ, silently staring at the screen after Cathy Lamb had switched off the VCR. His expression was sombre. Also present was DS Marriner. In the long moment that followed, Lamb wished she had spent her day finishing the paperwork on the burglaries.

'So you think there's a connection here?' Bartlett said eventually.

Lamb took no comfort from his tone. 'I did wonder, sir.'

'Spell it out.'

Lamb summarised her thought processes: the glimpse of the young man on the cycle at the building site in London and on the traffic camera in Northampton two years earlier; his link with Glebe Farm; his proximity to the Brandon killing.

'It's all very tenuous,' Bartlett said. He looked at Marriner. 'What do you think, Ted?'

Lamb realised she was holding her breath.

'It *is* tenuous,' Marriner agreed. 'On the other hand, I can see Cathy's point. What she's produced is at least some sort of evidence. We didn't see much of that on this case.'

'The thing is, Ted, are we even sure it's the same person?' Bartlett countered. 'Do we know who he is?'

'His name's Smith.' Bartlett raised a quizzical eyebrow. Marriner continued. 'Nikolaus Donovan Smith. We interviewed him a few months ago in connection with that death in the canal.'

Bartlett nodded slowly. 'I remember. Was he fingerprinted?'

'No call for it, sir,' Marriner said. 'One other thing, he's German, or at least part German. When he presented himself for interview, he produced a German ID card.'

'Your point being?'

'The Nazi connection.'

Lamb was glad the experienced, *male* DS Ted Marriner had said that, rather than herself. Coming from a woman, that might have been an intuitive step too far, even for her relatively open-minded boss.

'That's past history, Ted.' Bartlett sounded dismissive. 'And in any case, this guy is far too young to be part of all that. What is he … twenty something?'

'Early twenties, sir. But there are plenty of people around who still hanker after far-right ideas. And the bullets that killed Brandon were fired from a 9mm Luger pistol.'

Bartlett fell silent again. Lamb knew better than to speak.

'Was this chap interviewed about Brandon? Do we have *solid* evidence that he was around at the time, not just that image from the traffic camera?'

'I don't think anyone interviewed him back then, sir,' said Marriner.

'There's nothing on record,' Lamb confirmed.

More silence from Bartlett.

'Do we know how to get hold of him?'

Sensing that her boss was gradually taking the matter seriously, Cathy Lamb became more confident.

'He seems to be involved with that building project in Docklands, sir, or perhaps with the archaeologists.'

Bartlett was ahead of her. 'Where the Met investigated the death of the archaeologist in charge ...'

'Dr Fennimore,' Lamb said.

Bartlett nodded. 'So presumably they would have interviewed him and got his details on record.'

'Shall I check it out, sir?' said Marriner.

'You do that, Ted.'

On balance, Anne had no real regrets about missing out on trips to museums and galleries. Filming the dig had been an interesting experience. Fulfilling the role of sound engineer, she felt involved, carrying out her tasks with total concentration.

Watching Donovan at work, she admired anew his meticulous attention to detail. Every shot, every camera angle, he set up with infinite care, balancing the lighting to give the greatest advantage in the restricted space around the ships' remains.

And she had to admit that Zoë was an ideal presenter. Before each sequence, Donovan checked what Zoë would be saying before giving her ideas about when to point at an object or turn to look in a certain direction. She followed his advice scrupulously, but made her gestures and movements seem natural and unscripted. Zoë felt relaxed under Donovan's guidance, which made her performance confident and professional.

When Donovan set up two-shots, where Zoë discussed a find with a student, he devoted equal care to preparing both of them. The scenes unfolded like natural conversations between colleagues, not artificially staged performances.

The first half of the afternoon flew by, and when Zoë called out, *Clear up your loose*, Anne could hardly believe they had been working for two hours. Zoë insisted that everyone should go up to the surface for their half-hour break. After shepherding the students up the ladders, Zoë put an arm round Anne's and Donovan's shoulders, guiding them along. The body language was clear: they were a team.

When they stepped off the top of the ladders at surface level, Zoë went quickly to check her e-mails, leaving Anne and Donovan to make their way to the staff hut for refreshments.

'I think that went well,' Anne said, 'and Zoë's obviously pleased.'

'For the moment,' Donovan agreed.

'Oh? You think that's going to change?'

'Don't you, Anne? Don't you think she'll be less than delighted when Dick takes centre stage?'

'Ah, that …'

'Yes, that. And where is Dick?' Donovan said.

'Professor de Groot said he'd be here today or tomorrow.'

'Even so,' Donovan said, 'I'd have expected him to be here by now.'

'Why?' Anne asked. 'And don't give me your usual, *isn't it obvious?*'

Donovan grinned. 'Okay, but I would've thought it *was* obvious why he should be here.'

'Go on.'

'There's only a limited amount of time for him to complete work on the Saxon remains. His absence means that Zoë can use all the available manpower on her ships.'

'He must be really stretched at the moment,' Anne said, 'with his PhD thesis, the Saxon skeleton and now King John's treasure. It's like a lifetime's work all compressed into one bundle.'

'Like the skeleton and the tidal Thames,' Donovan said vaguely.

'That's fairly obscure even by your standards, Donovan.'

'Sorry. I was just thinking … Dick's in way over his head.'

Anne nudged him in the ribs and dragged him off for tea.

DS Marriner knocked twice on DCI Bartlett's office door and entered, followed by DC Cathy Lamb. Bartlett listened while Marriner outlined his phone conversation with DCI Bruere in London. It was not the result he wanted.

'Didn't interview him at all?' Bartlett said.

'No, sir. They established that this Smith character is a student at Brunel University doing some sort of filming with the archaeologists. He was nowhere near the site when the accident happened, so there was no reason to question him.'

'There were any number of reasons,' Bartlett growled. 'Smith could have provided information about the condition of the shuttering. If he'd spent time down there filming, they could have asked to see his footage as photographic evidence. He could have overheard conversations, seen things, at least gained some impression of what was going on. It all seems very lax ...'

'Yes, sir. I gather DCI Bruere had enough evidence to prove that it was just a case of partial collapse of the protective shuttering and scaffolding and he saw no point in further investigation.'

Bartlett sat forward with both elbows on the desk and rested his chin on his hands.

'Even so ...'

Marriner and Lamb stood in awkward silence, waiting for Bartlett to pronounce. Lamb had the feeling her idea of following up on Donovan Smith was about to go down the drain.

'I think ...' Bartlett began. 'I think we'll tackle this more thoroughly than the Met.'

Marriner cocked his head on one side. 'Sir?'

Bartlett sat up straight. 'Ted, I want you to track down this young man, find out where he lives. We're going to pay him a surprise visit.'

'It's in London, sir.'

'Don't worry about that. Leave the protocol to me. I'll talk to Bruere.'

Lamb could not prevent herself from smiling. Bartlett noticed.

'Don't get too carried away just yet, Cathy,' he said. 'It may lead nowhere, and we've got a long way to go on this.'

'To London, sir.' Her voice was filled with optimism.

'Yes, and while we're away, I want you to get all the paperwork on the burglaries well and truly wrapped up.'

Lamb tried not to sag visibly. 'Yes, sir.'

The final shoot that afternoon went well. Donovan showed Zoë and Anne the results on the small monitor at the bottom level while the students made their way up to the surface. Wearing a headset plugged into the machine, Zoë gazed at the screen with absolute concentration. She said nothing until the recording reached the end of the tape.

'Not bad,' she murmured appreciatively, removing the headset. 'You were right about the sound quality, Donovan. It is better with the new mic. It's a pity the earlier stuff sounded so poor in comparison.'

'I can camouflage that to some extent,' he said. 'I'll use some of the better quality soundtrack as voice-over as much as possible.'

'Good. Thank you for that.' A glance at Anne. 'Thank you both. So what next?'

'I'd like to get some of this material edited as we go along,' Donovan said, 'rather than save it all up for a huge job at the end. So unless there's something vital that needs to be filmed tomorrow …'

'No, that's fine,' Zoë said. 'We'll carry on down here. I want to get as much done as I can while the going's good.'

'Presumably you can only use all the students while Dick's absent,' said Anne.

Zoë shrugged. 'It's his loss … and my gain.'

Cathy Lamb did her best to hide her disappointment. Back at her desk, she set about finalising the report on the burglaries. The statements by the victims were complete and ready for filing. The lists of stolen property she divided into two files: one comprised those items for which the owners had provided serial numbers, the other contained those without. It always amazed her that so many people failed to take the most basic care of their possessions, as if they were convinced their homes were impregnable. Or perhaps that was normal; only the police expected burglaries to happen.

Then she made another connection. She rapidly bundled the burglary files into a single folder and focused her thoughts on that tempestuous summer two years before. The young man on the bicycle seen by the traffic camera flashed into her mind. Next, the report of a police search of the town centre that had produced no evidence considered useful or relevant at the time. But it had produced one or two unexpected finds, among them a baseball cap and a pair of jeans found in a skip and a bicycle wedged between the skip and the end wall of a back yard. There was something about that bicycle … Lamb was convinced that if she thought about it for long enough, she would remember what it was.

DS Marriner was not at his desk, but the cassette from the traffic camera was sitting in the middle of his blotter. Lamb quickly grabbed it and sped down the corridor to the meeting room. She fed it into the VCR and fast-forwarded till she reached the section showing the mystery cyclist. Several times she ran the tape backwards and forwards until she had isolated one image, showing the cyclist leaning over to turn a corner. It was far from sharp and gave no clue as to the identity of the rider. On the other hand, it gave a reasonably good view of the bicycle frame. Although little more than a blur, the picture enabled Lamb to make two deductions.

The first was that she was looking at a mountain bike. The shape of the frame, the handlebars, the chunky tyres, all these left her in no doubt. The second was the tubular construction itself. The image was black and white, but it was good enough to show that the frame was basically a light colour with the make of the bike woven into some sort of pattern in a darker shade.

And that was the connection.

The cycle found stuffed behind the skip had been a mountain bike with a dull yellow frame bearing the name, *Muddy Fox*, in black letters. On either side of the name was a pattern of pawprints. Now that she knew what she was looking for, Lamb could see that the bicycle on the traffic tape could be just such a bike.

Two minutes later, Lamb was back in the office phoning the County HQ. In response to her enquiry – *on behalf of DCI Bartlett* – she made two discoveries which intrigued her: the mountain bike had been checked for fingerprints when it was recovered and found to be clean. That was obviously suspicious. Of even greater interest was the fact that the bike itself was still in storage.

Lamb could feel her heart racing and knew she had to act carefully. If she put a foot wrong at this stage, she could look ridiculous. Proceed in an orderly manner, and she could advance her career.

With filming finished for the day, Donovan suggested to Anne that they might visit the Tower of London. It would include, among other things, a chance to see the Crown Jewels. Anne accepted, and the two set off like tourists to 'do' the Tower.

As they walked over Tower Bridge, Anne rang Marnie at Glebe Farm. She was pleased to hear that Walker and Co had not collapsed during her absence and that Marnie was managing to cope without her.

'When do you want me to come back, Marnie? I seem to have been away for ages.'

'Let's play it by ear,' Marnie said. 'I'm going to stay on here for a day or two, then rejoin Ralph in Little Venice. I'm thinking we might travel back up here together on *Thyrsis*.'

'So normal service at Walker and Co to resume next Monday?' Anne said.

'That's the general idea. In the meantime, you could stay in the flat for the rest of the week with Donovan, if you like, or maybe visit your parents on the way back. Up to you.'

Waiting in the queue to buy tickets for the Tower, Anne and Donovan discussed their options. They were both keen on the idea of staying in Marnie's flat, but Donovan needed to press on with editing his film material.

'How about this for a plan?' he said. 'Suppose I go back to my boat tonight, and spend all day tomorrow in the studio at uni?'

'Can you get the editing done in one day?'

'If I make an early start in the morning and go on for as long as it takes.'

'Okay. Will you come back to the flat in time for dinner?'

'Armed with flowers and a bottle of wine.'

Anne squeezed his arm. 'Then we have a plan.'

Lamb had caught DS Marriner as soon as he returned to the office. She presented him with the completed burglary report, and then as casually as possible, explained her thinking in relation to the cyclist and the mountain bike. Marriner wanted to see the traffic video again. He studied it for some time before walking along to DCI Bartlett's office.

The three detectives watched the footage again, this time pausing on the exact image that gave the best view of the bicycle frame. Marriner asked Lamb to tell her story to the chief inspector.

'You're not going to let this go, are you?' he said when she had finished.

'Sir, it's just that –'

He cut her off with a gesture. 'It's all right, Cathy. You've made your point.'

Bartlett stood up and crossed the office to look out of the window. When he turned, he spoke to Marriner.

'Ted, I want you to go over to HQ and fetch that mountain bike from storage.'

'Tomorrow morning, sir?'

'Now.' He turned to Lamb. 'Cathy, I want you to get on to Brunel University and get an address for this Smith character.'

'Yes, sir.'

'Oh and … I want you to go down to London with Ted Marriner. I'm going to be tied up here.'

Struggling to suppress a grin, Lamb headed for the door. In the corridor, she spoke to Marriner under her breath.

'Thanks, sarge.'

'We haven't done anything yet.'

'Thanks for giving me a chance.'

They went their separate ways, Marriner to the car park, Lamb to her desk. In a few minutes she was in contact with the student records office at the university.

'I'm afraid we can't give out personal details of students over the telephone.' The woman's tone was reasonable, the response not unexpected.

'As I said a moment ago, my name is detective constable Cathy Lamb. I'm with Northamptonshire County Constabulary. We're conducting an investigation into a major crime. Your student, Mr Smith, is believed to be a material witness and we need to speak to him as a matter of urgency.'

'Even so, we have rules on confidentiality, and I have no authority to give out the information you're asking for. I'm sorry.'

'May I know who I'm speaking to, please?' said Lamb.

'My name is Helen Gibbs.'

'Ms Gibbs, are you aware that it's a serious offence to withhold information from the police?'

The line went silent.

'Hallo?' said Lamb.

'I've ... I've never had this kind of enquiry before.'

Lamb realised this was new territory to her, too, and she wanted to play everything by the book. One false move could jeopardise the investigation and ruin all her good work.

'Could I speak to the person in charge of your department?'

'That's Mrs Bellamy, Monica Bellamy. I'll see if I can get her for you.'

When Mrs Bellamy came on the line, she was just as cautious as Helen Gibbs. Lamb was ready with her request.

'Can you give me your fax number, please. I'm going to send you a written request for the information at once. If you have a problem with that, you can phone me via the divisional HQ switchboard or speak to my chief inspector. We really do need to contact Mr Smith. It's important.'

Lamb typed the fax on headed notepaper in record time and sent it on its way. Ten minutes later her phone rang.

'Thanks for getting back to me, Mrs Bellamy.'

'I have information for you, Ms Lamb, but it may not be what you hoped for.'

'If you could just give me the contact details ...'

'The address is in Göttingen.'

'Where?'

'I think that's how you pronounce it. I understand it's a town in Germany.'

'No, no,' Lamb said. 'I must have his UK address.'

'I don't think that's going to help you very much,' Mrs Bellamy said.

'What do you mean?'

'It says here, *NB XO2*.'

'What the hell is that?' Lamb was beginning to feel the misgivings arising from any dealings with Glebe Farm and its associates. 'Can you say it again?'

Mrs Bellamy obliged.

'And that's the UK contact address for your student? That's how you get in touch with him?'

'We normally use the university pigeonholes in term time.'

Lamb was dismayed. 'So is that all you have?'

'Not quite ... there is something else. It says *c/o the Grand Union Canal*. Then we have a mobile phone number.'

'Grand Union ...? Ah, wait a minute,' said Lamb. '*NB* ... that could be *narrowboat*. You're sure that's all you have?'

'Positive.'

Lamb took down the remaining details, including the mobile number.

'Thanks for your help.'

Next stop, the British Waterways Board, the UK's licensing authority for inland waterways. Praying she would not meet the same obstruction from that organisation, Lamb found the number for the head office. The man who answered her call could not have been more helpful, but the result was no more enlightening.

'Yes, there is indeed a boat called *XO2*, licensed to a Mr N D Smith.'

'Great,' said Lamb, getting somewhere at last. 'And its mooring?' Her pen was poised over the pad.

'It's down as a CC.'

'Sorry, you'll have to explain. I'm not familiar with –'

'Continuous cruiser.'

'Meaning?'

'What it says. He doesn't have a mooring. He cruises continuously.'

'Does that mean you don't know where he keeps the boat?'

'We have over two thousand miles of waterways, Miss Lamb. He could be anywhere.'

Lamb was now losing the will to live. After hanging up, she put her head in her hands.

'You all right, Cathy?'

She looked up to see Sergeant Marriner hovering over her.

'I'm drawing a complete blank with this Smith character. He lives in Germany and his only address here seems to be a boat with a weird name somewhere in England.'

'But you've got his details, surely,' Marriner said. 'You interviewed him some months ago, remember? Didn't you get his particulars then?'

Lamb scrambled in the second drawer of her desk and began pulling out notebooks. She checked the dates and began flicking through the pages.

'Yes! Sarge, you're a genius.'

'True. Have you got it?'

Lamb's expression reverted to despair as she read her old notes.

'Oh no … He gave his address as *west London, on the canal somewhere between Uxbridge and West Drayton.*'

'That's better than nothing, isn't it?' Marriner said.

Lamb was incredulous. '*Somewhere between –*'

'Exactly. Isn't Brunel University in Uxbridge? Stands to reason he's going to be staying somewhere in the area. It's easier to check out the canal than all the streets in the borough.'

'I suppose it is, sarge. I hadn't thought of it like –'

'Cathy, get back to British Waterways. They must have someone responsible for each section of the canals. Give them a rough idea of where we think this boat may be. That might help them locate it for us. Then nip along to the boss and give him the name of the boat. He'll need it for the search warrant.'

15
Surprise Visit

For Marnie it felt very strange, sleeping alone on *Sally Ann* again, and she certainly missed the up-to-the-minute facilities of *Thyrsis*. She missed Ralph, too. When she awoke early on Tuesday morning, she found Dolly curled in a ball at the foot of the bed. Feeling Marnie stir, the cat made a quiet warbling sound that turned into a yawn. Marnie looked down to find her gaze returned by two large amber eyes.

'Good morning, Dolly. Time to explore our feeding bowls?'

The solid black cat agreed. They rose together and padded towards the galley.

Fifty miles to the south, on a mooring in London's Little Venice, Ralph was still sleeping. He would probably not be visiting the galley on *Thyrsis* for at least another hour.

In Docklands, Anne the early riser was already in the shower, her clothes for the day laid out on the double bed in the guest room. An initial viewing from the living room windows had revealed a hazy sun casting a glow over Docklands, bringing the promise of fine weather. She was humming an old favourite song, *Sunday Girl* by Blondie, and was cheerfully looking forward to the day ahead.

In the western suburbs, Donovan was also up and about. He had followed his usual routine of opening the stern doors of *XO2* and stepping out onto the deck for a blast of fresh air. In the background he was aware of the distant hum of traffic. As he breathed in, he checked over the boat, saw that his bike was padlocked in place on the roof under its all-weather cover and made a cursory inspection of the mooring ropes. Everything was as it should be. In half an hour he would ride off to the university for a long session in the editing suite. With luck, he would have his material completed by the end of the afternoon. It would be a normal day.

For Marnie the day unfolded as planned. By early afternoon she had dealt with all the outstanding matters in the office at Glebe Farm and phoned for a taxi to take her to the station. Issuing last-minute instructions to Dolly the cat while Rajeev the driver loaded her bag into the boot of the cab, Marnie looked around her at the honey-coloured stone buildings of the cottages and barns and at the farmhouse that would soon be her home.

Rajeev opened the rear door for Marnie to climb in.

'Taking a break, Marnie?'

'Going down to London to meet Ralph and bring our other boat back up.'

'A nice trip.' A broad smile split the friendly bearded face under its dark blue turban. 'You won't be needing my services for that, then.'

'Not unless you fit water-wings to the taxi and give us a tow.'

Rajeev laughed. 'Now you're giving me ideas. A new business opportunity.'

Marnie looked back through the rear window at Dolly washing herself outside the office barn, as the taxi crunched over the gravel in the courtyard, turned onto the field track and left Glebe Farm behind.

Anne had looked in on the building site on her way to the tube that morning. The students had just arrived and were being briefed by Zoë. She caught sight of Anne outside the perimeter fence and waved before turning back to the group.

After spending the morning among the British Museum's medieval collections, Anne sat out on the steps to eat a sandwich. The sun was high in the sky and all around the classical front of the museum people were sitting and lying about, enjoying the fine weather. She wondered if some day there would be a new exhibition devoted to the long-lost treasure of King John, with explanatory panels telling the story of how the royal regalia were discovered by a brilliant young archaeologist. Perhaps there might even be an audio-visual display produced by Donovan, showing Dick Blackwood at work, raising the finds from the sea.

There was one more section of the museum that she wanted to visit, the treasures of the Sutton Hoo ship burial. She had saved that till last, wanting to gain an idea of how the museum might in future display Dick's collection.

These were exciting times.

Ralph was keen to complete an article for *The Economist* magazine for which he had a deadline at the end of the week, so Marnie arranged to visit a friend in Little Venice. Mrs Jolly was an old lady who lived opposite *Sally Ann's* former mooring near Maida Hill tunnel.

'Come in, come in, my dear. I was just trying to work out how long it's been since you were last here ...'

Amid much hugging and general fussing, Mrs Jolly led Marnie through to the small, walled courtyard garden at the rear of the townhouse.

'The kettle's on and I'm making tea, or you can have coffee of course, if you'd prefer ...'

Under a vine-covered pergola and surrounded by cascades of climbing and rambling roses that filled the air with their fragrance, Mrs Jolly had laid the table for afternoon tea.

'I have Darjeeling, which I know you like, and there are slices of lemon. Of course, some purists would insist on Ceylon tea with lemon ...'

As her friend chattered on, Marnie smiled at the sight of sandwiches of white bread filled with salmon and pâté, each cut into neat triangles with their crusts removed. Beyond them, a mound of scones waited patiently beside a cut glass dish of raspberry jam – no doubt homemade – and a crock of clotted cream. To complete the scene, in the place of honour, stood a cake that Marnie guessed was coffee and walnut. Serene and magnificent, crowned with butter icing, it commanded the centre of the table.

'Oh, Marnie, I'm so delighted to see you again. I suspect you haven't been down to London because you've been busy. I do hope you haven't been working too hard ...'

By way of reply, Marnie turned and hugged the old lady, who smelled faintly of lavender. Just to be with Mrs Jolly again was like visiting a favourite aunt.

'It's wonderful to be back, Mrs Jolly. But tell me something.'

'Yes, my dear?'

'What time do they arrive?'

Mrs Jolly looked puzzled. 'Who do you mean?'

Marnie indicated the table at which only two places had been set. 'The bridge club ... or are you expecting your late husband's old regiment for a reunion?'

The old lady chuckled. 'Perhaps I have gone a little over the top. But today is a *special* occasion.' She kissed Marnie on the cheek. 'And you are a *very* special visitor, my dear. Come, have a seat. Tell me all about your marvellous project in Docklands. And will you take the Darjeeling?'

It was a day for visitors. Donovan had worked solidly in the university editing suite all day. When he arrived, the early morning cleaners were still at work in the department, and it was almost five o'clock before he was ready to leave. He had survived on a cheese roll and a cup of coffee in the studio at lunchtime and was looking forward to dinner with his friends.

In twenty minutes he was back at his mooring and lifted the bike into place on the roof under its cover. No need for the padlock; he would be putting it inside the boat before setting off by tube for Docklands.

He was pulling fresh clothes from the locker before taking a shower, when he became aware of movement on the towpath. Occasional joggers or passers-by were not unusual, but there was something about the sounds he heard that seemed out of place. It was as if a whole crowd of people was outside. He moved closer to the porthole to take a sideways look through the lace curtain. At that moment there came a loud knocking on the stern door. No-one was visible through the porthole, and for a few seconds he ran over his options. They were very limited.

'Who is it?' he called through the door, hastily dragging off his clothes. 'I'm taking a shower.'

'Police!' came the reply. 'Open the door.'

'Hold on,' he called back.

Racing to the bathroom, he turned on the shower, hung his clothes on the door and wrapped a towel round his waist. He turned off the shower and padded back to the stern, where he pushed open one of the doors. Two men were standing on the stern deck, staring down at him.

'I was just about to ...' Donovan squinted up at them. 'Can I see some ID, please.'

The nearer man began reaching into his pocket. Beyond them, Donovan saw several uniformed officers grouped together on the towpath. He made a gesture with his hands.

'It's okay. No need to bother with the ID.' He immediately recognised Cathy Lamb, then hastily adjusted his towel to make sure it was secure. 'What can I do for you?'

The nearer man held up a piece of paper. 'I'm DS Rigby, Metropolitan Police, accompanied by DS Marriner and DC Lamb from Northants. We have a warrant to search these premises ... er, this boat. We're coming on board.'

'Okay. May I see that, please?'

Donovan took the paper and read it quickly. He handed it back to Rigby.

'Can I put some clothes on? Is that all right with you?'

'Yes, but one of my officers will have to be in attendance.'

Donovan flashed a brief smile in the direction of Cathy Lamb. 'Do I get to choose which one?'

'Please step aside, sir ... now.'

Donovan backed away and walked quickly towards the bathroom where he hastily put his clothes back on. He emerged to find the boat filled with policemen.

'Can I get something from my bag?' Donovan asked.

Rigby nodded, carefully watching his every movement. Donovan took out his wallet and extracted his German ID card.

'You'll want to see this, I think.'

Rigby examined it before handing it back.

'Am I allowed to know what you're looking for?' Donovan asked. 'Perhaps I can help you.'

'That could count in your favour.'

Donovan realised he was no longer being addressed as *sir*. His mind was running in overdrive, trying to work out what lay behind this intrusion.

Watching the police quietly and efficiently going about their business, he made a supreme effort to present a calm exterior.

'So what is it you're looking for exactly?'

Another plain clothes officer turned from the bookcase. 'Are these your books?'

Donovan resisted the temptation to point out that they were on his shelves, on his boat. 'Yes.'

'They're in German, aren't they?'

'Some of them.'

The officer took out one volume. 'This is by Adolf Hitler.'

Donovan nodded. '*Mein Kampf*. It's his autobiography in which he sets out his political doctrine.'

The two Met officers looked at each other. Then they looked at Donovan. He was everyone's idea of Aryan youth: slim, with fair hair and blue eyes.

'Is that what you're looking for?' Donovan said. 'It's not illegal to possess it in this country.'

'Sympathetic to the cause, are you?' said Rigby.

'My boat has been compared with a U-boat, but that doesn't necessarily –'

'Sir.' A constable called across to his superior. He pointed at a set of shelves on the wall.

The detectives turned their attention to that part of the cabin. The unit was painted black and displayed three cameras and a coffee service.

'These are your property?'

'Yes.'

'You have receipts for them?'

Donovan shook his head. 'No. They're very old. I inherited them from a member of my family.'

'German?'

'Yes.'

Suddenly, both detectives homed in on three photographs mounted on the side panel of the shelving unit. They were old colour prints of silver racing cars from the 1930s, Mercedes-Benz and Auto Union. Each photo bore a faded signature. But it was not the impressive machines that had attracted their attention, rather the emblem clearly visible on the headrest of the middle car. It was a red circle surrounding a black swastika.

'He took these photos, did he, this member of your family?'

'He was a photo-journalist before the war,' Donovan confirmed.

'I don't suppose he got a snap or two of old Adolf, did he?'

Donovan was wondering where this conversation was going. He already suspected that it was linked with the killing of Garth Brandon, hence the presence of Marriner and Lamb. But were they interested in him as a possible Nazi or as an anti-Nazi? His best option was to tell the truth as far as possible and see where that led. If they were pursuing him as a potential Nazi, he had enough witnesses in Northamptonshire to swear that he was nothing of the sort.

'Adolf Hitler?' Donovan said. 'I'm not sure, though it is possible. My great-uncle certainly photographed Hermann Goering and other members of the top hierarchy of the Third Reich.'

'Are you proud of what he did?'

Donovan thought of his great-uncle, an honourable man who defied the Nazis and one day just disappeared, never to be seen again.

'He did what he believed was right,' he said, looking the detective straight in the eye.

'Mr Smith,' Rigby said, turning to walk back through the boat, 'would you come this way, please. There's something I want to show you.'

Donovan was immediately on his guard. He knew the police were sometimes accused of planting drugs or other compromising evidence on people they wanted to arrest. Could it be true? The officer beckoned him towards the stern doors. Once again playing for time to collect his thoughts, Donovan stopped by the bathroom to slip a pair of sandals on his bare feet.

Outside, he was asked to step down onto the towpath. The officer pointed at the roof of the boat, where a uniformed constable standing on the gunwale was starting to remove the waterproof cover from the bicycle.

Donovan said, 'That's just where I keep my ...'

As the cover was pulled away, his voice tailed off when he saw what was revealed. It was a mountain bike, but not the black one he had placed there ten minutes earlier. Donovan found himself staring at an older model, its frame painted yellow, with black pawprints running either side of the name, *Muddy Fox*. Seeing it for the first time in two years, and never expecting to see it again, brought a lump to his throat. Donovan forced himself to stay calm. He knew he could not trust his voice, so he resorted to the best alternative. He laughed.

'What is this?' he said eventually.

The police officers were watching him closely.

Rigby said, 'You were about to say that's where you keep your mountain bike, I believe.'

'That certainly is a mountain bike,' Donovan said, 'and it happens to be the same make as mine, but it's an older model and entirely the wrong colour for me.'

'You deny that it's yours?'

'We all know it isn't mine.' Donovan was still wary, but confident now of his position.

'What if I told you we can have you finger-printed to check your prints with those found on the bike?'

Donovan shrugged at the trick question. 'You won't find my fingerprints on that bike.'

'How can you be so sure of that?'

'I'd have thought that was obvious.'

Donovan knew he had only to suggest that they check the security cameras at the university, to prove that he had arrived and left on a black bicycle. But he said nothing, not wishing to appear too defensive or calculating. The confrontation on the towpath was taking on the appearance of a stand-off when an urgent voice called out from inside the cabin.

'In here, sir!'

The group returned to the interior, with Donovan sandwiched between the plain clothes officers while two constables hovered close behind on the towpath. Donovan knew what to expect as soon as he saw a policeman kneeling beside the bed.

'What is it?' said Rigby.

'There's a metal box concealed under here, sir. It's locked.'

Rigby turned to Donovan, an inquisitive expression on his face. Without a word, Donovan reached into his pocket and pulled out a small bunch of keys. Singling out one of them, he passed the bunch to Rigby, who gave it to the constable. A few moments passed while the man fiddled with the key in the confined space. They heard a lock turn and the sound of a container springing open. When the constable extricated himself from under the bed, he was clutching an iconic German shape. In his hand, wrapped in a yellow duster, was a Luger pistol.

The police stared at Donovan whose expression remained inscrutable. He broke the silence.

'The answer to your first question, Mr Rigby, is yes, it is my pistol. The answer to your second question is yes, I do have a licence for it. You'll find the firearms certificate in a slot inside the container. I have no ammunition.'

The kneeling constable laid the Luger on the duvet and returned under the bed.

'And the answer to my third question?' said Rigby.

Donovan knew exactly what the third question would be, but did not want to appear too clever. He remained silent.

Rigby reached down for the Luger and held it up in the cloth. 'Why do you have such a thing at all?'

'A memento from the war.'

'It belonged to your great-uncle?'

Donovan shook his head. 'No. It was found in my grandfather's house afterwards, along with an Iron Cross … second class. My father kept them as memorabilia, together with my great-uncle's medals from the Great War. You'll find them in a box in the bottom drawer of my desk.'

'We already have,' said Rigby.

'The answer to your fourth question,' said Donovan, 'is yes, by all means, you can take the pistol for testing.'

'That won't be necessary.' Rigby's tone was stern.

Donovan was on his guard. 'You don't want to take it?'

'I don't need to ask the question. We're taking it with or without your permission.'

In the kitchen area Anne was humming contentedly to herself as she prepared dinner, but her concentration was continuously interrupted by the desire to stare down at the river.

Numerous classic craft were coming and going in and out of Saint Katharine Docks opposite. She surmised that some sort of event was taking place at the weekend. Her attention had first been taken by an old Thames sailing barge approaching from downstream. Two others had followed shortly afterwards, their brown sails furled as they butted through the water under engine power. Most magnificent of all had been the sight of an oyster smack under full sail, its hull low in the water, speeding away, taking advantage of a light following wind.

Anne paused halfway through flaking smoked haddock onto a plate. She had baked it in the oven in milk in a closed dish, and it fell apart at the lightest touch. She checked the rice, which she had rinsed in cold water after boiling to prevent it from sticking together, then tipped into a colander to stand on top of a pan of boiling water to reheat. It was a tip she had learnt from Marnie who, in turn, had acquired it from an Indian friend in London. With six hard-boiled eggs cooling in a pan of cold water, and bowls of chopped spring onions, prawns, peanuts, parsley and potato sticks lined up ready to blend in, she was pleased to have everything under control when she heard the front door opening.

Marnie and Ralph had barely had time to put their bags down before Anne sprang out to meet them.

'Have you seen those lovely old barges?' she said.

Ralph kissed her on the cheek. 'We saw one as we came over the bridge. Are there more?'

'Lots. There must be some sort of rally or race coming up.'

'Something smells good,' Ralph observed.

'I'm making kedgeree for dinner.'

'Excellent. Just what I need after a hard day slaving over hot statistics.'

'How about you, Marnie?' Anne said. 'Are you hungry, too?'

Marnie tried not to think about Mrs Jolly's traditional English tea. The sandwiches, scones and coffee-walnut cake were not a distant memory.

'Sounds good to me.' She hoped she sounded enthusiastic.

Ralph was enquiring about the wine situation when the doorbell rang. He was checking the two bottles of New Zealand chardonnay in the fridge, and Marnie was washing her hands in the bathroom, when Donovan walked in. It was Anne who picked up on his demeanour.

'Has something happened?' she asked.

Marnie and Ralph appeared at her side. Donovan explained about the visit from the police, the search warrant and the questioning.

'The Met and the county force working together,' Ralph said. 'Interesting.'

'How worrying,' Anne said. 'Did you think they were going to arrest you?'

'For legal possession of a registered weapon kept in a secure locked cabinet in accordance with the rules? For having a Muddy Fox mountain bike?' Donovan shook his head. 'Not really.'

'Even so, it must've been scary.'

'My only concern was not knowing what they were looking for or why they had chosen that time to come after me.'

'Presumably it was in connection with ... Brandon?' Ralph suggested.

'That's my guess,' said Donovan. 'But they didn't give me any clues.'

'How did they leave it?' Marnie asked.

'They took the Luger away, and Rigby said I shouldn't leave London without notifying him of my destination.'

'Did you tell him you were coming here?'

'Definitely not. I didn't want to cause you any problems. Anyway, this is still London.'

'Donovan ...' Marnie looked uncomfortable. 'Please don't take this the wrong way ... I'm not sure how to put it ... but is there any reason for being concerned about them having the Luger?'

The question – with its implication – hung in the air as it had hovered over them for the past two years.

'I'm not sure, to be honest,' Donovan said in a calm voice. 'I don't know what's involved.'

'So what happens next?' said Marnie.

Ralph spoke first. 'I think I open a bottle of wine.'

16
Conclusions

Marnie and Ralph took the underground back to Little Venice early on Wednesday morning. Walking up to the pool from Warwick Avenue tube station, Marnie's eyes strayed along the towpath in the direction of the boat belonging to her solicitor and friend, Roger Broadbent. Seeing *Rumpole* gave her an idea.

Roger was on the speed-dial of Marnie's mobile for his home, office and mobile numbers. As she selected the first of these, she realised that storing all three numbers for her solicitor was in itself a comment on the way her life had developed in recent years.

A woman's voice came on the line.

'Marjorie, good morning, it's Marnie, Marnie Walker. Sorry to phone so early.'

'Hallo, Marnie. Do I take it this isn't a social call?' The friendly tone was edged with a touch of anxiety.

'That's right. I wonder if I might have a brief word with Roger.'

'I think he's just finished shaving. Hold on.'

There was a background sound of footfall on the stairs.

'What-ho, Marnie!' Roger was always alarmingly cheerful in the morning. 'Not been arrested again, I trust?'

'Listen, Roger, it's about Donovan.'

As concisely as she could, Marnie told Roger about the police raid on Donovan's boat. When she finished the story, Roger spoke without hesitation.

'What's behind all this, Marnie? The police don't just pounce on someone for no reason. Presumably it has nothing to do with the fatal accident at the building site.'

'No. We think it's probably connected with the Garth Brandon affair.'

This time, Roger hesitated for some seconds before replying. 'Are you suggesting that Donovan was in some way involved in that matter?'

'I'm not really suggesting anything, Roger, but it's the only thing I can think of that would bring detectives down from the county on a joint operation.'

'Hence the stunt with the bike-swap and their interest in the gun,' Roger said.

'Exactly.'

'Marnie, my advice to you as a friend is to be very careful what you might be getting yourself into. Tell me, does your friend have a solicitor?'

'Possibly the family has one, but they're all in Germany. Do you think he needs one?'

'It sounds like it to me, Marnie, and you think so, too. Otherwise you wouldn't be ringing me before breakfast.'

'What will happen now?'

'That all depends on forensics. Is Donovan worried that the Luger might incriminate him?'

'What you're asking, Roger, is –'

'We both know what I'm asking, Marnie. Putting it bluntly, did that pistol kill Garth Brandon?'

Marnie took a breath. 'To be honest, we've never broached the subject directly with Donovan. It's not really the kind of thing you can raise in casual conversation.'

'But I think you've given me my answer.'

'Possibly,' said Marnie. 'And we're back to my question. What do we do now?'

A pause. 'Frankly, Marnie, I think we wait for the police to renew their contact with Donovan. We're in their hands now.'

❖ ❖ ❖ ❖ ❖ ❖ ❖

Donovan rang the number on the card left with him by DS Rigby. It was too early to catch Rigby at the station, but he left a message: if Rigby needed to speak with him that day, he would be working at the Horselydown site. He left his mobile number and disconnected. The background sound for his call was clearly the underground, making the point that he was crossing London from his mooring. He wanted to keep a distance in all senses from Marnie's flat in Docklands.

On arrival at the site, he half expected to find the police waiting for him by Tower Bridge. But everything seemed normal, with the students stepping down from their coach and construction work in progress. He rang Anne who told him that Marnie and Ralph were long gone and that she would meet him by the staff hut in ten minutes.

'Oh, Donovan … is Zoë there?'

'Haven't seen her so far.'

'What about Dick Blackwood?'

'No sign.'

'Okay. Seeya!'

After disconnecting, Anne sat thinking. She felt sluggish, having slept fitfully that night, worrying about Donovan. He had done all he could to cover his tracks for the past two years, ever since the death of Garth Brandon, and she had a shrewd suspicion why. She had a dread feeling that a major part of her world was about to fall apart, and there was nothing she could do about it.

Even the biggest success of her short career, the huge contract at Horselydown, had become tainted with tragedy. And she had a sense of foreboding that all was not as it seemed with the dramatic discovery claimed by Dick Blackwood.

Anne stood up and walked over to the window, staring out over the river that was sparkling in the morning light. *Where are you, Dick?* she wondered. *And what the hell is going on?*

Cathy Lamb returned to divisional HQ in Towcester and went straight to the desk of DS Marriner, who was on the phone. There had been two more burglaries during the night, and she had been sent to investigate. But it was not the wish to report back to her sergeant that kept her hovering over him. As soon as Marriner replaced the receiver, she perched on the edge of his desk.

'No prizes for guessing what's on your mind, Cathy,' Marriner said. 'But first of all, what about the burglaries?'

'Could be the same: houses unoccupied, owners away on holiday, alarms disabled –'

'Inside knowledge,' Marriner interrupted. 'There's a link there somewhere.'

'I'll get on and write it up, sarge.'

'You do that. Is it the same make of alarm, Cathy?'

'Yes.'

'Leave the report till later. We've got some visits to make.'

'In the meantime, can I ask …?'

'The boss has spoken to the Met. We can expect a result on the Luger tests probably tomorrow. Rigby will phone to let us know.'

'Will he be brought up here following the arrest, sarge?'

'First things first, Cathy. Let's get the results back from ballistics.'

Lamb tried to conceal dissatisfaction, but her expression betrayed her feelings.

Marriner glared at her. 'You have a problem with that?'

'Well, I just thought, in view of the seriousness of the case …'

'Cathy, we need more than suspicion to hold someone in legal possession of a firearm. The boss says we do everything by the book. Okay?'

'I was just concerned he might make a run for it, sarge.'

'Don't worry. The Met'll be keeping an eye on him.'

Lamb grinned. 'When they pulled that stunt with the bike on the roof, I thought they might've startled him into giving the game away.'

'I think that was the idea, Cathy.'

'Yeah, but he's too cool a character for that,' Lamb said.

'That's what bothers me,' said Marriner. 'But don't worry. Once the report on the weapon is in, our young Mr Smith will have nowhere to hide.'

With no locks to negotiate until beyond Uxbridge, *Thyrsis* made steady progress after slipping her temporary mooring in Little Venice. After rounding Browning island in the pool, Marnie had looked back at the tree-lined waterway that had been her original base for *Sally Ann*. She still thought of it as a kind of home, still regarded this quiet corner of London as the most attractive section of urban canal anywhere in the country.

'Do you ever miss your life in London, Marnie?' Ralph was on the tiller. 'Ever miss Little Venice? Any regrets?'

'None at all. I did well here, but I came to realise I wanted something different. Anyway, we're not so far that we can't come back any time we want to, or need to.'

'True, and of course you have the flat in Docklands.'

Marnie nodded. 'And the project in Docklands.'

Ralph smiled. 'The best of both worlds.'

'Almost.' It came out before Marnie could stop herself. 'I mean –'

'I know what you mean,' Ralph said. He reached out and took her hand.

Marnie squeezed Ralph's hand and let go to turn and sit on the stern rail. 'It's strange, but every time I feel happy, something crops up to bring me down to earth with a bump. I can't help thinking about Dr Fennimore and now this business with Donovan and the police. I wonder what led them to him.'

'I don't suppose we'll ever know,' Ralph said, 'unless ...'

Marnie completed the sentence for him. 'Unless he's arrested and has to stand trial.' She frowned. 'I can't believe this is happening, Ralph.'

Ahead of them, another boat was coming their way. It was a fine modern craft with gleaming paintwork, a huge antique headlight in the bows and polished brasswork throughout. The steerer was a man with white hair, accompanied by a woman in a smock top with blue jeans. Both were smiling with contentment. As they passed, the steerer called across.

'Glorious day!'

'Wonderful!' Marnie replied.

Ralph raised a hand before turning to bring *Thyrsis* back into mid-channel.

'Wonderful,' Marnie repeated quietly to herself. 'But for how much longer?'

Anne and Donovan were growing impatient. After waiting for half an hour, Anne called in on the clerk of works. He confirmed he had had no word from Zoë Tipton and suggested to Anne that she might try the site agent in the next hut. The result was the same. She left the hut to see Donovan talking to the students who were sitting about on the ground. Most had removed their hard hats and were sunbathing or chatting.

Anne began walking over to Donovan who turned and met her halfway.

'Any joy, Anne?'

Anne shook her head. 'What about the students? Anyone been in touch with them?'

'No contact. Not a word.'

'The case of the disappearing archaeologists,' Anne said.

Donovan nodded. *'The Archaeologist Vanishes* – Alfred Hitchcock's lost masterpiece.'

'What are we going to do?' Anne asked. 'I don't fancy waiting around here all day.'

Donovan looked at his watch. Before he could speak, Anne read his mind.

'Good idea,' she said. 'Coffee. Let's go to that little place round the corner, or would you prefer to go back to the flat?'

Donovan indicated the students with a toss of his head. 'What about them?'

'It's tough, but I think they have to wait for Zoë or Dick. They don't have much choice, but we do. What d'you say?'

Donovan agreed. He went over to the group, gave one of the students a card and returned to Anne.

'I left my mobile number for Zoë or Dick to ring when they show up, if they want any filming. The students seem happy enough in the sunshine for now, so let's go.'

While Ralph steered the boat, Marnie went below to put the kettle on. Waiting for it to boil, on impulse she rang her sister.

'Got time for a chat?'

'When I regain consciousness,' Beth said in a cheerful tone. 'Two phone calls in the same month ... must be a record. Usually you're too busy with ... Ah, what's that?'

'What's what?'

'I can hear an engine running. Are you on the boat?'

'No, it's the Starship *Enterprise*. I've been abducted by aliens.'

'Shock, horror,' said Beth. 'Don't tell me you're *still* on holiday.'

'We're sort of *back* on holiday. But it's not quite as simple as that.'

'There's a surprise! So tell me more.'

Marnie brought Beth up to date on the Horselydown project and Dr Fennimore's accident.

'We saw it on the local evening news,' said Beth. 'They interviewed Philip. He looked really drawn.'

'With good reason,' Marnie said. 'He could've been held responsible as architect in charge.'

'But he wasn't, was he?' said Beth. 'So everything's back to normal, presumably.'

Marnie hesitated.

'Marnie? You there?'

'There are one or two things going on in the background, Beth.'

'Another surprise! Why is nothing ever straightforward where you're –'

'Seriously, Beth.'

'Give me a for instance.'

'For a start, one of the other archaeologists has made a big discovery –'

'The Roman boats, I know.'

'No, this is something quite different.'

'The Saxon skeleton? We've heard about that, too.'

'Same archaeologist, different find. I can't talk about it at the moment, but it seems to be very significant. I expect an announcement will be made quite soon.'

'That seems like good news to me, Marnie, but your tone suggests otherwise. Is something else going on?'

'It's … Donovan. The police have been questioning him.'

'About what?'

'We think it's in connection with the shooting of Garth Brandon.'

There was silence while Beth trawled her memory. 'That fascist politico?'

'Yes.'

Another pause. ' You're saying the police think *Donovan* had something to do with it? That's absurd.' No reaction. 'Marnie? It *is* absurd … isn't it?'

'Well …'

'My god … you think he –'

'Better not jump to any conclusions, Beth.'

'Sounds to me like you already have.'

They opted for the Italian café round the corner from the building site. Anne ordered a cappuccino, Donovan a mocha. While they waited to be served, Donovan reached across the table and touched Anne's hand.

'Something bothering you?'

She gave a grim smile. 'You've usually got everything worked out. What do *you* think it is?'

Donovan gave this some thought. 'Hard to tell. We're rather spoilt for choice. My guess would be, you're thinking about work.'

'This is the longest time I've spent away from Glebe Farm since that first summer. I went camping in Scotland with my folks.'

'So I recall. Was it good?'

Anne laughed. 'We got flooded out.' Her smile disappeared. 'I came back at the time of …' She remembered that first tragic death in the village. 'Let's talk about something else.'

'So I guessed right?'

'Not really. Look, Donovan, there's something I want to … or rather, I need to –'

Before she could finish the sentence, Donovan's mobile began warbling. He recognised Zoë's voice. Her tone suggested impatience that they were not at the site waiting for her to arrive.

'Hi, Zoë. We'll be with you shortly. Give us ten minutes.'

'Where are you … precisely?'

'In a café … *Fellini's* … just down the road from –'

'I know where it is. Wait for me there. Order me a double espresso.'

She was gone. Donovan pressed the red button.

'Boots and saddles?' Anne said.

Donovan placed a hand on hers. 'No rush. She's joining us here.'

He signalled to the waitress.

Bernard de Groot was at his desk reading through the morning post. It included three invitations. The first offered a three-year contract as principal guest lecturer with the Mediterranean shipping line, *Cruises of Distinction*. The second was a request to be keynote speaker at the next spring conference on archaeology at the University of York. The third invited him to take part in a television documentary on King Arthur entitled, *Avalon – fact or fiction?* The intercom sounded. He pressed a button on the receiver.

'Yes, Sarah?'

'I have a call on the line from Horselydown. It's Philip Everett, the architect. He says it's rather urgent.'

'Put him through.'

De Groot waited for the connection, wondering what else could go wrong at the building site. He tried not to appear too anxious when he announced himself. On the few occasions when they had met, de Groot had been impressed with Philip Everett, who seemed capable of handling problems with admirable composure. It was the same that morning.

Philip was concerned that the students had been waiting in the compound for over an hour with no sign of a site director to take charge of them. He had tried the numbers for Zoë Tipton and Dick Blackwood but had got no further than voicemail. De Groot assured Philip there would no doubt be a simple explanation for their absence and promised to investigate without delay.

When he hung up, he pressed the intercom button, called Sarah Lockyer in and asked her to make enquiries. She was back within five minutes with the news that someone thought they had caught sight of Zoë, but Dick had not been seen in the building that morning. De Groot asked her to enquire further: the local student hostel and the archaeology department in Cambridge for Zoë; his home address for Dick. She should also ring them on their mobiles and leave messages if necessary on their voicemail. They were to contact the professor at once.

When Lockyer went out, de Groot sat thinking. He did not like the way the situation was developing at Horselydown. It could get even worse once the news of Dick Blackwood's important discovery was made public. Above all, he was starting to feel that something about that discovery was not right. He would ask Blackwood for a thorough briefing on the project and would from now on take a direct personal interest in it.

But first things first. That morning's priority was Horselydown. Zoë and Dick had much to answer for. De Groot took the three invitation letters, scribbled *reply – yes* on each one and placed them in the tray marked *Secretary*. He got up from the desk, checked the car keys were in his pocket and headed for the door. He was not the only one who was much in demand that morning.

❖ ❖ ❖ ❖ ❖ ❖ ❖

Anne spotted Zoë through the café window, approaching at high speed. The sight made her think of a guided missile homing in on its target. Donovan noticed her expression and glanced over his shoulder. Obviously the same thought occurred to him.

'Incoming!' he said quietly.

Zoë opened the door, scanned the interior and marched towards their table. She stood over them, staring down like an avenging angel.

'Did you know about this?'

Zoë folded her arms in a posture of blatant antagonism. The other customers interrupted their conversations to focus on the newcomer.

'Good morning, Zoë,' said Donovan. 'Nice to see you. Shouldn't you be supervising the dig?'

'What? Oh … Bernard marched in, saw me, had a bit of a whinge, then buggered off. I got the students started and decided to do the same.'

Anne spoke in a hushed tone. 'Zoë, why don't you take a seat? We've ordered your coffee.'

'Well … did you?' Zoë persisted, staring at Donovan.

'Did I what?'

The stare became a glare. 'I asked you a question.'

In reply, Donovan stood up, pulled a chair out and took Zoë by the arm. She stiffened and, for a brief moment, it seemed as if she would resist. But with Donovan's urging, she relented and sat down. When she spoke, her voice was hushed, but only to the extent that customers at nearby tables had to strain a little to eavesdrop.

'Now look here, I want a straight –'

'Yes, we did.' Donovan's tone was unapologetic.

'Why would Dick tell *you* about it and say nothing to *me*?'

Anne pushed Zoë's coffee towards her and was not surprised to be ignored.

'He didn't.' Donovan's expression became thoughtful. 'But it's interesting you should see it that way.'

'Now you're talking in riddles,' Zoë said, bristling. 'If Dick didn't tell you, who did?'

'Donovan worked it out,' Anne said.

'Impossible!'

'Why impossible?'

'Because even the –'

'What did Fennimore tell you,' Donovan said, 'that day when Dick came back after being absent for a few days?'

Zoë narrowed her eyes. 'Is that when he told you? He was so full of himself. Everyone could see he was bursting to talk about his … *great discovery*.'

'Anne's already told you, he didn't tell us anything. I just thought about it and put two and two together. Sorry about the cliché. Your coffee's getting cold.'

Zoë looked momentarily off balance. She seemed to notice the double espresso for the first time and raised the tiny cup to her lips. She took a sip.

'I don't know what the hell's going on here.'

'You could try answering my question,' said Donovan.

'Your question?'

'That day, Dr Fennimore took you aside and spoke to you in private. We saw your reaction and assumed he'd taken you into his confidence. So what did he tell you?'

Zoë's eyes lost focus as she thought back. 'He just said … something like … Dick would be spending some time away from the dig as he'd made a major discovery … elsewhere.'

'No details?' said Donovan.

'When I asked him what the so-called *major discovery* was, he wouldn't go into detail.' Zoë was calmer now, speaking more slowly. 'But he did say he thought it would *rock the world of archaeology to its foundations*.'

'And overshadow your Roman ships find, presumably,' Donovan said quietly.

Zoë made no response.

'Have you actually found out about it now?' said Anne.

Zoë sniffed. 'I was in the department first thing this morning. I bumped into Miles's secretary and she mentioned it. She just came out with it, no doubt assuming I'd been told as a *senior* member of the team.'

'So you haven't heard anything from Dick.'

'Not a word.'

'Dick told us you'd saved his life,' Donovan said.

Zoë looked up sharply. 'What d'you mean? How?'

'You phoned him just before the scaffolding crashed down. He had to move away to get a better signal. That's why he was clear when the accident happened. Why were you calling him?'

Zoë thought back again. 'I wanted to have it out with him. I wanted him to tell me straight what he'd found that was so important.'

'Didn't you realise that was the exact moment when the scaffolding fell? You must've heard it.'

Zoë's expression was bleak. She shook her head. 'The line went dead. I thought Dick had cut me off.'

'Did you manage to get the whole picture out of Dr Fennimore's secretary?' Anne asked.

'No,' Zoë said. 'I couldn't really question her without letting on that I was in the dark. It would be too degrading. I just made appropriate noises. All I gathered was ...' She lowered her voice. 'Dick thinks he's found King John's lost treasure in the Wash.'

'That's about it,' said Donovan.

'I don't see how he could manage that single-handed,' Zoë said.

'He seems to have struck up some sort of partnership with an archaeologist at UEA.'

'Oh? Who's that?'

Donovan hesitated before replying. Zoë drew an impatient breath.

'You may as well tell me. I'm going to find out sooner or later. And I probably know this character anyway.'

'A guy called Parfitt.'

'Oh, Gerry Parfitt ... sorry, I mean *Gerald*.' Zoë pronounced the name with exaggerated emphasis. 'Actually, Gerald's quite sound, though I wouldn't have thought marine archaeology was his thing.'

'Do you think Dick's discovery is really major, Zoë?' Anne asked.

Zoë reflected. 'I suppose it is.' She picked up her cup and looked at them over the rim. 'If we can assume it's really true …'

For Marnie and Ralph it was a near-perfect cruise out of London. The occasional cloud took the sting out of the sun, maintaining a steady warmth, tempered by the faintest breeze. The engine on *Thyrsis* was fitted with a heavy-duty silencer, and the boat cut through the water with a deep muted burbling, a far cry, Marnie thought, from the clatter of the Lister on *Sally Ann*.

That afternoon, with one hand on the tiller and the other holding the cruising guide, Ralph suggested a pub supper. He recalled a place within walking distance of Cowley Peachey Junction that had a good reputation for its bar meals. Marnie agreed, and they made plans for the rest of their day. The aim was to take the boat up beyond the turn-off for the Slough Arm after eating, tie up for the night and tackle the first lock the following morning.

Once again Marnie thought of her first voyage on *Sally Ann* a few years earlier, when she was learning about boating. Perched on the roof by the hatch, she looked back at Ralph whose confident steering made everything look easy. She smiled inwardly at the memory of the many errors she had made in her apprenticeship on the water.

That journey had led her to a new life, a new direction in her career and several new relationships. Ralph was one of the most important of those. Now, on this trip, Marnie was glad she had put her solo days behind her. She was happy with Ralph, enjoying their easy-going manner of running the boat. It was a reflection of their life together as a whole. She hoped Anne and Donovan were equally enjoying being together … for the time that remained to them.

A feeling of anxiety engulfed Marnie as she remembered the investigation that was hanging over Donovan.

She was brought back to the present by Ralph pointing ahead, stretching up to his full height from leaning on the tiller. Marnie swivelled round. At first she could not see what had attracted his attention. Then she spotted it, the unmistakable shape of Donovan's boat. *XO2* lay at its mooring a hundred yards or so ahead, looking sinister in its dark grey paintwork.

Marnie turned and nodded at Ralph. '*Exodos*,' she said.

But Ralph was looking further ahead and pointing away from the canal. This time Marnie immediately saw what he intended. Parked on the road with a clear view of the waterway stood another unmistakable shape: its bodywork painted in white with yellow and blue chequers, surmounted by Perspex blue lights. The patrol car was clearly lying in wait, and Marnie was offering no prizes for guessing who its prey was likely to be.

17
New Scotland Yard

Next day, Anne experienced a new and unexpected sensation. She loved Marnie's flat. It was spacious, comfortable, beautifully furnished and equipped. But for the first time, Anne felt something akin to homesickness for Glebe Farm, her attic room and Knightly St John. No doubt it would have been different if Donovan had stayed with her, but he had returned to *XO2* after an early supper the previous evening. They were both keen not to antagonise the police.

Arriving back at the mooring, he had phoned to let her know he was still at liberty. Seeing the police car parked within view, he had left the porthole curtains open and turned on all the lights in the boat. Anne had laughed when Donovan announced he had commissioned a neon sign to put on the roof: *AT HOME WITH NOTHING TO HIDE*. But it had been half-hearted laughter, and Anne had felt a heavy weight in the pit of her stomach. *For how much longer would Donovan be free?* she wondered. When they were together she could not bring herself to raise the subject of the police investigation, and Donovan only hinted obliquely at the situation. It was as if they were both trying to put off the evil moment.

Her other call that evening had been from Marnie. She had been phoned by Philip Everett asking if she could take part in a site meeting with the client on Thursday morning. There was no specific request for interior design to be on the agenda, but the subject could be raised. Marnie explained where she was and offered to come back into town, but Philip had insisted that she continue on her journey.

'I can go,' Anne had volunteered. 'I'm here and I have my file with me. No probs.'

Marnie needed little persuasion. Anne could maintain a watching brief, and they went over the main aspects of the project in preparation.

Before ending the call, Anne had told Marnie about the conversation in the café with Zoë, and Marnie assured her they would soon be leaving London to return to the *real world* of their life in the country. The thought had consoled Anne when she went to bed that night, alone.

Looking out of the window at the riverscape below, Anne was determined to shake off her negative mood. She saw that the sky was overcast with a thin layer of clouds and read that as a sign of fair weather to come. Mentally changing her name to *Pollyanna*, she laid out her most cheerful summer clothes on the bed before taking a shower: a primrose yellow top, stone-coloured linen trousers and a matching linen jacket to give a note of formality for the meeting. On the floor she placed her tan deck shoes to complete the ensemble.

Turning her thin body in the hot turbojets of the shower, and permitting herself to use a small amount of Marnie's best *Chanel gel douche*, she thought of counting her blessings. Before she had made one complete turn she rejected the idea. *Let's not overdo the Pollyanna bit!*

Fragrant and refreshed, Anne picked up her shoulder bag, locked the flat and set off on the familiar route to Horselydown. The closer she drew to the compound, the firmer her state of mind grew. She realised she was tired of coping with the egos and tensions of the archaeologists. Her priorities were to give her best efforts to Marnie and the design project and to give her full support to Donovan for as long as she could.

With a spring in her step and a rod of tempered steel in her backbone, Anne said goodbye to Pollyanna, flashed her pass at the security guard and walked purposefully towards the staff hut. Before she reached it, a whistle pierced the air. She turned to see Donovan coming through the entrance gate. He waved and smiled as if he had not a care in the world. Anne smiled back as she waited for him to join her, and the sun began sweeping the clouds aside.

Good news and bad news were waiting for WDC Cathy Lamb when she arrived at divisional HQ that morning. The good news was there had been no further burglaries in the night; the bad news was there had been no results from ballistics in London.

She grabbed DS Marriner as soon as he came into the office.

'Any word from the Met, sarge?'

'You're keen, Cathy!'

'It's our most important case,' she protested, adding, '… after the burglaries, of course.'

'Wrong,' said Marriner. 'It's number three. A girl's been reported missing in the Hanford area. Grab your notepad. We've got work to do.'

Marriner asked Lamb to drive, and they set off at a fast pace, knowing it could be a grim enquiry. The village of Hanford was on the Grand Union a few miles north of Knightly St John, and inevitably the question would arise as to whether the girl had ended up in the canal. Lamb knew she had to give her full attention to the case in hand, but she could not help thinking of the residents of Glebe Farm and their friend in London who was top of her list of priorities.

For Marnie, that day came close to perfection. They had locked through at Cowley straight after breakfast, taking their second mugs of coffee with them to drink on deck as they cruised to the next lock at Uxbridge.

Ralph wanted to use the bathroom, so Marnie found herself alone at the tiller watching the suburbs slip by, thinking back to that first solo voyage on *Sally Ann*. Not quite solo, she reflected. She had in fact had one companion, a stowaway. A sturdy black cat had come aboard at Kensal Green and despite all Marnie's efforts to put her ashore, she had insisted on remaining a member of the crew. The cat eventually became *Dolly* and was even now in charge at Glebe Farm.

Although it was little after seven o'clock, Marnie had to reach into the cabin to take her sunhat from its hook by the control panel. She hitched herself up onto the stern rail and scanned the horizon in all directions. Then she thought of Donovan, and a wave of anxiety washed over her. Somewhere not far away was the modern campus of Brunel University where he was laying the foundations for the future. These were very much his home waters. But for how much longer, Marnie wondered. And what future?

No-one knew where the rumours began, but people were starting to talk. While Anne was checking with the site agent where the team meeting would be held, Donovan wandered across to the students to find out what was on their programme for the day. As before, they were uncertain, and this was causing them no little dissatisfaction. Understandably, they were gaining the impression that the dig lacked direction on account of events taking place elsewhere.

Neither of the two site directors had shown up so far that morning, despite the promises given the previous day by Professor de Groot. When one girl openly wondered if Dick Blackwood's absence owed more to the fatal accident of Dr Fennimore than to some other project, there was a general rumbling of assent from the group as a whole.

'What are you saying?' Donovan asked.

The student replied, 'Well, we think it's a bit odd that Dick has absented himself since Dr Fennimore was killed …'

'… and he was the only person down there at the time …' another student joined in.

'… the only witness to the accident,' yet another said.

'… if it was an accident,' a fourth added.

'But the inspectors have established that,' Donovan said.

The first girl stepped forward. 'But it was all a bit hasty, wasn't it? They were only down there for a day when they declared it an industrial accident. Next thing, the builders are called in and everything gets rebuilt.'

'You seem to be suggesting that the accident was something else and that the inspectors and contractors conspired in some sort of cover-up.' Donovan was trying to point out how absurd the rumours were, but even as he spoke he realised he was equally trying to convince himself. 'Why would they do that?'

'That's what I said.' It was another of the young women. 'It's all too improbable.'

'Yeah, but Dick can do no wrong where you're concerned –'

'That's not fair!'

'But it's true.'

Donovan raised a hand. 'I think you'll find the inspectors had to produce a rapid report because the site was unstable. The scaffolding was being reinforced when part of it collapsed. They had to rebuild it urgently before any more damage was done.'

'So it's just a coincidence that Dick's gone missing, is it?'

'Why not?' Donovan said. 'He's definitely involved with a major project outside London.'

'So we're told, but that's all gone very quiet, hasn't it?'

Some of the group were looking over Donovan's shoulder, and he turned to find Anne coming up behind him. The students looked at her expectantly.

'Any news?' one of them asked.

'Only that I've got a meeting with the contractors and client shortly.'

'*You* have?' The tone was puzzled. 'Why you?'

Anne adjusted the leather document folder conspicuously under her arm. 'Because I'm a member of the design team …' She spoke in a clear, confident voice. '… interior design consultant.'

The student indicated Donovan while still addressing Anne. 'You're not …'

Donovan said, 'No. Anne's not my assistant. She's just been helping me as a friend.'

Once again, the students shifted their focus. This time, Donovan and Anne saw Zoë Tipton entering the compound. Seeing the gathering of students, Zoë veered in their direction, quickening her pace, searching the group with her eyes as she drew nearer.

'Right,' she said decisively. 'Siân, Andy … I want you to take the group down to the lower level. Everyone is to return to their positions from yesterday and carry on. I'll join you in a couple of minutes. Any questions? Good. Let's get going.' As the students began moving off, Zoë turned to Donovan and Anne. 'I'll be back directly.'

Before either of them could react, she was gone. Anne drew breath but said nothing.

Donovan spoke quietly. 'She knows something.'

'Then why didn't she say anything?' Anne said.

'Zoë obviously believes in the old adage: *never apologise; never explain.* To do so in her view would be a sign of weakness.'

'On the other hand, it could be politeness,' Anne said, primly.

True to her word, Zoë reappeared a few moments later, decked out in the regulation safety gear.

'There you are,' she said briskly. 'Okay, I want to –'

'Good morning, Zoë,' said Donovan.

'What? Oh, yes. Good morning.' Zoë made to walk off. 'Now –'

'We were wondering where you'd been.'

Donovan remained immobile. Anne looked at her watch.

Zoë hesitated as if searching for a suitable answer. The implied question had clearly taken her by surprise.

'I wasn't aware that I had to explain myself.'

'Fine.' Donovan gave the impression he was in no hurry to move. 'Your students have been waiting for quite a while, but of course, that's not really my business.'

Zoë stared back. There was fire in her eyes.

House-to-house enquiries were already in progress when Marriner and Lamb arrived in Hanford. The missing girl's mother had reported her absence at breakfast time as soon as she realised her daughter had not come home the previous night. After a few quick calls to the girl's friends, she had phoned the police in near hysterics. A WPC in uniform was sitting with her when the detectives entered the house.

Normally, the police waited forty-eight hours before taking action on a case of this sort, but the authority had decided to step up a gear following a number of incidents earlier in the year when girls had been targeted by a sex offender. The media had at that time launched a major campaign, criticising the force for inactivity. This was the first time a girl had actually failed to reach home after a night out with friends, and the Chief Constable had issued instructions to take all necessary steps as a matter of urgency.

Search parties were fanning out across the fields around the village, and a television news crew was filming the action from a vantage point on raised ground. Another had set itself up on a bridge over the canal nearby, keeping watch over the teams roaming the towpath.

When Marriner and Lamb completed their interview with the mother, they left the house to review progress with the search.

'It's at times like this, you wish Marnie Walker was around,' Cathy Lamb said.

Marriner looked surprised. 'How's that?'

'Whatever you think of her, sarge, you know she'd be out here like a shot, helping us on that boat of hers. So would her professor.'

They arrived at the canal to find that one enterprising constable had already recruited a boat-owner to assist the operation. Navigating at slow walking pace in mid-channel, the narrowboat carried two officers who scoured the water on the opposite side of the canal from the towpath. Each of them carried a bargepole, hunting in the reeds and bushes.

Fifty miles to the south, Marnie and Ralph were cruising along, oblivious to the intense activity taking place near home, grateful for the regular succession of locks that punctuated their journey, making them concentrate on running the boat. In Rickmansworth they stopped off at a canalside supermarket to take on stores. Back on *Thyrsis*, Marnie changed into her shorts before they set off on the next stage of the voyage.

After casting off, Ralph joined Marnie briefly on the stern deck before tackling Batchworth Lock. He looked her up and down.

'You know, Marnie, that could be described as a hazard to shipping.'

Marnie pretended not to understand. 'Oh, I think there's plenty of room between the moorings and the lock. No-one's going to –'

'You know perfectly well what I mean.'

In reply, Marnie flashed him the heavy eyelids.

'And that Marlene Dietrich look could make it even more hazardous.'

Marnie smiled. 'Do I take it there's a compliment in there somewhere?'

'Not so's you'd notice.' Ralph draped an arm round Marnie's shoulders. 'Isn't this wonderful?'

'Yes.' Marnie took a deep breath. 'I love shopping at Tesco's ... the variety ... the special offers ...'

Ralph made a growling sound. Marnie reached forward to reduce speed at the approach to the lock and steered closer to the bank. Before Ralph stepped ashore, he patted her bottom.

'Ooh! Unhand me, sir.' She laughed. 'I wonder what your students would think if they could see you now.'

'They'd be jealous as hell.'

Marnie's expression became thoughtful. 'I hope Anne's getting on all right. I rather landed her in it with that site meeting.' She checked her watch. 'It's probably starting about now.'

'She'll be fine,' Ralph said. 'She's only got to maintain a watching brief.'

Marnie brought the boat to a halt by the bank. 'Even so, I'll make sure my mobile's switched on, just in case she runs into something unexpected.'

Zoë Tipton took Anne and Donovan to one side near the ladder leading down into the excavations. They could see she was seething with pent-up anger, or perhaps frustration.

'Look, it's difficult. There are times when you've got to prioritise. Needs must, and all that. And strictly speaking, I'm not supposed to talk about what's happened.'

'Even though Donovan worked it out anyway?' Anne said.

Zoë tossed her head. 'It's *complicated.*'

'Then don't tell us,' said Donovan. 'But if you don't mind me saying so, this whole excavation is going down the tubes because neither you nor Dick seems interested in running it.'

Zoë fixed him with a look that said, *you're just a student doing a filming project; you have no right to question my judgment.*

'That's not true,' she protested.

Donovan stared back with a look that said, *we both know my filming suits your personal agenda.*

He shrugged. 'You say you've made a find of national importance here, then you leave the students kicking their heels while you're off pursuing some other agenda.'

Zoë sighed. 'Okay, okay …'

Anne looked at her watch. 'Talking of agendas, you've got three minutes.'

Zoë frowned. 'What do you mean?'

'My meeting starts in just over five minutes.'

'Meeting? *You've* got a meeting?'

Anne nodded. 'With the client and all the contractors.'

'Why you?' Zoë seemed incredulous.

'You're forgetting, my firm is part of the design team. I'm representing them today.'

'But I thought you were just –'

'Two minutes,' Anne said in an even tone.

'But hang on,' Zoë began. 'I need you for the filming.' She turned to Donovan. 'What are we going to do about the sound recording?'

'We'll manage. I'll rig you up and keep an eye on it as we go along.'

'This is all very unsatisfactory.' Zoë looked pleadingly at Anne. 'Just when we'd got everything going so well …'

Anne could feel that Zoë was trying to make her seem unreasonable.

'Look, Zoë, this contract is as important to me – to all of us involved – as your Roman ships or Dick's lost treasure are to archaeology. This is one of the most innovative projects in the whole of Europe … maybe the world.'

'But surely someone else can deal with the meeting?'

Anne tucked her folder under her arm and turned to leave. 'There's a golden rule in Walker and Co. Never be late for a meeting, *especially* if you're a woman.'

'I thought you'd agreed to work with me ... and Donovan.'

'Yes, but like you, I sometimes have to prioritise when the need arises. Sorry, Zoë. Your time is up.'

The manhunt was over. DS Marriner took the call on his mobile as he was walking along the towpath. It was a brief message and after disconnecting, he waved to Cathy Lamb who was checking progress with a search party fifty yards up the canal. She arrived hot-foot, half walking, half jogging, her face a picture of concern.

'They've found her, sarge? Was she ... murdered?'

'The answers to your questions, Cathy, are yes and not yet, in that order.'

Lamb looked bewildered. 'I don't get it.'

'She has been found, or rather she's turned up.'

'She's alive?'

'For the moment,' said Marriner, po-faced.

'What does that mean?'

'It means, when she's recovered from her hangover, her mother has threatened to kill her.'

'Thank goodness.' Lamb let the relief wash over her.

'Cathy, pay attention.' Marriner spoke slowly. 'Call off the search.'

'Right, sarge.' She turned to go back to the search party. 'What about you?'

'I'm going up to the house. They may need assistance.'

Lamb grinned. 'To prevent the mother from killing her?'

'No, to help her do it. Get moving, Cathy.'

To her credit, Zoë Tipton offered to carry the sound equipment down to the lower level of the dig. She shouldered a backpack and walked in silence with Donovan, across the compound. At the top of the first ladder, she turned to face him.

'You were right to chastise me,' she said quietly.

'Past history,' said Donovan. 'We have work to do now. I've completed the editing of what we've done so far and –'

'Listen,' Zoë interrupted, placing a hand on his arm. 'I went in to LBU first thing to see if there was any news about Dick.'

She paused. Donovan waited. Zoë seemed to be wrestling with an internal dilemma.

'What do you know about Gerry Parfitt?' she asked, looking away.

'That he prefers to be called *Gerald*, for a start.'

Zoë screwed up her face. 'Yes, of course, he does. So what do you know about him?'

'Only that he's been working with Dick on the King John project. He has a boat up on the north Norfolk coast, so he's been able to help Dick in his search. That's about it.'

Another silence from Zoë. This time, Donovan spoke first.

'Look, Zoë, if there's something you don't think I should know, don't tell me. I won't be offended. I respect academic confidentiality. We can just get on with our own work and –'

'I don't believe Dick's made this so-called *major discovery*.' It came out in a rush. Zoë looked Donovan in the eye. 'There. I've said it.'

'Okay …' Donovan's brain raced through the implications. 'You've obviously given this a lot of thought.'

'Yes.'

'And you've come to the conclusion that Dick has made up the story? Why would he do that when it would all come out and do untold damage to his reputation?'

'That's the problem,' said Zoë. 'I can't fathom it out.'

'Then why the disbelief?'

'Well … for starters, you think Dick needed Gerald Parfitt because of his sailing expertise.'

'Correct.'

'But that isn't the case. Dick's an expert yachtsman.'

'That's not the impression I had.'

'Donovan, sailing is one of Dick's passions. He has a dinghy that he uses for racing on a lake somewhere. He used to own a small yacht but had to sell it to help finance the research course for his doctorate.'

'You're sure about that?'

Zoë nodded. 'A colleague at UEA told me that Gerald only bought his boat last year. My guess is that it was probably Dick who was teaching him about sailing.'

'I don't see what –'

'Dick has been using the boat by himself while Gerald's been off on some project or other.'

Donovan mulled this over. 'You're suggesting that Dick sailed solo, so we only have his word for it that he discovered the treasure?'

'Exactly. No corroboration.'

'Then what about the three pieces he brought up from the bottom?'

'They could have come from anywhere.'

'Surely not. Who keeps medieval objects like that lying around?'

'Universities and museums have collections of medieval artefacts,' Zoë said.

'But surely, they're catalogued or kept in secure storage,' Donovan protested.

Zoë raised both palms. 'It's not unknown for items to go missing, and a researcher would be in a position of trust.'

'So you think Dick stole them, or what?'

Zoë shrugged. 'What else would explain things?'

Donovan mulled over the possibilities in silence.

'But I come back to my question,' Zoë continued. 'What proof exists that Dick actually made his big discovery?'

'And I come back to mine,' said Donovan. 'What would be the point of lying? His deception would soon be uncovered, and he'd be disgraced. End of academic career.'

'Not necessarily. The fact that the treasure has lain undiscovered for the best part of a millennium would be on his side. He could simply claim that what he allegedly found was genuine, but that the underwater conditions were so unstable that finding more evidence was proving immensely difficult.'

Zoë left Donovan space to think over her hypothesis.

'So he'd have the kudos of finding the treasure ...' Donovan began, 'at least part of it, and nobody could deny that he'd made a major breakthrough because of the artefacts apparently recovered from the sea-bed.'

'You've got it.'

Donovan shook his head. 'But he could still be subject to challenge from his peer group. Knowing the academic world, that would be virtually inevitable.'

'Exactly.'

Zoë's reply took Donovan by surprise.

'You mean that's why he's gone missing?'

Zoë sighed. 'Come on, Donovan! You're supposed to be the one who works things out.'

Donovan closed his eyes, deep in thought. Eventually he stared at Zoë.

'Dr Fennimore?' he said, so quietly he was barely audible.

Zoë nodded. She looked deadly serious.

For once, DS Marriner opted to drive back to the station. Lamb sensed that he had a deal of pent-up energy for which he needed an outlet. Driving gave him something to occupy his mind and his hands.

Although everyone was hugely relieved that the missing teenager had turned up safe and well, no one could deny that a sense of anti-climax hovered over everyone who had taken part in the abortive search. She had simply walked into the kitchen while her mother was filling the kettle. The WPC had suggested that a cup of tea would do them good.

The girl looked the worse for wear and had broken down in tears when her mother embraced her, just as tearfully. It was as much as the WPC could do not to join them, struggling to keep her own emotions under control.

The prodigal daughter had asked to be allowed to go and lie down, accepting her mother's offer of painkillers. While the WPC phoned Marriner with the news, the mother had accompanied the girl upstairs. When she returned, a transformation had taken place; annoyance was starting to supplant elation.

In her emotional state, the girl had confessed between sobs that she had spent the night with a boy. It was the old, old story. They had been at a party; she had had too much to drink; the boy had taken advantage of her. His parents were away and, as the girl was in no fit state to go home, she had fallen into a drink-induced sleep and woken with a mighty hangover and a burden of guilt and regret.

At least no-one in the force could accuse Marriner of acting inappropriately. He had followed instructions to the letter and carried out orders by the book. The morning's activities had distracted Lamb from all other concerns, and it therefore came as a surprise on entering the station when the duty officer announced that Marriner had a message to phone DS Rigby of the Met.

Lamb had hovered behind Marriner while he rang New Scotland Yard. The conversation was brief and typically for Marriner, monosyllabic. He eventually thanked Rigby and hung up.

'Well, sarge?' Lamb tried to contain her impatience.

'Not quite what I expected, Cathy.'

Now fully occupied, the students seemed happy enough to be hands-on in the excavation. From time to time Zoë interacted with one or other of them, while Donovan filmed their conferring. In Anne's absence the sound recording was more complicated, but Donovan set up the camera on its stand, freeing him to watch over the dials on the sound equipment. Overall, he was reasonably pleased with the results. Zoë performed like a professional, and the students played their part.

Donovan was filming a scene with Zoë talking to two students in the foreground, while further back another was using flash photography on the remains, when he became aware of someone standing close behind him. He turned to find a builder watching him. Signalling to the man not to speak, Donovan crept towards the camera and switched it off.

'D'you want Dr Tipton?' Donovan asked.

'Donovan Smith?' the builder said without preamble.

'That's me.'

'You're wanted up top ... now.'

Donovan excused himself to Zoë and followed the man up the ladders. When they stepped off at surface level, the builder pointed to the staff hut.

'You're sure it's me they want?' Donovan said.

'That's the name the officer gave me.'

'Officer?'

The builder nodded. 'Copper.' He grinned. 'Hope you 'aven't been a naughty boy.'

The builder set off across the compound, leaving Donovan standing alone. He was about to move when he saw people exiting another of the huts, among them Anne. Her meeting had come to an end and, catching sight of him, she waved and smiled as she headed in his direction. By the time she reached him, the smile had faded.

'Something up?' she asked. 'You look serious.'

'I have ... a visitor,' Donovan said, '... a policeman.'

'Here?' Anne knew it was a silly question.

'Waiting for me in the staff hut.'

Anne took hold of his arm. 'I'll come with you.'

'No.'

'But I want to.'

Donovan glanced briefly away. 'Not a good idea ... for two reasons.'

Anne attempted a smile. 'You've always got two reasons.'

Donovan smiled back. 'At least. But I mean it. The first is that if there's trouble, I don't want you to be implicated.'

Anne squeezed his arm. 'I already –'

'No listen. It's important. As far as the police are concerned, my connection with you and the others is that Ralph and my father were colleagues.'

'But we're more than –'

'Of course, but they don't know that. Anne, this is about the shooting of Garth Brandon. No-one's going to try to connect Ralph with that.'

'So I'm under suspicion as some kind of gangster's Moll?'

Donovan laughed. 'Absolutely.' He looked at the thin, waif-like girl with the closely-cut blond hair and innocent blue eyes. 'You're type-cast for the role.' He reached forward and kissed her lightly. 'I've gotta go.'

Anne grabbed his arm. 'Donovan, I wish I could do something – *anything* – to help.'

'You can. Listen, if I'm … detained, get my filming equipment and take it to the flat. Keep it safe for me.'

'Sure.' She released his arm. 'You said there were two reasons?'

Donovan looked over towards the site entrance gate.

'There's the second.'

Anne turned to see Dick Blackwood talking to the security guard. They appeared to be deep in conversation. When she turned back to Donovan, he was striding towards the staff hut.

The constable was sitting at the table in the otherwise empty staff hut when Donovan knocked and went in. Someone had given him a cup of tea, and he was adding sugar to it from a tin. He looked about the same age as Donovan, with cropped hair that exaggerated the size of his ears. His distinctive helmet was resting on a chair beside him.

'Good morning,' Donovan said, taking out a small plastic card holder from his rear pocket and presenting it to the officer. 'I believe you want to see me.'

The policeman took the card. 'What's this?'

'My ID.'

The officer read it. 'Is this German?'

Donovan nodded. The PC looked up at him.

'Smith?' There was doubt in his tone.

'Long story,' said Donovan. 'What can I do for you?'

The officer handed back the card. 'You're to present yourself at New Scotland Yard.'

He drank from the plastic cup. Donovan looked on impassively. He knew what was coming next.

Dick saw Anne standing alone as he crossed the compound. He acknowledged her but made no attempt to approach or speak to her. When he was a few yards from the staff hut he was surprised when the door opened and a police officer came out ahead of Donovan. Dick stopped in his tracks.

Anne noticed that Donovan was no longer wearing his safety gear. She quickly moved to stand beside Dick. Mindful of Donovan's wishes, she made no direct contact, and Donovan did not even glance at her as he walked by.

'Morning, Dick,' he said in passing.

'Can we have a word some time?' Dick asked.

'Might be difficult.' Donovan indicated the constable. 'Later, perhaps.'

Still watching Donovan and the PC as they went out through the gate, Dick turned to Anne. 'Any idea what's going on?'

Anne could have told him she thought Donovan was being taken to the police station to be charged. Instead she said simply, 'Who knows?'

'Has something happened while I've been away?'

'You tell me, Dick.'

Dick shook his head slowly. 'Very odd. Is Zoë about, d'you know?'

'She's down at the lower level with the students. Everyone's been working on the Roman ships for a while now'

'I'd better get togged up, then,' said Dick.

'Me too.'

Dick looked at Anne and realised she was not wearing safety clothing. 'Have you just arrived?'

'No. I had a site meeting. You'd better get changed. We can talk later.'

Dick looked wary. 'What about?'

'About your absence, perhaps.'

'Sorry, Anne, no offence, but I don't see what that has to do with you.'

'You will when I tell you that Zoë is having doubts about your discovery.'

Dick's mouth gaped open. 'She what?'

'She was making disparaging noises about it yesterday.'

'What did she say?'

'She told us she had doubts, suspicions even, about what you said you'd found.'

'The *bitch*!' Dick glared at Anne. 'Who was there when she said it?'

'Just Donovan and me.'

'De Groot?' Anne shook her head. 'The students?'

'No. I told you. No-one else.'

'I'll bloody …' He clenched his fists at his side. 'That's typical of her.'

Anne stood her ground. 'Where have you been these past days, Dick?'

But she received no reply. Dick stormed off towards the site entrance and was through the gate and gone, leaving Anne to wonder once again what was going on. And what had happened to Donovan?

Marnie was starting to feel peckish, and Ralph readily agreed when she suggested they find somewhere suitable to stop for a bite in Cassiobury Park. Slowing to pass moored craft, she picked up the cruising guide to check the area ahead of them. A sudden flash of movement caused her to look up. Fifty yards off, a tube train was dashing over a functional modern bridge. At that range Marnie could just see the heads of passengers turning to look down at the waterway. For her, the Metropolitan Line of the Underground was the first sign of leaving

London behind. The second would be coming up later in the afternoon when they passed beneath the elevated section of the M25, London's Orbital Motorway.

Ten minutes later in a wooded parkland setting Marnie steered for the bank, and Ralph hopped ashore to attach the mooring ropes. When Marnie turned off the engine, she became aware that another was running, humming quietly elsewhere in the boat. Moments after Ralph climbed aboard at the cratch, the second motor cut out. Ralph had been running the generator to charge their mobile phones.

They were in the galley considering the major policy decision of what to eat for lunch when Marnie's mobile began chirping. Telling Ralph that her vote was in favour of a ham and salad sandwich, she went out on deck and took the call.

'Hi, Marnie, it's Anne.'

Something in the tone of Anne's voice put Marnie on her guard.

'Everything okay?'

'I've been trying to ring you, but I guessed you had the mobile on charge.'

'A brilliant deduction, Holmes. How are things? How did the meeting go?'

'Nothing to report, really. Just routine. We seem to be more or less on schedule at the moment. Philip wants to talk to you about designs, but he said it could wait till after the weekend.'

'Good. Anything else?' There was silence on the line. 'Anne?'

'A policeman came and took Donovan away.'

The baldness of the statement rocked Marnie's world. 'Was he arrested?'

'I don't know. They just went off together.'

'Was Donovan ... in handcuffs?'

'No.'

'How did he seem? Did he look worried?'

'You know Donovan, Marnie. He never gives anything away.'

'Did he say anything?'

'Not to me. He's trying to keep a distance from me as far as the police are concerned. He just said hallo to Dick and that he might see him some time.'

'Dick's back?' Another surprise.

'He looked in for a few minutes.' There was a pause. 'Marnie I ... I think I may have said something stupid.'

'Go on.'

'I, er ... told Dick that Zoë had said she wasn't convinced about his big discovery.'

'How did he take that?'

'Guess.'

'Right. And the outcome?'

'He was really angry. Oh, Marnie, I wish I'd kept my big mouth shut.'

'Where is he now, and where are you?'

'I'm in the flat. I came back for lunch. Dick went off in a state. I don't know where he's gone.'

'Okay. I think I'd better come back into town.'

'There's really no need, Marnie. I don't think there's anything you can do here.'

'I thought you could maybe use some moral support.'

'I'm fine, really. Sorry about this, Marnie. I think I've messed up.'

'Don't worry about it. Listen, Anne, you get some lunch and I'll give you a ring this evening.'

'Okay, but I think I've lost my appetite.'

Marnie was back in the galley just as Ralph placed her sandwich on a plate. As *pièce de résistance* he decorated it with a sprig of parsley. It was York ham, fresh and tender, on wholemeal bread, with lettuce and tomato, one of Marnie's favourites. As she looked at it, Ralph sensed the change in her mood, and she realised that she too had lost her appetite.

Donovan had been left sitting alone in a waiting room in New Scotland Yard for almost an hour. He suspected it was a form of intimidation, giving him time to fret about what was going to happen to him. If so, it seemed a very British way of applying pressure, and one which would not cause him any problems. Certain that he was being observed by hidden cameras, he sat quietly with both hands in his lap and contemplated the situation.

He knew it was only a matter of time before the police found out about his London house. There were occasions, he thought, when having the surname Smith was a positive advantage. Although the family home had been bequeathed to him by his parents, he had never notified the local authority that the occupier was now N D Smith, and the bills for council tax and utilities continued to be addressed to Dr W D Smith.

In normal circumstances it would not have troubled him that the police might be interested in his private affairs. They had no reason to disturb his privacy. But if for any reason they ever had grounds to search the house, it could be embarrassing having to explain why he possessed an officer's uniform from Hitler's SS. The fact that his late father collected memorabilia from the Third Reich would be difficult to prove, especially when it became clear that the uniform was an almost perfect fit for Donovan himself. *Try explaining that coincidence*, he thought.

Worse still, he had been wearing that uniform on the day when Garth

Brandon was gunned down in Northampton, and he knew there must have been CCTV footage from traffic cameras showing him cycling away from the scene.

Keep it simple and as close to the truth as possible, he told himself. The Luger, the German Great War medals, the Leica cameras, the books, even Hitler's *Mein Kampf*, had all been left by members of his family. Why did he keep them on his boat? He had explained that artefacts from the Nazi era were banned in Germany, and they had simply found their way to him when he had cleared out his late father's rooms at Oxford. So far no-one had worked out that at the time of his death Bill Donovan Smith was lecturing in London and Reading, with a house in west London convenient for commuting in both directions.

Donovan had told the police he had not had the heart to throw away any of his father's possessions when he was a boy. They had been stored in a trunk, impossible to take back to Germany. What else was he to do with them?

Eventually a uniformed sergeant came into the room, handed back the Luger with the firearms certificate and gave Donovan a form to sign for them.

'I'm free to go now?'

'Yes.'

Donovan pocketed the certificate and looked down at the pistol lying on the table, wrapped in its yellow duster. The officer read his thoughts.

'Not easy to carry it around like that. I might be able to get you a carrier bag.'

'Thank you.'

'You've had the gun a long time?'

'It's been in the family since 1945 ... a memento from the war.'

'You've kept it in good condition.'

'My father did before me, and I look after my things.'

'And you clean it regularly?'

Donovan shook his head. 'I never even look at it from one year to the next. I just keep it wrapped up in its box.'

'So it hasn't been fired for a long time?'

Donovan picked it up. 'Not since the war, I imagine.'

'If you'd like to wait here, I'll see if I can find a bag.'

The officer returned a minute later with a carrier from *Prêt à Manger*. 'Best I could do.'

'It's great, thanks.'

Donovan extended a hand, which the officer shook before escorting him out.

Anne stayed in the flat that evening and had two phone calls. The first was from Donovan. He only wanted to say that he was well and back on *XO2*. The police had treated him in a civil manner and told him he was now free to go where he wished.

'I'm thinking I might go home in a while …' he said, casually, '… take a break, you know.'

'Home?'

'Yes, I haven't been back to Germany for a while. It'd be good to see the family again.'

Why so stilted? 'That would be nice,' Anne agreed.

'Would it be okay for me to come back to the site tomorrow? I might have some more filming to do.'

It's like talking to a stranger. 'Of course. You've got your security pass.'

'Yes. Good night, then.'

'Bye.'

Anne had barely disconnected when the landline phone began ringing. It was Marnie.

'Hi. I just tried your mobile, but I got a strange message that your number wasn't recognised. Is it not working?'

'Could you have misdialled, Marnie?'

'You're on the speed-dial.'

Anne thought of the artificial conversation with Donovan, the impersonal way he had spoken to her, as if she was just a colleague, the reference to Germany as *home*, rather than his house in Uxbridge. Donovan, who never did anything without good cause, had been laying a smokescreen. There could be only one reason for that.

'Oh, I was on the phone,' said Anne. 'It was just one of the team saying he'd be back tomorrow … Donovan Smith, you know.'

A pause. 'Oh, yes. Yes. I'm thinking of looking in, too. Will Philip be around?'

'I think so.'

'Then I'll see you in the morning.'

After the call ended, Marnie sat wondering what was going on. Anne's warning signal – using both Donovan's names as if he was an outsider – had put her on her guard. Did she think the conversation might be bugged? Absurd idea!

Or was it?

18
A Sin of Omission

On Friday morning Donovan rang the local British Waterways officer to explain that he had to return home to Germany and would be gone for perhaps a couple of weeks. They had a good rapport, mainly because Donovan had always made a point of consulting the lengthsman on his movements of the boat. The BW officer knew that Donovan was studying in Uxbridge and was as flexible as he could be about mooring arrangements.

It was agreed that Donovan could leave *XO2* in her present location, which was in any case not a restricted mooring, and the lengthsman offered to keep an eye on the boat whenever he passed that way. Donovan left his e-mail address with him, plus the departmental phone number at the university.

Donovan lifted the bike down from the roof and brought it inside, checked that the mooring ropes were well secured and set off, carrying a black overnight bag and a rucksack. As he made his way to the tube station, he inconspicuously scanned parked vehicles, but saw no-one watching his movements. Perhaps the police were being true to their word and were no longer interested in him as a suspect in the Garth Brandon case. Perhaps, but he was taking no chances.

Marnie travelled into town from Watford on the Metropolitan line with the early morning commuters. Like most people on board she looked down at the canal as the train rumbled over the bridge by Cassio Wharf. She craned her neck to see if *Thyrsis* was visible, but they had tied up for the night in a secluded section of Cassiobury Park, where the waterway disappeared into an avenue of mature trees.

The carriage began filling up as the train passed through London's outer suburbs, and Marnie rested her head against the window and closed her eyes, dozing like her fellow travellers. She suspected that her reverie was very different from theirs. Her rambling thoughts ranged over a sudden death among ancient Roman vessels in the depths of a building site, the presumed discovery of a king's lost treasure, the investigation by the police of a friend on suspicion of murder. It was a normal day in the life of Walker and Co.

Marnie had to change trains at Baker Street, struggling through the throng at the busy intersection. As she battled her way along the corridors, up and down the crowded staircases and on the platforms with their tiles depicting the silhouetted head of Sherlock Holmes, she reminded herself that this was one of the reasons she had left London for a more tranquil existence out in the country.

At least, that had been the theory.

Donovan stayed on the tube for five stops before getting off at Ruislip. Minutes after exiting the station he was in a taxi heading back towards Uxbridge. Fairly certain that he was not being followed, he nonetheless asked the driver to drop him a short distance from home and set off to walk the last hundred yards once the cab was out of sight.

Inside the house, he dashed up to his bedroom, took the SS uniform from the wardrobe and folded it carefully into the overnight bag after removing the cushions he had stuffed in to make it look full. Gathering up the post and setting the intruder alarm, Donovan quickly left and made for the main road. Luck was with him, and he caught a taxi almost at once.

The fastest way to cross London is by tube, and Donovan rejoined the Metropolitan Line at Ruislip. Rattling through the tunnels, he turned his thoughts to disposal of the SS uniform. There was no question now of keeping it or of simply dumping it in the dustbin. Forensic examination would undoubtedly reveal traces of his DNA, and he would be hard put to explain that coincidence and how he had overlooked mentioning the uniform to the police.

The more he thought about it, the more he realised there was one perfect solution.

It was like a moment from a Hollywood romance. Marnie and Donovan emerged from the depths of the tube station at Tower Hill, and their eyes met across a crowded concourse. Unlike the Hollywood movie, Donovan gave Marnie only a restrained greeting, with not so much as a handshake.

'Shall we at least walk over the bridge together?' Marnie said.

Donovan shook his head. 'Probably not a good idea. Are you going to the flat?'

Marnie checked her watch. 'It's too early for my meeting, so yes.'

'I'll give you five minutes then join you there, if that's all right.'

'Sure. I'll put the kettle on.'

Donovan suddenly realised he had had nothing to eat or drink that morning. Close to the ticket machines he spotted a food stall.

'Good idea. I'll bring some breakfast.'

He watched Marnie walk away and reflected how much she had become part of his life. With Anne and Ralph they were almost like a family. He had no idea how long that situation would last, but he was grateful for it. He smiled inwardly. When you needed someone to turn to when you had an incriminating Nazi uniform to dispose of, that was when you found out who your true friends were.

He walked casually across to the food stall and made a selection. Would there be three or four of them? Was Ralph already at the flat or still on the boat? He erred on the side of generosity.

'What would you like, dear?' The stall-keeper had a cheerful London voice with a Caribbean lilt.

He pointed. 'I'll have two *pains aux raisins*, two *pains au chocolat* and four *croissants*, please.'

Donovan was pulling a note from his wallet when he heard a voice from beside him.

'You pronounced those like a true continental.'

He glanced up to meet the gaze of a tall young man beaming down at him. He was smartly dressed in the crisp navy blue uniform of a constable of the City of London police.

There was no restraint in the greeting Donovan received from Anne when he arrived at the flat. She threw her arms round his neck and squeezed him tight.

'Careful,' Donovan said, laughing. 'You'll crush my *croissants*.'

'Ooh! That sounds painful,' Marnie called from the kitchen.

Anne laughed too as she relinquished her grip and kissed Donovan warmly on the lips.

'So good to have you back,' she breathed.

'I've only been gone since yesterday.' As they drew apart Donovan noticed that Anne's eyes were moist with dark smudges under them. 'Hey, what's all this?'

'It's nothing, probably just a hormone thing. Or maybe I'm over-tired. For some reason I'm not sleeping properly right now.'

'Or eating properly, I suspect,' Marnie called out on her way to the table with the cafetière. 'Shall we put your *croissants* in the oven for a minute or two, Donovan?'

'I'll do it,' Anne said, taking the carrier bag from Donovan. 'You dump your stuff and have a seat. Won't be a mo.'

Donovan set his bags down on the floor. 'Marnie, I was wondering ...'

'Why don't you tell us the whole story while we eat?' Marnie said. 'We're dying to know what happened, aren't we, Anne?'

There was no reply. Marnie looked across the peninsular unit and saw that Anne was wiping her eyes on a piece of kitchen roll. Donovan saw her, too.

'Has something happened while I was away?' he asked.

Marnie shrugged and shook her head. She walked through into the kitchen and held Anne by the arms, searching her face. She was a picture of misery.

Marnie knew that expression. She had seen it once before, the day they first met when Anne, a fifteen-year-old schoolgirl, was running away from home.

'What is it, darling?' Marnie asked gently. 'What's the matter?'

Anne blew her nose loudly into the kitchen roll. 'I'm sorry … it's silly, I know, but …'

Donovan hovered in the background. 'Is there anything I can do?'

'This is more than relief, isn't it, Anne?' Marnie said. 'There's something else.'

Anne nodded. 'Donovan's going to work it out. He always does. And then …'

'And then what?' Marnie coaxed.

'And then he'll hate me.' She breathed in as if on the verge of sobbing. 'And I'll deserve it.'

Marnie glanced round at Donovan, who was concentrating intensely.

'Look,' she said, 'why don't we all just sit down, pour ourselves some coffee and have something to eat.' She began guiding Anne to the dining table. 'Whatever it is that's troubling you, Anne, I can't imagine there's anything you could do that would ever make Donovan hate you.'

When Anne was seated at the table, Marnie said, 'Donovan, would you like to pour the coffee while I get the *croissants*?'

'Sure.'

He did as Marnie had asked, laying a hand on Anne's shoulder before taking his place opposite her.

Marnie offered the basket of *croissants* to Anne, who shook her head. To her surprise, Donovan stood up, reached across the table and put a *pain au chocolat* on her plate.

'I know these are your favourites, Anne. That's why I bought them. I'm sure you can manage one. I nearly had a heart attack when I was getting them.'

Anne looked up sharply. 'You what?'

Donovan smiled. 'Just as I was paying for them a policeman came up and started talking to me. I thought it was going to start all over again. But it turned out he was just impressed with my pronunciation of French.'

'You were buying them in *French*?' Marnie said, uncomprehending.

'They were labelled with French names, so I … I used them.'

'Okay,' she said. 'So are you going to tell us what happened?'

'Of course.'

'Donovan …' Marnie began. 'I want to know how things turned out, but I'm assuming because you're here, everything's okay. What I think we should deal with first – for Anne's sake – is what she said about you working things out … and what your reaction might be. Can we do that?'

'Absolutely.'

'Have you worked it out, as she said you would?'

'Possibly.' A hint of doubt in his voice.

Throughout this exchange, Anne was sitting with her head bowed. 'I'm really sorry,' she murmured. 'I should've known …'

'Known what?' said Marnie. 'This is all a mystery to me.'

Donovan looked from Marnie to Anne and back again. 'At the risk of sounding like a cliché, I think it is fairly obvious what Anne had in mind. And actually, it's not her fault, it's mine … what you might call a sin of omission.'

'And can we clear it up here and now, once and for all, and set Anne's mind at rest?'

Anne was now staring at Donovan with eyes wide open. She and Marnie gave him their complete attention as he told his story, while the French *viennoiserie* went cold in their basket on the table.

Ralph was feeling rather proud of himself. He may not have won the Nobel Prize for Economics – yet – but he had managed to log on to the Internet with his laptop. Anne would be proud of him, too. He was delighted to be able to check financial and business websites around the world from the comfort of his study on *Thyrsis*, which was still moored in Cassiobury Park. He was reading an online article in the *Los Angeles Times* about new developments in the California computer industry when his mobile rang.

'Lombard.'

'Ralph, good morning. It's Philip … Philip Everett. Is Marnie with you?'

'No. She's gone into London to see you.'

'Pity. I was hoping to catch her.'

'She left ages ago. Aren't you meeting at eleven?'

'That's just it. The site agent wants to put it back till twelve.'

'I didn't realise anyone else was involved. Nor did Marnie, I think. But is there some reason why you aren't having this conversation with Marnie direct?'

'Her mobile seems to be unavailable.'

'That's odd. It's not like Marnie to switch it off when she's on the move. Look, Philip, I suggest you try the landline at the flat. Do you have the number?'

After disconnecting, Ralph sat thinking. Marnie never switched her mobile off. The only exception would be if something came up that was so important she could not be interrupted. Ralph's thoughts roamed over all the possible subjects that might fall under that heading. They came to rest on Donovan.

When Donovan reached the end of his story he picked up a *pain aux raisins* from the basket and peeled off a piece. Anne slumped forward with both elbows on the table and buried her face in her hands. Marnie sat quietly thinking while Donovan ate his pastry. He took a sip of lukewarm coffee.

'It's odd,' he said, 'but we'd probably call this a *Danish* pastry. The Danes call it *Viennese* bread, and the French group all this sort of thing together as Viennese.'

'What do the Viennese call it?' Marnie asked, absentmindedly.

'Not sure,' Donovan held up his half-eaten pastry. 'I suppose they'd call this sort a *Schnecke* – a snail – because of its swirling shape.'

Marnie reached across the table and laid a hand on Anne's arm. 'Anne?'

Anne drew back and sat staring ahead, looking drawn and weary. Donovan rose from his seat, walked to the other side of the table, knelt beside Anne and put an arm round her thin shoulders.

'There's no problem, Anne,' he said quietly. 'If there's any fault it lies with me. Maybe I should've explained things sooner. No-one could blame you for thinking I was … a murderer.'

'You've never invited discussion of what actually happened that day, Donovan,' Marnie said, 'but I think you can understand why we thought you probably had shot Brandon.'

'I had a good reason, Marnie. I thought you might've worked out what it was.'

Anne started to speak, but her voice was a croak. She cleared her throat. 'I think I've worked it out … for once.'

'Good,' Donovan said. 'It's no great mystery.'

Marnie gave Anne an encouraging look.

Anne said, 'Did you think that if you said nothing about it, we wouldn't be somehow implicated? If anyone questioned us, we could say honestly that we really didn't know what had happened.'

Donovan nodded. 'That's about it.'

'There's a part of your story that you missed out,' Marnie said. 'You managed to get in close to Brandon when his people were taking down his rostrum in the park, didn't you?'

'Yes, like I told you. I infiltrated the group by joining in with the work.'

'Then you tagged along with them as they walked back to his HQ nearby.'

'That was a stroke of luck, Marnie. I didn't know where his base was located, but it was fortunate that they could go on foot. If they'd had to use transport, I would probably have been left stranded.'

'And they just let you go with them.'

'Yes, for the inevitable two reasons, I think. One was that the members of the group that day had come from all over the country. They didn't all know each other. The second was that I was dressed as your total Nazi … in the black SS uniform that's currently in my bag in your living room, by the way.'

'Didn't they think that rather over-the-top?'

Donovan chuckled. 'You should've seen the rest of them. Half of them tried to look the part. Everyone was in black. I just looked more authentic.'

'And you were carrying a gun.'

'Not openly. I had the Luger in my rucksack.'

'Was it loaded?'

'I had five rounds in the magazine.'

'Where did you get them from?' Anne asked, her tone subdued.

'They were with the gun when my grandfather found it.'

'At the end of the war?'

'Yes.'

'Would the bullets still fire after all that time?' Marnie asked.

'I don't know … and I never found out.'

'That's the part of your story you didn't complete,' Marnie said. 'Who fired the shots?'

Donovan shook his head. 'I was reaching into the rucksack when the first shot rang out. A voice from behind me called out, *Get down!* At first I froze. I couldn't believe this was happening. That was when I saw Brandon. He'd pitched forward and was down on one knee, holding his neck. Blood was seeping through his fingers. Then the man next to me pulled me to the ground just as the next shot went off, quickly followed by a third. I heard someone running away, so I looked up in time to see a man disappearing round the corner of the street. I got up from the ground and ran after him.'

'Did you see who it was?' Marnie said.

'No. I was too slow. That was the strangest thing. He'd just vanished.'

'How?'

Donovan shrugged. 'He must either have ducked into a house or got into a vehicle.'

'A pre-planned execution,' Marnie said quietly. She looked at Donovan. 'Like yours, in fact. Did you have a getaway plan?'

Donovan hesitated. 'No. I didn't know where I'd be when it happened. And in any case, I didn't necessarily expect to get away …'

At that moment the phone rang. Marnie took the call in the kitchen area. It was brief, and she was back at the table within a minute, during which time neither Donovan nor Anne had spoken.

'That was Philip. The meeting's been put back to twelve.' There was no response. 'Why don't I make some fresh coffee?'

'Good idea,' said Donovan.

Anne was on her feet before Marnie could move. 'I'll do it.' She seized the cafetière and turned quickly towards the kitchen. 'It'll give me something to do.' She was filling the kettle when Donovan spoke.

'I'm sorry to have been the cause of so much … anguish. I told the BW officer I'd be going back to Germany for a while. I think that might be for the best.'

'But what about your project, the filming?' Anne said.

'I've got a lot of material in the can. I can probably round it off with shots of the completed dig when I get back.'

'Donovan …' Marnie began. 'I think what Anne really means is, she wants you to stay.'

Donovan shrugged. 'Then I'll stay. I just thought it might be easier if I –'

'No,' said Marnie. 'Nothing has really changed, has it?'

'I suppose not,' Donovan said. 'Though I don't think I have to worry about the police being interested in me any more. I think they've ruled me out of the equation.'

'I wasn't thinking of the police.'

'Up till now you thought I'd killed Brandon. Now you've found out that I didn't.' A smile crept across his face. 'I feel I've rather let you down.'

Anne called out from the kitchen. 'You can't get the assassins these days.'

There were three seconds of silence before they started laughing.

After breakfast Marnie opted to stay in the flat to take a shower and prepare for the meeting. Anne offered to stay and join in, but Marnie said it would just be routine. Anne could go with Donovan in case he had more filming to do and needed help with sound recording.

'Marnie,' Donovan said, 'there's something I want to ask you … about the programme for the building works.'

'Really? Why's that?'

'Do you need me to explain?'

'Are you being mysterious again?' Anne said.

'Not really.'

Marnie looked bemused. 'What is it you want to know?'

'Are they pouring concrete today?'

'Ah, I see. Yes, they're reinforcing part of the foundations this morning. You won't be able to go down into the excavations for filming until after lunch at the earliest.'

'We can still film up top if you want to,' Anne said.

'Good. That's what we'll do.' Donovan stood up. 'I'll collect my things.'

When Donovan emerged from the guest bedroom carrying his rucksack, it seemed a little bulkier than usual.

Anne and Donovan set off for the site without delay and had barely left the building when Anne spoke.

'I must say you played it very cool when that policeman came for you.'

'As soon as he said I had to present myself at New Scotland Yard, I knew it would be okay.'

'How did you work that out?'

'If they'd wanted to arrest me, he would've done it there and then. They'd hardly ask me to travel to the Yard unescorted. It would be like sending me to IKEA to get a flat-pack self-assembly arresting kit.'

Donovan chuckled. Anne remained serious. Suddenly she stopped and turned to him.

'Donovan, there's something I have to say.'

'There's no need.'

'Yes there is. I want to tell you how bad I feel about … what I've been thinking all this time.'

'It's fine, Anne.'

'But all along I've thought you'd …' She lowered her voice, aware of other people passing by in the street. '… done it. That's why I feel so awful.'

'Well don't. You've understood why I never spoke about what happened. I didn't want you to be implicated in any way. What I never said, you couldn't know.'

'That doesn't alter the fact that I believed you were capable of …' Anne shook her head, unable to finish the sentence.

Donovan took hold of her arm and stopped walking. 'Anne, what do you think I was trying to do?'

'Probably try to infiltrate Brandon's inner circle to …' She searched for the words. '… spy on him?'

'No. Don't have any doubt about it. I went there to shoot Brandon. To me, he was potentially another Hitler.'

'He wasn't as bad as that, was he?'

'That's what they thought about Hitler in 1933 when they elected him. What's that saying about hindsight always being twenty-twenty vision? The fact is, we don't know what Brandon might've done.'

'So you really would've done it.'

'Ultimately, Anne, someone has to take responsibility. I didn't want other families to suffer under the Nazi threat as mine had in Germany.'

Anne looked thoughtful. 'But someone beat you to it. Any idea who it was?'

'None at all.'

'But you think it was probably another anti-Nazi like you?'

Donovan shrugged. 'Or a rival from within the far right who thought Brandon was getting too powerful.'

'Would they do that?' Anne said, incredulous. 'They were all on the same side … weren't they?'

'These are dangerous people, Anne. Don't forget, the SS massacred the SA brownshirts in a power struggle.'

Anne frowned. 'It's funny, isn't it?'

'Funny?' Donovan's turn to sound incredulous.

'I mean, it's funny how nothing has changed over the years. Here we are standing near the place where river pirates murdered people and were hanged for it, and we're going off to film the remains of a man who was put to death for some unknown reason over a thousand years ago.'

'I suppose so. It seems to be the way of the world.'

Anne looked into his eyes. 'There's got to be a better way.' She reached forward and hugged him, whispering in his ear, 'I do understand, but I'm so glad you didn't do it.'

Passers-by smiled at the sight of the young couple in their embrace; the charm of young love. Donovan held Anne to him without speaking. He knew better than to say what was in his mind.

I may not have pulled the trigger, but – to borrow a phrase – I was just a shot away.

❖ ❖ ❖ ❖ ❖ ❖ ❖

Marnie was barely out of the shower, towelling herself dry, when Philip rang to ask if she was ready for the meeting. Glancing up, she caught sight of herself in the mirror. She was naked from head to foot and dripping water onto the bathroom tiles. Too professional to tell Philip the whole truth, she simply said she would be ready in fifteen minutes or so.

'The thing is, Marnie, we're going to hold the meeting in the hotel across the river.'

'Really? Why don't you just pop round to the flat?'

'The situation has changed. There are more people involved. I'd rather keep it impersonal … neutral ground and all that.'

'Is there a problem, Philip?'

'It's mainly a question of timing. The contractors are complaining about the dig as usual. They're worried about delays.'

'Well, at least we can say we're not holding them up.'

Philip paused. 'That's not quite how they see it, Marnie.'

'I don't understand.'

Another pause. 'I did wonder if something else was going on ... Anyway, they're muttering that our team is involved with the archaeologists and thereby contributing to the timetable being extended.'

'I don't see how they ... ah ... you mean Anne working with Donovan on the filming.'

'That must be it,' said Philip. 'The builders are saying there's nothing in the contract about filming on site.'

'But they're only recording the work as it goes along,' Marnie protested.

'Nevertheless, the contractors think we've got some sort of private arrangement favouring the archaeologists.'

'Why would we do that?'

'Prestige ... kudos ... reputation. Think of the publicity for the firm, Marnie, being involved in such a high-profile discovery.'

'But we're not involved, not directly. That's absurd!'

'Even so, the suggestion is it must be causing some delay. In addition, they're claiming that the site directors are often absent, leaving the students twiddling their trowels.'

'Will the archaeologists be present?'

'Not this time. The contractors want to prepare a united front in private.'

'Sounds like we're gearing up for a real confrontation.'

'I'm afraid so, Marnie. What we have to do today is assure them we're not contributing to delays. We need to be open and transparent ... show them we have absolutely nothing to hide.'

'I'll do my best,' Marnie said, suppressing a smile as she glanced again in the mirror.

The Horselydown compound seemed quieter than usual when Anne and Donovan arrived. Building work was proceeding apace, but there were no students in sight and no conflict surrounding Zoë. They quickly changed into safety gear in the staff hut, and Donovan asked Anne to wait for him there until he returned.

'You can leave your rucksack with me, if you like,' Anne said. 'No need to cart it around with you.'

Donovan hesitated in the doorway. 'Oh ... it's no bother. I won't be more than a couple of minutes.'

With that, he left, leaving Anne to wonder what was going on.

Donovan had scarcely exited the hut, when he saw a concrete mixer lorry by the site entrance. The security guard was pulling the gates wide open as it chugged patiently, its bulbous container revolving slowly behind the cab. Donovan hurried towards the ladder leading down into the dig, where three builders were standing together. Seeing him approach, one of them held up a hand and barred his way.

'No access to the dig this morning. It's out of bounds.'

Donovan frowned. 'What's going on?' His tone was nervous.

'We'll be pouring concrete down that tube as soon as the lorry gets here.' The builder pointed towards the gates, where the driver was exchanging words with the guard.

'Oh god ...' Donovan was wringing his hands.

'What's the matter?'

'I seem to have left a microphone behind yesterday. I must get it.'

'No chance.'

'You don't understand. It's exposed. Any dust or dirt getting in will ruin it.'

'Not my problem.'

'But it belongs to the university. I'm responsible for it.'

'You should've been more careful. We're not risking any more accidents on this job or any more hold-ups.'

'Look –'

Before Donovan could say more, one of the other builders called over.

'What's all the fuss?'

'He says he left a microphone in the dig,' the first builder explained.

'It'll take me two minutes to get it,' Donovan pleaded.

'Give the kid a break,' the second builder said.

Without waiting for a reply, Donovan leapt towards the ladder. 'Thanks. Two minutes. I promise.'

His head was out of sight in seconds. He had never descended so fast and soon reached the lower level where the huge yellow tube ended in a deep trough with shuttering to contain the concrete. Kneeling on the damp ground, he unzipped the rucksack and removed a microphone, which he laid beside him. Next, he pulled out a jacket, trousers and leather belt, all of them black; the jacket and belt bearing the insignia of Hitler's hated SS. Donovan dropped the uniform into the bottom of the trench row, pausing only for a second to look down at it.

In one motion he zipped up the rucksack and seized the microphone. By the time he reached the foot of the bottom ladder, he had the rucksack hoisted onto his back. From far above him, he heard a voice calling down. He ascended in record time and stood to get his breath back up at ground level, where the mixer lorry was already reversing towards the yellow tube.

'Thanks,' Donovan panted, brandishing the microphone. 'Got it. Two minutes, like I said.'

One of the builders urged him to step back as the pouring process began. Donovan watched until the first oozing of grey semi-liquid concrete slipped into the tube and began its fall down to the trough at the lowest level, where it would harden to form the foundations of the retaining wall and bury the SS uniform forever.

When Marnie reached the construction site a short while later a smart metallic grey minibus was waiting by the entrance, and a small group of builders and engineers was chatting beside it. She was about to join them when she spotted Donovan and Anne filming Dick near the dig. Dick was talking to camera in animated fashion, pointing down into the excavation. Donovan was bending forward looking into the viewfinder of the camera on its tripod, with Anne crouching to one side, holding the microphone in its furry jacket. After a few seconds she heard Donovan's voice ring out: *Cut!*

The contractors seemed to be in no hurry to board the minibus. Marnie asked one of the managers if she had time to speak with her colleague. With a glance at his watch he announced pointedly that they would be leaving in exactly seven minutes. Marnie gave him a brilliant smile and set off for the staff hut, signalling on the way to Anne to join her.

Anne was accompanied by both Donovan and Dick. Marnie explained that she had very little time before leaving for the meeting.

'I'm glad you're here, Dick. Listen, do you have a programme for the dig?'

'I've got a rough timetable.'

'How does it stand at present?'

'Fine. We've got till the middle of next month to complete our work.'

'And will you hit the target?'

'Should be no problem. Even with the Roman ships we should be okay, I think.'

'You sound doubtful.'

'That part isn't my project. You'll have to check with Zoë.'

'Presumably she's working on the ships?'

'No idea where she is. Haven't seen her this morning.'

'So who's directing the dig?' Marnie tried not to sound exasperated.

'I am. I've got two groups working on the two excavations, with postgrads supervising. Normal practice.'

Marnie glanced up at the clock. 'Gotta go.'

'Is that minibus taking you to the meeting, Marnie?' Anne asked.

'Meeting?' Dick sounded suspicious. 'Nobody's told me about a meeting.'

Marnie gathered up her bag and papers from the table. 'Technical stuff ... phasing and so on.'

'Has Zoë been invited?' More suspicion.

Marnie crossed to the door. 'Not to my knowledge. See you later.'

Dick dumped his hard hat on the table. 'I'm coming with you.'

If Philip Everett was put out by the arrival of Dick Blackwood at the meeting, he managed not to show it.

'I'm glad you've looked in, Dick. It gives me the opportunity to check a detail with you. Excuse me.' He broke off and called out to the uniformed young woman who had led the participants to the meeting room. 'Would you please ask the minibus driver to hang on a moment.' He turned back to Dick. 'I'll get him to give you a lift back to the site.'

Dick looked confused. 'Will Zoë Tipton be attending this meeting?'

'Zoë? No. This only involves contractors and consultants. However, there is one point I'd like to establish with you as representative of the archaeologists. Are your works proceeding on target?'

Dick hesitated. 'As far as I can judge, yes.'

'Something a little more definite would be helpful.' Philip's tone was diplomatic, but Dick noticed that everyone in the room was watching him. 'Do you think you'll be ready to hand over the whole site by the middle of August?'

'I'll need to confer with Zoë, but I'm assuming the answer will be yes.'

'Good. Thank you, Dick. Now I'm sure this young lady will be able to show you back to the bus. Thanks for dropping by.'

Dick had been dismissed, albeit with a smile. As soon as he was out of the room and walking up the stairs, the uniformed woman turned to him.

'I'm afraid the minibus couldn't wait. He had to get off to another appointment. Can I call you a taxi, sir?'

Dick sighed and shook his head.

If Dick Blackwood's morning had degenerated into a pit of annoyance and frustration, he consoled himself on the walk back over Tower Bridge that things could scarcely get any worse. He was soon to be proved wrong.

When he passed through the entrance gate the students were sitting out in the sunshine, eating and chatting. It was their lunch break, and he knew that on one level they were happy enough, enjoying sunning themselves on a summer's day. But he also knew there was underlying discontent. They were giving up some of their summer vacation for the dig. It was great experience to be part of something so rare and important – especially Zoë's damned Roman ships – but he knew they felt they were drifting without a rudder.

As he looked on, Dick became aware of shadows marching across the ground, and he was wafted by a sudden cool breeze. Some of the students were staring up at the sky, where grey clouds were passing over, filling in some of the gaps between the white fluffy cumulus.

Coming back to earth, Dick felt guilty, knowing he had been putting his own interests first. But he knew he had little scope for manoeuvre with so many pressures weighing on him. He paused and scanned the area, looking for Zoë, but she was nowhere to be seen. He was turning to continue on his way when a voice called out his name. Looking over his shoulder, he saw Bernard de Groot hurrying across the compound. Dick waited until the professor reached him, breathless and flushed.

'Dick, we need to talk.'

'Sure.'

De Groot gestured towards the staff hut. 'Not here. I want a word in private.'

Dick shook his head. 'Not in there. It'll be full of builders at this time of day.'

'Where, then?'

'Why not go down into the excavation?' Dick said. 'They've finished pouring concrete.'

Minutes later, the two men were standing on the middle level beside Dick's Anglo-Saxon skeleton. For a few moments they contemplated him, both of them moved by the pathos of his situation.

'Did you know the students have a name for him?' Dick said quietly.

'A name?'

'Yes. They call him *Stick-in-the-Mud.*'

In silence they regarded the cluster of bones. They did indeed look like little more than a collection of sticks protruding from the damp soil. Yet this had once been a man. Whatever his transgressions, they were long forgotten, and now the archaeologists were only able to empathise with a fellow human being who had suffered a terrifying death.

Perhaps the sobering atmosphere of the ancient killing ground affected de Groot. When he spoke, his tone was subdued.

'You've been away from the dig quite a lot recently, Dick. Why is that?'

'I didn't want to be.' Dick squatted down and gently touched the skeletal shoulder. 'It's ironic, you see. Did you realise that?'

'I don't follow you.' De Groot's tone was hesitant.

'*Stick-in-the-Mud* ... it's also their nickname for me.'

'For *you?*'

'It's because I'm such a stickler for procedure, apparently. They think I'm dogmatic ... set in my ways. The fact is, I like to do everything by the book.'

'That's why you're such a good archaeologist, Dick, thorough, conscientious. That's why I appointed you as joint site director here. That's why I need you to be here. So where have you been?'

Dick straightened up. 'Working, naturally, partly on the King John's lost treasure research, and I also have a deadline to meet on my thesis. They're two completely different projects, even if they are loosely related.'

'I can imagine the pressure of work,' de Groot said. 'But I have to remind you that you are being paid by Capital Archaeology. No-one's work is so important they can just ignore a contractual obligation. And let's not forget, the reputation of the university is involved here.'

'I'm sorry, Bernard. This was meant to be a routine summer dig. Instead, we've uncovered old *Stick-in-the-Mud* here, with all the reassessment that means, on top of my doctoral work and then this amazing discovery in the Wash.'

De Groot sighed. 'I'm not unsympathetic. It can't be easy having to juggle so much at once. The dig, the thesis, the treasure – for want of a better word – any one of those would be a full-time commitment in normal circumstances.'

'I'll try to manage things better,' said Dick.

'I'm sure you will.'

From above them, they could hear voices calling out. The postgrads were starting to shepherd the students down to the dig.

De Groot checked his watch. 'They're very early.'

'They've lost the morning because of the concreting,' Dick said. 'They want to make up for lost time,'

'That's good.' De Groot looked Dick in the eye. 'Perhaps you'd keep me informed if you're going to be absent from the site?'

'Of course.'

'Okay. Now let's get out of here while the ladders are still free. We don't want to get caught swimming against the tide, as it were.'

Waiting while de Groot climbed the first ladder, Dick turned to look at *Stick-in-the-Mud*, the words, *swimming against the tide* resonating in his ears. Looking upwards, a drop of rain struck him on the cheek.

Almost as soon as the contractors' meeting started, Marnie guessed it was just window dressing, unless there was some hidden agenda. True, it was useful to review the timetable of works, but that could have been achieved by a few phone calls and circulated e-mails. The real purpose of the gathering was to enable those present to cover their backs. In the event of slippage, the blame was to be laid firmly at the door of the archaeologists. That much was clear.

Philip chaired the meeting with his customary tact and skill, and he could not deny the contractors the opportunity to make their points. Neither could he deny that their points were valid. There had been days when at least one, sometimes both, of the joint site directors had been absent from the dig. The students had often been left milling about like lost souls. And then there was the matter of the filming.

It had not gone unnoticed that Zoë Tipton had been spending a considerable amount of time in front of the camera rather than supervising the students. Much the same could be said of Dick Blackwood. This extra activity was bound to have an adverse effect on progress.

Marnie was not slow to spot that this could rebound seriously on the architectural team, given Anne's role as temporary sound engineer. She raised a finger, and Philip invited her to speak.

'I do understand the concerns being expressed round the table,' she said, 'but I think some of your anxieties are a little premature. The filming is part of the dig's recording process. It's being carried out by a student from another university, so no resources are being taken away from the dig.'

'Sorry to interrupt …' the senior structural engineer began, 'but why is your girl involved in that?'

Sticking to formal protocol, Marnie did not respond direct, but looked at Philip, who nodded to her to continue.

'I'm glad you raised that point,' Marnie said, looking the engineer straight in the eye. 'Anne Price – *my girl*, as you call her – is in fact on holiday. She's helping Donovan as a friend.'

'That doesn't diminish the fact that the students are being left to get on by themselves for much of the time.'

Philip raised an eyebrow at Marnie. 'Would you say that's fair comment?'

'I have some experience of archaeologists myself, as it happens. We had a visit from the TV programme *Timeline* a short while ago, and they carried out a dig on my land. It's quite normal for the students to get on with their work for hours on end, independent of a supervisor. Much of it is just about scraping away soil.'

The engineer stood his ground. 'Even so, there have been persistent mutterings from the students.'

'Nothing new about that,' Philip intervened in a cheerful tone. 'Coming back to the central issue, the archaeologists have assured us that they're running on schedule. You all heard Dick confirm that at the start of the meeting. I'll keep in close touch with them, but I think we have to wait and see how things turn out as we near their deadline. There's nothing we can realistically do before then.'

There were murmurings around the table. Philip continued.

'I'm open to alternative suggestions,' he said in a reasonable tone.

The site agent indicated that he wanted to speak. Philip acknowledged him.

'You'll be putting our concerns in writing, presumably?'

Philip indicated Nigel Beardsley, sitting beside him taking notes.

'Nigel will circulate minutes after the meeting, as usual. I think a list of key points will suffice, if you agree.'

The site agent said, 'I meant, will you be writing formally to express our concerns to the archaeologists at this stage?'

Philip reflected. 'I'll be happy to include a sentence to that effect in my covering letter with the minutes.'

The site agent smiled. 'Thank you.'

'Now,' said Philip, 'back to the agenda. Do I understand correctly there may be some delays with the delivery of structural steelwork?' He looked across at the site agent. 'Would you like to comment on that first?'

The site agent's smile vanished abruptly, as the meeting took a new direction. Marnie quickly looked down at her papers to conceal her own smile.

19
Disaster Revisited

When Marnie parted the porthole curtains in the sleeping cabin on Monday morning, she was relieved to find that the rain had stopped. It had been a wet weekend, navigating up from Cassiobury Park, and they had tied up at Leighton Buzzard on Sunday evening, having made moderate progress since setting off after breakfast on Saturday. To console themselves for a damp voyage, they had changed into fresh, dry clothes and walked into town under a large, multicoloured golf umbrella to dine in an Indian restaurant. The food was good and the service friendly, and when they left to return to *Thyrsis*, their morale was restored. The rain scarcely bothered them.

On impulse, Marnie pulled on her dressing gown and went up onto the stern deck. It was barely six-thirty, and the town was still sleeping, with only the occasional vehicle crossing the bridge a short distance down the canal from the mooring. An underlying coolness gave an edge to the air, but the water was sparkling and smelled fresh and clean.

The trip down to London and back had been a good idea, and Marnie felt reinvigorated, her enthusiasm for life revived, but she was glad to be going home. In a few days Anne would join her, and life at Glebe Farm would return to normal. Thinking of Anne made her recall the underlying sadness of that summer, with the death of Dr Fennimore. And there was something else.

Marnie remembered that all was not sweetness and harmony at the archaeological site. The atmosphere between Zoë Tipton and Dick Blackwood was more than just a squabble over bragging rights between academics. It threatened the success of the whole building project. The contractors may have been trying to camouflage their own delays by casting blame on the archaeologists, but there was no doubt that real tensions between the principal players were bringing negative vibes to an otherwise magnificent venture.

A quiet voice behind her made Marnie jump.

'One point two cents for your thoughts?'

Marnie looked round at Ralph who was smiling up at her from inside the boat.

'What?'

'Am I being too obscure for you on a summer's morning?' he said.

'I'm totally bewildered by your gnomic utterance,' Marnie said evenly. 'Please repeat the question ... if it was a question.'

'I would've offered a penny for your thoughts, but I've been carrying out a study of issues relating to the euro ... hence the conversion at the current rate of –'

'Okay, okay. I get the picture. I was just thinking about going home.'

'Happy thoughts?'

'Yes.' An emphatically definite tone of voice. 'Absolutely. How could I be anything but positive?'

A few hours later that morning, Anne and Donovan stepped out on damp cobbles for one of their last days of filming. Along with their backpacks of equipment, each of them bore a carrier bag at Anne's suggestion: *we'd better take wellies. The site will be a quagmire!*

They had spent the weekend dodging showers, the odd downpour and even the occasional thunderstorm, determined to enjoy the time that circumstances allowed them to spend together. Visits to the Museum of London, the Horniman and William Morris museums had been interspersed with a boating expedition on the Serpentine and a soggy picnic in Regent's Park.

At Horselydown it was business as usual. As soon as they reached the perimeter of the compound they saw Zoë and Dick, and had advanced only a few yards when they heard Zoë's voice ringing out.

'Oh gawd,' said Anne. 'I wonder what it is this time.' She glanced at Donovan with an impish smile. 'I expect you've worked it out already?'

Donovan pulled a face. 'Could be anything. At a guess I'd say it was most likely about who gets priority on the dig.'

'Not recriminations about Dick's repeated absences?' Anne suggested.

'Also in the frame,' Donovan agreed.

The closer they got to the two young archaeologists, the more they heard. It was not difficult. Zoë as ever was in full flight.

'... taking us all for *absolute* bloody *fools*. I don't know how you have the *nerve* to –'

'What are you talking about?' Dick protested, waving his arms like a bad actor.

'You know *perfectly well* what I'm saying,' Zoë persisted. 'You must think we're all *totally* naïve.'

'Don't be *ridiculous*, Zoë. You've only got to think about the situation for half a second to realise what you're saying is *absurd*.'

'Really? You don't think I can't see through your ... your ... *charade*? It's obvious what you're up to. Well I can tell you, it isn't going to work. As soon as Bernard de Groot gets here, I'm going to put him straight.'

'You're crazy! You'll make yourself look like a *complete* idiot.'

Anne and Donovan were now standing just a few feet away, all their attention fixed on the rowing couple. Anne almost jumped when Donovan suddenly spoke up beside her.

'You might want to keep your voices down.' He spoke at normal pitch, but the two protagonists reacted as if he had bellowed at them through a megaphone. Dick spun round and stared uncomprehendingly. Zoë turned on him, her eyes blazing. Donovan was undeterred. 'It's up to you, but …'

He nodded in the direction of the site entrance. A coach stood by the gate, and students were spilling out. Some of the builders had stopped several yards away, spellbound by the vehemence of the argument or perhaps simply by the sheer volume of sound. Zoë opened her mouth to speak, but Anne cut her off.

'Do you realise the builders are looking for any evidence they can find to prove that you are causing delays to the contract?'

'What?' In one syllable Zoë conveyed the impression that the idea was fanciful and irrelevant.

Anne continued. 'There's a great deal at stake here. You don't seem to realise what's going on. You can't allow a personal argument to jeopardise the whole –'

Before Anne could complete the sentence, Zoë turned on her heel and hurried away towards the staff hut. Dick was breathing heavily and looked as if he had been struck in the face.

'That *bloody* woman,' he muttered under his breath. 'Someone should really put a stop to her wild accusations.'

'What *are* her accusations, exactly?' Anne said.

Dick turned to face her. 'I'm sorry you've got dragged into this, but you're right. We've got to get the students properly organised before everything goes down the tubes.'

With the flash of a grim smile, Dick turned and strode off to meet the group.

Watching him go, Anne said, 'I don't think I'm any the wiser about what they were arguing about.'

Donovan looked serious. 'It must surely be that Zoë is pooh-poohing Dick's treasure find.'

'But we knew that already, and so did Dick. I let it slip out last week, remember?'

'Sure, but this time there's a difference.'

'What can be different about that?'

'Well …' Donovan began. 'For a start, Zoë is actually confronting him about it in person. That's bound to give it an extra edge. And also, she's being much more forthright about it, much more up front.'

'Why d'you think that is?'

'My guess ...' Donovan hesitated, '... my guess is, she's found something out, something important.'

'You mean, like actual proof that he hasn't made the discovery after all?'

'Could be something like that.' He suddenly changed tack. Come on, let's get togged up. We don't want to delay things.'

From the doorway of the staff hut, Anne saw Dick talking to the students who were now assembled just inside the compound. She followed Donovan in and found Zoë sitting at a table speaking in animated fashion on her mobile. With her free hand she was gesticulating, waving a finger in the air to force home her points.

'... yes fine, fine. Good. I'll tell you more when you get here. See you soon. Bye.' She disconnected and looked up at Anne. 'Sorry. Sorry I turned my back on you, Anne. It's just ... *bloody* Dick Blackwood. He's such a *pain*. Anyway, that was Prof de Groot. He's coming over this morning and we'll have it out with Dick once and for all.'

'What are you hoping to achieve, Zoë?' Donovan asked quietly, setting down his bags.

'I'm going to prove it didn't happen.'

'*It* being ... Dick's big find?'

'Of course. What else?'

'It's sometimes hard to prove a negative, Zoë, especially when there's evidence to the contrary.'

Zoë's smile in reply contained neither warmth nor humour. 'Evidence? You mean a few artefacts that could've come from anywhere?'

'Artefacts that have been verified by experts from the British Museum.' Donovan's tone was reasonable.

Zoë shook her head. 'I'll tell you what's evidence. Dick says he made his discovery while out on the boat with Gerald Parfitt, right?'

'We know that,' Anne said.

'And if I told you Gerald Parfitt knew nothing about it?' Zoë paused for effect. 'What would you say about that?'

'Is that what Parfitt is actually saying?' Donovan asked. 'Are you sure?'

'Not in so many words, but I phoned him at the weekend. He was very coy about the whole thing.'

Anne looked at Donovan. She could almost hear his brain whirring.

'It doesn't add up, Zoë,' he said. 'Why would he make up something that could so easily be disproved?'

'Didn't I make myself clear?' Zoë persisted. 'Let me spell it out for you again.' She spoke slowly, emphasising every word. 'Parfitt had been out sailing with Dick. And yes, they had discussed the wetlands of that time. But of King John's so-called *treasure* ... Parfitt wouldn't be drawn. Is that clear enough?'

'Dick presumably didn't accept your view,' Donovan said.

Zoë glared at him. 'You saw how embarrassed he was. He was *furious* that his scheme had been rumbled. Surely you could see that.'

'There is another way of interpreting his reactions,' Donovan said. 'Parfitt could have been respecting confidentiality, and Dick could've been furious that you should question his integrity.'

'Integrity? *Huh!* What integrity? Anyway, why are you taking his side like this, Donovan? Is it some male pride thing ... solidarity between macho brothers?'

Donovan said nothing. Anne could feel static electricity crackling in the air between him and Zoë. She frantically searched for words that would defuse the tension in the atmosphere.

'Perhaps we could step back from the –' she blurted.

'*You* can step back,' Zoë spat out the words. 'I have work to do. If you want to do something useful to help, you can get yourselves into gear.' She pushed open the door, pausing briefly on the threshold. 'Time is running out ... I haven't got long.' The door closed itself smoothly behind her.

Anne and Donovan changed quickly. Anne sat to remove her wellingtons while Donovan took down the hard hats and pulled the jackets from the locker. Turning, he saw her stretch her legs and wiggle her feet in lime green ankle socks.

'Is that the latest fashion in the construction industry?' he said.

'Ask any of the builders,' Anne replied, unabashed.

They both donned protective boots before setting out. Five paces from the hut they bumped into Dick. Donovan thought he looked remarkably at ease for someone whose most important find was being held up to ridicule. In the background the students were trooping off to their hut to change into working gear.

'Any sign of the professor?' Dick asked.

'He's not here yet,' said Anne. 'He's coming later on.'

'D'you know when?'

Anne shook her head. 'Zoë didn't say.'

'Zoë?'

'She was talking to him on the phone just now.'

Dick turned and scanned the compound, holding up a hand to shield his eyes from the light. Without speaking he hurried away in the direction of the dig site. Donovan made to follow, but Anne took hold of his arm.

'I think Marnie ought to know what's going on this morning. Philip, too. We seem to be heading for some sort of showdown.'

'Got your mobile?' Donovan said.

Anne tugged it from her pocket. Marnie answered at once, and Anne succinctly outlined her concerns. While she spoke, Donovan was scanning the compound as the students trickled back from the changing rooms. He was frowning.

'Something wrong?' Anne asked.

'Not sure,' Donovan said vaguely. He continued his inspection, concentrating hard.

'What's bothering you?' Anne said.

By now they were surrounded by the students. Donovan pushed through the group and stood at the edge peering into the distance. Anne was about to repeat her question when he turned to the nearest students.

'Anyone seen Zoë Tipton?' he said.

Marnie was having problems with the switchboard operator at Everett Parker Associates. She tried the patient approach.

'Yes, I know he'll be in the management group meeting. I'm working with him.'

'Sorry, what did you say your name was?'

'Marnie Walker. I'm heading interior design on the Horselydown project.'

'Just a moment, please.'

Marnie sighed with relief. 'Thank you.'

After a brief pause the operator was back. 'I'm afraid you're not on my list.'

Marnie took a deep breath. It was intended to calm herself down. It failed.

'That's because I'm an external consultant. Will you please just put me through to the extension in the meeting room ... now.'

'But I'm not allowed to interrupt –'

'Trust me,' Marnie said firmly. 'Mr Everett will *want* to be interrupted. Tell him it's urgent.'

'But –'

'No, not *but*. This is really important.'

'I'm very sorry, but I can't do that. Those are my instructions.'

'You're new, aren't you?'

'Started this morning ... an hour ago.'

Another sigh from Marnie. 'Temping?'

'Yes, from the agency ... holiday relief.'

'And your name?'

A pause. 'Janice.'

'Okay, Janice, here's what I want you to do. Write a short note – *Marnie on phone urgent*. Trot across the foyer, take it into the meeting room and hand it to Philip. Wait for him to tell you to put me through, then go back and do it. Can you do that for me?'

Another pause 'I'm not supposed to leave reception.'

Marnie was now close to homicidal.

'Janice, I'm running out of two things. One if them is the battery on my mobile. I leave the other one to your imagination. I'll hold on while you go. You'll be in sight of the desk all the time.'

A minute later, Philip was on the line.

'Morning, Marnie. What's up?'

Marnie explained about Anne's phone call and her fears about the situation at Horselydown. At first, Philip made no reaction. When he spoke there was doubt in his voice.

'Is that so unusual, Marnie? I mean, Zoë in the middle of a row. I thought that happened fairly often.'

'It does, but there was something different this morning. I could sense that Anne was much more concerned than usual.'

'Fair enough. So what do we do?'

'I'm going down there.'

'Where are you at the moment, Marnie?'

'Not far from home, but I'll grab a train and get back as soon as I can.' No response. 'Philip?'

'You've got me worried, too, Marnie. I'll see you there.'

Anne and Donovan were standing with the students in the middle of the compound when the mobile rang. Anne had to press the phone tight against her ear to hear properly; it sounded as if Marnie was walking quickly as she spoke. She announced that she was on her way back to London and that Philip was probably already crossing the city to converge on the site.

Anne suddenly had a pang of misgiving. Had she exaggerated her anxiety? Was it all just business as usual at Horselydown, with Zoë in the thick of a row? But she knew Donovan had felt it too, a new edge to the tension that was so often in the air.

'Are you down in the dig?' Marnie asked.

'No, we're just sort of standing around with the students. Nothing's happening at the moment.'

'You're at surface level?'

'Yes.'

'Why aren't you in the excavation?'

'Hang on, Marnie.' Anne turned to Donovan. 'What's the hold-up?'

Donovan spoke to the students before replying to her. Anne raised the phone again.

'It seems we've been told to wait. Builders have gone down to make their routine check on the shuttering and scaffolding after all the rain. They just want to make sure it's –'

The sound that stopped Anne in mid-flow was a distant roar, like the whoosh of a gas jet igniting on the hob of a cooker. It was followed by a metallic clattering. In one movement the students leapt back, leaving Anne and Donovan momentarily isolated. Their eyes were drawn to the dig site as scaffolding collapsed inside the hole and a ballooning cloud of dirt and dust blew out like the eruption of a volcano. Donovan grabbed Anne's arm and pulled her away.

In a state of shock, Anne realised she was still clutching the mobile. As she raised it to her ear, she could hear Marnie's voice on the line.

'… was that sound? Anne? Can you hear me? Are you all –'

'Marnie, I'm here. The dig site … it's blown up, it's … I mean the scaffolding's collapsed … it's a complete mess … I don't know what to –'

'Anne, listen. Is everybody safe? Are you and Donovan okay?'

'Yes. I think so.'

'Is Dick there, or Zoë?'

'Can't see them at the moment.'

'Then get the students together and take a roll call. Assemble them by the perimeter fence well away from the excavation. Can you do that?'

'Sure. Right away.'

'We have to account for everybody.'

'I understand.'

'My train's coming. I'll be with you as soon as I can.'

Marnie's last words were instantly drowned out by the noise of a train pulling into the station. Anne caught the sound of a loudspeaker announcement in the background as Marnie disconnected.

Anne and Donovan wasted no time, shepherding the students towards the fencing. When everyone was well clear of the disaster area, Donovan went back to inspect the dig hole. Anne realised she had no list of the students to take a roll call. She swelled her meagre chest, took a deep breath and spoke out as loudly as she could above the students' excited voices.

'Can you please listen, everybody. Hallo? Can I have your attention, please?' The babble subsided. 'You may know that I'm part of the architects' team. We need to make sure everyone in the group is accounted for. Does anyone have a list of names?'

A black girl spoke up. 'Zoë and Dick both have lists ... probably in the staff hut.'

Anne looked round. There was a buzz of activity as builders milled about in the vicinity of the huts.

'Thanks, Debbie. But I think I might be in the way over there. Let's try another method. Could you group yourselves together according to who was with you yesterday in your pit or trench. I have to find out if anyone's missing.'

The students began reassembling, settling into groups of three or four. In minutes they had established that every member of the squad was present.

'That's great. Thanks, everybody.'

One of the postgrads asked if Anne knew what would happen next.

'The truth is, I've no idea. I expect the contractors will inspect the dig. Once they've done that, they'll tell us what has to be done.'

'What about us? Will we have to stay here?'

'Good question. I expect so.'

There were murmurings among the group. Clearly, the thought of another morning spent hanging around did not appeal. Anne had a sudden flash of inspiration.

'Look, would anyone fancy a coffee?'

The murmurings immediately shifted gear and became more positive.

'Okay. Here's what we'll do. I'll take six of you with me to the café. We'll get coffees to take away and you'll bring them back here. Then the next group of six will follow and so on, till everybody's got one. Is that all right?'

A cheerful voice spoke out. 'Sounds like a plan.'

Another voice said, 'Who's paying? I'm skint!'

Anne grimaced. 'I'll put them all on my credit card.'

A muffled cheer went up. Anne could see Donovan talking to some of the builders close to the point where the dig ladder still protruded from below ground. She excused herself briefly and rushed over to him. *Am I doing the right thing?* she wondered. Recognising the site agent, she veered off and collared him as he strode across the compound. She wanted to do everything by the book. At first she thought he was going to brush past her, but she stood her ground.

'Sorry.' She spoke rapidly. 'I know you're busy but I'm organising the students.'

The contractor slowed. 'About time somebody did.'

Anne outlined her plan to keep the archaeologists occupied and supplied with coffee. The agent agreed to their leaving the site in groups on the understanding that without exception each one of them returned directly to the collection point by the fence. Anne felt relieved to have his support. When she turned to go, she found Donovan behind her.

'I heard your plan,' he said. 'It sounds good.'

'What's happening here?' Anne asked.

'The builders are going to make an inspection. They'll wait for about twenty minutes. If there's no further subsidence, one of them will go down and carry out a quick visual.'

'D'you want coffee?'

Donovan smiled for the first time since the collapse. 'I'd have thought that was fairly obvious.'

Anne thumped him on the chest and legged it back to the students.

Janice the temp at Everett Parker Associates was not without her qualities. She had a taxi waiting outside the entrance to the building by the time Philip returned to the foyer with his briefcase. On the way across the city he tried to get Marnie on the mobile again, but each attempt was thwarted by a chirpy female voice inviting him to leave a message. By the fifth failure he was ready to strangle the voicemail woman.

He had more luck when he rang the site office. The clerk of works filled him in on the accident and assured him that as far as anyone could judge, no-one had been injured when the scaffolding crashed down.

'And you're certain you've accounted for everybody on site?' Philip said.

'Certain … well apart from the archaeologists.'

Philip could hear alarm bells ringing. 'Bloody hell, Terry, there are dozens of 'em!'

'No, no, Phil. What I meant was, Marnie's girl, Anne, has them all under control.'

'Well, thank god for Anne. Why aren't the two *so-called* site directors taking charge?'

'You know them, Phil. Never there when you need them.'

Philip admitted to himself that he had become profoundly disappointed with the archaeologists. When he had initially been briefed he felt a tremendous excitement at collaborating with Capital Archaeology, with their work as a central feature of the contract. It was ground-breaking, inspirational. The reality was that he found himself in the middle of a feud between rival interests, ambitions and egos. Worse than that, when calamity struck, the site directors proved inadequate to the task. It had fallen to a girl still in her teens to take the initiative and assume responsibility. *Yes, thank god for Anne*, he thought.

Another attempt to ring Marnie; another message, this time that her number was not available. Her battery was probably flat.

The taxi was making good time and was now passing through the City, the square mile of London's principal financial quarter. Soon, they were rounding the Tower of London, and the huge bulk of Tower Bridge came into view. At any other time he would have rejoiced to be associated with a development in such an iconic location. That morning he was dreading the thought of what might be awaiting him across the river.

Whatever Philip expected, he was completely unprepared for the spectacle that faced him as he paid the cabbie and turned to enter the building site.

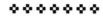

Anne's arrangements worked well. As one set of six students returned to the compound, another left for the café. Donovan waited with the main group by the perimeter and was delighted when one of them brought him a cappuccino with Anne's compliments. It was the pretty Afro-Caribbean girl who had swiftly volunteered to take the coffee back to Donovan, and she gave him her broadest smile as she handed over the beaker.

'It's Donovan, right?' She had a wide mouth, revealing dazzling white teeth.

'That's right.'

'I'm Debbie.'

'I know.'

'You've noticed me, then?'

Donovan chuckled. 'You're not easy to miss.'

Her smiled wavered slightly. There were no other black students in the assembly, and the only non-Europeans were two Asian girls, one of Indian origin, the other Chinese.

Donovan added, 'You're the only one wearing green denim fatigues.' Debbie laughed charmingly. 'It was nice of you to bring me the coffee,' he said.

'If there's anything else I can do for you, just let me know.'

'There is, actually.'

'Really?' The smile was even broader.

'We need a list of all the students in the group. D'you think you could draw one up?'

The smile became a little rueful. 'Sure.'

By the time Anne returned from the café with the last batch of students, Debbie's list was complete and Donovan was studying it. She had done an excellent job. From a first draft she had produced a second list in alphabetical order, with each name numbered. Her handwriting was attractive and easy to read.

'This is perfect,' Donovan said. 'Just what we needed. Thanks, Debbie.'

'Any time.'

Anne sipped her coffee. 'Any developments here?'

Donovan shook his head. 'Nothing so far. How about you, Anne? Coffee marathon completed?'

'Yeah,' Anne sighed. 'The good news is, the café owner let me have mine on the house.'

'Great. Is there bad news?' Donovan asked.

'I'm just hoping I can claim the bill on expenses. If not, you're looking at Glebe Farm's newest bankrupt.'

'I can pay you back for mine, Anne.' Debbie was reaching into her pocket.

Anne took hold of her arm. 'No, that's fine, Debbie. I'm sure I'll be able to –'

They were distracted by shouts from the dig site and turned to see men hurrying towards the ladder. Donovan set off at speed while the others looked on. Several builders were clustered at the edge of the excavation, some of them reaching down into the hole, others pointing. Anne followed in Donovan's footsteps, and the archaeologists began moving slowly forward.

As Donovan reached the builders, they parted and stepped back from the ladder. One man appeared from below, his hard hat tilted at an angle, climbing awkwardly under a difficult load. Over his shoulder, drooping like a broken doll, was the inert form of Zoë Tipton. The man was steadied and helped from the ladder by two of the builders. They lifted Zoë from his shoulder and laid her gently on the ground.

Behind him, Donovan heard a collective gasp from the students. Everyone seemed to freeze as they looked down at Zoë's body. Her hair was wet and matted, and she was streaked all over with mud. Her lips were parted, her eyes closed. Even in death she was beautiful.

'Oh my god ...'

No-one had noticed Dick Blackwood until that moment. No-one saw where he came from, though Anne noticed sub-consciously that unlike Zoë he was clean and not wearing protective clothing. He stood horrified, holding his face in both hands, mouth gaping open, staring down.

'Oh, Zoë, what have I done?' he muttered.

Still, nobody stirred. It was as if they had become a painting or a photograph, a scene of shock and dread. And then Donovan stepped forward. He knelt beside Zoë and gently took her wrist in his fingers. Anne joined him, kneeling on the ground.

'Any pulse?' she asked.

Donovan shook his head slowly. 'I can't feel anything.' He looked up at the builders who were standing in a group to one side. 'We need a first-aider here.'

No-one moved. They seemed paralysed with shock.

'Bit late for that, isn't it?'

Donovan insisted. 'Even so, we need someone with more experience than I have.' He reached forward and gently closed her mouth. To Anne, he said quietly, 'She wouldn't want people to see her crooked tooth. She was very particular about that.'

Anne remembered Zoë's instructions for filming her: *no shots of me talking from below the face, with the camera pointing up towards my chin* ... Into her mind came other words that Zoë had spoken. She repeated them now.

'*I will lay my bones here forever.* Do you remember her saying that?'

Donovan nodded without speaking. He was remembering something else Zoë had said: *Time is running out ... I haven't got long.* Removing his hard hat, he set it on the ground. As he did so he became aware of movement beside him and glanced sideways to see Debbie. She knelt down on the opposite side from Anne. One by one the students advanced slowly and followed her example. Like Donovan, they too removed their hats until every one of them was kneeling, with heads bowed. The scene now looked like a form of homage to the young woman lying on the muddy ground, the aftermath of tragedy.

The builders remained standing, self-consciously staring at the bowed heads before them.

Only one archaeologist refrained from joining the group on their knees. With an intake of breath that could have been a sob, Dick hurried away, stumbling across the compound to the entrance gate, brushing past the security guard, who was engrossed in watching the events around the dig site. He paid no attention to the man climbing out of the taxi. Vaguely aware of a coughing sound behind him, he rushed across the road causing alarm to drivers passing by, who braked hard and swerved to avoid running him down.

Philip Everett emerged from the taxi, stunned at the sight that met his eyes. The kneeling, bowed assembly could have been a vision from the ancient world, a ritual from Saxon or Roman times. He rushed into the compound, passing the security guard who seemed not to notice him.

Reaching the edge of the kneeling assembly, he spotted Donovan, rising from his knees, reaching forward.

Marnie did not have long to wait to catch a London-bound train at Bletchley and found an aisle seat near the doors. She had been formulating a plan ever since leaving *Thyrsis* and now switched on the mobile to talk it over with Ralph.

They agreed that she would probably stay in the flat for a day or two, but could only assess what was needed once she was on the spot.

'You're really worried about the situation at Horselydown, aren't you, Marnie?'

'It's more than that. I'm concerned that I don't know what's to be worried about.'

Ralph did not even try to work that one out. 'Okay. If you think you could use some moral support, just say the word and I'll come down at once.'

'That's sweet of you, darling. I'm hoping to find everything is normal and that Zoë and Dick are just playing their usual game of hunt-the-archaeologist.'

For the next few minutes Marnie briefed Ralph on what he needed to do when he reached the office to keep Walker and Co on the road.

'Leave it to me, Marnie. I shall relish being in charge … all that power. I'll take lots of important decisions.'

Marnie knew he was trying to lighten the atmosphere, but she found it difficult to respond in kind.

'Don't let it go to your head.' Her attempt at levity sounded flat.

Ralph picked up on her mood. 'There's probably nothing to worry about, Marnie. Next time we speak you'll probably be complaining that your journey was unnecessary and everything was normal when you got to the site.'

'I hope so, Ralph, but I trust Anne's judgment, and she was definitely worried. So was Donovan. I've got a bad feeling about this and I don't like leaving Anne to cope on her own.'

As she spoke, the mobile beeped – *battery low* – and they ended their conversation. While she raced south towards London, Ralph reached down to the map shelf from the stern deck and slotted the mobile into its holder. When Marnie had rung, he had brought *Thyrsis* to a halt by the bank, where the boat had waited patiently until it was time to move on.

Why now? Ralph wondered. What was it about that day's events that had caused Marnie so much concern? He realised that he had not heard Anne's tone of voice. *I trust Anne's judgment*, Marnie had said. And of course she had Donovan with her. Ralph could not imagine two more mature and level-headed young people. But, he reminded himself, Anne was still in her teens and Donovan was not much older.

He hopped onto the bank and pushed *Thyrsis* off at the bows. As the nose swung out into the channel, he stepped back onto the stern deck and pressed the accelerator.

Let's hope it's all a fuss about nothing, he thought.

The still body of Zoë Tipton brought a lump to the throat of those looking on.

Some of the girls were weeping openly, others were hugging each other for comfort.

Once again it was Donovan who acted first. He eased his arms out of his jacket and gently draped it over Zoë. Anne swallowed hard and suppressed a sob as she saw him covering her body but leaving her face clear. It was as if she was not really dead, and he was simply covering her to keep her warm like a sleeping child.

When Zoë suddenly coughed and retched violently, even Donovan started in surprise.

Anne's mouth flew open, and Debbie almost screamed. Some of the students at the back of the group began wailing in distress, unaware of the reason for the strange sound uttered by Debbie. But in seconds the word spread through their ranks.

Zoë was alive!

Everyone present was reacting to this new development, while Donovan was in action again. He grabbed the mobile from his jeans pocket and half-threw it sideways to Anne like a Rugby player in full flight.

'Three nines!' he called out. '*Ambulance!*'

Anne was pressing buttons as Donovan whipped off the jacket and rolled Zoë onto her side towards him. She coughed again, spluttering muddy water from her mouth.

'*Christ Almighty!*' one of the builders exclaimed. 'He's brought her back to life.'

'She was only unconscious,' Donovan called out.

Debbie crossed herself. As the hubbub rose behind them, Donovan struck Zoë firmly in the back. This brought on another bout of violent coughing to the extent that Zoë heaved and gasped even more. Donovan pushed a finger into her mouth and spooned out a glob of mud.

Anne winced at the sight, speaking into the phone. 'Ambulance please. There's been an accident ...'

As Anne gave details to the emergency operator, Donovan repeated the mouth-clearing exercise with his finger. Suddenly he jumped and exclaimed, turning to Anne with a smile.

'She bit me!'

Debbie threw her arms round Donovan and kissed him hard on the cheek. 'You're wonderful!'

Donovan could feel Debbie's tears against his face as he eased her back. Very carefully he looped an arm round Zoë and supported her as she leant forward. By now her eyes were fluttering and she was breathing heavily but steadily, like an exhausted runner at the end of a marathon. She began trying to hoist herself up on one elbow, but Donovan held her firmly.

'Zoë, can you hear me?' He spoke quietly into her ear. 'It's Donovan. Don't try to move.'

'What?' She coughed several times and struggled against Donovan, but he held on.

'Listen to me, Zoë. You've had an accident. You've got to lie still for a while. Help is coming.'

'What?' she whispered again breathlessly, her tone querulous and confused. She blinked several times and forced her eyes to stay open, trying to focus. 'What ... what's ... going ... on?'

'Take it easy,' Donovan said gently. 'You're going to be fine.'

'An ambulance is on its way,' Anne said.

Donovan turned towards Anne and saw she was looking away from him. She was talking to Philip Everett who had evidently joined them at a run. He quickly assessed the situation, nodded at Donovan and rushed over to where the contractors were standing. They began gesticulating as they explained what had happened.

By now, Zoë was breathing calmly, no longer resisting Donovan's embrace. He turned to Debbie.

'Can you take off your jacket.'

'Any time,' she said, grinning.

'Please, Debbie.'

'Sure.' Serious now. 'I can take off my jacket.' She passed it to Donovan.

'Can you roll it up. I need a pillow for Zoë.'

She did as he had asked. 'Anything else?'

'Yes, go to the entrance and get the guard to open both gates wide so the ambulance can drive straight in.'

Debbie got to her feet and set off. Without a word, Anne stood up and began shepherding the students aside to clear a direct route to where Zoë lay. Their actions were timely. The sound of a siren was heard in the distance, approaching at speed. Help was on its way. Zoë had survived.

When Marnie's train arrived at Euston, she headed straight for the stairs down to the underground taxi rank. Although there was a queue, the cabs drew up every few seconds, and she was quickly on her way.

The train journey had at first exasperated her, as the service from Bletchley stopped at every station, but it gave her time to think, and the nearer she drew to her destination the more convinced she became that her return was over-hasty. She was in no doubt that it would be a normal working day at Horselydown.

Sure enough, when the taxi pulled up by the site entrance, she saw only building work in progress. The overhead crane was turning on its axis, men were going about their tasks in an orderly manner, and on one side of the compound a group of students was being briefed by one of the leading postgrads. Standing by the excavation area, she saw Anne and Donovan in conversation. Marnie walked briskly into the compound and headed in their direction.

It was only when she saw the expression on Anne's face that she realised everything was not as normal as it appeared.

The rest of the morning was frantic. Philip and Nigel spent most of the time in talks with the builders while the health and safety inspectors carried out their initial examination. Ominously, the latter asked if anyone could have interfered with the scaffolding. This simple question produced a numb silence. Philip asked if there was any evidence of tampering with the structure. The inspectors, two men and a woman, exchanged glances.

'Early days,' said one of the men, who appeared to be the senior member of the team. 'What's clear is that the dig area has to be closed down until further notice. Also, we're informing the police.'

'You have serious grounds for suspicion?' Philip asked. He knew the answer before it came.

'Let's just say we have some doubts about the cause of the incident. That's all we need.'

Yes, that's all we need, Philip thought.

Marnie, Anne and Donovan went to the flat after the ambulance took Zoë away. As they walked, Anne briefed Marnie on the situation. She ended by describing Donovan's handling of Zoë's recovery.

'Looks like you're the hero of the hour.' Marnie smiled.

'She would've recovered anyway,' Donovan said.

'She could've choked on the mud,' Anne protested.

Donovan made no reply.

'So what now?' Anne said.

They arrived at the entrance to the block, and Marnie operated the security key system.

'I want to take a shower and change my clothes,' she said. 'But first, I'm going to ring Professor de Groot. It may not have occurred to anyone to keep him in the picture.'

Marnie was pleasantly surprised when de Groot's secretary told her that he had indeed been informed by *Mr Everett, the architect in charge*, of the morning's events. The professor was already on his way to the site. Marnie had not been surprised at the reaction when she asked if the department had had any word from Dick Blackwood.

After a long moment of silence, the secretary said, 'It would be best if you raised that with the professor direct, Mrs Walker.'

Twenty minutes later, Marnie emerged from the shower enveloped in a bath towel, with a second towel wrapped turban-style round her head, and laid out fresh clothes in the master bedroom. Within a few minutes the sound of the hairdryer ceased, and Marnie reappeared fragrant and groomed as the aroma of coffee wafted through the flat.

The three sat at the dining table to make plans. Marnie would return to the site for discussions with Philip, Professor de Groot and the contractors. Her own work would be unaffected by any delays, but she needed to be aware if there were changes to phasing and timing. Anne said she would join her.

'Donovan?' Marnie asked.

'I'd prefer not to be around when the police get here, but I don't have any choice. Everyone will tell them about me.'

'*Police?*' Marnie said. 'Why will the police be involved?'

'Two serious incidents on the same site, one fatal, another that could've been fatal. The inspectors are bound to notify them, don't you think?'

'I expect you're right,' said Marnie.

'And then there's the question of Dick Blackwood,' Donovan went on. 'Where is he and what did he mean when he said, *What have I done?*'

'What do you think he meant, Donovan?' Marnie asked.

'Who knows? He was in shock. Perhaps he felt remorse after his row with Zoë that morning. For him, it was his last contact with her before she was killed.'

'You don't suppose he could've meant something else?'

'That he himself had killed her?'

Marnie and Anne looked shocked. Neither spoke.

'Is that what you think he meant, Marnie?' Donovan asked.

'I wasn't there, of course,' she said. 'You were. What do you think? Or you, Anne?'

'We were all stunned at the sight of Zoë lying there,' Anne said. 'I'm not sure I'd place too much importance on his actual words. We were all feeling like we wished we could've done something – *anything* – to bring her back from the dead.'

'And he wasn't there when she, so to say, came back,' Marnie said. 'So presumably he doesn't know she's alive.'

When the three of them returned to the building site they found two squad cars drawn up in echelon by the entrance gate. Between them was a dark grey Ford Mondeo, which Marnie guessed was an unmarked police car. She was right.

'That's interesting,' Donovan said under his breath, as they walked into the compound. 'No crime scene tape round the excavations.'

'Why's that, d'you think?' said Marnie.

'Presumably, they haven't decided a crime has taken place.'

'And the health and safety people are probably still examining the site,' Marnie added.

Beyond the dig area the students were assembled outside one of the huts and were being addressed by Professor de Groot. When he saw Marnie and the others he broke off and came towards them.

'Ah, Mrs Walker … Marnie … Philip Everett asked me to tell you he's in the staff hut with the contractors. He'd like you to join them. A phasing meeting, I believe.'

'What's happening here?' Marnie asked.

'The police are interviewing the students, and then I'm sending them off, probably for the rest of the week.'

'The *week*?' Marnie said. 'There goes our timetable out the window.'

'I'm afraid it rather looks that way,' said de Groot.

'Who's here from the police?' Donovan asked. 'Is it chief inspector Bruere?'

'No. I gather these are from the City of London force, not the Met. Let me see … there's a DS Crosby and a DC Haig. The sergeant asked for you by name,' he said to Donovan. 'He wants to see you.'

At once Donovan excused himself and set off for the hut, where he surmised the interviews were taking place.

'Good luck in IKEA,' Anne called after him.

Donovan half turned and winked at her as he walked away.

Marnie and de Groot looked at her quizzically.

'Private joke,' she said.

An hour later the students had left the site. The architects' phasing meeting failed as they were unable to produce a revised programme until the investigation of the accident was completed. Meanwhile, work was in progress to make the dig area secure.

To his surprise, Donovan had found himself praised by the detectives for his prompt actions, which may well have saved Zoë Tipton's life. It appeared that to everyone present when she had been brought to the surface, Donovan was regarded as a hero. To some, he was nothing less than a saviour. Both officers had stood and shaken his hand when he left the interview hut.

Marnie and Anne were waiting for him when he came out and both noticed his change of demeanour.

'Do I take it the interview went well?' said Marnie.

'You could say that.' Donovan had a twinkle in his eye. 'I'm afraid it's going to mess up your plans.'

'Oh? In what way?'

'I wouldn't be surprised if they decided to put up a statue to me. You're going to have to redesign the entrance. Can we go while I'm still winning?'

Back at the flat Marnie rang Ralph to bring him up to speed. He was now cruising round Milton Keynes on the last leg of the journey and had nothing special to report. Only one lock remained before he hit the home stretch. Marnie was sorry not to be travelling with him, but she expected to be back at Glebe Farm some time the following day.

Ever practical, Anne was making sandwiches while Marnie was on the phone. Donovan, wanting to know how Zoë was faring, rang the A and E department at the Royal London Hospital. He told the duty nurse that he was Zoë's brother and wanted to know to which ward she had been transferred so that he could visit her.

To his surprise there was no need for subterfuge when he rang the direct line for Saunders-Mayhew ward.

'I'm phoning about Zoë Tipton,' he said. 'I'd like to visit her this evening.'

The nurse hesitated. 'Are you Donovan, by any chance?'

'Yes, I am.'

'She's been asking for you.'

'For me? Can I speak to her?'

'That's not possible. She's sleeping now. But you can visit her between seven and eight.'

That evening they went in different directions. Philip Everett needed to discuss the Horselydown situation with Marnie and invited her to dinner at his home in Islington. They left together by taxi. Anne opted to visit Zoë with Donovan, and a short bus ride took them almost to the hospital door.

Saunders-Mayhew turned out to be a grouping of individual rooms for patients requiring special treatment, rather than an open ward. When Donovan and Anne presented themselves at the nurses' station, the sister on duty looked from one to the other. She was young with short brown hair and an authoritative bearing.

'We'd prefer it if she had just one visitor.'

'Is her condition so serious?' Donovan asked.

'She's had a near-death experience and we've had to cleanse her system very thoroughly. It's not surprising that she feels weak at the moment.'

'When I phoned I was told she was asking for me,' Donovan said.

'That's correct.'

'But Anne and I both helped her at the scene, and it was Anne who called the ambulance.'

The nurse looked them over again before rising from her chair. 'Wait here, please.'

She walked a short distance down the corridor and entered a room without knocking.

'D'you think Zoë's all right?' Anne said quietly. 'I didn't think she'd have restricted visits.'

'*Cleanse her system very thoroughly,*' Donovan said under his breath. 'I wonder what that means.'

Anne agreed. 'Better not to think about it.'

Moments later, the nurse returned and led them to Zoë's room. Before opening the door she said, 'You can both go in. Ten minutes maximum. She needs plenty of rest this evening.'

Anne braced herself mentally, but was surprised to find Zoë lying back against the pillows looking relatively normal if rather weary. There were no tubes attached to her face, no drips, no hook-ups to equipment. Zoë gave them a faint smile and gestured to two chairs.

'Nice of you to come.' Her voice was hoarse and she swallowed after speaking.

'How are you feeling?' Donovan said. 'Or is that a silly question?'

Zoë attempted a shrug, and her expression changed to quizzical.

'I didn't realise before, but now I can see the likeness.'

Anne looked at Donovan then back at Zoë. 'Try that again.'

'It had never occurred to me that you and Anne were ... I thought you were just friends.'

'What makes you think we aren't?' Donovan asked.

'The nurse said you'd come with your ... sister.'

That evening Marnie arrived back at the flat at ten-thirty to find Anne and Donovan watching the news on television. Anne straight away turned off the set and asked about the meeting with Philip.

'First of all, tell me about Zoë,' said Marnie. 'How is she?'

'Delusional.' Donovan chuckled.

'You mean she's hallucinating?'

'Absolutely.' Anne laughed. 'The nurse told her we were brother and sister, and she believed her.'

'Actually ...' Marnie looked at them appraisingly, '... that's not an unreasonable assumption. But apart from that, how was she?'

'We couldn't stay long,' Donovan said. 'She was very tired, and we think they'd had to pump out her stomach.'

Marnie grimaced, her thoughts straying to pump-outs on *Thyrsis*. 'Oh god, how awful.'

'She'd ingested quite a lot of mud and river water,' Donovan said. '... horrible thought.'

'The nurse thought she'd feel better after a good night's sleep,' Anne said. 'We can go back tomorrow.'

'Did Zoë say anything about the accident?' Marnie asked.

Donovan said, 'We didn't press her on that. She really wasn't up to it. The police had seen her and decided she was unfit to be interviewed. We just reassured her that the Roman ships hadn't been damaged.'

'No mention of Dick?'

'Not a word.'

'How was your evening in trendy Islington?' Anne asked. 'What's it like? I've never been there.'

'Very mixed. Where Philip lives, the houses were built in the 1830s, three storeys plus a basement. Philip and Stella have a huge family kitchen at the lowest level, with a refectory table and a sofa for socialising while the meal's being prepared. It has French windows leading onto a patio.'

'Sounds lovely. Modern furniture or antiques?'

'Mostly modern, but with a few old pieces.'

'And Stella?'

'Small, dark and bubbly.' Marnie grinned. 'She's delightful. Teaches textile design at a college like yours, Anne.'

'Do they have a family? Sorry, I'm sounding like the Inquisition.'

'Two teenage sons. They're away at the moment, staying with Stella's parents in Dorset.'

'Were you able to talk about the project?'

Marnie leaned back against the cushions of the sofa and breathed out slowly.

'Philip's worried Willards might be getting cold feet about the design. They're asking if it was too ambitious to have the lower levels exposed to the tides.'

'But ... but surely that's the whole point of the scheme ... the archaeology being a living part of the building.'

'Quite.'

'So what do they want to do?' said Anne. 'It's a bit late to alter the whole concept when the work's in progress.'

'That's the line Philip is taking ... plus the extra costs.'

'I can't imagine the archaeologists are overjoyed,' Donovan said. 'And don't they have financial support from some sort of national heritage fund?'

Marnie ran a hand across her forehead. 'The whole thing's a mess. Two major accidents, one of them fatal, delays to the work, a cutting edge design now being called into question, a major archaeological project with two directors and no leadership ...'

'But can you just alter the whole thing at this stage?' Anne said. 'I mean, there are contracts and stuff.'

'Philip has agreed to talk to the contractors about modifying the lower levels. Instead of having openings where the tides will be visible as they come in and go out, they might opt for a more conventional structure with a retaining wall to keep the water out permanently.'

'So it becomes just like any other riverside building,' said Donovan.

Marnie nodded. 'That's about it.'

'How does Philip feel about this?'

'Cheesed off is the short answer. He's trying to persuade Willards that the consultants' calculations are correct and there should be no problem. He still hopes to convince them not to go back on the proposal.'

'So everything's up in the air,' Donovan said.

'Everything and everyone connected with it,' Marnie agreed. 'It's a disaster in the making.'

20
Revisions

With building work halted, Marnie found herself on Tuesday morning in back-to-back meetings, together with Philip and Nigel Beardsley. They discussed the interim findings of the health and safety inspectors, revised timetables with the contractors and possible redesigns with their clients from Willards Brewery.

Donovan phoned the hospital and was surprised when the duty nurse in Saunders-Mayhew ward told him they operated an open-hours policy in that unit. He would be allowed a visit of up to twenty minutes if he came that morning, with two conditions: he would have to leave if a doctor came to examine Zoë, or if the police came to interview her.

Donovan set off with Anne mid-morning, stopping briefly to buy some fruit. On arrival at Saunders-Mayhew they learnt that the doctors had already examined Zoë, and the police had not yet appeared. Reminding them of the twenty minute rule, the nurse indicated Zoë's room down the corridor.

Zoë seemed if anything even more weary than the previous day, but she cheered up when Donovan presented her with a bag containing a bunch of bananas and two peaches.

'What, no grapes?' She attempted a wan smile. Although she sounded tired, her voice was no longer hoarse.

'A cliché,' Donovan said, 'and very over-rated. These'll buck you up.'

'How are you, Zoë?' Anne asked, trying hard to conceal her feeling that Zoë looked poorly.

'You think I look bad,' Zoë said, 'worse than yesterday.'

'No, I –'

'We all know it's true. No need to spare my feelings. The truth is, I didn't sleep properly last night … hardly slept at all.'

'Couldn't they have given you something to help with that?'

Zoë shook her head and adjusted her position. 'I don't take pills … not if I can help it.'

Donovan stepped forward and put his arms round her shoulders to support her back.

'Anne, can you arrange the pillows to help Zoë sit up.'

When Zoë settled back, she looked more comfortable. She even smiled faintly.

'Look,' Donovan said, 'I think you need to rest. We didn't come to tire you out.'

'What did you come for?' Zoë realised she sounded sharper than she intended. 'Sorry, I didn't mean it to come out like that.'

'But you're right,' Donovan said. 'We did have a purpose. Naturally, we wanted to see how you were. But we wanted to know if you could remember what happened to you.'

'I've been trying to put it out of my mind.'

'Sorry, we didn't want to –'

Donovan cut Anne off. 'You know the police will be coming to question you. They could be on their way here right now.'

'Your point being?'

Donovan shrugged. 'It might help if you had things clear in your mind beforehand. They have a way of asking questions that can unsettle you.'

Zoë sighed, laid her head back and closed her eyes. 'I don't really remember all that much.'

'The brain shuts out what it can't cope with,' Donovan said.

'You think that's what it is?'

'I know how it works from personal experience. I was involved in a serious accident when I was a kid. It was a while before the event seeped back into my memory. Then I had nightmares for a long time.'

'You're really cheering me up.'

'Can you remember anything?' Donovan persisted.

'I was down at the lowest level inspecting the ships. Dick appeared and we had an argument. That's it … apart from …'

'Go on.'

'I heard … a tremendous rushing sound, then something like an explosion. Dick's words were ringing in my ears.'

'What was he saying?'

'*Go to hell!*' Zoë frowned in concentration. 'But he'd already gone before the explosion happened … I think.'

There was a tap on the door, and the nurse looked in. 'Everything all right?'

Zoë nodded. 'Fine.'

'Ten more minutes.' The nurse smiled and closed the door.

'Why were you arguing with Dick?' Donovan asked.

Zoë closed her eyes. 'I accused him …'

No-one spoke for several seconds. Donovan prompted.

'The King John treasure?'

Zoë sighed again, her eyes still closed. 'I said I didn't believe he'd found it. He was furious … you can imagine.' She opened her eyes. 'The colour drained from his face. I told him I had evidence that he hadn't made the discovery.'

'You have actual proof?' Donovan said, incredulous.

'Yes. Well, a kind of witness statement. I'd spoken to Gerald Parfitt. None of Dick's story was true. He'd invented it, at least the part that led to finding the place where the royal treasure lay.'

'But we know he was working up by the Wash,' Donovan said. 'He can't have invented all of it.'

'No. He'd been going on sailing trips with Gerald last year, and they'd been doing surveys along the coast, but that was it.'

'He really hadn't found the treasure?' Anne said. 'What about those pieces he produced?'

'I don't know where he got them,' Zoë said in a weary tone. '… nor did Gerald. Look, can we just drop this? I don't want to keep going over it.'

In the hope of cheering Zoë up, Anne told her about the steps being taken to protect her ships. Nothing more was said about King John's treasure. When it was time to leave, Donovan promised to make Zoë a copy of his film. Zoë managed a smile but seemed already asleep before Donovan closed the door.

On their way to the bus stop, Donovan remained silent. Anne knew the signs and did not interrupt his thoughts. He said nothing until they saw their bus approaching. As it pulled into the kerb, he spoke as if talking to himself.

'It doesn't add up.'

Marnie had never seen the Willards executives looking so anxious. Three of them attended the meeting with the contractors that morning: the head of planning, the deputy head of finance and Malcolm Cawdrey, deputy chairman of the board. Almost equally uncomfortable were the contractors and the structural and electrical engineering consultants. The only person who seemed unfazed was Philip, who greeted Marnie warmly and offered her a seat beside him. On the other side, Nigel Beardsley opened his notepad.

Marnie herself presented a calm exterior, nodding and smiling at the suits round the table in the hotel conference room. She knew she had only a minor role to play, if any. The main topics were the fundamentals of the design, the overall timetable and financial implications.

Cawdrey asked Philip to chair the proceedings. This at first surprised Marnie, as Willards were the main players. It was their hotel, with their name stamped all over it. But as soon as the discussions began, she understood the decision. All the issues were technical and complex. It made sense to have the talks conducted by an expert.

Willards' concerns were twofold. First, they were anxious about delays apparently caused by inadequate safety measures, which had resulted in two serious accidents. Second, they had misgivings about so much depending on the archaeologists, who had proved to be at least unreliable and at worst a complete liability.

As the consultants debated the merits and costs of revising the project, Marnie found her thoughts wandering. She realised that the absence of any archaeologists was no oversight. It saddened her to think that they had lost the trust of the clients and their contractors. What had once been the core feature of the scheme had now virtually become an irrelevance. Decisions would be taken on hard-nosed business principles, and the archaeologists would have to deal with the consequences. Zoë's strident opinions would not be heard in that gathering. And as for Dick, where was he and, more to the point, what was he up to?

Marnie arrived back at the flat to find Donovan's bags stacked near the front door and Anne mixing tuna and mayonnaise in the kitchen area. The fresh tang of cucumber in the air was a reminder of summer picnics and immediately lifted Marnie's spirits.

'Lunch will be ready in five,' Anne called out.

'Music to my ears,' said Marnie, 'What's cooking?'

Anne looked up. 'Strictly speaking, nothing. But I'm making pittas stuffed with tuna, lettuce and cucumber. To follow, we've got fresh figs and Greek yogurt with honey.'

Marnie raised an eyebrow. 'Don't tell me they've discovered a temple to Athena in the dig site!'

'It's to Apollo, actually,' Donovan chipped in. 'Quite a surprise.'

'I just thought it would cheer us up, that's all,' said Anne.

'You think we need cheering up?' Marnie said.

'You tell us. You were at the meeting. Has the archaeology gone down the drain?'

'Too soon to tell. That was the verdict this morning.'

Anne walked to the table carrying a large plate on which she had arranged the stuffed pittas, with a sprig of parsley in the centre.

'Ah, the pitta platter of tiny feet,' Donovan said.

Anne stuck out her tongue. 'My feet aren't that tiny. For your cheek, Donovan, you can fetch the tray.'

With the meal set out on the table with a jug of sparkling water and lemon juice, Marnie returned to her explanation.

'Willards want a plan B. Philip is to explore the possibility of a more conventional building with the archaeology preserved and displayed in a dry basement, with a galleried walkway for viewing the remains.'

Marnie reached for a pitta while Anne poured water into glasses.

'Presumably the decision will depend on costs?' Donovan said.

'To a large extent, yes. Anne, this is *delicious*. A great idea.'

'Glad you like it. Won't there have to be some special treatment to keep the remains in good condition?'

'We're planning a fine water spray anyway. It'll just have to be modified.'

'How does Philip feel about this plan B?' Donovan asked.

'Naturally, he wants them to keep to the original design. I think he believes the cost of changing things will scare them off. They'll lose most of their heritage grants.'

'I'll drink to that,' said Anne.

All three raised their glasses and drank.

'What about Zoë?' said Marnie. 'How was she this morning?'

'Not brilliant. She's still confused about the accident.'

'Post-traumatic shock,' Donovan added. 'I doubt she'll be able to give the police much help, not for a while at any rate.'

'Any news of Dick?'

'Not a peep.'

'Talking of plans ...' said Anne, '... do we have any?'

'Back to Knightly St John. I expect Ralph will be home by now.'

'When are we leaving?'

'I think this afternoon before the rush hour. I see you've already got the flat tidied up.'

'We gave everything a good going over,' Anne said. 'The beds are made. We've hoovered. The kitchen has to be finished off. You just have to pack, Marnie.'

'What about you, Donovan?' Marnie asked. 'Will you come with us?'

'Sorry but I've got things to do ... the final touches from both lots of filming. It won't take long. But there's the house to see to.'

'Would you like to join us at the weekend?'

'That'd be great.'

Marnie smiled. 'Let's hope for a nice quiet summer's day or two.'

'I'll drink to that,' Anne said.

This time, as they raised their glasses, all three of them looked thoughtful.

21
Quiet Summer Days

It must have been the season for the granting of wishes. The next few days brought sunshine interspersed with dappled shade from passing clouds drifting lazily through blue skies. Life back in Knightly St John settled into its habitual routine with Marnie steaming ahead on designs for various clients, Ralph engrossed in analysing statistics for a new book, Anne running the office and fitting in periods of reading for her future course at art school.

Exceptionally, the three residents of Glebe Farm took a lunch break each day to make the most of the fine weather. They ate out on the bank beside *Sally Ann* and *Thyrsis*, sometimes sitting at the table under the parasol, at other times picnicking in deck chairs, nibbling snack lunches in desultory fashion while sunbathing. They strove to put behind them all thoughts of horrible accidents, rivalries between archaeologists and the anxieties of clients with high-risk projects.

But however much the three of them relaxed, at the back of their minds they knew they would shortly be confronted by the tribulations of Horselydown. The one bright element was the steady recovery of Zoë Tipton. Donovan rang to say that she had kept in touch with him – she seemed to regard him as a guardian angel – and that she was now out of hospital, convalescing at home in Cambridge.

On the other hand, everyone was concerned that there had been no news of Dick Blackwood. As the days passed, Marnie and co began to grow increasingly worried about what might have happened to him.

They were soon to discover that their fears were well-founded.

22
A Restless Weekend

Donovan arrived on Friday evening. Marnie was tidying her desk after work when he knocked on the door of the office barn and entered. He was wearing a black short-sleeved shirt, dark grey jeans and black trainers.

Marnie rose from her seat and greeted him with a kiss on both cheeks.

'How did you get here?'

'I drove.'

'I didn't hear your car.'

'I parked by the garage barn.'

Marnie locked the office and they walked through the spinney arm-in-arm.

Anne and Ralph had prepared a *salade niçoise* with French bread and a sauvignon blanc from New Zealand. It was warm enough to sit out at the table on the bank, with the fresh smell of the water and the sound of birdsong to accompany the meal. A pair of dragonflies buzzed around them briefly, swooping over the table, then rising up to hover beneath the parasol before darting off.

Donovan asked if they had heard anything from Dick, or about Dick, but there had been no word. No-one seemed to have any idea of his whereabouts. Donovan announced that Zoë had been discharged from hospital on Thursday. He had rung her number in Cambridge with no result. When he tried the Institute of Archaeology, the secretary informed him that Zoë had gone to stay with her parents, but regretted she was unable to 'divulge her phone number'.

'It's funny, isn't it?' Ralph observed. 'The way we use certain words only in specific contexts.'

Everyone at the table was used to Ralph speaking like a text book.

'You mean like *divulge*?' Marnie said.

'Yes. If we want to let someone have a phone number, we don't say we can *divulge* it. We just say we can give it. *Divulge* has a sinister, negative quality. It's the same with a word like *withhold*. We *withhold* information. Then there are words like –'

'Yes, darling,' Marnie interrupted the flow before it became a lecture. 'I think we get your drift.'

Ralph chuckled. 'Quite.'

'So back to the vanishing archaeologists,' Marnie said. 'Zoë's gone to stay with mum and dad. Dick's gone ...' she shrugged, '... who knows where?'

'Where does that leave us now?' Anne asked of no-one in particular.

Donovan began, 'At the risk of sounding like a cliché ...'

The refrain of *I'd have thought that was rather obvious* was voiced by Anne and Marnie in unison. Donovan laughed, unable to join in the chorus.

'Speak words of wisdom and enlighten us, O Sage,' said Marnie.

Donovan's turn to shrug. 'Someone has to go to East Anglia to try and trace Dick. He has questions to answer.'

'Isn't that a matter for the police?' Ralph said.

Donovan looked thoughtful. 'I think they'll just want to find out if he had anything to do with Zoë's accident.'

'You have something different in mind.'

'Of course. I'm sure he did nothing to harm Zoë. I'm much more interested in getting to the bottom of this whole business of King John's lost regalia and to finding out what has actually happened to Dick himself.'

Marnie thought of her workload, meetings with clients, the need to keep Walker and Co on track.

'Getting away might be difficult,' she said.

Ralph, who was immersed in several projects simultaneously as usual, agreed.

Anne looked in Marnie's direction. 'We've got a lot on right now,' she said.

After a long moment, Donovan spoke. 'My film editing is completed, so I'm free and flexible. I've promised my aunt in Göttingen that I'll go and spend a week or two there, but that can be any time before term starts in October.'

'You mean you could go to East Anglia?' Marnie said.

'Sure.'

'How would you organise the trip?'

'I've brought my camping gear with me in the car.'

Marnie looked at Anne. 'Everything's ticking over quite nicely here. I can manage things. There's nothing to prevent you going.'

Anne frowned. 'There's always plenty to keep us busy in the office, Marnie.'

'But there's no better time to take a few days off than mid-July.' Marnie smiled. 'I can cope here ... and we know how keen you are on camping ...'

Donovan glanced quizzically at Anne. She returned his gaze.

They loaded the VW after breakfast on Saturday. One overnight bag each fitted snugly in the cramped front luggage compartment. The rear seats were already occupied by the camping equipment. Marnie and Ralph waved them off at eight, with Donovan at the wheel and Anne riding shotgun, the road atlas resting in her lap.

Marnie linked her arm through Ralph's as they watched the Beetle burble off up the field track. 'I wonder how long it'll take them to get there.'

'Best part of three hours, I expect,' Ralph said. 'You can reach the coast in almost any direction in three hours from here.'

Marnie tilted her head on one side. 'The Beetle sounds different somehow, more growly. D'you think it's all right?'

'I wouldn't mind betting Donovan's been working on it. Just look at that bodywork. A quarter of a century old and it looks like new.'

When they left the village and joined the dual carriageway Anne gave her first directions.

'We'll be taking the by-pass round Northampton, the Nene Valley Way, following signs to Wellingborough then Peterborough. Okay with you?'

'Sounds fine.'

Anne relaxed and began taking stock of her surroundings. 'The car seems … *different*. The seats sort of grip you … very comfortable.'

'Ergonomics.'

'Really?' The name meant nothing to Anne, but it sounded impressive. 'So you've been doing things to it.'

Donovan tapped the steering wheel. Anne noticed for the first time that it had a polished wooden rim in a rich, attractive colour like cherry wood. He tapped the gear lever. It too had a cherry wood knob, and the stick itself was chrome, protruding from a leather cuff.

'Did you fit these?'

'Yep.'

'It seems different in other ways.'

'Alloy wheels?'

'Oh yes. I did notice them.'

'New mats on the floor,' Donovan suggested.

'No, I mean the sound of the engine. It seems quieter but its note is sort of … deeper … more like *Thyrsis* than *Sally Ann*.'

Donovan laughed. 'That sound you hear …'

'Yes?'

'It's Dr Ferdinand Porsche turning in his grave.' He pronounced the name like *Portia*.

'What? I mean, who?'

'The man who designed the original Volkswagen.' He pronounced the name the German way, like *Folx-vargen*. 'I'm not sure he'd be pleased at the comparison with a narrowboat engine.'

'Sorry, Ferdy,' Anne said. 'But am I right? Has something changed?'

'I'm glad you noticed. New parts on the engine … a new exhaust system.

And I've fitted insulation inside the car.'

Anne fell silent for the next mile or so. When she spoke again, there was a hesitancy in her voice.

'Donovan ... hope you won't mind me saying this ...'

'You're wondering how I can afford to do things like that.'

'Well ... yes ... really. Of course, it's none of my business. Sorry. Forget I said anything.'

'It's no great mystery, Anne. When my parents died, my father had life insurance. It paid off the mortgage on the house in London and left quite a large lump sum. On my mother's side there was a legacy from her parents in Germany. And when my uncle died two years ago, he had no children, so Uschi and I were his sole beneficiaries.'

'I see.'

'You're wondering if I'm rich.'

'For once, Donovan, your assumption is wrong.'

'Oh?'

'I was thinking that ... No. I don't think I should say any more.'

'Say what you want, Anne. You know you can be frank with me.'

'Well ... I was sort of thinking ... a sad thought ...'

'Ah, yes. And you'd be right. I would rather have my parents and my uncle alive than all the inheritances in the world.'

After making love with Ralph that night, Marnie felt restless. Listening to Ralph's steady breathing as he drifted off to sleep, she quietly slid her legs out from under the duvet, walked to the stern doors and pushed them open. The cool air wafted over her as she stood looking out across the water. It took a while for her eyes to adjust to the darkness. There was no illumination except starlight over Glebe Farm, but gradually she made out the form of the trees and hedges on the opposite bank. Somewhere nearby a fish jumped, and she saw the ripples spreading on the surface of the water.

She began thinking of Anne and Donovan, of the strange events at Horselydown. It seemed to be a place marked for death and tragedy, a place of grisly executions over hundreds of years. And now it had claimed the life of Miles Fennimore and almost killed Zoë Tipton. If she had been a believer in omens and portents, she would be having serious doubts about building a hotel in a place like that. Instead, she believed – or rather hoped – that the hotel project would bring new life and a fresh start to that corner of London.

In a way, that was precisely what she was trying to do at Glebe Farm. It too had known its share of tragedy, with a suicide and bodies in shallow graves.

It was the way of the world, Marnie thought. Everywhere could probably testify to tragic events in the past. And then she realised what was keeping her awake. She was wondering what Anne and Donovan would discover on their journey to East Anglia. Was the disappearance of Dick Blackwood going to be the next tragedy?

Everything about Dick was exaggerated, his discovery – or otherwise – of the lost treasure of King John, his disappearance, his strained relationship with Zoë. They would know his fate soon enough.

Marnie tried to focus on positive things. Somewhere in the dark fields beyond the waterway a fox barked. Before she moved to the country she would not have recognised that sound. Now it was as familiar as traffic noise in London. It was pleasant sleeping on the boat, but she could feel that phase of her life coming to an end. Soon she and Ralph would be moving into the farmhouse, and their life would settle into a new pattern. The question was, would their life be any more settled than it was now?

'This is like playing house,' Anne said, rolling out a sleeping bag on an inflatable mattress. 'I didn't realise you had a proper frame tent, Donovan, with *two* rooms. Do you call them rooms?'

'Chambers, I think. We used it to go on holidays when I was a kid.'

'Gosh, is it that old?' Anne sniffed the air. There was none of the mustiness she had expected. 'It seems like almost new.'

'It must be well over ten years old,' Donovan said. 'We only used it a few times and I've looked after it properly since then.'

They had found a camping site on a farm, where half a dozen caravans and a handful of tents were scattered about in a field. Donovan chose a slightly elevated position some distance from the outbuilding which housed the showers and toilets. When Anne asked why they weren't setting up the tent nearer to the facilities, Donovan simply smiled and said all would be revealed in the fullness of time. Anne let it go as just Donovan being enigmatic as usual.

'What are we going to do about eating?' Anne asked, plumping the pillows at the head of the sleeping bags. 'Are we going to try and find a pub or a chippy or something?'

Donovan was outside, fetching a large plastic box from the car. 'Were you talking about food, Anne?'

Anne stepped out of the tent. 'What's that?'

The box was bright blue plastic with a stout red handle that extended over its full length. Anne noticed that a wire was protruding from one end, and that Donovan had wound it round his hand.

'We can go out if you like, but I packed some basics in case we ended up somewhere remote.'

He laid the box on the ground. It was almost the size of an overnight bag. Anne was intrigued.

'Is it a coolbox?' she said. 'Did you have it plugged in in the car?'

'Yes. Also quite old, but it still works. The car didn't have a cigarette lighter, so there's no socket to plug into, but my father fitted an extension lead behind the driver's seat.'

'Clever man, your father.'

'Yes, he was. But the extension was just basic D-I-Y. So, what would you like to do?'

'Since you've brought the stuff, let's eat here. Then we'll be proper campers.' Anne laughed.

'Why are you laughing?' Donovan said.

'This reminds me of camping out in the garden with my brother when we were children. Summer nights at home. We treated it like an adventure.'

'An adventure in the garden at home,' said Donovan. 'Why not?'

'Absolutely. Sorry, I'm starting to sound like the *Famous Five* or *Swallows and Amazons*.' Anne's accent became *frightfully uppercrust*. 'I say, Dee, what a *spiffing* adventure!'

Donovan smiled at her, but only faintly. 'You know, Anne, you might want to be careful about *adventure*. You know my father lectured on German literature. He told me that *adventure* in medieval times meant whatever might befall you ... might come your way.'

'Was that good or bad?'

'Either was possible, but it usually meant ... sinister happenings.'

They fell silent while Donovan took plastic containers out of the coolbox.

'But for now,' he said, holding up each container in turn, 'why don't we concentrate on smoked cheese, rye bread, cucumber salad, coleslaw, hard-boiled eggs, yogurts and apples? And there's a choice of beer – German of course – or red wine. What is your pleasure, *madame*?'

Anne helped Donovan open the containers and set out their meal on melamine plates spread on a dark tartan picnic rug. The atmosphere had lightened, but both of them were thinking of Dick Blackwood and their mission the next day ... whatever might come their way.

23
Chinese Whispers

On Sunday morning they were the first people on the camp site to be up and about. It came as no surprise to Anne that Donovan had the tent dismantled and packed away in a matter of minutes while she rolled up the sleeping bags, and the air mattresses were deflating. They had showered the previous evening after supper, and Donovan, keen to be away, suggested they find a café somewhere for breakfast.

They stopped off near the shower block to use the toilets before leaving. Anne was the first to emerge and she stood by the car, looking out over gently rolling fields, enjoying the view. The VW was covered in beads of condensation, and a mist hung over the landscape. As she surveyed the area, she understood why Donovan had chosen the spot to erect their tent. The nearer part of the field which had seemed ideal, close to the facilities, lay in a slight hollow and was now cloaked in a dense blanket of mist.

Moments later, Donovan joined her. She pointed out the fog hollow. His only reply was a smile and a nod. Before driving off, he asked for a few minutes to finish preparing the car. From a plastic box under the bonnet he produced a large chamois leather and proceeded to wipe over the bodywork and windows while Anne studied the atlas and checked her notes. A few minutes later they were ready to leave.

'You said we were meeting Dr Parfitt in Norwich near the cathedral,' she said. 'Look's like an easy run from here.'

The engine rumbled into life. Donovan put the car in gear, and they trundled over the grass, through the field gate and out onto the open road.

For the first few miles they were on minor country byways, but soon reached the A148 and within minutes came upon a large filling station with a mini-market attached. Donovan pulled in and filled the tank while Anne investigated the shop. It boasted a coffee machine near a display of pre-packed Danish pastries. They breakfasted in a lay-by a mile down the road and when they set off again Anne produced bars of Kit Kat to sustain them on their journey.

The Beetle ticked off the miles, cruising solidly on the highway, with Anne noting passing villages to track their position. Donovan drove smoothly, treating the car with the respect due its not inconsiderable age. After rolling in silence for a while, Anne spoke.

'How did Dr Parfitt seem when you talked on the phone?'

'Friendly enough … quiet spoken … approachable, once he understood that I'd been working with Dick at Horselydown.'

'I wonder what he'll be able to tell us,' Anne said.

'I'm hoping he'll fill in some of the gaps.' Donovan negotiated a roundabout before continuing. 'At the moment we're faced with too many unknowns.'

Anne said, 'We know Dick was teaching Parfitt to sail. That's not in doubt. Also, we know he'd found some artefacts that could be part of the treasure.'

'Not sure Zoë would agree with that last bit,' Donovan observed.

'D'you think he lied about finding those things?' Anne asked.

'I don't understand why he'd lie. Zoë's theory is that he could only enhance his reputation, even if nothing else came to light. Somehow I don't see Dick doing something so blatantly dishonest. You saw him, Anne. He was genuinely excited by what he'd found.'

'Yes, he was. I've always thought of Dick as a totally dedicated archaeologist. So you believe he really had found King John's lost treasure, Donovan?'

'He found something.'

'Then why's he gone off like this? What's he up to?'

'I'm hoping he'll tell us that himself.'

'You think we're going to find him?' Anne said.

'I hope we are. And I hope he'll give us a simple explanation for everything.'

'So for once you haven't got it all worked out.'

Donovan laughed. 'I'm touched by your faith in me.'

'No, really. You always seem to be one jump ahead of everybody else.'

Donovan became serious. 'Anne, there's something we're all missing.'

'What?'

'That's just it. I can't put my finger on it. But it's probably staring us in the face.'

Marnie spent an hour that morning inspecting the farmhouse, leaving Ralph to his research on *Thyrsis*. She took a clipboard to list all the work still outstanding. To her surprise, the list was not long. Bill and his mate had made good progress during her absence. She saw too that the joiner was well advanced with his work. The fitted oak bookcases were almost complete, and shelving was in place in all the cupboards. Only the kitchen remained unfinished, and even there she estimated there was only another fortnight's work till completion.

Marnie stood for some minutes in the kitchen – the *farmhouse kitchen*, she told herself – a generous space, with windows looking out over the garden on two sides. That morning it smelled of freshly sawn timber and new putty. She tried to imagine other smells there: bread baking, bacon sizzling, a hint of garlic, cucumber being sliced, coffee filtering.

She walked through to the living room, which gave onto the rear terrace through French windows. At the sight of the garden – *garden to be* – she grimaced. It was a jungle, no doubt home to as yet unidentified species of wildlife. Anne had once told her she was convinced gorillas were living in there.

Thinking of Anne made Marnie wonder what progress she and Donovan were making. They would be well on their way by now, she thought. Pressing number two on the mobile's speed-dial, she heard the ringing tone. After three rings, Anne came on the line sounding crackly but reasonably clear.

'Do I hear road noise?' Marnie asked.

'Yes. ETA is about half an hour.'

'All well?'

'Fine. How about you?'

'I've just reached a major decision, actually *two* major decisions.'

'You're starting to sound like Donovan! Where are you?'

'I'm standing in the kitchen.'

'D'you mean the galley?'

'No. I'm in the farmhouse.'

'Your decisions concern the house?'

'Yes. The first is that I'm aiming to move in this autumn.'

'That's great. And the second?'

'I'll tell you when you get back.'

'Even more like Donovan! A *woman* of mystery.' Anne paused. 'Well let me tell you something. Deciding on the colour could be tricky ...'

'What d'you mean?'

'I'm guessing the front-runners are dark blue or red,' Anne said. 'Tough choice.'

Marnie laughed. 'I don't know what you're talking about.'

'Of course you don't,' said Anne.

'Safe journey and keep me posted. Give my love to Donovan.'

As Marnie disconnected, she looked up from a brochure lying on the workbench beside her to see Ralph walking into the kitchen.

'All quiet on the eastern front?' he said.

Marnie grinned. 'She's a witch, that girl, I'm convinced of it.'

'What's your evidence this time?'

Marnie pointed at the brochure. Ralph looked over her shoulder at a catalogue of Aga cookers open at the page illustrating the range of colours. Marnie had written question marks against two of them. One was dark blue, the other, red.

'So you've decided on an Aga?' Ralph said.

Marnie nodded. 'They're so expensive. I suppose it's now or never. And this place is made for one.'

Ralph put a hand on her shoulder. 'You know about the four adult ages of Man?'

'Would Man embrace woman?'

'Any time.' He held her by the waist. 'The four ages are, in this order: lager – Aga – Saga – gaga.'

Marnie groaned and hugged him tight.

Hearing Anne give Marnie their estimated time of arrival, Donovan calculated they had about an hour in hand before the rendez-vous with Dr Parfitt. He pulled into a lay-by and asked to see the road atlas. The coast was not many miles north of their current position, and he traced a line up to a point where the name seemed familiar.

'Isn't that where the marina is, where Parfitt keeps his boat?' he said.

Anne looked at her notepad. 'Whittleham, yes. That's the place.'

'Why don't we look in? We've got bags of time to spare. I'd like to see the boat and get the lie of the land … or the sea.'

'Fine by me,' Anne said. 'Take the next left.'

Donovan put the car in gear and pulled out onto the highway.

'Donovan, do you have another reason for going there?'

'Such as?'

'You're hoping we might find Dick there, aren't you?'

'The thought had crossed my mind. But even if we don't, I'd still like to do a recce. I like to be prepared.'

As they drew nearer to the coast it became noticeably breezy, and at their first sighting of the sea they could see white tops on the waves. Anne pointed towards the rolling grey waters.

'Look … white horses.'

Donovan looked but said nothing. Anne directed him to turn right along the coast road, and within minutes they saw the sign to Whittleham Marina on their left. The road stood at a slightly higher level than the harbour, and instead of driving down to the car park, Donovan pulled off onto the grass verge. They had a commanding view of the pontoons where dozens of white-hulled sailing boats were tied up, their sails furled under covers. The village of Whittleham lay to their left at the mouth of a creek, and with the tide in, a host of small boats rode at anchor in the channel.

Donovan switched off the engine and let down his side window. Immediately a salty breeze buffeted the inside of the car, and a tinny, rattling sound assailed their ears.

'They could make a better job of that,' Donovan murmured.

'Do you know about sailing boats?' Anne asked.

'We used to have one when I was little, a twenty-eight footer. Kept it at Gosport.'

'So you're knowledgeable about sailing.'

'Not really. Both my parents enjoyed it, but the time they died was about when I would've started to learn, so I never really ...'

Anne bit her lip, regretting that she had introduced a painful subject.

'So what could they make a better job of?' she asked, indicating the boats in the marina.

'Some of the boats have their halyards loose. My father would've thought that was sloppy. He'd never have left them to clank against the mast like that. That's the noise you can hear. He always tied them back to the spreaders to keep them clear.'

Donovan reached across and opened the glove box. He took out a compact pair of field glasses and began sweeping the marina. Watching him, Anne found herself remembering her first impression of him and *XO2*: Donovan, the U-boat *Kapitän*.

'What can you see?' she said.

'I'm looking for ... ah ... what did you say Parfitt's boat was called?'

'*Arabella.*'

Donovan leaned forward, adjusting the focus of the glasses. 'Got her. There she is. Nice boat.'

Anne muttered under her breath. 'Half ahead both, come left two points, flood forward torpedo tubes.'

Donovan lowered the binoculars and stared at her. 'Sorry?'

Anne shook her head. 'Nothing ...' She grinned at him. '... *Herr Kapitän.*'

Donovan raised the glasses, shaking his head slowly. 'Funny girl!' he said, smiling.

'What now, then?' Anne said.

Donovan lowered the glasses. 'Presumably, fire one ... fire two?'

'Something like that.'

'She looks deserted, but I'd like to go down and take a quick look. I don't think Dick – or anyone else – is on board.'

'Can we just do that?' Anne said. 'Don't we need permission?'

'We'll soon find out. Anyway, it's easier to ask forgiveness than permission.'

Donovan gave Anne the binoculars and started the engine. The road led down to a car park beside the moorings. Large signs stated that access was strictly reserved for those with genuine business on the boats. They parked as close as they could to where *Arabella* was moored, and Donovan set off walking assuredly along the pontoon while Anne remained in the car. She was to start the engine if anyone came to investigate them.

A quick inspection told Donovan all he needed to know. The cabin was locked shut with a padlock on the outside. An inflatable dinghy, also secured by padlock was stowed on the deck. They were soon heading back to the main road, confident that their visit had gone unnoticed.

In the marina office another pair of binoculars was lowered, and the registration number of the black Beetle was noted in the daily log.

Ralph was glancing through the *Observer* magazine as relief from the business news, when he spotted an article about eating habits. It was one of those lifestyle pieces that reveal changing trends under the heading, *The Way We Live Now*. The discussion of food tickled his taste buds, and he rang Marnie in the office.

'Had any thoughts about lunch?' he asked.

Marnie reflected. 'Nothing ... specific. Why? Are you hungry already?'

'I was wondering if you fancied going out for a traditional British Sunday lunch, the country's favourite meal.'

'Roast beef and Yorkshire pud?' Marnie said.

'Not even close ... it's chicken tikka masala.'

'Really? Since when?'

'I've just read about it in the *Observer*.'

'Oh well, then it must be true. But will we get a table at such short notice?'

'I'll ring the Maharajah Tandoori.'

'Give him my regards,' said Marnie.

The road atlas had a section at the back giving street plans of the centres of major towns and cities, which included Norwich. Anne guided them to a car park that was free on Sundays. They walked to the cathedral precinct in five minutes and took another minute or two to locate the pub suggested by Dr Parfitt. As they walked towards it, they saw a man in shirtsleeves coming from the opposite direction. He was of average height and medium build, with a shock of sandy hair and carrying a briefcase. His trousers were khakis with patch pockets, and his shirt was chequered in cream and green.

'I bet he's our man,' Anne said quietly.

She was right. The man smiled hesitantly as the three of them converged on the pub's front entrance. Anne was determined to resist the temptation to say *Dr Parfitt, I presume*, and she hoped Donovan would do the same. As soon as they got within speaking range, Parfitt extended a tentative hand.

'Would I be right in thinking ...?'

'I'm Anne, Anne Price.'

'Donovan Smith.'

'Gerald Parfitt. Good to meet you.'

Parfitt nodded towards the pub's door. 'Is this okay for you? They do a rather good Sunday lunch.'

'Are there vegetarian options?' Donovan asked.

'Of course.'

Anne smiled. 'Thank you. It's fine.'

Parfitt led the way inside. The pub was cool and beamy, and even though it was barely noon, the place was filling up. Parfitt found a vacant table near the inglenook fireplace, which at that time of year boasted a huge display of summer flowers. The menu was chalked up beside the bar.

'We can leave some things here to keep our table.' Parfitt placed his briefcase on one of the chairs. 'You're my guests today, by the way,' he added, in a tone that was almost apologetic.

'Oh no, really –' Donovan began.

Parfitt raised a hand. 'No arguing. I insist. You're here at my invitation.'

He walked off towards the bar, and the discussion was at an end. After placing their orders, Parfitt held back while Anne and Donovan took their places at the table. He joined them a minute later clutching a bottle of wine and three glasses.

'I've got the house red. Is that all right? If you'd prefer something different ...'

Agreement was unanimous, and Parfitt began pouring.

'It's good of you to agree to meet us,' Donovan said.

'And to offer us lunch,' Anne added. 'That's very generous of you.'

'Not at all. You said you wanted to talk about possibly doing some filming for a university project? I'd be happy to help.'

They clinked glasses and drank to each other's health.

'Actually ...' Donovan said, 'we'd like to talk to you about Dick Blackwood's project.'

'Oh yes? Which one?'

'Which one?' Anne repeated.

'Well, there's the Saxon find in London,' Parfitt said, 'and his doctoral research topic, concerning revolts against the Normans in the wetlands hereabouts.'

'What about the King John's lost regalia project?' Donovan said.

'Okay ...' Parfitt looked thoughtful. '... though I'm not sure how much I can help you with that one.'

'Could you tell us what you do know about it?'

'Certainly, but you may find my knowledge rather limited. You really need to talk to Dick for the details.'

'That's just it, Dr Parfitt –'

'Call me Gerald.'

'Right, Gerald,' Donovan continued. 'Dick seems to be away at the moment, and I'd like to prepare myself for working here before we begin.'

'I can understand that from the filming point of view. The light up here is very ... how can I put it? ... extraordinary luminosity ... big skies and all that.'

'Could you fill us in on some of the background, perhaps?' Anne said.

Just then their food arrived. Parfitt topped up their glasses and they began eating.

Donovan said, 'We understand you spoke to Zoë Tipton about Dick's discovery of part of the king's treasure.'

'Oh well, I couldn't really say much about that,' Parfitt said hastily.

'Do you mean to us now or to her then?' Donovan asked. 'We do understand about the need to respect confidentiality, especially in relation to something as major as this. But if there's anything you feel you could tell us ...'

Parfitt looked up from his meal and fixed Donovan with a stare. He took another forkful of roast pork before replying.

'I'm not sure what to say. How much do you know already?'

'That you helped Dick with his research on the rebellion that took place in this area at that time ...' Parfitt nodded. Donovan continued. 'That you provided him with documentary material to show how the land had changed over the centuries ...'

Parfitt glanced down at the briefcase on the floor beside him. 'That's right, and I've brought some things to show you.'

'That's great,' said Donovan. 'We also know that you went out in your boat with Dick ...' Murmurings of agreement from Parfitt. 'That you possibly involved marine archaeologists from your university that led to Dick bringing up artefacts that have since been identified by experts as part of King John's regalia.'

Parfitt put down his knife and fork and took a mouthful of wine. It was difficult to read his expression.

'Are we on the right track so far?' Anne said.

Parfitt placed the glass carefully beside his plate and frowned.

'Sorry, but I haven't the faintest idea what you're talking about,' he said.

Several seconds passed in silence. Anne realised she was gaping and shut her mouth so quickly that the snap of her teeth could be heard at the next table. Even Donovan was momentarily lost for words. He took a sip of wine before speaking.

'Which part don't you know about?' he asked. 'You did go out in the boat with Dick?'

'Yes.'

'And the marine archaeologists?'

Parfitt's frown deepened. 'I don't know where you got that idea.'

Donovan looked at Anne as if asking for help.

'Was it Dick who told us that?' she said uncertainly. 'Or Zoë perhaps ...'

'Dr Parfitt ...' Donovan began, '... Gerald ... can we go back a step or two? I'm not sure now where our understandings diverge.'

'I think that would be a good idea,' Parfitt agreed.

'You went out sailing with Dick. That much is fact.'

Parfitt nodded decisively. 'Correct.'

'And you produced material about the changing nature of the landscape up here during the period in question?'

'Yes.' Parfitt picked up the briefcase, opened it and produced a bundle of maps and other documents. 'These are the things I showed Dick.'

'And he used that information to work out the route King John took on what was to be his last journey.'

Parfitt looked bewildered. The corners of his mouth turned down and he shook his head.

'You don't know about that?' Donovan said.

'Absolutely not. What made you think I did?'

'You're making me doubt if that is in fact what I heard.' Donovan looked back to Anne. 'I didn't imagine it all, did I?'

Anne shrugged. 'Perhaps ... actually, now that you mention it, I'm not sure any more what Dick said and what we were left to guess.'

Donovan turned to Parfitt. 'I found out from LBU sources that you and Dick were involved in a project together and that you'd been staying in a bed and breakfast somewhere between Wisbech and King's Lynn.'

'You're right. That was last autumn.'

'And you've not been involved since?'

'How could I?'

'I'm sorry, Gerald, I don't follow.'

'I've been out of the country for half a year, seconded for a semester at the University of Roskilde in Denmark. I'm deputy director of the Danelaw project. That's a joint Anglo-Danish study of the invasion of England and its impact on the economy of Zealand in the ninth century ...'

Parfitt went on describing the work of the project and his part in it, but for Donovan and Anne all their thoughts were on their misconceptions about Dick Blackwood and his *big discovery*. Could Zoë be right? Was Dick's story about the find of the century – of *eight* centuries – a fabrication from beginning to end?

As they continued their meal, Anne and Donovan feigned interest in Parfitt's work in Denmark while he explained it in some detail. When the table was cleared and they waited for coffee, he opened out the maps and photographs he had produced for Dick and showed them how the wetlands along the coast of the Wash had ebbed and flowed down the ages.

It was small wonder that no-one had ever located the lost treasure. The baggage train could be anywhere in a vast area covered at different times by water, marshes, mudflats and farmland. It could lie buried beneath twenty or thirty feet of soil either on the seabed or under fields planted for grain or beet. Had the dream of making such a discovery preyed on Dick's mind like an obsession? Not unlikely, they thought. Perhaps that gleam in Dick's eye held a glint of madness or at least fanaticism.

Coffee arrived. Parfitt gathered up the papers and put them back in his briefcase.

'I suppose you've no idea, Dr ... er, Gerald, where Dick might be?' Anne said.

'None at all, I'm afraid.' He closed the briefcase and set it down on the floor. 'Mind you, one odd thing has happened. One of the other boat-owners in the marina did say he saw Dick recently.'

'At Whittleham?'

'Yes. He assumed Dick was there checking over *Arabella*. He's been keeping an eye on her during my absence.'

'Do you know where Dick lives?' Donovan asked.

'Of course, but I've tried phoning his mobile without success. ... the usual voicemail reply: *caller-not-available.* I've left messages for him in the department at LBU. No response.'

'What about his family?' Anne said.

'There's no-one in this country, as far as I know. When his father retired, his parents moved to Canada a few years ago – his mother's from Toronto – to be near Dick's sister. She moved there when she got married, and there are no other siblings.'

Anne looked at Donovan. 'Could he have left the country?'

'I was just wondering …'

After lunch they took leave of each other with handshakes outside the pub.

'Thank you very much for seeing us, Gerald,' Anne said, 'and for your hospitality.'

'My pleasure. I'm only sorry I couldn't help you further with your enquiries. I'm sure Dick will be able to clear up any misunderstandings when you see him. There'll probably be a perfectly simple reason for his absence.'

'We hope so, too,' Anne said. 'Somehow we managed to get it all wrong.'

They watched Dr Parfitt walking off before they turned back to find the car park. Anne linked arms with Donovan as they strolled along in bright sunshine.

'What are you thinking?' she said.

'Nothing fits. We're none the wiser.'

Marnie had her mobile switched off in the restaurant, so she missed the call when Anne phoned to report on their meeting with Parfitt. Anne left a message that she would ring back later.

Although Ralph tried to give his full attention to the chicken tikka masala and Marnie did her best to focus on the lamb tarka dal, both of them found their thoughts wandering.

Eventually Ralph said, 'I wonder how Anne and Donovan are getting on.'

'They're on my mind too,' said Marnie. 'And I was thinking about Zoë as well. She's lucky to be alive. The whole Horselydown project is starting to feel doomed.'

'It's funny, isn't it?' Ralph began. 'In ancient times in some countries they used to slaughter an animal and let its blood run into the foundations of a building. They still do that in some countries, I believe, a sacrifice to the gods.'

Marnie got the inference. 'Dr Fennimore …'

'And Zoë, too, almost,' said Ralph. 'A sobering thought.'

Marnie looked down at the succulent pieces of lamb on her plate and felt her appetite fading away.

The rest of the day lay before them, and they were free to do anything they wished. Anne suggested they head for the sea. Donovan pointed the VW northwards, and they chugged along until they found a broad beach, sparsely occupied, fringed by dunes and pine trees. Although the sky had become opaque and a light haze hung over the coast, they were happy just to unwind and do nothing in the warmth of the afternoon.

While Donovan spread out the picnic rug on the white sand and inflated the air mattresses, Anne sat in the car and changed into shorts and a skimpy tank top. She walked down to the beach, where Donovan produced sunblock. When he came back after donning shorts, he found her smoothing the lotion on her legs. She passed it to him.

'Lovely smell,' she said.

Donovan nodded. 'Always reminds me of family holidays.'

'How do you pronounce the name of it?' she asked.

Donovan read the maker's name, *Piz Buin*, and pronounced it for her. 'It's like *Pits Boo-een*.'

'German, of course,' Anne said, smiling.

'Swiss, I think. Very popular for winter sports holidays … sun reflected off mountain snow and all that.'

They idled away an hour or two reading magazines. When it was time to rub suntan lotion on each other's backs, Donovan suggested Anne might take off the tank top. After a moment's hesitation, she pulled it over her head and rolled onto her stomach. Both of them had naturally pale skin and after lying in the sun for part of the afternoon, they turned an unimpressive faint shade of shrimp.

Anne looked at Donovan and laughed gently. 'Even the Germans, I mean the Swiss, can't guarantee a Mediterranean tan,' she said, 'or even an Alpine one.'

But Donovan was not smiling. Anne could see that his thoughts were miles away, and she knew what was occupying his mind.

It was a happy afternoon in spite of all their concerns about Dick Blackwood's disappearance, and they were relaxed and contented when they carried their beach things back to the car. Donovan said he had noticed a camping site not far from the sea that morning, and they set off to find it. When they arrived, it had plenty of space. The amenities were modern and clean and the charges reasonable.

They set up the tent together and soon had their temporary home in good order. After their lunch with Dr Parfitt, neither felt hungry, and Anne was taking out a book to read when Donovan remarked that they were not far from the marina.

'Do you want to go back there?' Anne asked.

Donovan's expression was thoughtful. 'I wouldn't mind a second look. You never know, he might be there this time. He has to be living somewhere secluded.'

'But surely Dr Parfitt would know about it, if Dick was staying on his boat.'

'Who says he doesn't?'

They put the camping chairs inside the tent and zipped it up. A minute later they were back on the road to Whittleham. Taking the turning to the marina, Anne was reaching to unbuckle her seat belt when Donovan continued past the grass verge where they had stopped earlier in the day. He drove straight into the car park, making no attempt to be inconspicuous. They climbed out and walked onto the pontoon leading to *Arabella*. Since their previous visit the tide had turned, and the boat was now resting on its twin keels.

'Are you expecting things to have changed since this morning?'

Donovan studied the boat intensely, seeming not to have heard Anne's question. *Arabella* was one of the craft which had its halyards properly tied to the spreaders; the dinghy was securely in place; the sail was tightly covered and stowed away; the hull, decking and topsides were clean. Everything about *Arabella* was neat and tidy. The words *ship-shape* and *Bristol fashion* ran through Donovan's mind. Most important of all, the padlock was still firmly in place.

'Donovan?'

'Look at the boat, Anne. What does she tell you?'

'She looks … orderly. Whoever looks after her is very competent.'

'Does she look to you like a boat that's been lying idle for most of the year?'

'Now that you mention it, I suppose she does give the impression of being well maintained … definitely not neglected.'

'Exactly.'

'But it doesn't look as if Dick's staying on board.'

'No, it doesn't. Now I'm wondering if we've got the story wrong or if maybe someone's been paid to keep the boat in good order during Parfitt's absence.'

'I think you're about to find out.' Anne was looking over Donovan's shoulder.

He turned to see a man approaching them down the pontoon. He was wearing a check shirt and jeans and had the weather-beaten tan of someone who spent much of his time in the open air.

'Can I help you?' It was the standard phrase used to demand what you were doing, with the implication that you shouldn't be doing it.

'Good afternoon,' Donovan said. 'We were rather hoping to find a friend here.'

He held out a hand, which the newcomer shook with a grip that would bend mild steel. Anne followed suit, trying not to wince.

'And who might that be?'

'Our friend is Dick Blackwood. He's an archaeologist and sails from here.'

'Oh?' Another standard response, conveying the meaning, *I'm trying to give you the benefit of the doubt, but you'll have to do better than that.*

'My name's Donovan Smith, by the way, and this is Anne Price.'

Anne smiled, grateful that the blood was beginning to circulate in her hand again.

'Guy Horsfall, manager of the marina. So, this friend of yours ...'

'Dick comes here to sail with Dr Gerald Parfitt of the University of East Anglia.'

'Ah ...' This message signified, *Okay, you're on the right track.*

'*Arabella* belongs to Gerald, of course,' Donovan added.

'She does. What made you think your friend might be here?'

'Just a thought. We came by on the off-chance. We had lunch with Gerald today and –'

'Where was that?'

'A pub round the corner from the cathedral in Norwich ... *The Mitre*, I think it was called.'

Horsfall nodded. 'I know it. They do a pretty good Sunday lunch by all accounts.'

Donovan turned and began walking slowly along the pontoon. 'I was wondering ...'

'Yes?'

'Has the boat been laid up for a while?'

'*Arabella* laid up? What gave you that idea?'

'I thought Gerald said he'd been away a lot this year. She doesn't look as if she's been abandoned for months on end.'

'She's been out regularly.'

'You've seen Gerald quite often, then?'

'Not exactly,' said Horsfall. 'Now I come to think of it, I'm not sure when I actually last set eyes on him.'

Donovan stopped. 'Sorry, I'm not with you.'

'It's a funny thing, but some days when I arrive I find she's already gone out. If I spared her a thought it was to assume Gerald had taken advantage of the tide, but ...' Donovan and Anne waited while Horsfall collected his thoughts. '... I'm not really sure if the tides had anything to do with it.'

They began slowly walking on again.

'So what are you saying, Mr Horsfall?' Donovan said.

'If there is a pattern it's that Gerald chooses to take her out some time between my going home and my coming back in the morning.'

'Is that a normal pattern of sailing here?'

Horsfall blew air through his lips. 'People are all different, but I would say Gerald's the only one in this marina who tends to do that.'

'So you haven't seen him around with our friend, Dick Blackwood?'

'Can't say I have. I don't in fact recognise the name.'

Donovan stopped in the car park a few yards from the VW, and Horsfall stared at it, appraising it from end to end.

'Thank you for your time, Mr Horsfall,' Anne said.

'My pleasure.' He returned his gaze to the car, which was shining in the late afternoon sunlight. 'That's a little beauty. Was she in that condition when you bought her?'

'Better,' said Donovan. 'We've had her from new.'

Horsfall looked sceptical. 'That car's older than you are ... seventy-one plates, aren't they?'

'By *we*, I meant my family.'

'Well, you've certainly looked after her ... and added quite a few extras, I see. I like the wood-rimmed steering wheel ...'

While Donovan patiently answered Horsfall's questions about the merits of Twin Hot Spot exhaust systems and Koni shock-absorbers, Anne knew he really wanted to know more about Parfitt and *Arabella*. He seized his chance when Horsfall gave him an opening.

'You've been here before, of course.'

'Here?' Donovan said. 'Oh, today, you mean. Yes, we dropped by this morning. I was curious to see the boat and, as I said, perhaps run into our friend who sails with Gerald.'

'This other archaeologist ...' said Horsfall, 'Dick, er ...'

'Blackwood,' Donovan supplied. 'Yes?'

'Well, as I said, he's not known to me.'

'I'm guessing, but I think Dick may be one of the reasons why *Arabella* is in such good order.'

Horsfall looked puzzled. 'What makes you say that?'

'She's in very good shape, considering her owner's a novice. Everything about her looks just right.'

'A novice?' said Horsfall. 'Gerald Parfitt? What makes you think that?'

Donovan frowned. 'I thought he'd only recently acquired *Arabella*.'

'That's true, but she's not his first boat. He's had others over the years. He's a fine sailor, very experienced.'

249

Anne finally got through to Marnie that evening and gave an outline of the day's findings. After their conversation had ended, Marnie ran through everything in her mind. Nothing seemed to add up.

She was sitting out in a deckchair on the bank while Ralph was in the galley on *Thyrsis*. He had offered to make a small treat to round off the weekend, and when he appeared carrying a tray containing two glasses of Pimm's, she congratulated him on his choice. They settled down to watch the sun dipping towards the horizon in sybaritic bliss. As they sipped, Marnie gave Ralph an account of what Anne and Donovan had learnt that day.

For a while Ralph made no reaction. He put his glass down on the picnic table between the deckchairs and sat gazing ahead.

Eventually he said, 'You know, Marnie, I can't make head or tail of what's been going on. Everyone who's spoken about the events of this summer seems to be describing a *completely* different set of circumstances.'

'I'm reassured to hear you say that, Ralph. I was beginning to wonder if it was just me.'

'Perhaps it's all a case of Chinese whispers. We hear part of the story and it changes each time it gets passed on.'

Marnie frowned. 'But the versions we hear are by the actual participants. Dick says one thing, Zoë says another. We see one side of things, Donovan and Anne come up with something else. This Dr Parfitt has a different take on it altogether.'

'Curiouser and curiouser …' Ralph said quietly.

Marnie shook her head. 'This isn't a fantasy, darling. Something's going on that we're not seeing.'

'Perhaps it's just a matter of differing perceptions of the same thing,' Ralph suggested.

Marnie looked sideways at Ralph, who was sipping his drink. *Spoken like a true academic*, she thought. She kept that to herself.

'You know what I think, Ralph? Someone's lying. It's as simple as that.'

'But do you know who that person is?' Ralph said.

Marnie shrugged. 'I don't think we'll be any the wiser while Dick's gone to ground.'

'Well, one thing seems certain,' Ralph said. 'He doesn't appear to have gone to sea.'

24
Donovan's Plan

Anne could not help feeling guilty the next day. To be having a leisurely breakfast before packing up the camping gear felt like playing truant on a Monday morning. Donovan was in no rush to be away early. He wanted to give the *so-called-rush-hour* traffic, as he put it, time to clear the roads. Although he was as attentive to her as always, Anne noticed that when she glanced in his direction, his mind was elsewhere. She knew he was not just trying to understand the situation, but seeking to move beyond the immediate.

They drove out of the camp site just after nine and turned westwards. Anne opened the road atlas on her lap.

'Home, James, and don't spare the horses,' she said in a la-di-da voice.

'Yes, madam.' The reply came with clipped vowels.

Anne smiled. 'It is home, I assume.'

'Where else?' said Donovan.

'Just checking. I'm never quite sure with you.'

'I'd like to call in at Dick's digs in London, but first we need fresh clothes and ...'

'And what? Come to think of it, how can we call in at his digs when we don't know where he lives?'

'That's what I've been thinking about.'

'And have you come up with an answer?'

'I might have.'

'I've been wondering about it, too,' Anne said.

Donovan continued. 'The only people who know where he lives are at the university.'

'But they won't *divulge* his address, will they?'

'No.'

'Then how will you get hold of it?'

'Is there any chance you could be free over the next few days?'

'That depends on Marnie and on how much there is to do at the office, but these are the summer holidays, so I suppose I might. What do you have in mind?'

'I'm still working on it.'

'But this is where the university comes in, is it?'

'More specifically, Anne, it's where *you* come in.'

Marnie was standing on the newly-laid terrace at the back of the farmhouse, surveying the *jungle*, when she heard the familiar burble of the Beetle coming down the field track. Inside the building a cacophony of banging could be heard. From the kitchen came the sound of units being knocked into place. From upstairs she could hear nails being hammered into slatted shelves for the airing cupboard. This was the chorus of the finishing touches. After two years of steady progress on the renovation, completion was in sight. Soon the action would shift to the garden. Marnie grimaced at the thought.

Round by the garage barn, car doors were slamming shut. Next came footsteps on gravel and voices, Anne calling out to Steve the carpenter. A minute later, Anne and Donovan joined Marnie on the terrace. After hugs all round, Anne turned to face the garden.

'Well, it's obvious what has to be done here,' she said.

'That's good news,' said Marnie. 'I've been puzzling over it for ages. Tell all.'

'First step, we send for Dr Livingstone to lead the expedition.'

'Do you design gardens as well as interiors, Marnie?' Donovan said.

'I've got some ideas, but I want to talk to some friends in London first.' With a sigh, Marnie turned and walked them round the side of the house. 'Let's change the subject. Just thinking about all the work that has to be done out here makes me feel weary. What I want to know is if you found out anything in darkest Norfolk. Why don't you tell us all about it over lunch?'

Ralph joined them on the bank for a light meal of scotch eggs, cheese rolls and fruit. They accompanied this with chilled lemonade that Marnie had made the day before. Anne gave an account of everything they had learnt on their trip, which added little to what Marnie and Ralph already knew.

'So all rather inconclusive,' Marnie said.

'At least we've now heard all sides of the story,' Donovan pointed out, 'even if they all contradict each other.'

'All sides except one,' Ralph observed. 'Strictly speaking.'

'I was counting what Dick had told us before as his version,' said Donovan.

'And that seems like all we're going to get,' Marnie added.

'Not really.' Donovan paused. 'The next step is to get the whole picture – and the whole truth – from Dick.'

'If it was that easy …' Marnie said quietly.

'Donovan's got a plan,' Anne piped up, 'or at least an idea. Haven't you?'

They looked at Donovan. He hesitated, choosing his words with care.

'It's a long shot, more the *germ* of an idea at the moment …'

'For contacting Dick?' Ralph said.

'Yes.'

'Do you know where he lives?' Marnie asked.

'That's the problem,' said Donovan.

'I expect some of the students might know,' Ralph said.

'Are they back on the site?'

'I think they must be,' said Marnie.

'Then that's our first port of call,' Donovan said. 'That would make everything much easier.'

'I'll ring Philip and find out.' Marnie reached for her mobile and pressed buttons.

The conversation was longer than they expected. Yes, the students were on site. They were working under the supervision of the two postgrads with Professor de Groot looking in from time to time. No, Dick had not reappeared. When Marnie mentioned that they would like to find out if anyone knew Dick's address in London, Philip gave her an immediate answer. None of the students knew where he lived. Philip had asked the group if they could let him have contact details, but they only had his mobile number. When he made the same request to de Groot, the professor simply said his secretary was chasing him up.

'So that's another dead end,' Marnie said.

'Not necessarily.'

They all looked at Donovan again.

'Second port of call?' said Anne.

Donovan nodded. After a moment's pause, he sat forward and outlined his plan. When he finished, Marnie was the first to respond.

'Sorry to say this, Donovan, but it strikes me as a bit … well, flaky.'

'I'm open to any other suggestion,' Donovan said mildly.

'Have you thought about security?' Ralph said.

'I'm hoping it's the same as at Brunel in the long vacation. There are lots of new faces around, attending summer schools and the like.'

'True.'

'What about you, Anne?' Marnie asked. 'How do you feel about your part in it?'

Anne took a deep breath. 'Well … the bit that bothers me isn't so much smearing my face with shoe polish, abseiling down the side of the building at midnight wearing a black jump suit and breaking in through the office window …'

'So what is the problem?' Donovan said, deadpan.

'I'm not sure if I'm up to disabling the alarm system and cracking the combination code on the safe to get the personnel files out.'

Donovan shook his head dismissively. 'Piece of cake.'

Anne smiled. 'So ... all systems go, then.'

They put the first phase of Donovan's real plan into action that afternoon. Anne typed a brief note on Walker and Co headed paper, asking Dick to get in touch with her at the office as a matter of urgency. She was plucking an envelope from the stationery rack when Donovan stopped her.

'Don't you have something in a different colour?'

'Colour?' Anne looked up at him. 'All our envelopes are this cream vellum.'

'No. It has to be coloured ... the brighter the better.'

'We only ever ... ah, just a mo ...'

She opened a drawer in the desk, rummaged around and tentatively produced an oversize envelope in bright blue. 'Will this do?' Her tone was doubtful.

'Absolutely. It's perfect. Will it fit in the printer?'

'Should do.'

It did. On it Anne printed Dick's name and the address, care of the archaeology department at LBU and sealed the note inside. Then she stamped **FIRST CLASS** in bold letters in the top left hand corner, and underneath in smaller letters she stamped PERSONAL and CONFIDENTIAL. She completed the operation with a first class stamp and held it up for inspection.

'I think that looks imposing enough,' she said.

'Almost.'

'Almost? What more do you –'

'You've got nice handwriting, Anne. I want you to write in black felt-tip ...'

Anne picked up a marker pen and waited.

'To the left of the address write URGENT in capitals, then *Please forward* underneath it.'

When this was done, Donovan pronounced himself satisfied, and they went hand-in-hand together up to the village to post the letter with the rest of the office mail.

25
A Busy Day

They left after breakfast on Tuesday morning, with Marnie assuring them she could survive in the office without Anne for another day. They all wanted to get to the bottom of what was going on, and this seemed their best bet. Anne packed her overnight bag and once again climbed into the Beetle with Donovan.

It was an easy trip. The VW cruised steadily in moderate traffic, and their progress seemed effortless. Donovan had installed a cassette player beneath the dashboard and made up some compilation tapes to create a soothing atmosphere as they rolled along. Anne enjoyed the mixture of flowing instrumental music from all ages on guitar, lute and keyboard.

It was only when she thought about what lay ahead that she felt uneasy.

Their first stop was at Donovan's house, tucked away in its quiet cul-de-sac not far from the Grand Union in Uxbridge. Donovan sifted through the post while coffee filtered in the kitchen and Anne used the bathroom. She liked his house. It was like another country, filled with objects that seemed exotic and foreign. Many of them *were* foreign: the books on the shelves in German and Swedish – Donovan's mother had spent several years in Sweden where her parents were refugees from the Nazis – certain items of furniture, table lamps, paintings and wall hangings. Even the smells were foreign. *Especially* the smells, she realised.

In the kitchen, the rich aroma of coffee blended with a background smell, possibly vanilla. The storage jars on the workbench, the crockery, the equipment, all made her feel as if she had passed through a curtain to a place hidden from the outside world.

Donovan came in and dropped junk mail and discarded envelopes into the recycling bin. Without a word, he returned to the hall. Anne heard him press the button on the answerphone. After a beep a message played, a young woman's voice. Anne could not make out what was being said, but she recognised it as German. Whoever it was – and Anne could make an educated guess – she did not sound happy.

When Donovan came in a second time, he sat at the table with a sigh and began pouring coffee.

'Problem?' said Anne.

'That message was from Uschi. Onkel Helmut is in hospital.'

Uschi – short for Ursula – was Donovan's cousin living in Germany. Anne had met her when she came over to stay with Donovan in London the year before. Onkel Helmut – presumably *uncle* – was her father.

'Is it serious?' Anne bit her lip. 'Sorry. Silly question. You know what I mean.'

'Could be. He's having tests. Seems he collapsed while out walking in the forest.'

'How old is he?'

'Fifty something.'

'Do you need to go?'

'I might. Uschi's going to keep me posted.'

Donovan withdrew into his thoughts while they drank coffee. Anne thought it best not to intrude. Eventually, Donovan stood up and cleared away the cups and saucers. He quickly washed them and Anne dried. While she was putting them back in the cupboard, Donovan checked the rooms upstairs and came down to record a new message on the answerphone in German, giving his mobile number.

'I want to look in on the boat … make sure she's all right.'

'Fine,' said Anne. 'We've got plenty of time.'

When they arrived at the street with a view onto the canal, Donovan drove slowly down its full length. He asked Anne to look unobtrusively into each of the cars parked on her side of the road to see if anyone was sitting in them. At the end, he turned back and, satisfied that they were not under surveillance, parked in a gap from which they could clearly see *XO2* at her mooring.

They opened all the windows, portholes and doors to air the boat, and Donovan went from bow to stern checking that everything was in order. He turned on the gas and the water pump, switched on every lamp and turned every tap on and off. He tried the shower and asked Anne to let him know when the Paloma came on.

'*Alles in Ordnung, Herr Kapitän,*' she said, grinning.

'*Danke,*' he replied. 'Though I think I'd more likely be a *Kapitän-Leutnant* on a U-boat.' He smiled. 'Have you been taking German lessons?'

'They showed an old film on the telly, *The Spy in Black*, and I picked up some useful phrases.'

Anne refrained from telling him about the teach-yourself course of tapes and book that she had been following for several weeks.

On their way to the mooring she had also picked up some sandwiches and fruit, and they ate an early lunch on *XO2* sitting in the comfortable dinette. Anne recognised the same range of smells on the boat that she had noticed in the house, and suspected that Donovan tried to carry a little piece of Germany with him as a reminder of home. She asked him if he felt more German than British, to which he replied he felt he was a mixture of both and reminded her that he also had Irish connections on his father's side.

After lunch they methodically shut up the boat and walked back to the car. Anne felt a twinge of nerves as she realised her moment was coming. Donovan reassured her that if the plan went wrong, nothing could happen to her. They would just have to find some other way of tracing Dick. But deep down inside, she had a feeling that time was running out.

By the time they reached the campus of London Barbican University in the City, the lunch break was ending and staff and conference delegates alike were returning for their respective afternoon sessions. Donovan took a chance on getting into the underground car park and turned in to find the attendant away from his post.

'Good omen, perhaps?' he muttered to Anne, as he tucked the little car into a corner slot out of view, as far away from the entrance cabin as possible. On the top of the dashboard where it would barely be legible in shadow, he placed a parking permit from Brunel University and beside it a card marked VISITOR with another university's crest. He had used it once when attending a seminar at the University of Southampton.

'Neither of those is strictly speaking valid,' Anne observed as they climbed the stairs out of the car park.

'No.'

'So what will you do if the cark park attendant sees you … make up an excuse?'

'Just returning books to the library,' Donovan said, unabashed. 'And by the time he catches up with me, I'll be leaving anyway.'

'*Immer eine Antwort*,' Anne said. Always an answer.

'You have been taking lessons!'

'I learnt that from Uschi last year. That was her opinion of you, too.'

Donovan pulled open the car park exit door. 'Got all your things?'

Anne patted her shoulder bag. 'All present and correct.'

'Good luck,' he said quietly as he kissed her.

They emerged into the open air. Donovan immediately took Anne by the arm and inclined his head towards a group of young women walking ahead of them on the pavement.

'Attach yourself to them. They'll be good cover.'

Anne quickly caught up with the group and asked the nearest girl which way was the library. She offered to show Anne and asked which summer school she was attending. Anne took a folder out of her shoulder bag and held it under her arm. She replied vaguely that she was involved in an archaeological project. They were chatting amiably together as they reached the security booth, and the guard on duty barely spared them a glance as the girls strolled through.

Marnie looked up at the wall clock in the office. Anne and Donovan would probably be on campus by now, she thought. She knew no harm could come to them. At the very worst, they might find themselves unable to get into the university complex, or they might be identified as *unauthorised persons* and asked to leave. Both of them were highly resourceful, and she knew they were capable of bluffing their way out of most situations. On the other hand, she had an uneasy feeling that they absolutely *had* to find Dick Blackwood.

Ralph had followed her back to the office for coffee after lunch, knowing that as she was short-handed, Marnie would not want to leave the phone unattended for any longer than necessary.

'No prizes for guessing what's on your mind,' Ralph said, sitting at Anne's desk, draining the last of his coffee.

'Aren't you thinking about them, too?' Marnie said.

'It's not them that you're concerned about, is it, Marnie?'

'No. I'm really concerned about Dick. I don't like not knowing what's become of him.'

Ralph reached for the phone, checked a number on the pad beside him and pressed buttons. Marnie looked on.

'Philip? Ralph here. Don't suppose Dick's turned up today, has he?'

Marnie could tell what the answer was from Ralph's expression.

Anne sussed out the location of the archaeology department from a plan on the wall outside the library. Inside, she asked a librarian if there was a post-box nearby. There was apparently only one in that part of the campus, situated in the entrance to the central admin block. Anne asked if she could leave her folder on a desk while she posted a letter. The librarian, herself a trainee little older than Anne, offered to keep it for her behind the counter. The name *Sandra* was printed on her identity badge.

Anne checked the plan outside and located the admin block about a hundred yards away. She had no difficulty in finding the post-box. As she went through the entrance doors, a young woman was feeding a bundle of letters into it. Without hesitation Anne approached her.

'Excuse me. What time is the post collected from here?'

'Three forty-five in the long vac.'

Anne frowned. 'Oh … I don't think I'll have it ready by then.'

'It is a bit early, isn't it?' the young woman replied. 'Any later and your only bet is to take it to the post office, and that's quite a step away, off-campus.'

'Is the collection here always prompt?' Anne asked.

'Spot-on every day. You could set your watch by it. The postman sits in his van at the kerb sometimes and waits till the exact time before emptying the box.'

'Right. Er ...' Anne pulled a face and lowered her voice. 'Is there a loo in this block?'

The young woman turned aside and pointed. 'Just over there.'

'I'm new ... temping.' Anne hurried away, calling over her shoulder. 'Thanks.'

She lurked in a toilet cubicle for five minutes, hearing other people come and go, before retracing her steps to the library. The young trainee was nowhere to be seen, and an older woman had taken her place at the main desk. Anne walked confidently to the counter.

'Hallo. Earlier when I was here I left a folder. Sandra put it aside for me. It has a pale blue cover.'

The librarian looked up and down the desk below the counter.

'Is this it?'

'Thanks.'

Before leaving, Anne looked at her watch. She stopped, as if thinking.

'Could I possibly just read through my notes in here? I'm ages early for the next session.'

'Do you have your visitor's pass, or temporary library ticket?'

Anne patted her back pocket. 'Ah ... it's with my other papers in the car. Not to worry, I'll go back to the car park and get it.'

'The main car park?'

'The underground one,' Anne confirmed, turning to go.

'You don't want to borrow any books, presumably?' the librarian said.

'No.'

'That's all right, then. Take a seat. There's plenty of room.'

Anne thanked her and found a vacant study carrel. Three o'clock. Forty-five minutes to wait. Allowing five minutes for the walk and five minutes in the toilets, she took off her watch and set it down in front of her on the desk, as she did when taking exams. The time dragged slowly by while she tried to read the notes she had made on one of Marnie's projects. Normally she would be so engrossed in her work that the time flew by, but on that day she could barely take in a single sentence. It took all her efforts to give an outward appearance of calm concentration.

Just before three-thirty she gathered the papers together and slotted them into the folder. No-one paid her the least attention as she walked out of the library. She took a deep breath. It was time for more subterfuge.

Anne made it to the admin block within the time she had allocated and headed straight for the toilets. Once inside a cubicle, she tugged off her T-shirt and hung it on the hook on the door. She opened her shoulder-bag and took out a blouse with a tiny floral pattern and buttoned it up before folding the T-shirt and placing it in the bag. The transformation was almost complete. She left the cubicle and stuck her head out of the main door. There were four minutes to go, and in the distance she could see the red post van coming down the road.

She ducked back in and rapidly applied a coating of pink gloss to her lips and pale blue eyeliner to her lids. She inspected herself in the mirror while running a comb through her hair. The finishing touch was to loop the security pass for the Horselydown site over her head. Would she pass muster as a junior secretary? She took three deep breaths and hurried to the door, leaving her shoulder bag on the floor just inside.

The postman was pushing the first entrance door open as she exited the toilets. She took a few paces in the opposite direction before turning and scurrying towards the post-box. Her arrival coincided with the moment when the postman put the key in the box and opened the door.

'Oh, I'm so glad I caught you,' she said breathlessly.

The postman barely moved his head, but continued opening the cage that held the letters in place in the box.

'Oh yeah?'

'I think I've made a mistake. Can I just check?'

'You what?' He seemed disinclined to pay her any attention, reaching in to scoop the letters out of the box.

'No wait ... please. I need to check one of the letters.'

He glanced round at her. 'You are joking, love?'

'No, really. I think I've put the wrong postcode on a letter I re-addressed.'

'Sorry. No can do. I haven't got time to let you sort through all this lot. Tight schedule.'

'But it was marked *urgent.*'

'I don't care if it was marked for the Queen of Sheba.'

'It *was* marked for the Queen of Sheba,' Anne pleaded.

'Eh?'

'Look, I'm new here. I don't want to make a mistake in my first week.'

'Sorry I can't help you, love. No way I can spare time to go through the whole –'

'I can see it! Look, it's that one.'

'Are you kidding?'

'No. It's that big blue envelope. I only want to see if I've put the right postcode on it. Two seconds, that's all I need.'

With a sigh, the postman muttered, *you office girls*, and handed her the letter, turning to scrape the rest of the mail into his bag. As soon as he finished, he held out his hand. It was Anne's turn to sigh.

'What a relief! False alarm. Thanks ever so much.'

Tut-tutting, the postman took the letter from her outstretched hand. He looked at Anne appraisingly. In smart blouse and linen slacks, she was every inch the well-groomed office worker, trying to make a good impression in her new job. Not bad looking, either, he thought. As his eyes began straying to her security pass, she self-consciously tucked it between the buttons of her blouse.

'Must be off,' she said and turned on her heels. 'Thanks again.'

Before the postman could say anything else, she ducked into the toilets. Picking up her bag from the floor inside the door, she muttered, *14 Wilberforce Street, E1 7JJ*, over and over, like a mantra. Anne returned to her now familiar cubicle, swiftly wrote the address in a notebook and changed back into her T-shirt. The conversion from office worker to student took barely two minutes, and she was pressing buttons on her mobile as she left the building.

She arrived at the exit to the car park a minute before the distinctive engine note of the VW could be heard as it climbed the concrete ramp up to street level. Donovan pushed the passenger door open and waited at the roadside while she fastened the seat belt. They parked in a side street where Anne searched for the address in the A to Z.

'Well done,' Donovan said. 'Brilliant.'

Anne breathed out audibly, studying the street atlas. 'Mission accomplished, skipper ... *Herr Kapitän-Leutnant*,' she said, without looking up.

'Were you nervous?' Donovan asked.

Anne chuckled. 'Well ... I don't want to be indiscreet, but I think I qualify for residential status in the loo in the admin block.'

Donovan laughed, reached forward, turned her face towards him and kissed her.

'Is that my reward?' she said.

'Yes. Iron Cross, second class.'

'Huh! After what I've been through, I expect a gold medal with crossed swords and oak leaves.'

'You got it. What about Dick's address?'

Anne pointed at the map. 'It's about a mile from here, I reckon.'

Donovan started the engine. 'Which way?'

'Turn left at the end of the street.'

Anne dug out her mobile as Donovan pulled away from the kerb.

Marnie was putting stamps on the day's letters ready for the afternoon mail run when the phone rang. She scribbled Dick's address on her notepad while Anne gave an account of their activities. Anne kept it brief to preserve her phone battery.

'You did well, Anne. So what's next?'

'We're on our way there now. I'll phone later.'

Marnie immediately rang Ralph on *Thyrsis* and gave him the news before locking up the office and making for the field track. On the way up to the village her mind was filled with thoughts of what they should do if Anne and Donovan got to Dick's place only to find that the cupboard was bare.

Wilberforce Street was narrow and treeless, a Victorian development, probably once occupied by poor working class families in miserable conditions. Now, it was by no means in the *des res* category, but the proliferation of satellite dishes, fresh paintwork, the occasional window box and Venetian blinds told a story of modest gentrification.

Anne peered out to read the numbers on the front doors. The first to be clearly visible was an enamel plaque with a white 46 on a blue background, the classic French design that told of upward mobility aspirations on the part of the owner. The next legible number they passed was a 40 in black iron digits fitted on a cream front door.

'It's on this side,' Anne said, 'down towards the far end.'

They found a parking slot on the opposite side to the house a few doors along. There was no movement in the street.

Donovan climbed out. 'I won't be a minute.'

Anne watched him approach the house and bend forward to read the names beside doorbells. He pressed one and stood back to wait. Evidently there was no response. After two minutes on the doorstep Donovan tried again. The result was the same. He walked slowly across the road to the car, glancing back as he reached the pavement.

He slid into the driver's seat. 'You know how you sometimes get a feeling that a house is empty ...'

'But you saw his name?'

'Bottom bell,' Donovan said. 'I guess that means the ground floor.'

'Do we wait?' Anne asked.

'Now that we're here ...'

'Presumably he's got to come back sooner or later.'

Donovan yawned. 'Not necessarily. He could be anywhere, but I don't see what other options we have.'

After half an hour Anne suggested they might listen to the radio. Donovan pressed a button and they found themselves halfway through a programme on Radio 4 giving a detailed analysis of inflation in Zimbabwe. Donovan looked at Anne for a reaction.

'Too light-hearted?' she said, raising an eyebrow.

He tried the other channels. Radio 3 was playing what seemed to be Stockhausen. Within less than a minute it was jangling their nerves. Classic fm offered a selection of Wagner's *greatest hits*, with a thunderous orchestral crescendo giving way to Brunhilda in full lamentation mode.

'At least it's German,' Anne said, generously.

Donovan was already hitting the next button. 'Some other time, perhaps.'

Radio 2 featured a phone-in of favourite cookery recipes. The theme for the day was creative dishes based on root vegetables. Listeners were being invited to give suggestions on what they could do with carrots. Donovan was on the brink of giving his own personal suggestion when Anne quickly prodded another button at random. They were almost blown out of their ergonomic seats by a blast from Radio 1.

'What the hell?' Donovan was reaching for the volume control.

'Hey!' Anne caught his arm.

'You *like* the Sex Pistols?' he said, incredulously.

'No. Look, *look!* Anne pointed across the street.

Donovan pressed the off-switch on the radio as they stared out to see a bicycle parked at the kerbside. They both sat up in their seats. Someone was at Dick's front door. Wearing a close-fitting outfit of blue lycra, a girl was pressing one of the bells. She was small and compact, with leg muscles that told of regular exercise.

'This could be interesting,' Donovan said quietly.

The newcomer pushed the bell a second time.

'Can you see which bell she's pressing?' Donovan said.

'I think it's the bottom one.'

Like Donovan before her, the girl got no reply. They watched as she stood back with hands on hips, clearly pondering what to do. She turned towards the front window and pressed her face to the glass, hands cupped either side of her eyes, peering in.

'Dick's place?' Anne said.

'Could be.'

The girl tapped several times on the window.

'She's not giving up easily,' Anne observed.

'Nor would you if you'd cycled through London traffic to get here.'

It was the voice of experience from Donovan, the cyclist.

As they looked on, the girl crossed the narrow pavement and fiddled in a small, pouch-like container attached to the back of the bicycle seat. When she returned to the door, she fitted a key in the lock and went in.

'Why didn't she just use the key straight away?' Anne said.

'Discretion? Last resort, maybe? Come on!'

Donovan was out of the car before Anne could react. She scurried after him, and he was already pressing the bell when she reached the pavement. Within seconds the door flew open.

'Where the *hell* ...' The girl stopped in mid-flow. 'Oh ... who are you?'

'Friends of Dick,' Donovan said.

The girl had taken off the cycling helmet to reveal short spiky dark hair. She was frowning as she surveyed them.

'I've never seen you before,' she said.

'Why did you think I was Dick when you opened the door?' Donovan was seizing the initiative. 'If this is his place, surely he'd use his key.'

The girl tossed her head. 'I knew that was stupid as soon as I said it. Who are you anyway?'

'Donovan. This is Anne.'

'Donovan ...' she repeated in a far-away voice.

'We've been filming Dick's excavation.'

The girl's eyes widened. 'Where?'

'Horselydown,' Anne said. 'The Saxon remains.'

'Oh, those ...' The girl gave them an inquisitive look. 'Why are you here?'

'You didn't tell us your name,' Anne prompted.

'Judith.'

'Well, Judith, we've come to see Dick ... find out if he's all right. We've been worried about him.'

'Welcome to the club.'

'D'you think we might come inside?' Donovan said.

Judith stepped back and pulled the door open. 'The sitting room's on the right.'

The room was small, furnished with cast-offs. Anne remembered Zoë's disdainful tone when she had invited her back to the flat in Docklands.

Student digs ... But there were shelves built in either side of the chimneybreast, filled with Dick's books and box-files. Under the window stood a simple desk, with three drawers on each side, presided over by a red anglepoise lamp. Spread out on the desk were maps and charts, the largest of them overlaid with tracing paper on which dotted lines and arrows made a criss-cross pattern. For all its meagre furnishing, the room had an atmosphere that was at the same time cosy and purposeful.

'You too were worried about Dick?' Donovan said. 'Don't you know where he's been this past week?'

Judith looked at them, as if weighing up whether they could be trusted.

'It's important we find him,' Anne said.

'What if he doesn't want to be found?' Judith's expression wavered between defiant and wary.

'He has nothing to fear from us.' Donovan's tone was reassuring.

'Probably not. You don't look like the police.'

'The *police?*' Anne was shocked. 'Why should Dick worry about the police?'

Judith looked uncomfortable. 'Since Zoë Tipton was killed –'

'Zoë was *what?*' Anne shook her head.

'Dick said it was all his fault and the police would be looking for him. He was –'

'Judith, listen,' Donovan said firmly. 'Listen to me.'

'You can't blame him for –'

'Listen!'

'You don't understand,' she persisted.

'No, Judith. You're the one who doesn't understand. Zoë Tipton isn't dead. Okay? She was slightly injured. It was an industrial accident. No-one's blaming Dick.'

'What are you saying?' Judith sounded unconvinced.

'We were there,' Anne said. 'Zoë looked dead, it's true. But she was only unconscious and came round just after Dick ran off.'

Donovan said, 'Don't you think it would have been on the news if she'd been killed and the police were hunting for Dick as a suspect?'

'I don't have a radio on the boat, and Dick didn't want me to buy any papers.'

'On the boat?' Anne repeated.

Judith nodded. 'He's been staying with me on my narrowboat since Zoë ... since the accident. But yesterday he went out and didn't come back.'

'Did he say where he was going?' Donovan asked.

'No, but he looked very troubled.'

It felt as if they had reached a dead end.

'Perhaps you could tell us about Dick.' Anne looked around. 'Is there a kitchen? Could I make us all a cup of tea?'

Judith led them to a small kitchen at the rear of the house that was evidently shared by the tenants. It was clean and tidy, and Anne guessed that Dick was the only occupant currently in residence. Judith found tea-bags and mugs, while Anne filled the kettle and set it to boil on the hob. There was no milk in the fridge, but they found a lemon in reasonable condition among over-ripe apples in the fruit bowl. They returned to the sitting room and made themselves at home while Judith told her story.

Marnie took it as a good sign that Anne had not phoned back after an hour had elapsed since her earlier call. It made her no less impatient for news, but it was better than a swift message that they had drawn a blank. She had hoped Anne would eventually phone to say they had found Dick at his digs in bed with a chesty cold brought on by the damp conditions of the excavation, or something of the sort. But Ralph had thrown a bucket of icy water over that idea. He pointed out that Dick was conscientious enough to have contacted Professor de Groot to let him know, if that had been the case.

It was not in Marnie's nature to sit around waiting for somebody else to let her know what was happening. She knew Anne and Donovan were quick-witted and resourceful, but that did not make it any easier. It did not make her any more patient.

They sat in the little room, each clutching their mug of tea, while Judith gave her account without interruption.

She had been Dick's girlfriend for much of the past year, after meeting him when she visited the Glebe Farm excavations. Travelling down the Grand Union Canal on her parents' boat, she stopped by when she discovered a full-scale dig on her journey south. The plan was for her to live on the boat while studying in London for a Master's degree in history at University College. Her father had arranged a mooring for her in Islington, and she was competent enough to run the boat solo from its usual base in Braunston down to its new home.

Dick had given her a guided tour of the excavations in Knightly St John and asked if they could stay in touch when he returned to continue studying for his doctorate at LBU. Their relationship had grown from then on.

She knew about Dick's work in Norfolk and had accompanied him on one of his trips, but despite her love of boats, she was a poor sailor – *I prefer to do my boating in a vertical position, rather than hanging over the side feeling sick, getting soaked by spray* – and was happy for him to go on his expeditions alone or with his friend, Gerald Parfitt, whom she had not met. Her knowledge of Dick's discovery in East Anglia seemed no greater than what Anne and Donovan had learnt. Judith's MA course was intensive and demanding, and when she and Dick were together they had other things on their mind than their fields of study.

Judith was well aware of the problems being caused by Zoë Tipton and how she sought to manipulate every situation for her advancement. Dick had told Judith it was just like Zoë to steal the limelight at Horselydown with her Roman ships and simultaneously cast doubts on his finds – *his earth-shattering discoveries* – in East Anglia. When he finally confronted her face to face, just the two of them down at the lowest level of the excavations, she had taunted him. She said he would be held up to ridicule by the archaeology establishment and would become a national laughing stock. In his fury, Dick had picked up a long-handled mattock and hurled it at the wall. He wanted to stun Zoë into shutting up, but it made no difference.

Zoë had rounded on him, yelling that he couldn't bully her into silence. She told him he was a disgrace to the profession. Dick told Judith he became numb all over. He stopped hearing Zoë's words. Her voice was just a series of sounds breaking over him like a tidal wave, battering his eardrums till he could suffer it no longer. He had fled up the ladder, aware that she was yelling after him.

Desperate to assert his position before Zoë's version became accepted as fact, he had stormed off and phoned Bernard de Groot from the staff office. For twenty minutes or more he had poured his heart out, begging the professor to believe him. Eventually he had calmed down, reassured by de Groot that he would be given every opportunity to explain his discoveries in full and without prejudice. Totally absorbed in the conversation, Dick was unaware of the dramatic events unfolding outside.

When he left the office, he had found the students crowded together beside the dig hole. Zoë's body was lying lifeless on the ground and everyone was kneeling. With a sense of horror he thought back to the moment when he had hurled the mattock at the wall. Could he have caused the shuttering to become unstable and collapse? It was unbearable. Dick was convinced that Zoë's death was his fault. His world, like the excavation, had fallen apart.

'The first I knew about it was when Dick came hammering on the side of my boat,' Judith said. 'He'd come back here, packed some things and ... well, fled. He told me he'd killed Zoë. He hadn't meant to do it but she'd driven him mad. Those were his words.'

'We all thought she was dead,' Anne said. 'But suddenly she had a sort of coughing spasm. We called for an ambulance and they took her off to hospital.'

'And she's really all right?' Judith said. 'No serious injuries?'

'Nothing worth talking about,' said Donovan. 'She was hit by flying debris and collapsed in the mud. One of the builders brought her to the surface, unconscious.'

Judith's shoulders slumped. 'I can't tell you how relieved I am. We were convinced –'

'Sorry, Judith,' Donovan broke in. 'The question facing us now is, what's happened to Dick?'

Judith shook her head. 'I thought he must've come back here.'

'He hasn't. So where else would he be likely to go? You know him better than we do. Think.'

'Er ...'

'Does he have relatives he could go to?' Anne asked.

'Not really. His parents live –'

'In Canada,' Donovan interrupted. 'We know that. Is there anyone else?'

Judith looked blank. 'I can't think ...'

'Did you have a row?' Donovan said.

'No.' Judith looked affronted. '*No*. What are you getting at?'

'Could he have gone to see an old girlfriend, perhaps?'

Judith spoke slowly and firmly. 'We did not have a row.'

'Donovan's only wanting to explore possibilities,' Anne said soothingly.

To their surprise, Judith gave a weary smile.

'What is it?' Anne said.

'It's ironic, really. I've always felt I was second best where Dick was concerned.'

'There is someone else?' Anne prompted.

'In a way. When I first met Dick and told him I was a graduate in history, he said that was the next best thing to archaeology. I've always had the feeling I came second in his life, *after* archaeology.'

'I'm sure that's not right,' Anne said.

'Really?' Judith looked pointedly at Anne. 'Did Gerald Parfitt mention me when you spoke to him?'

Anne hesitated. 'Not actually, as far as I remember ... but I may be –'

'There you are then. I doubt if Parfitt even knows I exist. When those two get together there's only one topic of conversation. Trust me.'

Anne began, 'I'm sure you're –'

She stopped in her tracks as Donovan leapt to his feet and made for the door. Judith gaped at his retreating back.

'Of course,' they heard him say as he rushed out into the narrow passage and threw open the front door.

'Sorry, Judith.' Anne rose hurriedly from her seat. 'Gotta go.'

'Is he always like that?' Judith said, bewildered.

'You get used to it.'

Once again, Judith was left behind, wondering.

Marnie put the phone down after taking Anne's call and sat for some minutes, lost in thought. Eventually she phoned Ralph and filled him in on the latest developments. Ralph was impressed. He was intrigued to learn that Dick had taken refuge with his girlfriend on her boat, but pointed out that this new information had brought them no nearer to finding Dick himself.

Marnie said she didn't think Donovan would entirely agree with him about that. He had a very definite idea of what to do next. When Marnie told him, Ralph was surprised.

'*Where?*' Anne said, hastily fastening her seat belt as Donovan accelerated down the road. 'What ... now, right now?'

'When else?'

'You're intending to drive all the way back to *Norfolk* this afternoon?' She looked at her watch. 'This evening, this minute?'

'That's where we'll find Dick. Don't you think that's what we have to do?'

'Not without fresh knickers!' Anne protested.

Donovan brought the car to a halt at the end of the street and burst out laughing. Anne had never known him react like that before, and she found it infectious. The two of them sat helpless with mirth until a van drew up behind them and Donovan had to drive on. He found a space twenty yards down the road where he could stop the car.

'What's so funny?' Anne said, wiping her eyes.

'You are.'

'I was being practical, Donovan. If we're going all the way back to Norfolk it'll presumably mean staying overnight. If we're to do that, I'd like some clean ... clothes.'

'Knickers!' Donovan exclaimed.

'I don't see what's so funny about my knickers.'

Anne tried to remain po-faced, but failed. She snorted, which set Donovan off again.

'It's a good job you're not Ferdinand Magellan,' he said.

'I often think that,' Anne replied without hesitation. 'Any particular reason this time?'

'I can just imagine him turning back from rounding Cape Horn.' Donovan changed to what he hoped was a Portuguese accent. 'I 'ave no zee clean underpants. Back to Lisbon! We do zees journey some ozzer time.'

Anne sniffed. 'But I was being serious. I would like some fresh undies. Wouldn't you?'

Donovan gave in. 'We'll find a Marks and Spencer somewhere.'

'No need. We've still got clean clothes at Marnie's flat. It's just over the river. We could grab a quick shower, too.'

'You're serious, aren't you?'

'Steer course zero-two-zero,' Anne said. 'Come right full rudder – after the Tower of London – then full ahead both.'

Donovan recognised the U-boat allusion as an order. He didn't like to remind Anne that U-boat crews scarcely changed their clothes at all when on tours of duty. He sighed and steered the Beetle towards Tower Bridge.

It was an hour or so later when Marnie took the next call. This time it was Donovan, and she was surprised to hear that he and Anne were about to leave her flat in Docklands. He explained that Anne had needed some things from the flat and wanted to shower before they set off back to Norfolk. She was using the hairdryer, so he offered to phone to save time. He apologised for whisking Anne away, and Marnie assured him the office would survive without her for another day.

Before hanging up, Marnie asked what things Anne had needed from the flat. Donovan gave a one-word reply. Marnie smiled.

There was heavy traffic heading north-east out of London, and they resigned themselves to making only slow progress. They listened to the news but soon tired of the car radio and drove for a long time in a silence only interrupted by Anne's navigational instructions as they gradually picked up speed.

Eventually she said, 'I could use some of that tracing paper on the atlas to mark our route.'

'Yes.'

'Did you notice it at Dick's place?'

'On the desk covering the map of the area.' Donovan sounded vague and distant. He was concentrating on the traffic.

'When my brother did the map reading on long car journeys, he'd mark the route with a pencil … drove my dad mad. He didn't like smudgy pencil marks on his nice clean atlas.'

'I expect Dick was plotting King John's journey across the wetlands,' Donovan said. 'I'd like to have had a chance to examine the markings more closely.'

'Are you coming round to believing his story?' Anne said.

Donovan's silence was so long that Anne wondered if he had heard the question.

'On balance, I think I do,' he said. 'His elation was genuine. I don't really go along any more with this idea that he could claim the discovery, produce artefacts and rest on his laurels.'

'I don't either really,' said Anne. 'But something's not right.'

'You think he was lying about his collaboration with Gerald Parfitt? There's definitely something strange about that.'

Anne made a signal to go straight on as they approached a roundabout. 'Parfitt looked completely baffled when you told him what Dick had said about them working together. That must prove something.'

'It could only mean either Dick was telling the truth and Parfitt was mistaken, or that one of them was lying.'

'Yes,' Anne agreed. 'And Parfitt can hardly have been mistaken about being away in Denmark.'

'Not the sort of thing that slips your mind,' Donovan said. 'And easy to check.'

They retreated into their thoughts as the miles rolled by and they cut across country with the sun slowly going down over their left shoulders. Somewhere near Peterborough the rumble of the engine was joined by another rumbling. Anne put a hand on her stomach.

'Sorry, that was me. I think I must need something to eat.'

'Can you hold out for another hour?' Donovan said.

'I s'pose so. I don't expect you've got one of your German picnic meals hidden away somewhere in the coolbox?'

'Not this time. But didn't we pass a pub on our way to the marina on Sunday? They'll probably do food. We could look in quickly at the marina and see if Dick's there on *Arabella*. If he is, we can all go and eat at the pub.'

It seemed a reasonable plan, and they hurried on their way.

'What do you think, Ralph? Any ideas about where Dick's gone?'

The meal that evening on *Sally Ann* was a modest affair. Marnie had bought salmon filets in the expectation that Anne and Donovan would be eating with them. When Donovan had phoned with the revised plan, the filets had gone into the freezer, and the menu changed to omelette and salad.

'I think Donovan's probably on the right track,' said Ralph. 'I can't think of anywhere else he might have gone.'

'But why has he run away in the first place?' Marnie shook her head. 'What *is* going on?'

'Perhaps he's on the verge of another revelation. It would resolve everything if he suddenly came up with irrefutable proof of his discovery.'

'And how would he do that?'

Ralph steepled his fingers. 'To make the maximum impact he might contact the local TV stations and get them to film him *in situ*, holding up pieces recovered from the ground or under the sea or wherever.'

'Yes, that would be irresistible ... a tale of buried treasure, the solving of a mystery eight hundred years old ... a *huge* news story for the region.'

'For the *country*,' Ralph said.

Marnie looked thoughtful. 'I hope Donovan's got his cameras with him.'

Anne forgot all feelings of hunger as Donovan turned off the highway onto the access road for the marina. Without hesitation he drove into the car park and pulled up at the end of the pontoon leading to *Arabella*'s mooring. The engine note had barely died before Donovan was out of the car striding towards the boat. Anne had to admire his stamina. It had been a long and tiring day, and she had to make a supreme effort to drag herself from the seat.

The first inkling that something was wrong was the sight of Donovan standing motionless halfway along the pontoon, staring out to sea. The tide was in. Beyond the harbour wall in the mouth of the river, craft were bobbing among gentle waves. In the marina, the boats were floating on still water. But not all the boats. One of them was missing. Where *Arabella* should have been lying, there was an empty space. Donovan turned and looked towards the marina office. It was obviously closed. Horsfall and his staff must have left long ago.

The cark park was almost devoid of vehicles, but at the far end a solitary figure could be seen pulling equipment out of the back of a Land Rover. Donovan dashed past Anne without a word and made his way towards the stranger. Anne waited, too lacking in energy to pursue him. After a brief exchange, Donovan walked back. Anne could tell from the body language that he was not overjoyed by what he had learnt.

'No luck?' she said.

'No. She said she'd been here for about an hour, working on her boat.'

'She?'

'Yeah. She's the vice-commodore here, or something like that. She can't recall seeing anyone going out, but she's been busy replacing some of the sheets on her boat and splicing the ends.'

These details meant nothing to Anne, but she judged that it was not the time to ask for explanations.

'So maybe Parfitt's taken *Arabella* out,' she suggested. 'Perhaps he's gone with Dick.'

'One way to find out.' Donovan pulled out his mobile and pressed buttons.

It surprised Anne that Donovan rarely looked up numbers. He had the knack of retaining them in his head.

'Gerald, it's Donovan, Donovan Smith.' He held the mobile so that Anne could hear both sides of the conversation.

'Donovan, yes. What can I do for you?'

'We're at the marina.'

'You're still in Norfolk? I thought you were returning home.'

'We did. We went to Dick's place in London, but that's not why I'm phoning. Gerald, your boat's not here. Her mooring's empty. Were you aware of that?'

Silence.

'Can you hear me? I said –'

'Yes, I can hear you. I'm just rather taken aback.'

'You didn't know she'd gone, obviously.'

'Well, no. You're sure you're looking in the right place?'

'Certain, but we'll check everywhere. Could someone have moved her for any reason?'

'Not to my knowledge.'

'Have you had any contact from Dick? Could he have taken her out?'

'I suppose it's possible, but he hasn't been in touch with me.'

'Look, Gerald, there's a woman here … Helen somebody … vice-commodore or something. I asked her, but she's seen nothing. Presumably the only person who might know what's happened would be Guy Horsfall.'

'Yes. I'll ring him straight away.'

'Is there anything we can do while we're here?' Donovan said.

'No, not really. Thanks for tipping me off, Donovan. I'll deal with matters from here on.'

'Okay.'

'Before you go … did you say you've been to Dick's lodgings?'

'Yes. We had a look around but –'

'You went in?'

'We were let in by his girlfriend.'

'Girlfriend? I see …' His tone suggested otherwise. 'But you don't know where he is.'

'No. The girlfriend doesn't know, either.'

'Did you see anything of interest at his place?'

'Not really. We were only there for a short while, though we did notice there were maps on his desk.'

'Ah, yes, probably the ones I gave him.'

'He seems to have marked out some routes on tracing paper.'

'Across the wetlands?'

'I presume so.'

Parfitt hesitated. 'It seems odd he should be away, when those tracings were still there. They're rather important.'

'That's what we thought.'

'It sounds as if he must still be living there, don't you think?'

Donovan paused before replying. 'To be honest, Gerald, I'm not sure what to think.'

By the time they found the pub, Anne declared she had gone through the hunger barrier and was no longer in need of food. Donovan persuaded her they both had to eat, and she chose a goat's cheese salad from the menu. While Donovan ordered drinks at the bar, she phoned Marnie with the latest news.

As soon as Anne had her first taste of salad, her appetite returned. Donovan too set about his scampi with enthusiasm, and for a while neither spoke. Taking a break from eating, Donovan summed up what they had both been thinking.

'If Parfitt was unaware that his boat was missing, it's likely that Dick came and borrowed it. Does that make sense?'

'He would have told you if he'd let anyone else use it,' Anne said.

'Yeah. Then we have to ask ourselves why.'

Anne frowned. 'What could he do if he's alone on the boat? It's hard enough keeping *Sally Ann* in the same place on a canal if there's a lock opening or closing nearby. The least movement of the water and she starts wandering about.'

'So he can't have gone diving on the treasure if he's alone. That's what you're saying?'

'I think so.'

'He could use an anchor, I suppose. But setting that aside, we're left with other possibilities.'

'Plural?'

'Of course. He may have taken the boat as a refuge to get away from everything.'

'That doesn't seem very rational,' Anne said.

'If he's as desperate as he seems, he's way past rational.'

'Mm ... Any other ideas?'

'He could've gone out to check a marker buoy or maybe to set a marker buoy.'

'But I got the impression he'd found the treasure somewhere inland.'

'Let's face it, Anne, we don't honestly have a clue where he found it, always assuming he did actually find it. What we really know about what did or did not happen is frankly anybody's guess.'

Darkness had fallen by the time they arrived at the camp site, but Donovan erected the tent without difficulty on the same pitch they had occupied before. They used the showers, which revived them briefly, and Anne made one last call to report back to Marnie, while Donovan prepared the air mattresses and laid out the sleeping bags and pillows. It was an overcast evening but the air was warm, and the countryside lay peaceful around them.

Anne made herself comfortable while Donovan was switching off the lantern. Instead of climbing into his sleeping bag, he began slithering into hers.

'Oh, and what's this?' she said.

'I thought you might like a little comforting after the energetic day we've had,' he said quietly.

'And what if I said I had a headache?'

'I'd find you some tablets and then get in my own sleeping bag.'

He began wriggling his way out. Anne put a hand on his shoulder.

'It's a good job I haven't got a headache, then, isn't it?'

26
Uschi

It was Wednesday morning, and Marnie had arranged to phone Philip to check on progress at Horselydown. She was surprised to be told by the firm's receptionist that Philip was temporarily working every day at the site. He had taken over one of the huts and was using it as his main office. In addition, Nigel Beardsley was based there most afternoons. Marnie rang Philip on his mobile.

'You're babysitting, Philip. That tells me you're worried about the project.'

'The official line is, I'm maintaining a close personal interest in this as our flagship development. But the truth is yes, Marnie, I'm worried.'

'What in particular's bothering you?'

'Where do you want me to start?'

'Bad as that? I thought we were just about on target.'

'*Just about* isn't good enough for a job of this size, Marnie, with so many imponderables. I built in some flexibility on timing to give us breathing space, but that's all been used up. We've had delays on the archaeology, the time taken out for health and safety inspections, the fatal accident enquiry, remedial works after two disastrous structural collapses ... need I say more?'

'You could mention the loss of the two archaeology site directors.'

'I rest my case, m'lud.'

'So any more delays and the programme goes out the window.'

'And costs more money,' Philip added. 'I don't suppose there's any chance you could come down some time in the next few days?'

'Relief with the babysitting? Belt and braces? Or are there real issues concerning my designs?'

'One or two questions have been raised by the client, but they're minor matters.'

'You're in need of moral support, Philip.'

'If you could come for a day it would be a great help. Just the sight of you will reassure the directors of Willards, Marnie. You know they think the sun shines out of –'

'Okay, fine. I'm sure I can come down. Give me a day or so to get things sorted out here.'

'You've got problems, too?'

'No. It's just that I'm short-handed at the moment. Anne's away trying to track down Dick Blackwood. I don't suppose he's turned up on site, has he?'

'Not a sign, Marnie. I'd have let you know.'

'Sure. I'll see you as soon as I can get away. Those questions you mentioned ...'

'Oh, that ... Willards would like some clarification of certain parts of the design.'

'No problem. Everything's under control.'

Philip sighed. 'You don't know how wonderful that sounds.'

Breakfast for the campers was a polystyrene cup of machine coffee and a fruit pie, standing in a filling station on the way to the marina. Showered, fed and watered and with a full tank of petrol, they were ready to face whatever the day produced. Arriving at the marina, they found it produced no change. *Arabella* was still absent and the admin office was not yet open. After a slow walk round the marina, Donovan suggested they head back to Knightly St John. It was too early to phone Parfitt. They would speak later.

It was soon after seven o'clock when Donovan slipped on his aviators and they hit the road, with Anne plotting their best route while Donovan steered south and west. As soon as she was ready, Anne recited what she called her *stepping stones*, the main landmarks of the journey, to give Donovan a feel for the general direction. She calculated a total drive time of around three hours, traffic and road works permitting.

Donovan's preferred driving style was to cruise, and once they had settled into a steady rhythm, Anne voiced a question that had been preying on both their minds.

'You don't suppose this could all be just a big fuss about nothing, do you?'

'That thought did cross my mind when we were waiting outside Dick's lodgings, but now I'm seriously concerned about him.'

'You don't think he's ... done something stupid, do you?'

Donovan chuckled. 'I love the British way of putting things.'

'What d'you mean?'

'The Brits say something like, *If anything happens to me*, when what they mean is, *If I'm mown down by the number 93 bus and get horribly mangled with bits of me scattered all over the road ...*'

Anne grimaced. 'You don't think that's what's happened to Dick, do you?'

'I don't think the 93 bus runs in that part of London.' Deadpan Donovan.

Anne giggled. 'Idiot! But you know what I mean.'

'You mean do I think he might have committed suicide? It seems to me something's wrong about the whole situation, but we've heard so many sides to the story that I'm really not sure what to think.'

'Nor me.'

They came to a series of roundabouts near Peterborough, which required Donovan's full attention. When they were finally following their new direction, Anne posed another question.

'As a matter of interest, what do Germans say for *If anything happens to me*, and that sort of thing?'

Donovan chuckled again. 'Actually we say, *Wenn etwas ist*, which in literal translation means, *If something is ...*'

'That's even more of a euphemism than we use,' Anne said, 'even more obscure.'

Donovan was grinning. 'Yes. My German side is often worse than my British side.'

'It must be very confusing being you, Donovan.'

'Tell me about it ... as we Brits say.'

Not long after reaching her desk, Marnie's phone rang.

'Walker and Co, good morning.'

'Good morning. Is Donovan there, please?'

A woman's voice, young, lightly accented.

'I'm afraid he isn't here at the moment. Can I help you? I'm Marnie Walker.'

'Oh yes. He has spoken of you. Will you see him today? I've tried his London number and his mobile, but no success.'

'He's in Norfolk, or rather on his way back from there. He's driving, so his mobile's probably switched off.'

'It's important I speak with him ... urgent.'

'Certainly. Your name, please?'

'Ursula.' Her pronunciation was unfamiliar to Marnie's ear.

'Sorry?'

'Just say *Uschi*. I'll spell it for you.'

Marnie wrote down the strange name. She thought she had heard Anne mention it before.

'I'll get him to ring you the minute he arrives. He has your number?'

'I'm at home. Thank you.'

Anxious to get back as quickly as possible, they made just one brief stop at a service station. While Anne used the loos, Donovan ordered coffee and rang Gerald Parfitt.

'I was wondering if you'd called the police,' Donovan said.

Parfitt sounded uneasy. 'No, or rather, not yet. I asked myself what if Dick had just come and borrowed her for a trip. He's been through a lot lately. Sailing can soothe the troubled mind.'

'Presumably Dick has a set of keys for *Arabella*?' Donovan said.

'Yes. We've spent so much time working together we both have a set of each other's keys. It makes it easier when coming and going.'

'So what will you do now?'

'Dick's a strange chap,' Parfitt said. '… very unpredictable. That's why I'm hesitant about contacting the authorities. I think I might give it till tomorrow morning and see if he's returned by then. That's when I'll make a decision.'

Anne reappeared as Donovan was ending the call, and he brought her up to date. She bought two Mars bars at the newsagents on the way out, and they were on the road again within a few minutes.

Her map reading was faultless, and the Beetle gobbled up the miles. The sunshine of recent weeks had been replaced by cooler, cloudier weather, ideal for long journeys in a car without air conditioning. With the added comfort of the ergonomic seats and the sound-damping of the interior, they arrived back at Glebe Farm without fatigue at the end of their journey.

When Marnie passed on Uschi's message and added that it was urgent, Donovan's face clouded over. He reached in a pocket for his mobile, but Marnie pointed at the phone on her desk and invited him to use it. She went with Anne to the utility room at the back of the office and helped unpack her bag. While they loaded used clothes into the washing machine, Marnie asked for an update. They commiserated with each other at the lack of progress.

Returning to the office they found Donovan sitting in Marnie's chair, deep in thought. He did not look happy.

'Are you able to talk about it?' Marnie said gently.

'It's Helmut, my uncle. He's had another heart attack.'

'*Another*?' Anne said.

'It seems the time he collapsed was a minor attack. This one's more serious. He's having an emergency operation this morning.'

'Will you go to see him?'

'I must.'

'Of course,' Marnie said. 'You'll want to leave straight away.'

'Yes. I can get a Lufthansa flight to Hanover from Heathrow.'

Marnie grabbed the phone, asked directory enquiries for the number and rang the airline. They confirmed there was a flight that afternoon and seats were available. Marnie passed the handset to Donovan who made a reservation there and then. When he came off the line, she offered to take him to the airport, but he preferred to drive himself, so that the car was available for him when he got back.

Minutes later, Marnie and Anne waved Donovan off up the field track. Marnie put an arm round Anne's shoulders as they watched the squat black car climbing the slope. They both shared the same thought. Could anything more go wrong that summer?

They were soon to find out.

27
Homeward Bound

For Anne, early starts were becoming the norm. At supper the previous evening Marnie had announced she was finding it increasingly difficult to settle into her normal pattern of work in the office. Most of her local clients were still on holiday, and she was ahead of herself on her entire programme. And she had to admit, she was fretting about the problems with Horselydown in general and Dick's absence in particular. She wanted to return to London at the earliest possible moment.

When Anne offered to join her, Ralph volunteered to hold the fort in the office. That meant in practical terms working at Marnie's desk and taking phone calls. Marnie felt guilty about imposing on him, but when he pointed out that he would have support from Dolly, the matter was settled.

Bags had been hurriedly packed that evening in readiness for an early start on Thursday morning. The Discovery lumbered up the slope under a cloudy threatening sky, with puffs of pale grey smoke emanating from the exhaust. Marnie steered the chunky car round the tussocks and bumps in the field, determined to overcome all the issues that were bothering the clients in London. At the same time she would track down Dick Blackwood and get to the bottom of his story once and for all.

Beside her, with no lesser resolve, Anne allowed her thoughts to stray to a small town in Germany where a man she had never met was fighting for his life and another man who was becoming ever more important to her was willing him to survive.

At that early hour they made rapid progress on their drive south. Traffic on the motorway was moderate, and even in London it was less heavy than outside the holiday season. With the Disco occupying its slot in the underground car park, Marnie and Anne had time in hand to take a shower and a cup of coffee. They entered the building site fresh and ready for the day ahead.

Philip's delight at seeing them told its own story. He embraced Marnie and Anne warmly, and the light came back into his eyes when Marnie confirmed that she was confident there were no questions about her scheme that she could not answer.

And so it proved to be. Marnie, Anne and Philip were joined at the meeting by two senior managers from Willards, plus the site agent and chief quantity surveyor. Marnie guided them through each part of the design scheme, step by step, so comprehensively that the few questions she had to handle were on minor points of detail. When she came to the end of her presentation there were smiles all round the table. Philip commented that it had been some time since that had been the case on this project.

'Good old Marnie,' he said. 'It's great to see you haven't lost your touch. The old magic is still there.'

Amid murmurings of appreciation he asked, 'Any other business, gentlemen?'

There were no takers. Marnie raised a finger.

'You wish to add something, Marnie?'

'Just one thing, Philip … Go easy on the *old*, okay?'

As the participants emerged from the meeting, Anne found herself standing alone on the threshold of the hut. Holding the door open for Marnie, she noticed that one of the Willards managers had taken her aside for a quiet word. Not wishing to intrude, she decided to wait at a discreet distance outside. By chance, the end of the meeting coincided with the archaeologists' morning break, and the students were climbing out of the excavation. Anne wandered over towards them and discovered a new development. A refreshment stand had been set up by the contractors since her last visit to the site, and drinks and snacks were being distributed free of charge.

Anne spotted Debbie in the queue. The Afro-Caribbean student was wearing her familiar green denim fatigues.

'Debbie, remember me … Anne?'

The sparkling white smile. 'Course I do. How's things?'

'Okay. You? I see the facilities round here have improved.'

'Started this week. Actually, everything's better these days.'

'Who's in charge of the dig now?' Anne asked.

'Andy and Siân … you know the two postgrads?'

'What about Dick Blackwood? Is he back?'

Debbie shrugged. 'Haven't seen him for ages, not since …'

'No, right. I expect things have quietened down a bit since then.'

'Absolutely. I don't want to speak ill of … you know …' She mouthed *Zoë*. 'But we don't have the daily rows any more. No warring factions, no hassle to look forward to every day. And the prof looks in from time to time. It's cool.'

'That's great.' Anne turned to go.

'Anne? Your friend not with you?'

'Which one?'

'Donovan?'

'He's … away at the moment.'

'Pity. Tell him he's welcome back any time.'

'You miss the filming?' Anne said casually.

Debbie paused and flashed the brilliant smile. 'Something like that.'

Marnie turned down Philip's offer of lunch, saying she had to get back to base. Walking back to the flat, Anne asked if they would be driving home straight away. Marnie's reply surprised her.

'Home? No. Too much to do here.'

'But I thought you told Philip –'

'Anne, we have to sort out the Dick Blackwood business. And I have other reasons for wanting to be away from the site.'

Anne waited for Marnie to explain, but she added nothing.

'Can I help with anything?' Anne asked, hesitantly.

'If you can solve the problems with the Horselydown project, that would be a good start.'

'But I thought you'd done that, Marnie ... at least as far as our part of the job's concerned.'

Marnie stopped and turned to face Anne.

'Can't you sense it, Anne? Can't you see that just below the surface this project is on a knife edge? The atmosphere is still poisoned. That's why I don't want to be here any longer than I have to.'

'Well, the archaeologists seem happier.'

'I'm glad to hear it. This job needs all the help it can get. We can't afford for it to fail.'

Anne was alarmed. 'I thought it was going to be all right from now on. Philip seemed more relaxed about things.'

'It's called *window dressing*, Anne, putting on a brave face, smiling in adversity.'

'I thought your presentation was really positive, Marnie. The clients loved it.'

Marnie made a sound between a snort and a cough. 'I'm the brave face. That's why Philip wanted me here.'

'I'm sure they think you're a very attractive face, Marnie.' Anne bit her lip. 'Sorry, I mean –'

'It's okay. I know what you mean. And I'm sorry to say, it does help. It shouldn't, but there it is. The main thing is not to exploit being a woman in a man's world too often, or it can backfire on you.'

They reached the entrance to the flats, where Marnie used the key card to open the outer door into the lift lobby. On their way up to the fifth floor, Anne asked how Marnie proposed tracing Dick Blackwood. They would simply act systematically on all the leads they had. The first step was to phone Gerald Parfitt in the hope that he might have some news. Anne rang his number at the university as soon as they entered the flat.

But there was no news. In fact there was no contact, only ...

You've reached the number of Dr Gerald Parfitt, UEA. Please leave a brief message after the tone and I'll return your call as soon as I can. Thank you.

Anne mouthed *answerphone*. Marnie shook her head, and Anne disconnected.

'The case of the vanishing archaeologists,' Marnie said. 'It's like an Agatha Christie. Soon there'll be none.'

Anne grimaced.

'Sorry ...' Marnie began, 'I shouldn't joke about it.'

'So are we going home after all?' Anne said.

Marnie bit her lip and considered the options. 'Well, since we're here, we may as well make the most of it. Do you have Dick's girlfriend's number? I'd like to meet her and see Dick's place for myself.'

Anne checked in her notebook and made the call. After three rings it went to voicemail.

'Shall I leave a message?'

'Don't bother,' said Marnie. 'We'll try another time.' She walked over to the window and looked down at the river. 'Fancy an early lunch?'

'Sounds good to me. Then what?'

Marnie turned to face Anne. 'There's an exhibition I'd quite like to see at the V and A – Krazy Kat – interested?'

Anne grinned. 'Why not? Sounds fun.'

And so they took time out that afternoon, losing themselves temporarily in the vintage comic strip world of Krazy Kat, Ignatz Mouse and Offissa Bull Pupp, trying not to see too many parallels in the strange love-hate relationship between cat and mouse. The classic designs helped take their mind off their worries, but only sporadically. Their thoughts drifted all too easily back to the disappearance of Dick Blackwood and the concerns that would not go away.

What was going on? What was it all about?

28
Arabella

When they arose on Friday morning, Anne was keen to phone Gerald Parfitt on his mobile at breakfast time, but Marnie suggested that they wait until normal working hours. She urged a softly-softly approach, without anxiety or apprehension.

'D'you think he'll be at uni by nine?' Anne asked.

'I doubt it. Let's give him till ten o'clock. It is the long vac, after all. Let's keep everything calm and unhurried.'

'Right.' Anne tried to sound cool and composed. 'I think I'll read a magazine until then.'

'Good idea. Me too.'

They settled on the sofas to pass the time with the *Architects' Journal*, *Domus* and *Schöner Wohnen*, though Marnie observed without comment that Anne was not turning the pages as often as might be expected. A brief call to Ralph to check that all was well at Glebe Farm, then it was time to phone Parfitt. Marnie suggested that Anne should make the call as she had already met the archaeologist. Anne pecked out his direct number at UEA and was relieved when he answered almost at once.

'Dr Parfitt ... Gerald, it's Anne, Anne Price. I was wondering if you'd heard from Dick Blackwood or if you had any news.' She held her breath.

'Yes, I have some news.' His voice was expressionless. '*Arabella* has been picked up by the Coastguard. They found her abandoned, eight miles out at sea.'

Anne froze. Try as she might, she could not unscramble her thoughts. Seeing her reaction, Marnie asked what had happened and took the phone from her hand. She could hear Parfitt speaking as she put the receiver to her ear.

'... someone there with you?' he was saying.

'Dr Parfitt, my name is Marnie Walker. I'm Anne's employer, a friend of Donovan and of Dick Blackwood. Would you mind telling me what's happened?'

Parfitt repeated his news.

'Did the Coastguard say anything about Dick?' Marnie asked.

'Nothing. The boat was spotted drifting under light sail in the early hours of this morning. There'd been a heavy sea and they fear Dick ... He was a good sailor, but in those conditions ...'

Marnie asked Parfitt to keep in touch if there were any developments. Disconnecting, she looked at Anne, who was stunned and close to tears.

'He was so full of life, Marnie ... so enthusiastic about his work. It meant so much to him and –'

Marnie took Anne by the arms. 'Listen. I don't want to sound hard, but we have to go on until we know for sure what's happened.'

'But Dr Parfitt said –'

'He said nothing that changes anything. There's more we have to do.'

Anne blinked. 'What d'you mean?'

'I still want to see where Dick lived ... where he lives. Can we arrange that?'

'Er ...'

'Think, Anne. You've got Judith's number.'

Anne checked in her notebook, gathered herself together and made the call. Marnie told her to say nothing about *Arabella* being found abandoned at sea. They were in luck. When Anne asked if she could go to Dick's rooms again, Judith agreed after some hesitation. It appeared she already had in mind to go there that afternoon after work. She had a part-time job waitressing and was working the lunchtime shift that day. They arranged to meet soon after three.

The three women stood in Dick's living room in an awkward silence.

'I'm not quite sure what your reason is for coming here.' Her tone bordered on the querulous.

'Good question,' said Marnie. 'I'm not entirely sure myself.'

'I was wondering what's driving you to try to help him now – if that's what you had in mind – when so many of his *so-called* friends have abandoned him at a time when he really needs them.'

'Judith, we're more colleagues than friends. I only met Dick last summer and caught up with him again as a result of this project at Tower Bridge. That doesn't make my concern for him less genuine.'

Marnie's voice was calm and gave no hint that she might have taken offence at Judith's rebuke.

'Marnie *has* been helping,' Anne said. 'She has a business to run. I work for her, but she's been giving me time off to go with Donovan to try to trace Dick in Norfolk. Now that Donovan's out of the country –'

'What's happened to him?' Judith looked startled.

'He has a sick relative in Germany and he's gone to be with his family. Now Marnie's getting more involved herself.'

'I hope you can see we're all on the same side, Judith,' Marnie said quietly.

To their surprise, Judith suddenly burst into tears. One moment she was confronting them, petulant and hostile, the next, she was sobbing convulsively. Anne reached forward to hold her in her arms. Marnie gestured towards the sofa, where Anne led Judith and sat her down.

'Is there anywhere we can make a cup of tea round here?' Marnie asked.

Anne pointed at the door and indicated down the hall. 'Kitchen.'

By the time Marnie came back into the room carrying a tray, Judith was sitting up straight, drying her eyes. With milk still unavailable, they sipped hot black tea with sugar.

'Don't be in any doubt that we want to help locate Dick,' Marnie said.

Judith blew her nose. 'I'm sorry. I shouldn't have said what I did. It was –'

'It was understandable. Forget it. You came here today for the same reason that we did. You hoped to find Dick. Am I right?'

Judith nodded. She was more composed now, but still looked miserable. 'He's not here, and there's nothing we can do.'

'I'm not so sure about that.' Marnie cast her eyes round the room. 'Has anything changed since your last visit? When was that, by the way?'

'The day I met Anne and Donovan here.'

'And is everything the same as it was?'

'You think Dick might've been back?'

'I'm asking you, Judith.'

Judith swept the room with her eyes. 'I don't think anything's changed. It's all just as it was.'

Marnie began speaking. 'Are you sure about –'

'No, it isn't,' Anne interrupted her.

'What d'you mean?' said Judith.

Anne stood up and walked over to the desk. 'Things *have* changed.'

'What things?' Marnie was rising to her feet.

'There was tracing paper on top of this map.'

Marnie was at her side. Judith stood up to join them.

'Do you remember, Judith?' Anne laid a hand on the maps on the desk. 'There were arrows marked in pencil on tracing paper … King John's last journey back to that abbey in Lincolnshire … different ways he might've travelled the day he lost the baggage train.'

Judith peered down. 'Yes … you're right, Anne. I'd forgotten about that.'

'But you're certain now, Judith?' Marnie said.

'Absolutely. There was definitely tracing paper here, unless … I don't suppose Donovan might've taken it?'

'Definitely not,' Anne said. 'He'd never touch anything.'

'And you're sure you haven't moved them, Judith?' said Marnie.

Judith looked horrified. '*Me*? You're joking. I'd never even *touch* Dick's work papers. They mean *everything* to him.'

Marnie and Anne stared at each other. Judith looked at them and read their thoughts.

'So he *has* been here,' she said in a half-whisper.

❖ ❖ ❖ ❖ ❖ ❖

In the car on the way back to the flat, Anne noticed Marnie resting her head against her hand when they stopped at traffic lights.

'You okay, Marnie?'

'Bit weary. Slight headache. I'll take a tablet when we get in … lie down for a bit.'

'You didn't tell Judith about *Arabella* being found abandoned. Was it because you didn't want to worry her?'

'Partly that. Also, I wanted her to keep thinking about Dick in a positive way.'

'Not sure I follow.'

'My guess is that if she thought Dick had been lost at sea, she might just retreat into her shell … give up. We need her to stay focused if she's to be of any help.'

Back at the flat, Marnie went straight to the bedroom to take some tablets and lie down while Anne checked messages on her mobile. There was just one text.

OH holding on. D

Hang in there, Onkel Helmut, she thought. Feeling at a loose end, she rang Ralph at Glebe Farm. He answered on the first ring. His *Walker and Co, good afternoon*, delivered in an authoritative tone sounded impressive. But his next words, following Anne's greeting, froze her blood.

'Oh, Anne. Thank *god* you've phoned.'

'What is it?' The alarm in her voice registered 6.4 on the Richter scale.

'I can't get my computer to work. The bloody thing's seized solid and I can't wake it up.'

'Oh …' Relief flooded over her. 'Is that all? You had me worried. I thought –'

'Is that *all*?' Ralph repeated. 'Anne, I have the text of my new book in it, not to mention drafts of articles, research papers, notes for conference lectures …' He stopped to draw breath.

'Okay. I get the message. Tell me what happened.'

'Well I … I was just pressing the keys when everything went off.'

'What *exactly* were you doing at the time?'

'Er ... dragging and dropping figures into a table of statistics, I think.'

'Could you have touched something?'

'Anything is possible.'

Too true, Anne thought. 'Did you try booting it?'

Ralph hesitated. 'I must say I was sorely tempted.'

'Sorry?'

'To boot it ... into the canal ...'

For the next several minutes Anne guided Ralph through a series of steps to try to reawaken the machine. Nothing he did brought any reaction. Hearing the prolonged conversation, Marnie came out of the bedroom and stood beside Anne.

'Hang on, Ralph. Marnie's here. I'll see if she has any ideas.'

Anne explained the problem and passed the handset to Marnie.

'Hi, Ralph. I think Anne's suggested everything I'd try doing.' She heard a loud sigh at the other end. 'Look, there's an IT firm in Stony Stratford – *Extreme PCs*, or something of the sort. Perhaps you should give them a call. The number's in my address book under C for computer.'

'Ah, Marnie, that reminds me. There's a message on the answerphone from Beth. Hang on. I'll just play it through.'

Marnie waited, asking Anne quietly if she had any other bright ideas. Anne was shaking her head despondently when Ralph came back on the line.

'It's not my day. Bloody answerphone's on the blink now.'

A pause before Marnie spoke again. 'Try turning on your desk lamp, Ralph.'

'What good will that –?'

'Indulge me ... please.'

Silence. A faint click in the background.

'No luck?' Marnie said.

'Oh god ... it's a power cut, isn't it?'

'Tell me about Beth's message.'

'I feel like a complete –'

'The message, Ralph.

'Well, I think the gist of it was, she just wanted a chat.'

'I'll ring her some time. Thanks, Ralph.'

'Marnie –'

'It's all right, darling. These things happen. See you later. We're coming home.'

29
Wild Horses

It was a quiet weekend at Glebe Farm. By common consent, Marnie and Ralph opted to set their work aside and potter about on the boats. When Marnie and Anne had said goodbye to Judith on Friday, she promised to be in touch as soon as she heard from Dick. But there was no call, and that surprised no-one. Ralph articulated what they were all thinking.

'It looks as if the worst has happened.'

They had taken up the decking on *Sally Ann*, and he was packing the stern gland with grease. Marnie had donned rubber gloves and was scooping dead leaves out of the bilge, dropping them into a plastic carrier bag.

Anne came out of the spinney to join them, wearing overalls and wellingtons. She had spent Saturday morning giving her Mini a thorough wash, wax polish and general clean-up and came to ask if Marnie wanted her to give the same treatment to the MG. The classic sports car, dating back to 1936, spent most of its life under a tarpaulin in the garage barn. Marnie accepted Anne's offer with alacrity and promised to take her for a ride in the two-seater after lunch to give it a good airing and shake out its cobwebs.

The weather varied all weekend between sunshine and scudding clouds, a good mixture for getting to grips with odd jobs. By Sunday afternoon a feeling of modest satisfaction had settled over Glebe Farm, and its three residents put their cares behind them to embark on a tootle on *Sally Ann*, with glasses of Pimm's for the crew, while Dolly perched on the open hatch cover.

On Sunday evening, as they were preparing supper in the galley, Marnie had a phone call from Philip Everett.

'You're not going to believe this,' he began.

'Oh god, break it to me gently, Philip. Should I be sitting down?'

'It's good news, actually. I've had a phone call from Bernard de Groot.'

Marnie pricked up her ears. 'About Dick Blackwood?'

'Oh no ... nothing like that. The archaeologists have virtually finished their work – amazingly – and they want to make a handover presentation to the clients and their contractors.'

'Ahead of schedule?'

'Yep.'

'And on budget?'

'Absolutely.'

'I think I do need to sit down. When do they want this meeting?'

'The prof's suggested Wednesday morning, ten-thirty. Can you make that?'

'I can hear wild horses in the background,' Marnie said. 'No problem. I'll be there.'

30
Grim News

On Monday morning Marnie spotted the note to ring Beth when she reached her desk. Feeling guilty at not phoning sooner, she called her sister at nine o'clock.

When Beth picked up the phone she sounded agitated. 'At last!'

'What's up, Beth? I'm sorry. Ralph gave me your message and I meant to phone over the weekend, but –'

'That doesn't matter. I just felt like a chat. The thing is, have you been listening to the news?'

'Not really. What is it?'

'Apparently a body's been washed up some place on the east coast.'

Marnie felt her cheeks go numb. Anne saw her expression and felt a knot in her stomach.

'When was this?' Marnie said.

'Some time early this morning, I think. I picked it up on the eight o'clock news.'

'Did they give any details … location, sex, age, anything at all?'

'Somewhere on the Lincolnshire coast, I think it was. Nothing else.'

Marnie looked at her watch. 'Thanks, Beth. I'll catch the next bulletin at ten.'

After disconnecting, Marnie told Anne what had happened, and they digested the news in silence. Simultaneously they decided to contact Gerald Parfitt. Anne had several numbers for him and began with the mobile. *Not available.* His home number connected immediately to voicemail. Not a good sign. The last chance was the university department.

'I'm afraid Dr Parfitt isn't in today.'

'I've tried his other numbers but couldn't reach him. It's very important I speak with him.'

'Are you a student? Can anyone else help?'

'I'm involved in the Horselydown excavations in London. I need to contact Dr Parfitt on an urgent matter.'

'And your name, please?'

'Anne Price. I'm a colleague of the joint site directors, Dick Blackwood and Dr Zoë Tipton.'

'Ah, I see. Well, Miss Price, I have to inform you that Dr Parfitt is out of the country.'

'But I spoke to him just a few days ago, on Friday. He didn't say he was going away.'

'That's all I can tell you, I'm afraid.'

Anne's mind was racing. 'He's returned to Denmark, to Roskilde, presumably?'

'I believe so.'

'Do you know when he'll be back?'

'He has a meeting here on Wednesday, so he should be back by then.'

'Thank you very much. Goodbye.' Anne hung up.

Marnie took the phone. Muttering, *we can't just sit around waiting*, she asked directory enquiries for the Lincolnshire Coastguard Service and was given the number of the nearest regional station. She might have known she would draw a blank. The duty officer in Great Yarmouth confirmed that the yacht *Arabella* had been located off the coast the previous Friday and that a body had been washed up that morning near the village of Wainfleet St Mary. If she had any information that might help the police identify the person in question, she should contact them at their office in Skegness. No other details were available at that time.

Ralph was sitting at the computer in his study on *Thyrsis* digesting a set of statistics when he caught sight of Marnie passing the window. Seconds later she entered the study. He could tell from her expression that something was seriously wrong. Without preamble she told him about the body being washed up.

He groaned. 'You're thinking it's Dick Blackwood?'

Marnie looked downcast. 'I don't know, Ralph, but after all that's been going on in that part of the world, it's an awfully big coincidence if it isn't.'

During the course of the afternoon clouds built up over Glebe Farm. Ralph, whose powers of concentration were normally considerable, felt at a loose end. Try as he might, he could not take his mind off the body. He imagined it lying on wet sand as the waves rolled in. Curiously, he saw Dick Blackwood dressed in eighteenth century clothes like a buccaneer and thought how fitting it seemed for one like him, with his swashbuckling, devil-may-care approach to life. Now, he was convinced that that life had been stubbed out, and the waters had washed over his inert shape like an executed pirate left to the mercy of the tides at Execution Dock.

The weather matched Ralph's feelings, as clouds gathered in the afternoon. An air of gloom seemed to hang over Glebe Farm following the latest news. More than anything, he resented the sadness it caused to Marnie. He felt powerless and would do anything to lighten the atmosphere and cheer everyone up.

And then, at the moment when he felt at his lowest ebb, he had a spark of inspiration.

Marnie and Anne were glad when the time came to close the office for the evening. Marnie locked the door behind them while Anne stood beside her in the courtyard, stretching and breathing in deep lungfuls of clean country air. They linked arms and set off through the spinney to the docking area. There had been a light shower during the afternoon, and everything smelled clean and cool. Both had tried to shake off feelings of despair and regret, and the overcast weather did nothing to raise their spirits. Under a leaden sky that threatened more rain, lights were visible in both boats as they emerged from the trees. They guessed that Ralph had left them burning deliberately to create a welcoming sight. As they boarded *Sally Ann*, their nostrils were assailed by aromas of cooking, a heady mixture of aromatic delights, blending savoury and creamy ingredients with a whiff of herbs and spices.

Ralph broke off from stirring a pan to kiss Marnie on the lips and Anne on the cheek.

'Perfect timing,' he said. 'Are you ready to eat?'

'How can I put this ...?' Marnie began.

Anne merely groaned.

Ralph smiled. 'Don't bother. I get the picture. Have you enough strength left after a hard day's work to take a bottle of wine out of the fridge and open it?'

Marnie summoned up her energy. She found a chilled Italian *rosé* from Veneto and set to with the corkscrew. Ralph was adding cream to onions and mushrooms frying in the pan and transferred the mixture to a jug after a few seconds' more stirring.

'Ready in three minutes,' he said, turning his attention to the wok that was resting on the hob. He poured in a tablespoon of olive oil and swirled it round. 'I'll be ready by the time you've poured the wine.'

He was as good as his word. While Marnie filled the glasses, Anne chopped a baguette into chunks. Ralph tipped a bowl of chopped vegetables into the wok and worked them round with a wooden spoon. At his request, Anne lit nightlights under plate-warmers on the table. Leaving the vegetables on a reduced heat, Ralph knelt at the oven and removed a dish covered with baking foil.

The evening was drawing on rapidly under dark clouds, and Marnie lit the oil lamps to counteract the gathering dusk.

'Ralph, what *have* you been doing?' she said in wonder. 'You must've been cooking all afternoon.'

'Just my usual peasant food,' he replied. 'Dead easy. The salmon's been marinating for a couple of hours and baking for the past fifteen minutes or so. I made my mother's favourite sauce ...' He offered Marnie the jug. '... plus a few stir-fried vegetables. Simple.'

'What peasants had this?' Anne asked, serving herself from the dish.

'Various ones, really.' He pointed at the salmon and vegetables. 'Those are basically Vietnamese and Chinese ...' He raised the jug to pour sauce over the salmon on his plate. 'This is ... well, St John's Wood, I suppose.'

'Ah ... *those* peasants,' Marnie said, raising her glass. 'To our master peasant chef. Long live the paddy fields of north London.'

By the time they were clearing the plates from the main course, rain was streaking the windows. Ralph declared he could banish the dismal weather in a trice. With a fanfare he produced a bowl of summer fruits, a medley of strawberries, raspberries and redcurrants, which he served with whipped cream. Over a second glass of *rosé*, the day gradually seemed not so bad after all.

They dealt with the washing-up while the kettle boiled for coffee. Sitting in the saloon by lamplight, they began to feel they had regained their strength, ready to phone the police the next day. All three of them were ready for a shower and an early night.

Anne retired to her attic room to phone Donovan, hoping for more good news about Onkel Helmut. Marnie and Ralph lit sandalwood joss sticks in holders on the draining board in the galley to freshen the atmosphere. Feeling pleasantly drowsy, they crossed the docking area to *Thyrsis*. Marnie lit another joss stick – snow jasmine – on the shelf over the bed in the sleeping cabin, while Ralph used the shower.

That night under the duvet they made love languidly to the drumming of rain falling on the roof. For a short while they were able to banish from their minds all thoughts of the body lying under a shroud on a steel rack in a mortuary a hundred miles away.

31
The Morgue

On Tuesday morning while Ralph and Anne prepared breakfast on *Sally Ann*, Marnie stayed on *Thyrsis* and dialled directory enquiries to ask for the phone number for the police service in Lincolnshire. The operator offered several divisional HQs around the county. The obvious choice was the Coast Division, and Marnie rang the number at once. When the switchboard operator asked the nature of her enquiry, she replied that it concerned the body washed up on the beach at Wainfleet St Mary the previous morning.

The operator put her through to a woman officer whose manner was business-like but not unfriendly.

'You believe you can assist our enquiries, madam?'

'I don't know for sure, but it's possible.'

'Your name, please?'

'Marnie Walker.'

After noting all Marnie's contact details, the officer continued.

'Briefly, what leads you to think you might know the identity of the deceased?'

'A colleague ... a friend ... has gone missing, and the boat he was probably using has been picked up by the Coastguard several miles out from the marina at Whittleham. That's in –'

'I know where it is. And the name of this boat?'

'*Arabella* ... owned by Dr Gerald Parfitt of the University of East Anglia.'

'You said your colleague was *probably* using it?'

'We have reason to believe he may have borrowed it from Dr Parfitt, who's a friend of his.' Marnie almost winced at her use of the phrase, *reason to believe*. It felt like playing a part in a TV drama.

'Did your friend normally use this boat?'

'Yes, he did, regularly ... either with the owner or solo, with his permission.'

'Are you speaking on behalf of the owner?'

The question caught Marnie off-guard.

'In a way, I suppose ... well, no, not as such. Dr Parfitt is out of the country at the moment, in Denmark on business.'

'And your reason for contacting us?'

'I wondered ... if the body had been identified.'

'Can you give me a description of your missing colleague, and a name.'

'He's called Dick Blackwood … mid-twenties, medium height and build, short brown hair … grey eyes.'

'If required, would you be willing to identify the body?'

This was the part Marnie had been dreading. 'If necessary … yes.'

Five minutes later Marnie crossed the docking area and stepped aboard *Sally Ann*. Two expectant faces looked up at her from the table as she made her way through to the saloon.

'You've spoken to them, haven't you?' Ralph pulled out a chair for Marnie.

'Is it that obvious?'

'What did they say?'

'No-one has yet come forward to identify the body.'

'Did they ask you to do it?'

Marnie nodded. 'Apparently, they took the … they took him to a mortuary in Boston.'

The last place Marnie wanted to go that Tuesday morning was to a mortuary two hours' drive away, but the decision had been taken. Filling the Discovery at the local garage, she consoled herself with the thought that at least they would be bringing that sad episode in their lives to a conclusion. The Horselydown project would now forever be tainted. What should have been a great achievement in her professional life, bringing a degree of renown plus not inconsiderable financial rewards, would always remind her of the untimely death of two talented people – Miles Fennimore and Dick Blackwood – and the near-fatal accident to Zoë Tipton.

The smiling Bangladeshi at the till took her credit card, ran it through his machine and handed the payment slip to Marnie to sign.

'Going anywhere special, Marnie?' he asked.

'Not really.' She wrote her signature and gave him back the slip and pen.

'Oh well, have a good day anyway.'

'Thanks. You too, Nalak.'

During the pit-stop Ralph had remained in the car, studying the road atlas. When Marnie climbed in beside him, he outlined a route and offered to split the driving with her, but she said she preferred to have something to do that demanded all her concentration.

'You don't have to do it, Marnie.'

'Honestly, Ralph, I'd prefer –'

'No. I mean, you don't have to do the identification. I know Dick. I'll handle it when we get there.'

'But, Ralph –'

'No arguments. I've made up my mind.'

Marnie leaned over and kissed him. Without a word, she palmed the car into first gear, released the handbrake and steered towards the highway.

Meanwhile, back in the office at Glebe Farm, Anne sat at her desk trying to keep occupied, a bundle of mixed emotions. As she caught up with the filing, her thoughts continuously strayed to Marnie and Ralph on their grim mission. She dreaded the call they had promised at the end of the morning.

There were designs to examine – a key part of her training programme – and bank statements to check and enter into the accounts. Anne soon realised she lacked the concentration for either activity. Instead, she applied herself to cleaning and tidying the office.

First, she assembled the equipment in the middle of the kitchen area, arranging the vacuum cleaner, brooms, brushes, mop and bucket in a neat row. They reminded her at once of the orderly methods of the archaeologists, who always lined up their wheelbarrows, picks, mattocks and all the other paraphernalia in regimental fashion at each refreshment break on a dig. Anne banished this further association with Dick Blackwood from her mind and set to work.

She pressed on for an hour or so, interrupted only by the arrival of the morning post and the occasional phone call. When she finished, the whole place looked good enough for a photo shoot. Anne smiled to herself, imagining Marnie walking in and walking straight out again, joking that she must be in the wrong office. But she knew there would be no smiling or joking that morning.

They met light traffic on their cross-country route, and Marnie suggested a short break for coffee after an hour on the road. She took the opportunity to phone Anne and ask how things were going. Anne reported nothing significant in the post and relayed messages from two clients just back from their holidays.

The good news had come from Donovan. Onkel Helmut was making a steady recovery, and all the indicators were so far positive. Marnie could hear the relief in Anne's voice. Before disconnecting, she promised to phone again as soon as their business in Boston was concluded. In little more than an hour they would have a result.

At the police station the duty sergeant gave Marnie directions to the morgue, a short drive away. She turned into the access road leading to a pleasant modern brick building, stopped at the pole barrier and pressed a button on the control panel. A metallic voice invited her to state her business and instructed her to park by the entrance.

As soon as she stopped the car, a man in a white coat came out to meet them. Ralph explained that he would be carrying out the task, while Marnie waited in the car park. The man introduced himself as Dr Wiseman, senior pathologist, and he led the way into the building. His expression was friendly, no doubt intended to put visitors at their ease in what would certainly be one of the most unpleasant experiences in their lives.

'I understand you're not actually related to the deceased, Professor Lombard.'

'No. He was an acquaintance.'

Dr Wiseman pushed open a door leading into a short corridor. The place smelled like a hospital.

'But there's no doubt you would recognise him?'

'None at all. I first met Dick last summer, and I've seen him again these past few weeks.'

Dr Wiseman stopped outside a door and turned to face Ralph. His expression was a blend of serious and reassuring.

'This is the viewing area. I'd like you to go in and stand by the internal window. The deceased is in the next room. When you're ready, I'll pull aside the sheet covering the body so that you can see his face. When you're satisfied, just turn away and I'll come back to collect you.'

'Fine.'

'Are you okay?'

'Yes.' Ralph swallowed.

'Just one other thing. There are some signs of predation. It's quite normal when death occurs at sea, even after just a day or two. I'm afraid parts of the face have been subjected to scavenging. It's unfortunate, but there's nothing we can do to conceal it.'

'I understand.'

Ralph forced himself to appear calm, wishing he was a million miles away. Wiseman opened the door and stood aside to let him enter.

Waiting outside in the car, Marnie attempted to cheer herself up. In her bag she carried a cologne stick by 4711, not much bigger than a lip-gloss, and she ran it across her forehead and round her throat. The car instantly smelled fresh and clean, and the evaporating perfume cooled her skin. She closed her eyes and shut out the horrors of the world around her. But even the sharp tang of *eau de Cologne* could not lift her sense of guilt at letting Ralph perform the identification. She was hugely grateful to him for offering to undertake the awful task.

When she opened her eyes again, Ralph was exiting the mortuary. He looked tense, and her heart went out to him. She at once climbed out and went round to open the tailgate. In the luggage compartment she pulled open a hold-all and, by the time Ralph joined her, she produced a small bottle, unscrewed the cap and held it out to him. It was a miniature of brandy from the emergency supplies. Without hesitating, he took the bottle and swallowed half its contents in one gulp.

'I should've been in there, Ralph. Thank you so much for doing that.'

Ralph looked puzzled. 'You? Why should you?'

'I was the one who said we'd do it. It was cowardly of me to –'

'It wasn't Dick.'

Marnie thought she had misheard. 'Sorry?'

Ralph shook his head. 'Whoever it was, it wasn't him. It was some other poor ...' His voice cracked.

Marnie nudged his elbow, and Ralph needed no second bidding to down the rest of the bottle.

'Not Dick? You're sure?'

'Absolutely. I'd rather not go into detail, if you don't mind.'

'Of course.'

Marnie took him in her arms and hugged him tight, aware of an exotic mixture of smells: cognac and cologne.

'You smell nice,' he said.

Marnie attempted a smile. 'So do you. Come on, darling, let's get out of here.'

Back in the car, Marnie phoned Anne to let her know the outcome, while Ralph stared ahead through the windscreen. When Marnie ended the call he opened the atlas to plot the route for home. Marnie manœuvred the car out of its space and drove up to the barrier. The car was still rolling when the bar rose, and she accelerated out into the street. As she changed gear, she noticed Ralph shudder.

'I'm so sorry you had to go through that. You're a hero.'

'One of us had to.' He gently smoothed her thigh with his hand. 'I'm glad it wasn't him.'

'Yes, that would've made it even worse.'

Ralph indicated she should take a left at traffic lights. 'But it still leaves him out there somewhere.'

Marnie made the turn just as the light changed to amber. 'Yes. This isn't over yet.'

Anne replaced the receiver and sat quietly for a few moments feeling numb but relieved. She understood what Ralph had gone through. A little more than two years earlier she herself had been asked to perform the identification of a dead girl. It was the most traumatic experience of her life. She was rising to make a cup of tea when it occurred to her that the task could have been even more harrowing for Ralph. It would have brought back memories of the time his wife had died. Ralph had been at Laura's bedside when she succumbed to illness a dozen or more years earlier.

Anne was pouring freshly-boiled water into the teapot when the phone rang. She skipped across to her desk and picked up the receiver. It was Donovan.

'The doctors are pleased with Onkel Helmut's progress.'

'Brilliant!'

'His condition is stable. They said this first week or so after an attack is critical, but he's doing well.'

For a few minutes they spoke about Onkel Helmut and the family.

'Hold on, Anne. Uschi's saying something.' Anne heard a German voice in the background. The voice came nearer as Donovan raised the phone again. 'Uschi wants to speak to you. Here she is.'

'Hallo, Uschi? I'm really sorry about your dad. I hope he's feeling much better.'

'Hi. Thank you, Anna. He's going to be fine. The doctors are very pleased with him. Oh sorry, I called you *Anna*. I meant, Anne, of course. Forgive me.'

'No probs.'

'You see, we always say your name the German way when we talk about you here.'

'You talk about *me*?'

Uschi laughed. 'Oh yes. My mother interrogates Nikki – I mean *Donovan* – all the time.'

'Oh ...' Anne was taken aback.

'German women ...' Uschi left the rest of the sentence unsaid, as if it was unnecessary. 'She asked Donovan how your German was coming on.'

In her mind's eye, Anne saw the book and cassette tapes she kept in the bedside cabinet that she worked on every night.

'How did she know about that?'

'So you *are* learning German?' Uschi sounded elated. 'Mutti will be so pleased. She's also been asking him when you are coming to see us in Germany.'

'Say hi to Mutti.' Anne pronounced it to rhyme with *sooty*. 'But I'm afraid I don't really have any plans to visit you.'

'Yet.' Uschi laughed again.

On that enigmatic note, Uschi passed the phone back to Donovan.

'It must be nice for you to be in Germany again, Donovan, with your family.'

'Yes, though my aunt makes a big fuss of me. She's always plying me with questions about my life in England, my studies, my friends. You get the picture.'

'Uschi says she asks about *me*.'

Donovan laughed. 'Incessantly. She's very curious. Germans are like that … nosy.'

'Donovan, listen, I er … I've got some news for you.'

Donovan noticed the change of tone and immediately became serious.

'About Dick?'

'Yes … sort of. Early yesterday morning a body was washed up on a beach opposite Whittleham. Marnie and Ralph went up to Lincolnshire this morning to see if they could identify it.'

'And?'

'It wasn't Dick … just some other young man.'

'They were sure of that?'

'No doubt about it. I suppose there was only an outside chance it might've been him.'

'So still no sign of Dick?'

'Nothing.'

Donovan paused for a moment. 'I can't get my head round it just now. Let's talk about it when I get back.'

'D'you know when that will be?'

'Now Onkel Helmut's out of danger, I'll return in the next day or so.'

'As soon as that?'

'I have a lot of preparation to do for the new term at uni.'

After disconnecting, Anne poured her tea and sat looking round the tidiest office in the western world. She was sure even Donovan's aunt would approve.

In Göttingen, Donovan refocused his thoughts on the situation awaiting him in England. On impulse he checked the speed-dial on his mobile and found Dick's number. The call went straight to voicemail.

The voicemail memory for the number you are calling is full. Please try later.

32
A Visitor

Marnie and Anne saw the gathering inside the construction site when they arrived for the meeting on Wednesday morning and their hearts sank. They had barely entered the compound when a cheer went up, then another, then another.

'I thought ...' Marnie looked bewildered.

'Don't tell me,' said Anne. 'You thought Zoë was in there having her usual rant with the builders, right?'

'Got it in one. Come on. Let's see what's going on.'

A cry went up as soon as the students spotted Marnie and Anne, and some of them broke away from the bunch to usher them into their midst. They found themselves alongside Professor de Groot and the postgrad site directors lined up for a group photograph.

'Isn't Donovan with you?'

Anne recognised the voice at once. Turning, she found Debbie in her green denim fatigues, smiling broadly.

'He's still away.'

'That's too bad.'

Before the conversation could go any further, they were called together for more photographs, and Philip Everett waved to them from the site office. The students punched the air as several camera buttons were pressed by helpful builders. As the fists were lowered, Marnie excused herself and took Anne off for the handover briefing.

In the office Bernard de Groot explained that the two post-grad site directors would each give a short PowerPoint presentation, one on the Saxon skeleton, the other on the Roman ships. One site, two important finds. Although touched by tragedy, it had been a memorable excavation. Before the presentations, de Groot asked those present to observe one minute's silence in memory of Dr Fennimore. Everyone rose and bowed their heads, standing round the table with the muted sounds of construction work seeping in from outside. When de Groot murmured a subdued *thank you*, they resumed their seats and the meeting began.

After the archaeologists finished their talks, Marnie and Anne stayed behind to review developments with the contractors. There were no serious issues to address, and the discussion lasted barely an hour. Marnie was asked to give an update on her side of the work, and she impressed as ever with a succinct, off-the-cuff résumé of progress.

As they were leaving the hut, Marnie saw de Groot emerging from the dig site. He walked over to thank her and her 'young colleagues' for their help with recording the excavations. He gave Marnie his card and asked if Donovan would get in touch to arrange for copies of the film material to be handed over in due course. They would form an important part of the archive.

'Are you happy with how things have turned out, professor ... apart from the dreadful accident, of course?'

'Call me Bernard, please. Yes, it's been an extraordinary excavation, and we're all delighted with the plans to keep it, so to say, alive *in situ*.'

'And have you heard anything from Zoë Tipton?'

'Only that she's submitted the report on her findings here, and I gather she's making a good recovery.'

'What about Dick Blackwood?'

De Groot shrugged and lowered his voice. 'Not a word. Have you heard anything?'

Marnie was silent for a long moment. 'No. We did think, at one point ... Well, let me just say we know he's gone missing, and there's a possibility that he may have met with an accident at sea.'

'You think so, too? Yes. I've been informed though that a body washed up was found *not* to be him. That's all I know at present.'

Marnie refrained from describing the visit to the morgue in Boston and said simply, 'He's been working apparently with an archaeologist from UEA.'

'That would be Gerald Parfitt, yes. I'm keen to speak with him, but I gather he's not available, either.'

'No. He's away in Denmark.'

'Ah, yes ... the Roskilde project. Do you know when he's coming back?'

Marnie glanced sideways at Anne, who replied.

'Quite soon, I think.'

'You're obviously more in touch with things than I am,' said de Groot. 'Let me know if you hear from him, would you?'

They agreed to keep in touch, and de Groot took his leave.

'Why doesn't the prof know what's going on?' Anne said on their way back to the flat. 'He's supposed to be the one in charge of everything.'

'Beats me,' said Marnie. 'I don't know what to make of these archaeologists sometimes.'

'What do you think we should do now?'

'Have lunch.'

Anne laughed. 'Is that the sum total of your plans, O Wise One?'

'How about this? We grab a sandwich from the deli and phone Judith.'

'Okay by me. What's the idea?'

'I want another talk with her. I think she knows more than she's saying.'

'Amazing ... and she's not even an archaeologist.'

Judith agreed to see them at Dick's rooms after her lunchtime shift ended, but with one proviso. She had noticed that the lock key on her parent's boat was not in its usual place and, after searching high and low, had no idea what had become of it. She wanted to call in at the chandlers to buy a replacement, so they agreed to meet at Dick's place at four.

Marnie booked a minicab, and they arrived in Wilberforce Street to find Judith dismounting from her bicycle. Anne had bought a box of tea bags, a bottle of milk and two packets of biscuits, determined that their encounter this time would be more congenial.

As soon as they shook hands on the doorstep it became clear that Judith's demeanour had changed. There was a gleam in her eyes. While Anne occupied herself in the kitchen, Marnie and Judith carried out an inspection of Dick's living room and bedroom. Nothing seemed to have changed since their last visit.

Judith turned to face Marnie, taking hold of her arm.

'Listen. I've found out something. It may be important.'

'Go on.'

'Dr Parfitt's been here.' Judith paused, waiting for a reaction. 'Well, what d'you think of that?'

'Has he been in touch with you?'

Anne came in carrying the tea tray. For a few seconds they were distracted, clearing space on the low table, passing round cups and taking biscuits. Marnie took up the thread.

'You were saying, Judith ...?'

'Apparently he showed up here one morning, out of the blue.'

'How do you know this?'

'Jonathan was in his room upstairs. He's one of the housemates ... came back to collect something. Anyway, he heard someone come in and thought it must be Dick.'

'Why did he think that?'

'Because he came in here. Only Dick has his own sitting room-cum-study. Jonathan came downstairs, just to say hallo. He knocked on the door but got no reply. So he pushed the door open and found this chap standing in the middle of the room looking sheepish.'

'Did Jonathan recognise him? Does he know Parfitt?'

Judith frowned. 'Er … no. I mean … I don't know for sure. But he said he was a friend of Dick's and had permission to fetch a book he'd lent him and now he wanted it back.'

'Why do you think it was Parfitt?'

'Jonathan described him. I've never met Parfitt, but I've seen photos of him with Dick, so I know what he looks like. I'm pretty sure he was the man who came here that day.'

'When was this exactly?' Anne asked.

'Towards the end of last week.'

'And this Jonathan just let a complete stranger come into the house and walk out with what could have been Dick's property?'

'When you put it like that, Marnie, it does sound suspicious. But he had a front door key and he told Jonathan the title of the book and where Dick had said it would be.'

'They found it?'

'Yes, on the bookcase exactly in the right place. It was just an ordinary text book – ethno-archaeology or something – and the man seemed pleasant and friendly, so Jonathan thought no more about it.'

'Did he say if he left this man – let's assume it was Parfitt – alone in here for any length of time?'

Judith considered the question. 'He didn't say.'

'Pity.'

'You think it's important?'

'Don't you?'

'Then why don't we ask Jonathan?' Judith said.

'Is he here?' Marnie asked, surprised.

'No, but he has a mobile and I've got his number.'

Judith rang the number and had an immediate reply. The only time the visitor was alone in the room was when he first arrived. Judith thanked Jonathan and asked if he could remember anything else from their conversation. The answer was simple: nothing. Marnie asked if she could have a word. Judith explained who Marnie was and passed her the phone.

'How long was it before you came downstairs that morning?'

'No time at all. I was coming out of the bathroom when I heard the front door shut. I went straight down.'

'Didn't you think it was odd that you got no reply when you knocked on Dick's door?'

'I suppose I did.'

'Did you remark on that when you found the man in the room?'

'I didn't actually say anything, but we both knew it was an awkward situation. I think the other guy said something like he'd been surprised to hear a knock as he believed the house was empty. He felt rather embarrassed, like an intruder.'

'After you located the book he wanted ... who did that, by the way, you or him?'

'I did.' No hesitation. 'It was exactly where he said it would be.'

'Okay, and then he just went away?'

'Yes.'

'Immediately? He didn't ask to use the loo or anything?'

'What an *odd* question. No, he didn't. He had his book, thanked me and said he ...'

'Hallo?' Marnie frowned. 'Jonathan, are you there?'

'Just a minute.' A pause. 'There was something ... let me think ...'

Marnie waited patiently before he continued.

'Yes ... he said he just wanted to make a quick phone call before he left. I said we didn't have a phone in the house, but he had his mobile with him. Not wanting to intrude, I went out of the room and left him to it.'

'For how long?'

'Hardly any time. I went to sit on the stairs to give him some privacy, but he came out almost as soon as I sat down.'

'Had you heard him talking?'

'No, but he said there was no reply. We made some remarks about the dreaded voicemail and I showed him out.'

'Just two more questions.'

'Okay.'

'Was he carrying a briefcase?'

'Er ... yes.'

'Are you sure?'

'Positive. He put the book in it.'

'And did you check the room after he left?'

'Funny you should say that. I did have a quick look round, but everything was the same as before.'

'No doubt about that?'

'None at all ... I think.'

Back at the flat, Marnie phoned Ralph in the office. The main news was that Donovan had rung to say he was back. He had managed to get a flight that morning and was going to call in at the university library. He would phone again in the evening. Ralph had asked after Onkel Helmut and learnt that he was doing well.

Anne tried Donovan's mobile but only got as far as the message that he was not available. They both felt strangely unsettled and, as usual, stared down at the riverscape from the window. The sky was still cloudy, casting a dull workaday atmosphere over the scene. In the distance the tallest skyscraper in Canary Wharf flashed a laser beam like a beacon from the glazed top of its pyramid roof.

In the bedrooms the overnight bags lay unopened on top of the duvets. For a few minutes neither of them spoke, gazing down at the Thames, mulling over what they had learnt that afternoon, trying to make an intelligible pattern of recent events.

Eventually, Marnie suggested that they return to Glebe Farm. Neither could see any merit in remaining in London that evening. Both had the niggling feeling that something did not add up, but neither could work out what it was.

33
Donovan Returns

Anne woke early in her attic room on Thursday morning and immediately felt happiness wash over her for two reasons. The first was the sight of a narrow shaft of bright light cutting across the room from the thin slit in the gable end, her only window. The sunshine had returned and would be bringing Donovan with it. He had phoned the night before and arranged to drive up from London. Anne looked at the clock before rolling out of bed. Six-forty. Knowing Donovan, he might already be on his way.

Over supper on *Sally Ann* the previous evening, they had examined every aspect of Dick Blackwood's disappearance. Ralph had surprised Marnie and Anne by playing devil's advocate. Had it occurred to them that the visitor to Dick's house might have been some other student? Gerald Parfitt was not the only archaeologist he knew, or who might have lent him a book. Nor was he the only person who answered to the description of a youngish man of medium height, medium build with sandy hair.

Marnie was perplexed. She had so convinced herself the visitor was Gerald Parfitt that she had closed her mind to other possibilities. Biting her lip, she brought her clenched fist lightly down on the table. Determined to fill in the gaps of Judith's account of the conversation with Jonathan, she had overlooked a key question. Had the stranger in fact given his name? Ralph pointed out that that would be normal when confronted by an unknown person in a strange house. Surely, he reasoned, it would be the first thing you'd say to establish your *bona fides*.

Anne climbed out of bed, descended the wall ladder and went through to the shower room. Turning under the hot jets, rinsing away the lather from the shower gel, she tried to clear her mind of all thoughts of Dick, Gerald, Zoë, Horselydown and the whole sad affair.

After breakfast Marnie and Anne went through all the papers in their in-baskets. For two hours they dealt with correspondence, finance and designs and were so engrossed they put all other thoughts out of their minds. By the time Anne returned to her desk, armed with a to-do list and a bundle of filing, Marnie announced that it was time for action, time to phone Gerald Parfitt. She picked up the handset to dial the direct line for the departmental secretary at UEA.

'I'm afraid Dr Parfitt can't be reached at the moment, Mrs Walker.'

Something about her tone rang an alarm bell in Marnie's head.

'I understood he'd be back by now. It's really rather urgent that I speak with him.' Marnie looked across at Anne, crossed the fingers of her free hand, grimaced and added in an authoritative voice, 'It concerns a multi-million pound project in London.'

'Oh my goodness. I … I just don't know what to say.'

'You could tell me when it will be possible to speak to him. Sorry, I didn't catch your name. I'd like to make a note of it.'

'Oh heavens …'

'You were saying?'

'It appears that Dr Parfitt … hasn't in fact been in Denmark.'

'I see.' Marnie did not see. 'So where *has* he been?'

'I don't know, Mrs Walker. But he wasn't here for a meeting yesterday and then Dr Rasmussen from Roskilde University phoned to talk to him this morning. That's when we realised he'd not been there at all.'

Ralph had an appointment that morning and was unable to spend much time discussing this latest development. He was meeting an American academic at his cottage in Murton, near Oxford. The professor from Northwestern University in Chicago would be renting the cottage from August to December, and Ralph had arranged to meet her to give her the guided tour and hand over the keys. They would then be having lunch with the Master at Ralph's college, All Saints.

Before leaving, he suggested that they discuss with Donovan that evening what, if anything, they should do next. When Marnie and Anne returned to the office after seeing him off, Marnie sat immobile at her desk for some time. It took Anne a while to notice this, being totally occupied with routine clerical tasks. Eventually she spoke.

'Planet Earth to Marnie. Come in, please. Over.'

No reaction. Anne picked up her mobile and hit the speed-dial. Marnie's phone rang and she picked it up. Before she could announce herself, she heard a strange voice with a drawl worthy of the Deep South, Kentucky or Georgia.

'Anybody home?'

Marnie looked totally mystified. 'Sorry? Who is this, please?'

'It's me, you idiot.' Normal voice this time. 'Anne with an 'e'. Remember me?'

Marnie looked up to see Anne waving at her from across the room. She laughed.

'What are you playing at?' She put down the receiver. 'Oh … was I somewhere else?'

'In outer space, by the look of it, probably heading for the planet Tharg.'

Marnie's expression became serious. 'It's no use. For once I can't agree with Ralph, can't wait till we can all discuss it rationally. Sometimes you just *have* to take action.'

'Royal Marines School of Management?' Anne suggested.

'Exactly ... seize the high ground.'

'What are you going to do?'

Marnie stared at Anne. 'Much as it goes against the grain, I'm going to contact the police.'

'You're kidding!'

They both knew that Marnie's relationship with the police in the past had been ... erratic.

'I don't see any other way. Do you?'

Some time later Anne took coffee out to the builders working in the farmhouse. On her way back to the office a familiar rumbling sound stopped her in her tracks in the courtyard. It was unmistakably the burbling of an air-cooled flat-four-cylinder engine. Donovan's VW Beetle was coming down the slope. She rushed to the garage barn to meet him.

'You're later than we expected,' Anne said, hugging him warmly.

'Jetlag.'

'From *Hanover*?'

Donovan kissed her a second time. 'I had things to do before driving up.'

In the office, after enquiries about Onkel Helmut, Marnie switched on the answerphone, and the three of them made their way through the spinney to sit out on the bank beside *Sally Ann*.

'So what's new?' Donovan asked.

Marnie brought him up to date on events surrounding Dick's disappearance, including the news about Parfitt not going to Denmark and her contact with the police.

'Let me get this right,' he said, raising an eyebrow. 'You, Marnie Walker, phoned the police for advice?'

'Yes, this morning.'

Donovan sat back in his chair. 'It's gotta be a first. How did you get on?'

'I got through to Sergeant Marriner ... told him we were seriously worried about Dick.'

'Let me guess how he reacted,' Donovan said. 'He told you Dick was a grown man and could go where he wanted. Being away for a few days after so much happening at the dig was no surprise.'

Marnie sighed. 'Yes. That's more or less what he said.'

'Did he point out that it's not unusual for people to go on holiday in July, even to take a break on impulse?'

Marnie nodded. 'He said that, too.'

'Did you tell him about Parfitt going off?'

'I did. Actually, he seemed interested in that. Also, he couldn't come up with any reassuring theory on why Parfitt's boat was found adrift out at sea.'

'So how did you leave it, Marnie?'

'He said we should give it a while before doing anything else. He thought Dick would come back with a reasonable explanation of where he'd been and why, and the same went for Dr Parfitt. He suspected they might be doing something together on what he called their *secret treasure project.*'

Donovan looked thoughtful. 'He could be right about that. You did well to get so much out of him.'

'Yes, he was only partially interested, of course. The whole business is well outside his jurisdiction.'

'Do you have a plan for what to do next?'

Marnie shrugged. 'Ralph thinks we should sit down together and talk through the options. He'll be back this evening. I'm not sure he thinks we have any options, in fact.'

Donovan stared out at the canal. Two hire boats went by, one of them flying a Swedish flag attached to the tiller. The crews waved a friendly greeting.

'We need to think everything through, step by step,' Donovan said. 'While I've been away I've been trying to get things clear in my mind.'

'Have *you* reached any conclusions?' Marnie said.

'This absence of Dr Parfitt from Denmark seems to me significant. Personally, I don't think Sergeant Marriner's comments have added anything new.'

'Can you add anything new, Donovan?'

'Before we go any further, I think we need to establish the latest situation from every angle.'

'I thought we just did that,' Marnie said wearily.

Donovan shook his head. 'Not as of now, this morning. The situation's changing all the time. We need to check with the Barbican archaeology department in case they've heard anything, in case Dick's suddenly turned up. We need to check out UEA in case they have fresh news of Parfitt this morning. Same goes for the marina.'

'Okay.' Marnie began rising from her chair. 'We'd better make a start. Shall we take one each?'

'That's not where we start,' Donovan said emphatically.

Marnie sat down again. 'No?'

'No. The key point of contact is Judith. She's the closest relationship he has. Her boat is his temporary base. If anyone's going to have news of him, it'll probably be her.'

'But only yesterday she said –'

'That was *then*.' Donovan cut Marnie off. 'The situation could've changed completely overnight.'

Anne, who had remained silent throughout their exchange, put her mobile on the table.

'I've got Judith's number on speed-dial.'

'Go for it,' Marnie said.

Anne pressed buttons and held the phone to her ear. The conversation was short. Anne thanked Judith and disconnected.

'No contact. Not a word. She's also spoken to Jonathan at the house, and he said Dick hadn't been back there.'

Marnie rose again. 'Okay, so at least we know the situation as far as she's concerned. Now we can tackle the others.' She turned to Donovan. 'What if we don't get anywhere with any of them?'

Donovan ignored Marnie's question and spoke instead to Anne. 'Was that all Judith said, nothing else?'

'That was it. Well, she did mention she'd tried Dick's mobile again, but no luck there. She left yet another message on his voicemail – a forlorn hope, she said.'

'Something's not right.' Donovan frowned. 'Say that again, Anne.'

'Only that Judith didn't expect to get a reply from Dick to her message.'

Marnie and Anne sat watching Donovan who seemed lost in his thoughts.

'That's odd ...' he said. 'It doesn't add up.'

'What doesn't add up?' said Marnie. 'It's nothing new that Dick probably won't reply. He's been incommunicado for the past two weeks.'

Donovan closed his eyes. 'Let's go back a step.' He opened his eyes and stared at Anne. 'Judith said she'd left a message for Dick on his voicemail, right?'

Anne nodded. Neither she nor Marnie had any idea what was troubling Donovan. They waited patiently.

'When was that?' he said.

'Late last night, I think.'

'On his mobile.'

'That's all he has.'

Donovan shook his head slowly. 'No. I tried to phone him from Germany two days ago … Tuesday. His voicemail wasn't accepting any more messages. Its memory was full.'

Marnie immediately grasped the implication. 'So Dick *must* be alive!'

'Yes!' Anne exclaimed. 'He must've been checking his messages, then deleting them.'

The three of them digested this latest development. Donovan broke the silence.

'Or someone else has his mobile,' he said quietly.

Marnie was pinned down on the phone for the rest of the morning and most of the afternoon, while Anne caught up with paperwork in the office. This left Donovan free to pursue the leads relating to Dick Blackwood.

He rang London Barbican University: no contact from Dick. He tried the University of East Anglia: still no news from Gerald Parfitt. It was the same picture at the marina. *Arabella* was back on her mooring, but no-one had seen Parfitt for some days, nor had anyone else apparently been to the boat.

Anne was preoccupied with business matters, and it bothered her to see Donovan struggling with the Horselydown situation while she could do nothing to help. Midway through the afternoon he offered to take *Sally Ann* for a tootle to give the machinery some exercise and clear his head.

He returned an hour or so later, seeming more relaxed than before, announcing that he had filled the boat's water tank, lubricated the tiller tube and packed grease in the stern gland.

Marnie grinned at him. 'I thought you wanted time to think. What next … servicing the engine?'

'I did want time to think.'

'Have you reached any conclusions?'

'Yes. I know now what has to be done. Is it all right if I stay tonight?'

Marnie glanced at Anne for a reply.

'Sure … and you won't need to put up your tent.'

It was warm enough to eat outside that evening. As Ralph had had lunch in college, Marnie proposed a buffet supper with a please-yourself medley of dishes clustered together on a *lazy Susan*. They helped themselves to asparagus, king prawns, Russian eggs, salads and dips with chunks of crusty baguette, while Marnie gave Ralph an update. The table was decked with nightlights sparkling in crystal glass holders. Anne poured glasses of a dry *rosé* wine from Provence. It reflected the candlelight, adding a cheerful glow to the setting, but no-one proposed a toast.

When Marnie had finished her narrative, Ralph accepted some more wine from Anne.

'I think what you've told me reinforces what I've been thinking all day,' he said. 'It seems to me most likely that Dick and Parfitt are away somewhere together. I think they *both* want to make an impact with the King John treasure. For my money, it's the only explanation that makes sense.'

'What about the boat?' Marnie said. 'We know for a fact it's at the marina.'

Ralph nodded. 'Okay, but didn't we know already that the treasure may not be located out at sea at all? Didn't Dick tell us the whole region had changed unrecognisably? I think that's why Parfitt went to get the tracing paper showing the routes across the wetlands.'

'And have you reached any conclusion on why Parfitt went to Dick's house to collect the tracing paper rather than Dick himself?' Marnie said.

'There could be any number of reasons. For example, perhaps Dick didn't want to be seen in London at that time. The element of secrecy seems to be important to him.'

Marnie nodded. 'Well, that all seems to add up.'

Anne glanced at Donovan, whose expression was impassive.

'I suppose so,' Anne said. 'It makes as much sense as anything else.'

Marnie spoke tentatively. 'Have you any thoughts, Donovan?'

After a long moment he said, 'There may be another possibility.' He drank from his glass and sat staring into the distance.

'Are you going to elaborate on that?' Ralph asked.

'We could be looking in the wrong place.'

34
Another Blank

When Donovan set off the next morning, Anne watched the Beetle rumble up the field track with a sense of unease. He had seemed more than usually preoccupied ever since his return from Germany and had withdrawn inside himself. The previous night, he had showered while Anne busied herself with mundane chores in the laundry room. When she eventually climbed the wall-ladder she found him fast asleep in her bed.

At breakfast she realised that at other times she would have teased him again that he was being a *man of mystery*, but all her instincts told her he was really troubled.

When lunchtime came and there had been no word from Donovan, Anne voiced her anxiety to Marnie, who confessed that she too was concerned about him. She suggested that Anne should take the initiative and phone him. Anne hit buttons straight away. The mobile rang several times before Donovan replied. He explained that he was driving and had had to pull over to take the call.

'We were worried that we hadn't heard from you, Donovan. How's it going?'

'Nothing to report so far.'

'Where are you?'

'Not far from Wisbech. I've been to that B and B where Dick and Parfitt used to stay.'

'No luck?'

'No. They haven't been there for some time.'

'That was where you thought Dick might've been hiding out ... the place we hadn't been looking in?'

'Just a long shot.'

'So what now?'

'I'm ... following up another lead.'

'Can you tell me about it?'

The silence lasted some seconds.

'Look, Anne ... I'd rather not say anything till I'm sure of my ground. I'm not trying to be mysterious, really. It's just ... well, let's see what happens.'

'Okay. Will you phone in later?'

'As soon as I have some news, but it may not be until tomorrow.'

'*Tomorrow*? Right. Well, good luck. Drive safely.'

'Yeah.'

35
Explanations

It had been Anne's turn to have a restless night. Half hoping that Donovan might ring sooner than expected, she had stayed up till midnight waiting for a call. After turning out the light, she lay awake in the darkness trying to work out what Donovan had in mind that had not occurred to anyone else. Eventually her brain switched off and she faded into a disturbed slumber of weird dreams, with pirates being dragged to the gibbet at Horselydown to be hanged in chains and left dangling for the tides to wash over their rotting corpses.

On Saturday morning at seven, bathed in sweat, Anne crawled down the wall-ladder and yawned her way zombie-like to the shower where she gradually regained full consciousness. To complete the process she turned the temperature control knob to full-cold for a five second blast. With a yelp and a squawk she leapt out and grabbed the towel.

The first call of the day came in just after nine. Marnie looked across at Anne to find she already had the receiver in her hand. The caller was not Donovan, though the voice sounded familiar.

'Is that Anne?'

'Yes. Who is this, please?'

'It's Judith … Dick's –'

'Hi, Judith. Is everything all right?'

'More than all right, Anne. Dick's come back!'

For a few seconds Anne was speechless. She only realised she was sitting with her mouth open when Marnie held up a hand and made a shadow-puppet mime of a crocodile snapping its jaws shut.

'Er … sorry, Judith. I'm just finding it hard to take in. It's *wonderful* news.' For Marnie's benefit, she added. 'I'm so glad Dick's back. Is he okay?'

'Sort of … I mean, yes, really. He's had a bit of an ordeal, but he's fine.'

'Is he with you there?'

'He's on my boat, sleeping. I've got to go shopping, then on to the restaurant later this morning.'

'Lunchtime shift?' Anne said.

'Yes.'

'Judith, when can we see him?'

'Some time this afternoon, if you like. D'you want to fix a time and place?'

'It's not just down to me. I need to check with Marnie. Can you hold on half a mo?'

Anne held the phone to her chest and gave a quick summary to Marnie, who reflected briefly, looked up at the clock and came to an instant decision. Could Judith and Dick come to Marnie's Docklands flat for three-thirty? Anne relayed this to Judith who accepted at once.

Anne had scarcely disconnected when the phone rang again. This time, Marnie took the call. It was Donovan, and he sounded tense. She gave him the news about Dick and was surprised at his reaction.

'Okay.'

Marnie waited for more but nothing came. She could hear road noise in the background.

'Are you driving?'

'Yes.'

'Where are you?'

'On the A1 southbound.'

'We've arranged to meet Dick and Judith at my flat this afternoon.'

'What time?'

'Half past three.'

A pause. 'I'll be there. Gotta go.'

Marnie was listening to air.

'What's up?' said Anne.

'Donovan seemed somehow … distant.'

'He doesn't like to use the phone when he's driving.'

'But he rang us.'

'Mm … probably just hit traffic,' Anne said.

'Yes. I'm sure you're right.'

Marnie, Ralph and Anne grabbed a quick sandwich at Milton Keynes station and caught the first available train to Euston. They were going to London for a happy occasion, with Dick back safe and sound, but at the back of Marnie's mind she had an uneasy feeling. Donovan's reaction had unsettled her.

They reached the flat with an hour to spare. To keep all options open they had taken overnight bags, and they dropped them in their bedrooms on arrival. The contract cleaners had paid their weekly visit since the last time they were there, and everything was neat and tidy, with fresh towels hanging in the bathrooms where all the fittings were polished and gleaming. The perfect order was only disturbed by a carton of milk standing on the kitchen worktop. Marnie had bought it in passing at the mini-market. Anne picked it up and put it in the fridge, then surprised Marnie by checking the cupboards in the kitchen.

'Everything all right?' Marnie asked. 'I'm sure we have coffee and tea already.'

'Marnie, could I make something for tea-time to offer Dick and Judith when they come?'

'*Make* something? Like what?'

'Don't take this the wrong way, please. I mean, the flat is absolutely lovely … really elegant and stylish and all that. But …' Anne's voice faded.

'You think it looks too spruce, like something in a magazine or a catalogue?'

'In a way, yes. I don't mean to be rude or –'

'No, Anne. You're right. It is a bit impersonal.'

'I thought it might feel more welcoming, more lived-in, if it smelled of something baking. This is meant to be a celebration, after all.'

'*Baking?*' Marnie reflected for a moment. 'Okay. So what do you have in mind?'

'We've just got basic ingredients, so I was thinking about something really simple, like Welsh cakes. They only take a few minutes. They're delicious and they smell great.'

'Excellent idea,' said Ralph. 'Do you have the recipe?'

Anne tapped her head. 'In here. My Grandma Price taught me to make them when I was eight. It's dead easy.'

By the time Dick and Judith arrived, followed a few minutes later by Donovan, the atmosphere had been transformed. With sunlight pouring through the windows, the flat was filled with the homely smell of hot cakes. They took their places on the wide deeply-upholstered sofas facing each other. As they made themselves comfortable, Anne lit a chunky cream candle in the middle of the low coffee table before handing out plates and Welsh cakes. Judith sat close beside Dick and held his hand briefly before they broke off to sip their tea. As celebrations went, it was low-key, but there was no disguising the relief they all felt at Dick's safe return.

The scene was set for him to tell his story and bring the episode to a happy conclusion.

'Where shall I begin?' he said in a hesitant voice.

'Why not start with what happened after you left the site the day of Zoë's accident?' Ralph suggested.

Dick shuddered. 'I thought she was dead and it was my fault.' He looked desperate.

Judith squeezed his hand. 'Well she *wasn't*, and it was *nobody's* fault.'

'Tell us about your disappearance,' Marnie said.

'Okay. I took off to Norwich to see Gerald. I thought the best thing I could do would be to relocate the treasure. I know it's silly to call it treasure – *Indiana Jones* and all that – but you know what I mean. I wanted to restore my reputation. It's very selfish, but it was all I could think of as a way out of a horrifying situation ... something *positive*.'

'And Dr Parfitt could help you with that?' Marnie said.

'Yes. The plan was to go out on *Arabella* and bring up more artefacts. That's when we hit a snag.'

'You realised you didn't have all your maps and notes.'

'Exactly. I was in such a state when I came away that I left some important material behind. We agreed that Gerald would go to my digs and collect what we needed.'

'Why didn't you just go yourself?' Ralph said.

'I couldn't face going back to London, not at that time ... didn't want to see anybody. I wanted to wait till things settled down after Zoë's ... accident ...'

Ralph nodded. 'You thought she was dead.'

'Yes and, like I said, I wanted to come back with something tangible ... some more finds.'

'A return in triumph,' Marnie said quietly, 'to outweigh the tragedy.'

'It sounds bad, I know, but it's all I could think of. So Gerald went to the house where he bumped into Jonathan. I hadn't expected anyone else to be there at that time. He managed to get the tracing paper with the routes marked, but that was all. He thought it was enough and we could overlay the tracing on an Ordnance Survey map of the area. The trouble was, there were a dozen or more maps. He didn't realise we had to have the actual master map – a copy of a medieval one – to make sense of everything.'

'Didn't you know enough to be able to make an informed guess about the location?' Marnie asked.

Dick shook his head. 'That was my big mistake. I thought I could. We studied the tracings of the routes, and I was convinced I could find the right spot, so we set off on *Arabella* with a feeling of cautious optimism.'

'If anyone could find it, you could,' Judith said. 'You're brilliant.'

Dick gave a self-deprecating smile. 'That's what I thought, too. Huh! When we got out and were faced with that flat featureless coastline and that grey empty sea I realised how hopeless it was. It was all so vast. I got annoyed, mainly with myself. But Gerald took it personally, said I was blaming him. The weather started to deteriorate, and we ended up shouting at each other. It was stupid. Gerald said he'd taken the tracing paper because that's what I said we needed. I yelled at him that he should've known we'd need the maps as well.'

'So you fought?' said Ralph.

'Yes.' Dick fell silent, as if reliving the event over again. 'That's when it happened. The boat was heaving about in the wind, and the waves were getting bigger. I'd just put on my lifejacket when there was a sudden lurch and I got knocked over the side. I quickly lost sight of *Arabella* ... don't know how long I was in the water, but I must've passed out. Eventually I was picked up by another boat. They landed me in Skegness – that's on the Lincolnshire side of the Wash. They wanted to take me to a hospital, but I said I wasn't injured. Luckily my wallet was in a zipped pocket. I found a shop and bought some new things to wear.'

'Where did you stay?'

'That wasn't a problem. I bought a small tent and got a bus to a camp-site on the edge of town. I had enough cash to keep myself for a while, using the shop on the site.'

'Why didn't you come back to me?' Judith said. 'I would've taken care of you.'

'I wasn't thinking straight all along. I was worried about Gerald ... what he might do. He was in a dreadful rage with me.'

'All on account of the tracing paper?' Marnie could not keep the scepticism out of her voice.

Dick swallowed. 'There was more to it than that. Gerald wanted to claim more credit for finding the treasure than was really justified. It's ironic, because at first he didn't even believe it could be found. He said without his boat and his collaboration I'd never have done it. When I told him his demands were out of the question, that's what really started the quarrel. He was absolutely furious.'

'So what's brought you back now?' Donovan spoke for the first time.

Dick shrugged. 'I had to come back sooner or later. I've got work to do.'

'And you're not worried about Gerald any more?' Marnie said.

'Well, I'm giving Norwich a pretty wide berth at the minute, just to be on the safe side.'

'I don't blame you,' said Judith. 'Sounds like a good idea.'

Dick squeezed her hand. 'But I had to return to take up my life again. I'm ready to take my chances ... hoping Gerald will have cooled off by now.'

'I'm sure you're right,' Donovan said.

'You think so?'

'Absolutely.'

'I'm glad you're optimistic, Donovan.'

'I don't know if it's optimism, but I'm certain he'll have cooled off by now ... literally.'

Everyone looked at Donovan, their expressions curious. He returned their stares calmly.

'I don't follow,' Dick said. 'What do you mean, *literally?*'

'Just that. You've no need to worry about Gerald Parfitt. He poses no threat.'

'Donovan,' Marnie said gently, 'you're talking in riddles.'

'You're right, sorry. Let me put it more plainly. Gerald can't harm you, Dick. I identified his body at the morgue yesterday.'

Silence. For a few seconds they sat as if captured in freeze frame. Then, with a sob that made Anne start in surprise, Dick thrust his head into his hands. At that moment the room darkened, and they heard the first raindrops lashing the windows. A summer storm had broken.

Judith hugged Dick and pulled him gently to her. Anne was next to react, standing to pour more tea from the pot, while Marnie got up to switch on the table lamps.

'What should we do now?' Judith said softly.

Donovan replied. 'Dick should go to the police.'

Judith looked startled. 'Why?'

Dick raised his head. 'Yes, why? I haven't done anything wrong.'

'I'm not saying you have,' Donovan said. 'The point is, you've been reported as missing. There's been a fatality. You're the nearest thing to a witness, at least the last person to see Dr Parfitt alive.'

Dick absorbed this and nodded slowly. 'You're right.' He looked at Judith. 'Who reported me as missing?'

'I suppose I did,' Marnie said. 'We were all concerned about you. You were gone so long and you left so abruptly, without a word ... even to Judith.'

Dick breathed out audibly. 'I'm so sorry. It was thoughtless of me. I'll go to the police tomorrow. Right now I could use a shower and a good night's sleep. I feel shattered.'

'Nervous exhaustion,' Judith said. 'It's hardly surprising.'

Dick looked at Donovan. 'What do you think the police will ask me?'

'They'll certainly want to know what happened on *Arabella*. Also, they'll want to check out the camp-site. Do you have receipts for the things you bought? Can you tell them who picked you up ... the names of the people, their boat?'

Dick looked thoughtful. 'I think I've probably got receipts for the tent, maybe the clothes, but as for the people who picked me up ... their boat ... I'm not sure about that. I was in a daze ... barely conscious ... disoriented.'

'Don't worry,' Donovan said. 'If the police want to speak to them they'll put out an announcement and hope they come forward.'

'But what if they don't?'

Donovan shrugged. 'Then they don't. There's nothing they can do about it.'

'The main thing is, you're safe and well,' Judith said. 'It's awful about Dr Parfitt, but accidents do happen at sea, especially in rough weather.'

'I know that, but all the same, I feel –'

'Don't,' Marnie said firmly. 'First Zoë, now Dr Parfitt … you can't take responsibility for every bad thing that happens.'

Dick said nothing, staring bleakly ahead. Judith took his arm and made to leave. As they were about to stand, Donovan spoke.

'Dick, did you need to use the inflatable dinghy on *Arabella* for any reason?'

Dick looked puzzled. 'The dinghy? I don't think so … don't think we ever used it. Why d'you ask?'

'No reason. It just occurred to me … I don't remember seeing it when I visited the boat yesterday.'

'Sorry, can't help you. I'm pretty sure it was on board when we went out … at least I think it was. Could it be significant?'

'Possibly, possibly not. Just a thought.'

They all stood as Judith led Dick to the front door.

'Perhaps it's best if I don't mention our quarrel when I speak to the police,' Dick said. 'What d'you think?'

'Not really relevant, is it?' Marnie looked at the others for a reaction. 'I'd just keep to the bare essentials. You were out sailing, a storm blew up, you had an accident.'

'That makes sense. Thanks, Marnie.'

More rain struck the windows.

'It's pouring down,' Marnie said. 'Let me lend you an umbrella.' She grinned at Dick. 'You've had enough soakings.'

'Yeah, right. That'd be good. But how will I return it to you?'

'I'll be in touch. You must come to dinner … both of you. I'll call you soon.'

Judith kissed Marnie on the cheek. 'Thank you so much, for everything.'

Marnie kissed them both. 'It's good to have you back, Dick.'

'What about King John's treasure?' Donovan asked, as they shook hands. 'Did you manage to keep your tracings?'

'Luckily, I did.' Dick smiled ruefully. 'That's the one good thing to come out of this tragedy.'

'And the master map and the other papers?'

'I'll collect them when I go back to the house.'

'Oh?' Donovan frowned. 'You mean Dr Parfitt didn't give them to you?'

'He couldn't. Don't you remember? He just took the overlay … the tracing diagram. That's one of the reasons why we quarrelled.'

'I'm confused here.' Donovan looked from Anne to Marnie. 'I understood he'd gone back and fetched that folder and the maps.'

'What gave you that idea?'

Donovan shrugged. 'I called in at the house on Thursday morning. They weren't there then. I assumed he'd retrieved them earlier ... or you had.'

Dick stared at Donovan and shook his head. 'No. That can't be right.'

'There's an easy way to find out,' Judith said. ' We can go to the house on our way back.'

'It's teeming down,' Ralph pointed out, 'and a long walk in the rain ... in the opposite direction.'

'You could phone Jonathan,' Donovan said. 'Is he still in London? He might be there.'

'It's worth a try,' Judith said. She took out her mobile. 'I've got his number. Shall I ring?'

'Yes.' Dick spoke without hesitation.

Judith pecked out the number and handed the mobile to Dick. 'You speak to him. You'll know what to say.'

They were in luck. Jonathan was in the house. Dick told him where to look in the living room-study. He described the yellow folder containing various documents in the top right-hand drawer of the desk. After an extensive search, Jonathan confirmed that the relevant folder was definitely absent. Also, the maps were no longer on the desk. They disconnected.

Dick had turned pale. 'He must've had them all along. Why didn't he tell me?'

Everyone looked blank, except Donovan.

'At the risk of sounding like a cliché ...' Donovan began, 'I would've thought that was rather obvious.'

Dick's head snapped round. 'Why?'

'I would've thought he'd want you to agree to his recognition in the venture before handing over the documents and maps that would guarantee your success.'

Dick stood transfixed. 'Yes,' he breathed. 'Of course ...'

'But you can work it out, can't you?' Judith struggled to sound reassuring. 'You know where to search.'

Dick looked horrified. He closed his eyes, inwardly imaging the endless coastline, the vast expanse of wetlands, the wide grey empty sea under the enormous sky. 'You don't understand. Those maps, those papers ... many of them were irreplaceable. They represented years of work, years of my life. Without them ...'

'You think Parfitt carried them to his death?' Donovan said.

Dick's eyes widened. '*Arabella*! They're probably on the boat. Yes. They *must* be.'

Donovan shook his head. 'I checked her over pretty thoroughly. That's when I noticed the dinghy was missing. There were no papers on board.'

'Of course not,' Dick said hastily. 'They'll be in his study or at the university. He wouldn't want to risk them getting lost or damaged. That's why he didn't produce them when we sailed.'

'That's it,' Judith said. 'That *must* be it.'

Marnie squeezed his arm. 'Let's hope so.' She looked into Dick's eyes. 'You still look off-colour. Are you sure you're well enough to go out? You could have a lie-down here for a while, till you feel better.'

'No, it's all right.' Dick attempted a smile, but it fell flat. 'I suppose I'm still upset about Gerald. I hate to think of him drowning like that. And it could so easily have been the same for me.'

'Dr Parfitt didn't drown.'

Once again, all eyes swivelled towards Donovan.

'What d'you mean?' Marnie looked confused.

'Which part didn't you understand?'

'Any of it. Can you explain?'

'I asked the mortuary technician what was the cause of death. He showed me a very nasty wound to the back of the head. Dr Parfitt was probably unconscious by the time he went into the water. He died of a fractured skull.'

'Oh god ...' Dick looked distraught. 'Poor Gerald. He must've hit his head as he fell in. Perhaps ... I will sit down for a minute or two, Marnie.'

They resumed their seats. Anne fetched Dick a glass of brandy, and he downed it in one gulp.

Ralph looked at Donovan. 'So that's what they believe happened? He hit his head on the side of the boat as he fell?'

'The technician checked the autopsy report. It described the wound as being made by a small object, nothing as broad as the deck or gunwale of a yacht.'

'What sort of object? Could they be more specific?'

'He said it was like a hammer head or a spanner or ... perhaps a lock key ...'

'But you don't have a lock key on a sailing boat, do you?' Anne said.

Judith made a sharp intake of breath.

'What is it?' Marnie asked.

Judith's cheeks flushed. 'It's nothing ... just that ... you know I had to get a new lock key the other day. I couldn't find ours, so I replaced it.'

'It was that day we saw you at Dick's house, wasn't it?'

'Yes. I expect it'll turn up some time, but I couldn't risk not having one on board. Sorry, I know it's nothing to do with what we were talking about ... just a horrible coincidence.'

The rain lashed the windows again as they sat in silence. Dick was staring into his empty glass.

36
The Lost Regalia

On Sunday morning when Marnie woke, as her eyes focused for the first time that day she saw Ralph's dark head on the pillow beside her and heard his rhythmic breathing. Round the edge of the curtains the light was not as bright as usual, and her first thought was that summer had ended. She slipped out from under the duvet, put on a dressing gown and padded into the living room. From the large windows looking out to the river six floors below, she saw that the rain had stopped but a thick blanket of grey was spread over the great city, and the Thames looked like shiny pewter. It was one of those quiet London Sunday mornings that she so disliked, and she found herself longing to be back home in the country.

After Dick and Judith had left the previous evening, she and Ralph had taken Anne and Donovan to a restaurant in Saint Katharine Docks on the Tower side of the river.

When they had finished their meal, Donovan surprised them by announcing that he needed to get back to deal with various matters at his house and on the boat. He had brought some food back from Germany and invited them to join him for what he called *Kaffee und Kuchen* the following afternoon to return their hospitality. They arranged to meet on *XO2* at three. Neither Marnie nor Ralph had ever been on board, and both were curious to inspect the interior of the *stealth narrowboat*.

Marnie went back to the bedroom and laid out her clothes for the day before taking a shower. Ralph was still sleeping. Nothing ever seemed to disturb his slumbers, whereas she had spent a troubled night dreaming of tsunami waves crashing down on the decks of helpless sailing boats, sweeping their hapless crews overboard. The drowning sailors had been surrounded in the water by swirling maps and papers that gradually disintegrated in the turbulence.

By the time Marnie made her way to the kitchen to prepare breakfast, she could hear the faint hissing of another shower. Anne was up and about. Soon the two of them were chatting together as coffee brewed and toast browned. When Ralph joined them they laid their plans for the day. He had brought his laptop and would work in the flat during the morning while Marnie and Anne walked along to see what progress had been made on the Horselydown project.

When they reached the entrance gates a security guard recognised Marnie.

'Can't you keep away from the place? All the keen ones are on site today.'

'What do you mean?' said Marnie. 'Is Philip Everett here?'

'No, but the professor is. Are you coming in?'

Marnie glanced at Anne. 'I think we might.' As they walked through the compound she murmured, 'I wonder what Bernard's doing here.'

'We'll soon find out,' said Anne. 'There he is now.'

Professor de Groot was standing looking down into the excavation and did not hear them approaching. Marnie called out softly, not wishing to startle him into falling into the hole. He turned in surprise.

'I didn't expect to see you – or indeed anyone – here today, Marnie. What brings you to the site?'

'We were just curious to see how things were going.'

'Look around you,' de Groot said. 'It's amazing. You must be used to this kind of thing, but I didn't realise works proceeded so quickly.'

Marnie was impressed with the progress of construction, and Anne was astonished to see how much of the building had been extended since their last visit. The archaeological site was now entirely enclosed within the structure, and many of the deep trenches carrying services around the site had been filled in as all attention was now focused on raising the steel framework skywards.

'I wanted to have a final look before I set off,' de Groot explained.

'You're leaving … going on holiday, perhaps?'

'Actually I'm off for three weeks to lecture on archaeology on a luxury cruise liner … the major sites of the eastern Mediterranean. It sounds like a holiday, but I try to persuade myself – and others – that it's really work.' He smiled. 'Someone has to do it.'

Marnie and Anne obligingly laughed politely, as required.

De Groot was delighted when Marnie gave him the news of Dick Blackwood's return. She wondered how long his good humour would last once he knew the whole situation.

They adjourned to the staff hut where Marnie outlined what had happened. Bernard de Groot sat silently listening while Marnie narrated the whole story from the time Dick had left the site believing Zoë Tipton to be dead, to his return the previous day. The professor was deeply distressed to learn of the death of Gerald Parfitt. They had met at numerous conferences over the years, and de Groot held his colleague in high regard.

When Marnie reached the end of her narrative de Groot announced that he too had some news, though nothing as shattering as the events that Marnie had described. It was still highly confidential, but the Roman ships had been recognised by English Heritage as a find of national importance. He assured Marnie that this would in no way delay the construction of the hotel. In fact, he believed it would add to the prestige of the project and all concerned with it.

'Zoë must be mightily pleased about that,' Marnie observed.

'*Pleased* is not the word.' De Groot tapped the side of his nose in conspiratorial fashion. 'Strictly off the record, I can tell you that contract negotiations are in hand as we speak for Zoë to present a television programme inspired by the Roman ships. In fact, I have it from an impeccable source ...' He raised both eyebrows.

'Professor Barney Guthrie, by any chance?' Marnie suggested.

'Ah, so you're in the loop, Marnie.'

'Just an inspired guess.'

'A good one,' de Groot confirmed. 'It seems likely that our young lady could well be fronting a whole TV series telling the story of how London grew from earliest times to become the major city it is today. What d'you think of that?'

'Amazing.'

'Quite. She's confidently being tipped as the new face of archaeology in Britain.'

'Won't that put a lot of noses out of joint?'

'Naturally. But if someone like Zoë can raise the profile of archaeology, that has to be good for us all.'

Marnie and Anne could both think of one archaeologist who might not share that opinion.

'*That*'s a sting in the tail!' Ralph exclaimed when Marnie recounted de Groot's latest news. 'I can't see Dick Blackwood queuing up for Zoë Tipton's autograph when she becomes a TV star.'

They were sitting at the dining table in the flat, having a sandwich lunch so as to leave space for coffee and cakes on Donovan's boat that afternoon.

'Dick's not going to be overjoyed,' Marnie agreed, 'though I suppose a lot will depend on whether he can get hold of those maps and papers that Gerald Parfitt seems to have taken with him.'

'Do you think finding King John's treasure will outscore Zoë's TV series?' Anne said.

Ralph swallowed some mineral water. 'It'll make big headlines and possibly outshine her success ... if he can truly locate it.'

'That's the big question,' Marnie said. '*If* he can locate it. What if he can't get hold of the maps and the other documents?'

'I expect he'll ask Bernard de Groot to make contact with the archaeology department at UEA and get permission for Dick to check out his study to see if they're there.'

'Or they could be at Dr Parfitt's home, Ralph. Do you know what his domestic situation was? Did he have a wife and family, a partner or anything?'

'No idea. But in any case the whole thing is a longshot. I wouldn't be at all surprised if Parfitt took them with him to a watery grave.'

'That's a bit unlikely isn't it? If he'd had them on him when he and Dick went out on the boat, Dick would've seen them. We're talking about a bright yellow folder stuffed with material. It couldn't go unnoticed.'

'That's a fair assessment, I suppose,' Ralph conceded. 'On the other hand, why would Parfitt leave them behind when they sailed? I thought the whole idea was to go off and find the treasure. My thinking is that he did indeed take the folder with him, but somehow it got lost when the storm hit them. Perhaps he was trying to go through the papers after Dick went over the side, but then got struck by a wave himself and they all ended up in the drink.'

Marnie felt a chill sweep over her.

'Are you all right, Marnie?' Ralph asked. 'You've gone rather pale.'

Marnie put a hand to her face. 'You've broken my dream. That's exactly what I saw ... Parfitt and all the papers in the sea ... everything being destroyed.'

'Sorry, darling, I didn't realise ... Still, it was just a dream. It doesn't mean anything. This has been preying on all our minds for the past few weeks. We'll soon know for sure what really happened. Then we can put it down and get on with our lives.'

Marnie sipped her mineral water. 'I hope so.'

They crossed London by tube and took a taxi for the last part of the journey from Hammersmith Broadway to Uxbridge. Donovan had given them a rendez-vous and had brought the boat as close as possible to the road. As the cab cruised slowly along, Anne was first to spot *XO2* at her mooring. It was just a short walk under a grey sky through the access gate and along the towpath, stepping round puddles left behind by the latest shower. The rain had eased off, but felt as if it could return at any minute.

As they drew nearer, a familiar waterways smell reached them. Mingled with the cool, damp air was the unmistakable aroma of wood-smoke. Ahead of them they saw wisps of pale grey issuing from Donovan's chimney.

Donovan must have seen them coming, for the stern doors swung open and he came out onto the deck to welcome them aboard. Dressed in black sweatshirt and black jeans, he complemented perfectly the dark grey paintwork of his boat. Marnie noticed that even the mooring ropes were black, though faded slightly to a shade of charcoal grey.

Anne led the way down into the boat, past the shower room, through the sleeping cabin, on into the galley which in turn opened into the dining area and saloon. Behind them, Donovan closed the stern doors and slid the hatch back into place. With all four standing in the dining-saloon space, the interior felt crowded. Donovan invited his visitors to sit at the dinette while he completed preparations for *Kaffee und Kuchen.*

'This is delightful, Donovan,' Marnie said, twisting in her seat beside Ralph to survey the interior. 'I'm not quite sure what I expected. Your design scheme is very functional, but you've made it really cosy and welcoming.'

'I've never seen it with the stove in action,' said Anne. 'It creates a lovely atmosphere.'

Donovan laughed. 'A U-boat with a wood-burning stove! It's gotta be a first.'

'D'you mind if I look round?' Marnie said. 'I feel so curious about what you've done with the boat. I've never seen anything like this before.'

'The U-boat is certainly unique,' Anne chimed in.

'Go ahead.' Donovan gestured towards the saloon. 'Make yourself at home.'

Marnie stood and walked towards the front of the cabin. On the left was a desk unit with shelving above and fitted drawers either side of the knee-hole below. Beyond it, beside the cratch door, the blacked wood-stove glowed orange-red with yellow flames flickering behind the glass. The side wall to the right was lined with bookshelves.

Nearest to the dinette was a unit made of metal painted matt black. The top shelf held three classic Leica cameras. On the two lower shelves crockery was displayed, which Marnie guessed might be *Rosenthal* or *Hutschenreuter* from years past. On the end panel were attached three photographs of silver racing cars from the 1930s.

The whole interior was monochrome in shades of grey, just as Marnie imagined an actual U-boat might be. Even the upholstery was in a dark grey tweed that was both functional in appearance and comfortable to use. Portholes were the only source of external light, and on that dull overcast afternoon, Donovan had drawn the curtains. The only lighting inside the boat was provided by candles, thick and chunky, some of them decorated with carvings like the friezes on medieval rood screens.

Marnie admired Donovan's sense of design and his success in bringing all the elements together in a cohesive style. She took her place with the others just as Anne was helping Donovan set out the refreshments.

In the German way, he had filled a large vacuum jug with coffee, which he set down in the middle of the table. Beside it was a bowl filled with vanilla-flavoured whipped cream. There were three sorts of cake on offer: a *Streusel*, a sort of apple and blackberry crumble, a *Linzertorte*, a tart made with raspberries, and a cake topped with plums, which Donovan called *Zwetschgenkuchen.*

He looked at his guests. 'It's decision time, perhaps in more ways than one.'

'Hearing you pronounce their German names like that seems rather exotic,' Marnie said, studying the plates before her, 'and rather daunting.'

Donovan smiled. 'Don't worry about the names, Marnie. It's the taste that counts.'

'They all look delicious,' said Ralph. 'May I ask, without indiscretion …'

'My aunt made them all. She likes nothing better than baking. So, please … what will you have?'

They set to, and soon the only sound heard at the table was groans of pleasure. When they had finished their first slices of cake, Donovan invited them to take another. Marnie suggested a small pause to let the first pieces go down. At that point, the conversation turned to the questions that were on their minds.

'So where are we with King John's treasure and all that?' Marnie began. 'What do we know for certain, and what remains to find out?'

Donovan astonished them all. 'I think it's all quite clear.'

'Why am I not surprised to hear you say that?' Marnie laughed. 'Even though I'm rather bewildered.'

Ralph joined in. 'Surely there are some questions that are still unresolved.'

'I think Dick is hoping that's the case,' Donovan said quietly.

'Isn't he the one who has all the answers?' Marnie said. 'He's the only one who knows what really happened on *Arabella* that day. No-one else can ever know for certain about that head injury to Dr Parfitt … whether it really was an accident or … he was struck with a blunt object …'

'Like a lock key,' Donovan added. 'Yes. It's impossible to know exactly what happened and therefore impossible to prove things one way or another.'

'You really do suspect Dick, don't you?' Ralph said.

'That's not entirely the point.'

It was a stock Donovan reply. Ralph smiled.

'Then what is?' said Marnie. 'Surely that's at the heart of everything.'

'Of course. But the real point is, what do we do about it?'

'Do we all think Dick killed Parfitt?' Marnie asked.

'It's probably the only solution that fits all the facts, as we know them,' Ralph said. 'We know he's fanatical about his discovery, that he sent Parfitt to get the maps and papers, that he was furious with Parfitt for trying to muscle in on his hour of glory. He's admitted as much.'

Marnie agreed. 'But what he doesn't know is what became of the maps and other documents. He absolutely *must* have those in order to pinpoint the exact location of the treasure.'

'Coming back to my question,' Ralph was looking at Donovan, 'do you believe Dick killed Parfitt?'

'Yes, I do. I'm certain of it. What we can't know is in what circumstances he did it. I mean, was there a sudden flare-up? I don't believe Dick's a violent person, but he might lash out if provoked ... as he did with Zoë.'

Marnie sipped her coffee. 'It could never be proved, as you said, but if that's the case, how can you be so sure?'

Anne spoke for the first time. 'The lock key.'

Donovan nodded. 'The lock key. There's no need for a lock key on a boat sailing in the Wash, and *Arabella* was never going to cruise on inland waterways, so she was never going to enter a canal lock.'

'You believe he took the lock key from Judith's boat,' Marnie said.

'There's no evidence to prove it, but yes I do ... and so I think does Judith.'

'So it was premeditated on Dick's part?'

'Why else would he take it with him when they went sailing?' Donovan said.

He reached forward and offered Marnie a slice of the raspberry tart, the *Linzertorte*. It was covered with lattice pastry and looked very tempting. She topped it with a spoonful of whipped cream. The others followed her cue, while Donovan poured them all a second cup of coffee from the flask.

'Presumably,' Ralph began tentatively, 'the police would come to that same conclusion, so Dick wouldn't get away with it.'

'I'm afraid that's not quite the point, either.' Donovan screwed the cap back on the vacuum flask. 'And before you accuse me of being mysterious, I owe you all an explanation. This morning I took it on myself to go to the police. I went to see Inspector Bruere.'

'That was a bold move,' said Marnie.

'I didn't want anything to jeopardise a potential enquiry, so I presented him with my conclusions on what happened between Dick Blackwood and Gerald Parfitt.'

'How did he react?' Ralph said.

Donovan shook his head. 'He asked me what proof I had, which is what I expected him to say. He pointed out that there was no evidence to support my *theory* – as he called it – that Dick had taken Judith's lock key and used it to assault Dr Parfitt with fatal results. He dismissed my idea that Dick had then used the dinghy to make his escape in the direction of the Lincolnshire coast.'

'Surely the facts relating to his being picked up by another boat could be ascertained. That could corroborate his story.'

'Bruere didn't think so, Ralph. He thought it highly unlikely the police would ever be able to locate Dick's rescuers.'

'What about the receipts for the new clothes and the stay at the camp site?'

'I think the expression, *so what?* would sum up his opinion of that as evidence of anything. What could it possibly prove?'

'When you put it like that, it does all sound rather flimsy,' Marnie agreed.

'I suppose the dinghy might turn up,' said Ralph.

Donovan said, 'My guess is, the lock key and the dinghy are now lying at the bottom of the sea, for all we know keeping company with King John's treasure. They could be there for another eight hundred years. Finding a needle in a haystack would be easy in comparison.'

Ralph frowned. 'And if Dick does find his papers in Dr Parfitt's study, either at the university or at his home, he'd be able to use them to his advantage and achieve international fame and fortune.'

'That would be *so* unfair,' Anne said.

'Not necessarily.' Donovan drank some coffee and took a small forkful of *Torte*.

'This is you being enigmatic as usual,' Marnie said, smiling.

'Sorry. I meant it would only be unfair *if* he got away with it.'

'But you've just told us the police thought there was no evidence against Dick.'

'That's right. Bruere said they needed actual solid *proof* before they could take anything to the Crown Prosecution Service. A missing lock key and a lost dinghy weren't good enough.'

'No smoking gun,' said Ralph. 'Or rather in this case, no windlass with Dick's fingerprints and Parfitt's DNA on it.'

'So I'm the only one who thinks he's guilty,' Donovan said quietly.

'You said you thought Judith might suspect him,' Anne pointed out. 'Or at least she thought he'd taken the lock key.'

Donovan shrugged. 'That still doesn't amount to proof, and in any case I can't imagine she'd ever speak up against Dick.'

'For what it's worth ...' Anne began hesitantly, 'I think you're probably right ... I mean about Dick ...'

'There is no evidence,' Ralph said, 'Let's be clear about that. But I have to admit ... I go along with your ... theory.'

'Why?' said Marnie.

'Dick's account of the events ... it was all so convenient. I never met Gerald Parfitt, so I don't know if he was capable of that kind of violent outburst, but it struck me as a rather over-the-top explanation.'

'He seemed quite a kindly sort of man to me,' Anne said softly. 'A mild sort of person ... rather like you, Ralph, in some ways ... a man of intellect.'

'I come back to where we started,' said Donovan. 'None of this actually proves anything.'

'Nevertheless, we all suspect Dick did it,' Marnie said. 'We do, don't we? Something about Dick's version of events … his body language … He didn't manage to convince us that his story was true, did he?'

'You're right, Marnie.' Ralph took her hand across the table. 'We all think he's guilty, and there's nothing we or anyone else can do about it. Case closed.'

'A perfect murder,' Anne muttered.

For a few moments they sat in silence and heard the rain falling again on the boat's roof. Marnie eventually spoke.

'So that's it? Dick gets away with it, produces King John's treasure and becomes a national celebrity while poor Gerald Parfitt lies on a slab in the morgue?'

Anne recalled the account of the execution of Daring Jake Pepper in Marnie's pirate book. 'In the olden days criminals were hanged at Horselydown and left to swing in chains. I'm not saying they should do that nowadays, but there should be some punishment for such a dreadful crime.'

'If Dick can get hold of his maps and papers and use them to locate the rest of the treasure, he'll be home and dry.' Marnie frowned. 'No sticky end for him … no penalty at all, in fact.'

'That's a rather crucial assumption, Marnie,' said Ralph.

Marnie thought of her dream, with Parfitt under the sea and the papers dissolving around him. 'You think Dick isn't going to retrieve his papers … that they may be lost forever?'

'That's in the lap of the gods, no doubt,' Ralph said.

'No, it isn't, really.' Donovan stood up. 'Excuse me. The stove needs attention.'

Marnie swivelled in her seat and followed him with her eyes. 'What are you up to, Donovan?' Her voice was edged with suspicion. 'Is there something you're not telling us?'

Donovan crouched by the stove. He picked a log from the basket and examined it for a few seconds before blowing a spider away to one side. It scurried off to safety. He opened the stove door and pushed the log in. A current of warm air drifted down the cabin, carrying with it a tang of burning wood. Donovan closed the door with a snap and stood up.

'I've been trying to work out what's best to do. That's why I wanted you all to come here today. It can't be my decision alone.'

'Decision?'

'Yes. The police and the Crown Prosecution Service have washed their hands of the whole affair, so what's a fitting punishment for someone who takes the life of another? Sorry to sound so grandiose, but that is the question.'

'You said yourself nothing could be proved in a court of law,' Marnie said. 'So your question is presumably hypothetical.'

'No, it isn't.' Donovan smiled faintly. 'Sorry. I keep saying that.'

He turned towards his desk, opened the top drawer and pulled out a folder. It was yellow and stuffed thickly with papers.

Ralph sat up with a start. 'Is that what I think it is? Are those Dick's maps and documents?'

Donovan held them up. 'Everything is here. Everything he needs to help him find King John's lost regalia.'

Anne stared in amazement.

'Blimey,' said Marnie. 'How did you get hold of them?'

'You remember I took longer than usual travelling up to visit you on Thursday? I called in at Dick's place and found Jonathan there. He let me in. He'd just come out of the shower and was wearing a dressing gown. I told him I had some questions, so he invited me to sit in Dick's room while he got dressed. To cut a long story short, I found the folder in the top drawer and tucked it into my rucksack, together with the master map from the desk. Jonathan suspected nothing.'

'You could've given them to Dick when we saw him yesterday,' Marnie said, 'but you wanted to be sure, wanted to hear what he had to say, didn't you?'

'And he convinced you that he was guilty,' Ralph added.

'That's right. That's what decided me to go to the police.'

'But Bruere dismissed your theory out of hand,' Ralph said.

'Exactly.'

'So where does that leave us now?' Marnie asked.

'Now I come back to my question,' Donovan said. 'What price do we put on Gerald Parfitt's life? Is it more important than solving the greatest unsolved mystery of the Middle Ages, as Dick called it? Does it count for eight hundred years of waiting?'

'What do you have in mind?' Marnie said.

Donovan shook his head. 'I told you. It can't be my decision alone.'

He clasped the folder to his chest and looked down at the wood-burner. The fresh log had taken light, and flames were licking round it behind the glass door. Donovan laid the folder on top of the stove, knelt down again and slid open the vent. They heard a faint roaring sound as the flow of air quickened and the log began to blaze more brightly. They all stared at it as a smell of warm paper began to float on the air.

'What about the treasure?' said Marnie.

'What about it?' Ralph smiled. 'We've managed to live without it for eight hundred years. It's still there waiting for someone to find it.'

'What do we think?' Donovan continued. 'It's down to all of us here. No-one else can decide for us.'

'A punishment to fit the crime,' Anne said.

Donovan nodded. 'Well? Do we consign the folder and all it represents to the fire?'

Marnie looked from Ralph to Anne and back to Donovan.

'That,' she said, 'is a very good question.'